Christopher Ransom is the author of internationally bestselling novels including *The Birthing House* and *The People Next Door*. He studied literature at Colorado State University and worked at Entertainment Weekly magazine in New York, and now lives near his hometown of Boulder, Colorado.

Visit www.christopherransom.com to learn more.

CHRISTOPHER RANSOM

THE ORPHAN

sphere

SPHERE

First published in Great Britain in 2013 by Sphere

Copyright © Christopher Ransom 2013

The moral right of the author has been asserted.

A CIP catalogue record for this book
is available from the British Library.

ISBN 978-0-7515-5130-3

Typeset in Caslon by M Rules
Printed and bound in Great Britain by
Clays Ltd, St Ives plc

Papers used by Sphere are from well-managed forests
and other responsible sources.

MIX
Paper from
responsible sources
FSC® C104740

Sphere
An imprint of
Little, Brown Book Group
100 Victoria Embankment
London EC4Y 0DY

An Hachette UK Company
www.hachette.co.uk

www.littlebrown.co.uk

For Cowboy
Sweet stray who took us in,
best dog, best friend

The past is hidden somewhere outside
the realm, beyond the reach

of intellect, in some material object (in
the sensation which that

material object will give us) which we
do not suspect. And as for that

object, it depends on chance whether
we come upon it or not before

we ourselves must die.

MARCEL PROUST,
In Search of Lost Time

SPRING

The stranger showed up around noon and ruined what was left of a beautiful day.

Darren had only himself to blame. The bicycle auction was Beth's idea, to support Fresh Starts, the non-profit she worked part-time for, but he had agreed, experiencing an initial blast of selflessness and good will that carried them through the planning stages, past the point of no return. Once Beth arranged for the local newspaper, *The Daily Camera*, to cover the event and the appointed date drew near, he found himself dreading the attention. He was not looking forward to stirring up old acquaintances in his home town, but there was nothing to be done. The auction was happening, and it had somehow fallen on his shoulders to carry the day.

Of course, without his collection, there never would have been an auction, and he might never have encountered the man in the park.

It was a Saturday in middle April, Colorado's bright sun pushing the temps into the mid-seventies. The tent was up, a cheerful red and white striped affair large enough to host a wedding, presently sheltering each of the twenty-four bikes he had selected. The bikes were standing atop the rented banquet tables, each with a placard denoting the manufacturer and model, original release date, breakdown of components, a bit of lore if the bike could claim any, as well as the bidding charts and pens Beth had set out.

Raya was working a smaller card table, bedecked with a signboard she had painted herself, selling lemonade and batches of cookies she'd baked with her mother, giving background on the cause. Darren couldn't help noticing that his daughter was more interested in the decorations and treats than in the bikes themselves, but he was not surprised. Raya had grown as tired of hearing about the bikes as her mother had.

Darren made a continuous circuit of his ponies on display, adjusting brake cables, dusting rims with a shop rag, dabbing a touch of green Phil Wood grease from a newly plumbed stem bolt, nervous as a dog owner gunning for best in show. This, he supposed, was a male thing, the aspect of the event only a son or another bicycle geek tended to appreciate. Chrome was sexy. To men.

His anxiety increased as he realized for the tenth time today that, if the event succeeded, he would be letting go of some of his best bicycles. Oh, he knew he had plenty, but he had spent hundreds of hours assembling and restoring this lot of vintage BMX bikes, and in one manner or another, each was dear to him.

Not wanting to intimidate the bidders, but also wanting to ensure the event raised a meaningful amount of money, he had selected a variety of stock and custom rides ranging in value from $350 to $4,000. He had others at home worth twice as much on the collector's market, and much more than that to him. Who would have ever thought these relics of his youth – bikes that were, back in the late Seventies and early Eighties, a suburban staple as common as today's video game consoles – would be worth three times what he had paid for his first car?

Not Darren. Not twenty or even ten years ago. He hadn't been collecting for the investment value. He simply loved BMX bikes, ever since he hopped on his first Schwinn Sting back in 1977, and he had never outgrown that love.

The event was being billed as 'RAD Kids: Raising Awareness for Disadvantaged Kids', Beth's clever touch. Fresh Starts was a way station and counseling center for troubled youth, teen runaways, pre-teen kids living in abusive homes, drug and early-pregnancy prevention, as well as a resource for referrals to other state-funded health services. A noble cause.

Yet at first he had found himself asking, 'The bikes aren't actually going to the kids, right? Please tell me some stoner punk's not going to be thrashing one of my two-thousand-dollar vintage rides around town before he hocks it to fund a bag of weed and the last panels of his full-sleeve tattoos.'

'No, honey, and stop being so awful,' Beth had said. 'There are a lot of bike freaks in Boulder, even some collector snobs like you. But most of them will probably go to people who love to brag about their philanthropical contributions and need something to show for their donations on the tax forms. We don't care where the money comes from. The center needs a bunch of repairs, clothes for the kids, maybe a couple extra counselor interns to man the phones over the summer. No one is going to hurt your precious little dirt bikes.'

'Sorry. You're right,' he admitted. 'I need to thin the herd a bit.'

This made her happy, hearing him say it. Because honestly, how many BMX bikes does one grown man need? Good question, to which he had always responded, How many flowers does a constant gardener need? How many books does a lifelong reader need? How many photos of her children does a mother need?

By the time the reporter from the *Camera* showed up, Darren had resigned himself to the event, but his heart was not in it. He was vaguely aware of Beth and Raya hovering off to his right, giggling over his moment in the spotlight. He felt like a heel and wanted to shoo them away.

'Kristen Meade, lifestyle and entertainment beat reporter,' she said, and began to walk him through her boilerplate questions to complete her profile of him. The first was clarifying for her what BMX stood for, bicycle motocross, and he soon found himself launching into an abbreviated history of the sport before she cut him off with an 'I got it now, thanks.'

The intrepid Ms Meade seemed more like an aspiring *National Geographic* writer–explorer than a small-city reporter, slumming in community events until Nairobi called. Her button nose and broad cheeks were wind-chapped, her brown hair short and unfussy. She wore a weekend rock climber's sleek hiking boots and tight-fitting thermal shorts. Her nod to the traditional adventure journalist's safari vest was a Patagonia fleece filled with camera batteries, GPS, light meter, phone, and energy gummies. She used her blocky digital camera to take lots of photos of the bikes and Darren as she talked, and he was never sure if she was really listening to his answers. She must have had a microphone attached to a digital recorder somewhere in her backcountry layers, or a very good memory, for he didn't see her take a single note.

'So, Darren Lynwood. Entrepreneur turned BMX bike guru.'

'I guess that's about right.'

'You're a Boulder native?'

'I am. Or was. For the past twenty-two years I lived in the Midwest – Milwaukee and Chicago. We just moved back about nine months ago.'

'Who's we?'

'My wife Beth and our daughter Raya.'

'How old's Raya?'

'Fifteen.'

Kristen saw Raya waving and snapped a few shots of her. 'She ride BMX too?'

'I tried to get her into the sport when she was about ten, but it didn't take.'

'And you've been collecting bikes for how long?'

'Ever since I was a kid, ten or twelve. Of course, I didn't think of it as collecting back then. I just wanted more bikes, could never make up my mind which one. I always had to have the newest, coolest bike, the most innovative components. Drove my parents crazy, but they taught me to work for new parts and how to save for things, so I guess you could say it became a life lesson of . . . some kind.'

'That's great. How many bikes do you own now?'

Darren squinted. 'Mmm, probably a hundred and twenty, maybe one thirty before today. Plus a few road bikes, three motorcycles, a bunch of other stuff. But yeah, around one twenty complete BMX from the Seventies and Eighties.'

'Wow. So, you've been working in cycling all this time? Our editor mentioned something about a company you sold a year or two ago for, like, millions?'

'Revolver,' Darren said. 'That was a fashion apparel label I started, yes. Jeans and shirts and a few other things.'

'Revolver jeans?' Kristin lowered her camera. 'The ones with the blue leather tape inside the fly? You started that company?'

Darren nodded, embarrassed for reasons he didn't fully understand.

'No way! I used to love those jeans. Why'd you sell a cool company like Revolver?'

Used to? Darren bristled. He didn't want her to turn this into a discussion about his business or their 'millions', which weren't that many, or relevant to today's event. He attempted to steer the interview back to the bikes.

'Well, it's like this. When I was a kid, I spent half my free time at Dave's Bike Shop, which used to be on 30th Street here in town. There's nothing like that bike shop smell. Chain oil, bearing grease, fresh rubber tires. Some of my best memories were going down to Dave's with my dad, or riding down there with a gang of friends. The manager was a guy named Arnie, crazy old Italian with a huge mustache, and he loved us. He'd let us hang out there all afternoon, feed us pizza. Sometimes he'd even come out and ride with us in the vacant lot behind the store. I always dreamed of owning my own bike shop when I grew up, so I could spend my days surrounded by bikes and people who understood the simple, innocent pleasure of riding them.'

Kristen looked a little bored. Was he starting to sound like a flake? Connect the dots for her, he reminded himself. This was about the collection, how we got here today.

'But in high school I discovered a talent for design, and in college I started screen-printing my own T-shirts, selling them out of my dorm room. A few snowboarding jackets when that sport was still young. My dad saw what I was doing, my knack for design and the entrepreneurial side, and he convinced me to major in business. Why not? I figured I could always keep designing on the side.'

He paused, noticing a man standing about thirty feet behind Kristen, just outside the edge of tent shade, apparently hanging on his every word. Tall, very thin,

7

dressed in plain brown work pants and a white T-shirt, hands stuffed in his pockets. There was a handsome man in there somewhere, but his shaggy hair was no-color brown and he looked like he hadn't shaved for a month. His skin was pale everywhere but the cheeks and nose, which glowed from sunburn or alcoholism. His eyes were bulging with surprise or disbelief. How long had he been standing there?

'Anyway,' Darren continued. 'Along the way I became an operations manager and a CEO. I was no longer a designer, and I wasn't having any fun, so I sold the company. Revolver was a cool brand, but once they reach a certain size, every company becomes a company. A corporation. And I never forgot about the bikes.

'When BMX nearly died in the late Eighties and so many kids switched their allegiances to either mountain biking or skating, bike-shop owners were left sitting on thousands of dollars in "worthless" BMX inventory. So I started making calls, accumulating in bulk. Then eBay happened, all this stuff started showing up online, at relatively sane prices. For a few years there, I actually hired two assistants to monitor auctions, call bike shops around the country, hunt down rarities on my hit list, and in general keep everything organized while enabling their boss's crazy obsession.'

The onlooker crossed his arms and stiffened, raising his chin like a priest who has just heard the damning portion of the confession. He seemed relatively harmless, but his eyes were still intensely focused. Maybe he always looked that way.

'So then you retired and rediscovered—'

'More of a hiatus,' Darren said, cutting her off. 'Twenty years later, I finally had enough time to bring everything out of storage, and I couldn't believe how much stuff I had accumulated. I built a showroom at the house. The bikes are part of me, my history ... well, anyway. Maybe too much history isn't always a good thing. My wife said it was time to put some of it to a good cause.'

'Fascinating,' Kristen said a bit too quickly. 'That's a great story, and this certainly is a good cause. I hope the auction is a smash success. Thanks for your time.'

'Don't you want to talk about Fresh Starts?'

'I got all that from your wife.'

'All right. Thanks for coming out.'

Kristen moved off to shoot the bidders who had begun scribbling on the auction forms. Darren was relieved but felt like he had skipped something important. Had he come off like a spoiled rich boy-man with a hoarding obsession? He glanced back toward the stranger with the obscenely large eyes, hoping the guy had moved on.

He was still there. Staring. Not grinning. None of the other twenty or thirty people milling about the tent seemed to have noticed him. He appeared to be on the verge of shouting, but he didn't. His eyes looked wet and filled with too much white.

Darren maintained eye contact, tilting his head as if to say, Yes, I see you, and you see me. Now what?

After a few seconds, the lanky weirdo mouthed

something, just four or five words that Darren failed to understand, and then he smiled so wide Darren could see most of his teeth. It wasn't a grin. It was predatory, a display.

'What was that?' Darren said, loud enough to be heard. Something about the guy was familiar, and not in a good way. 'You need something?'

The man repeated the phrase in silence, his thick chapped lips forming several 'O's' and, a sharp 'S' and, judging by the snarl twisting off at the end, some form of expletive.

You're such a fucking liar.

Stop pretending, you think I'm stupid?

You haven't earned any of this.

It could have been any of these things, or none.

But to be sure, and to head off trouble before the guy made a scene in front of Beth's co-workers, dampening the spirit of the auction, Darren decided to say hello. He took a few steps before Beth grabbed his arm, halting him.

'Hey, honey, how'd it go? Were you nervous? Raya said you looked too serious.'

Darren blinked down at his wife and instinctively pivoted to put himself between her and the creep.

'Do me a favor,' he said. 'Without being obvious, look past my right shoulder and tell me if that guy who looks like he's been living in a log cabin for the past ten years is still glaring at me. Is he being weird or do we know him from something?'

Beth frowned, leaned sideways a bit.

'Don't give it away,' Darren said. 'Pretend you're scanning the crowd.'

She swept her gaze across the tent slowly, glanced up at Darren again, and then to the other side.

'What's he wearing?'

'Dark pants, white shirt, scruffy wino beard. Manson eyes.'

She stood on her toes. 'I don't see anybody like that.'

'Oh, for Christ's sake.' Darren turned around. Looked directly at the spot outside the tent where the man had been standing, around all the bikes, across the park's broad expanse of green grass.

The stranger was gone.

'Who was it?' Beth said. 'Did he do something?'

'He was staring at me during the entire interview. Then he mouthed something, but I couldn't make out the words. He looked angry, excited in the wrong way.'

'Did you recognize him?' she said.

'Something about him seemed familiar, but I might've just assumed that because of the way he was watching me.'

Beth did not seem overly concerned. 'Probably just some Boulder crackpot. There's a lot of those around here.'

'Maybe so.' But Darren didn't believe it.

The auction was a smash success. Twenty-two of the twenty-four bikes went for a total of thirty-one thousand and change. The follow-up article in the *Camera* netted a few more inquiries from vintage bike collectors around Colorado and one in Utah, and Darren agreed to let go of five more bikes for an additional eleven thousand. Beth was awarded Hero of the Month at Fresh Starts. Raya earned a hundred-dollar bonus on top of the seventy-six bucks she made hawking lemonade and cookies. She donated it all to the center, and turned the experience into a report for her health studies class at Boulder High, for which she was given an A.

As spring gave way to summer, Darren couldn't stop looking over his shoulder, wondering who the stranger in the park could have been, and why someone he could not remember might harbor such reserves of ill will.

Part 1

THE LAST DAY OF SCHOOL

1

It was early June when Darren Lynwood fell asleep breathing in the scents of summer rain and wet grass drifting through the master bedroom's open windows, and awoke several hours later with the deep black smoke of burning wood and charred insulation coiling inside his nostrils. His eyes opened to a stinging furnace of orange and black phantoms feeding their way toward him. Streams of tears immediately blurred his vision and wet his cheeks. He thrashed in bed, tangled as if his limbs were in the grip of invisible forces who wanted him to surrender to the billowing layer of dusty ceiling smoke and the flames licking up his bedroom walls.

He tried to scream but his throat was dry, rough, constricted. His lungs heaved and ached for fresh oxygen. A lattice of fire snaked across the floor, igniting the bedding, up over his legs and flash-fried his hair to oily ash in seconds. His skin blistered and bled in rivers, but still he could not scream. All around him the house fed itself to the roiling inferno, until the walls buckled and the roof caved in, the beams crushing Beth and Raya as they screamed for the help he could no longer provide. Before the searing flames stole his life, he had time for one last coherent thought:

I did this. It was my fault. I started the fire that killed my own family.

The flames howled, and death was upon—

Darren bolted awake, unable to breathe or cry out. His fists clenched the sweat-soaked sheet bunched against his throat and he kicked away the thin cotton blanket that had ensnared him. He sat up, swatting at flames that were no longer there, and blinked in the cooling darkness, his eyes and mind working to assert the more peaceful reality of the bedroom.

The bed frame. The tall oak dresser. The dark windows behind their curtains of yellow gauze, rippling with the faintest summer breeze. Tint of rain from the evening, but the rain had stopped now. His throat opened and his lungs resumed their work.

The other half of the blanket was draped over Beth. His wife was sleeping blissfully on her stomach, turned away from him, one arm reaching above her head and over the pillow like a swimmer who'd frozen in ice mid-stroke.

Thank God she's all right, he thought.

And with nearly as much relief, *Thank God I didn't wake her this time.*

Even though he had experienced the same nightmare almost a dozen times in the past five weeks, part of him still refused to believe it was only a dream. The fire had been too real. The nightmare's intensity, combined with its repetitive nature, convinced him that sooner or later it must come true.

He wouldn't be able to go back to sleep now, not for hours, so he got up to check the rest of the house. Checking always made him feel better, at least until the next dream inferno occurred. Darren shuffled across the master bedroom, careful to avoid knocking over a lamp or a chair that would wake up the girls. He felt a chill as he pulled on a T-shirt and the heat-sweat from only minutes ago began to dry. He found the doorway and began the trek into the main house.

The master suite, reachable only through a long hall that forked off the main house, had been added to the house six or seven years ago by the previous owners. They must have had kids or a mother-in-law, Darren figured. Someone they wanted to get away from. The hall itself was anything but ordinary, and the girls had taken to calling it 'the bridge'.

With its bamboo flooring, decorative hand railing and eight-by-four panel windows providing a view to the immediate backyard, it wasn't difficult to imagine you were standing outside, or maybe staring at a zoo exhibit, waiting for some creature to drag itself from the depths of the koi pond that twisted beneath the floor. A Japanese rock garden ornamented the north view; to the south lay the flagstone patio, flower gardens and the bocce court with its lane of rolled clay and crushed shell. During daylight hours, the views were a reminder to slow down and enjoy the natural splendor of one's property, find some tranquility.

At night, however, the experience of walking the bridge was more like a spaceman's journey between pods of unearthly gravities. The series of dim amber-toned night lights set close to the floor were of little help and in fact confused his eyes as to the depth of the actual floor, making him goofy-footed. The massive panes of pitch-black glass only seemed to confirm the tissue-thin membrane standing between his family and the darkness waiting on the other side.

Tonight he was glad to be out of it, back in the house's true center, where the sunken great room opened to the expansive chef's kitchen. One visual sweep was enough to confirm there was no fire raging about, but he was still glad he'd left the small halogen lights under the kitchen cabinets turned on to guide him. The kitchen's slate tile flooring was cold against his bare feet, a welcome sensation that nudged him closer to total alertness.

The black ceramic stove top was not glowing orange at any of the six burners, but he waved a palm over them anyway. Feeling no warmth, he sidled along the granite countertop and ascertained that the espresso machine, four-slot bagel toaster and Raya's panini press – an item she had picked out of the Williams-Sonoma catalog for her last birthday and now used for grilling Velveeta and smoked prosciutto sandwiches almost daily – were unplugged, as he had left them before going to bed.

He was tempted to check the fire alarms, but he'd changed out the batteries and tested each unit last

Sunday while Beth and Raya were out getting frozen yogurt. Darren still possessed enough self-awareness to know that checking them again tonight would confirm he was no longer operating with mere excessive caution but had in fact slipped into the land of outright paranoia and genuine pyrophobia.

He checked the alarm panel in the front foyer instead. The combination burglar alarm and carbon monoxide detector showed only stable green indicators, no red bulb alerts. He checked the front door anyway, making sure it was locked. The door to the attached garage was also locked. What about Raya? What if she'd left a curling iron on? Darren doubted their daughter even used a curling iron, but he was already on his way to what they had come to refer to as Raya's wing of the house.

Being an only child with a strong independent streak, Raya had inherited her father's love of good design and her mother's addiction to reality shows that catered to notions of how to feng shui oneself into a healthier 'space' (Beth's word for moods), and then proceeded to commandeer – and direct the remodeling of – the largest remaining bedroom, the attached full bath, as well as a second room for her office.

It's not that she's spoiled, Beth liked to remind him, she just knows how she likes things to be and has her own vision for how to get there. What's wrong with allowing your daughter to take responsibility for her own environment? Nothing at all, Darren had replied. I'm just not sure it has to cost more than a fast food manager's annual salary for her to do that.

Darren cupped one ear to her door, listening for what he did not know. The exhale of smoke, hushed cell-phone chatter, another of her awful teen romances on the TV. He heard nothing and, in truth, he didn't really want to know what his daughter got up to after 10 p.m., as long as she was behaving responsibly. Which, Beth always assured him, she was. Even so, he fought the urge to open the door, make sure Raya was home, in bed, safe.

Returning to the kitchen, Darren considered making a coffee, but the espresso machine went off like a Panzer division on maneuvers just to brew four ounces of the stuff, and that was before the hissing choking whine of the milk frother kicked in. 1:17 a.m. according to the clock on the stove. No matter. The last thing he needed was another wake-me-up. He'd never had much use for sleep anyway. Four hours per night were usually enough, even when he had been running the company seventy and eighty hours per week.

He moved to the sliding glass door that faced the back yard, debating whether to venture out to his true den. The house had been built in the Sixties, a long ranch-style home of white brick, with Southwestern archways along the front and rear fascia, something of a hacienda here on Linden Street, in the heart of North Boulder. The two-acre lot lent it more of a rural feel than most properties located within the city limits. On the back half of the long green lawn stood the kind of outbuilding seen on a farm, a place for parking tractors, working on your car, storing tools and other equipment.

And that was where, a full acre away, a light now glowed in the night. The illumination was not, however, the flickering orange of a fire. All three windows along the side of the outbuilding were glowing soft yellow, from the interior.

Darren specifically remembered turning off the lights and setting the alarm out there, as he did every night before turning in, after he finished working on whatever project had captivated him that day.

'Son of a ... '

Someone was in the Bike Cave.

Darren hurried to the laundry room, pulled on a pair of drawstring sweatpants, and slipped into his blue canvas Vans. Taking a flashlight from one of the kitchen drawers, he deactivated the house's alarm, yanked the sliding glass door open and jogged out across his backyard to confront the intruder.

2

The fragrant smell of damp earth. The music of running water. A tingling, almost electrical sensation pulsing throughout his limbs. In his core, a sinking despair and the broken feeling of detachment, that he had been split into parts by some terrible incident, his true self lost to another place, a better realm.

The boy perceived each of these things as he stirred and opened his eyes, and the darkness surrounding him did not alleviate the feeling he was lost. When he tried to move, the ground seemed reluctant to give him up. A moist suction along his thighs and belly, the wet seeping into his clothes. Fragments of the scenery returned and he remembered this was where he had come to rest. Near a stream, in the hills. But he couldn't remember anything else. Where he had come from, why he was here. Questions piled up, each more frightening than the last. What happened, where am I, and then most alarmingly – who am I?

What came to him wasn't an answer, only a label.
Adam.

Or so a voice prompted inside him, but it didn't sound like his voice.

Adam who?

Adam.

Okay, then. Adam for now. It wasn't a bad name, he supposed. Maybe it felt wrong because there was nothing attached to the name – no last name, no family, no friends, no colored-in life. Only the name and his cold self, face-down in the mud and pine needles and long grass. Rising, he saw that he was in a sparse forest.

He needed to find shelter.

Not *home*, because he couldn't remember where home had been or if he'd ever had one. Even the idea of home was too vague for him to latch onto.

When Adam sat up, every muscle protested the change of position. His thighs felt knotted with rocks. His calves, arms, shoulders and back were sore. What had he done earlier today? Yesterday? A week ago?

Running. He was sore because he had been trying to get away from something. On his feet were a pair of severely worn sneakers that appeared two sizes too large because they were caked with mud, and maybe the mud was all that was holding them together. His Puma Baskets, white with the black stripe. He remembered them as new, but they looked ten years old. How could that be? Somehow the plight of his shoes conveyed everything else that was wrong. This was his life. Soiled. Lost.

He looked at his T-shirt, threadbare blue with a cartoon screen of the Creature From the Black Lagoon standing in a swamp, the thought bubble above his head reading, 'Who peed in the pool?' His favorite shirt. But how could he remember his shirt and shoes but not where he lived, what had happened to him? Had he been beaten up and left for dead? Drugged by some kidnapper and thrown away like trash? Neither felt true but both seemed possible.

A strap slipped down his shoulder and Adam pulled it back up before pausing to consider what it was attached to. A cloth-grained weight shifted between his shoulder blades. A backpack, not too heavy, but another thing so familiar he'd forgotten it was there, like it was a part of him. He had no idea what was in it, but he'd find out later, when he had gotten out of here and into some light.

His eyes adjusted to the darkness and he got to his feet. He was standing on a slope, not a riverbank. The stream must be on the other side. He set one leg straight to brace himself and surveyed the woods. They weren't very deep, or at least all the trees were small, mostly young pines. He saw no houses or roads, no lights or other signs of civilization. He noticed a fallen log angling down the slope, leaves and loose ground cover that had been piled up beside it, like a burrow. He'd chosen this spot.

'Hiding,' he said softly. There was no other explanation. 'You were hiding.'

From . . . ?

His heart drummed and his thoughts raced in a fight-or-flight response, even though he had no idea who or what he had been running from.

Adam turned and saw a deer standing on the slope, not more than twenty-five feet away. The deer was small, like him, but it didn't look frightened or even curious. It had no spots, just brown fur that looked gray in the night.

'Hey there,' Adam mumbled to the deer.

The deer craned its head around to its opposite flank, smoothly. It took two small steps toward the peak of the slope and held very still. It wasn't interested in him now. Something else in the woods had become the priority.

Adam felt the change before anything happened, before he saw any movement. The air came alive with another presence. A moment ago he had felt lost but hidden, safe from the eyes of the world. Now he felt watched, him and the deer, and he knew something was in the woods with them, and that it was a bad thing.

He listened for the crunching of twigs and leaves underfoot, the snap of a branch, the growl of something large and predatory, something that might like to eat a deer or a boy. But it did not announce itself.

'It's all right,' Adam whispered to the deer.

The animal's ears rotated like radar dishes. Adam cinched the straps of his backpack tight against his chest.

Go. Run now, the voice warned him, speaking from a place of knowledge. *Gonna have to run again, might as well get a head start.*

Hunt for shelter, find help.

But who could he turn to? Everyone, people of all kinds, seemed far away and faceless to him. When he tried to remember even one person he knew, kids or adults, all he could see were plain blank faces, yellowed like dried candle wax. They had no voices and their eyes were black sockets. He meant nothing to them.

The deer bolted, broke into a full gallop before Adam could turn around, bounding over the slope, down and splashing through the stream, only to emerge hopping like a jack rabbit up the other side. Vanished.

Adam wished he could move so quickly, for now he could hear the thing that stalked them, coming from behind the thin screen of nearest trees. A low keening at first, then building to a strained howl. Adam's vision magnified and jumped wildly around the woods but found nothing.

Something full of full of dead weight clomped over the ground, dragging through dry grass and brush, growing louder, coming closer.

Adam threw himself forward, scrambling up the slope and over the bank, following his deer. He slipped going down the other side and his backpack braced his fall. He dropped down a steep slide, hard root branches tripping his heels, cold water covering his shoes, soaking into his socks, halfway to his knees. He jammed one palm into the mud and shoved himself upright and leaped, hoping to clear the stream. He landed midway and slipped on the stream-bed rocks, water sloshing up to his waist as he hop-stepped across, the splashing loud, blowing his cover completely.

The thing loosed a heart-rending scream, the sound of a lamb being quartered by a pack of wolves.

The toe of one sneaker snagged on a heavy rock and Adam pitched forward, his entire front side smacking down in the water before his hands caught the edge of the other bank. He crawled out, his fingers digging in cold mud and raking at rocks as he imagined something the size of a bear and twice as angry coming down behind him.

I'm going to die here tonight. Whatever's chasing me isn't just an animal, frightened because I wandered into its territory. It's smarter than that. It has another purpose, and that purpose is to kill me.

This was more than his fear talking. Adam knew in his guts that he and the thing chasing him shared a connection, their fates set in motion by some terrible event. He had wronged it somehow and it wanted to make him suffer for what he had done.

Adam scaled the second bank, gasping. There were no trees on this side, the stream was a border at the end of the woods. He ran downhill and quickly leveled off into a huge field, the prairie grass knee-high in all directions. He could run faster out here without fear of slamming into a tree or slipping on rocks, but he also knew the thing would be able to spot him in an instant.

Adam looked in every direction for a building or street light, some marker of civilization. But there was only the land. He ran as fast as he could.

The beast loosed another series of hateful shrieks, sounds neither human nor animal but more wretched than either. Adam imagined a monster eight feet tall, covered in dirty white fur, skeletal, with a mane of black hair and flat snout, its mouth racked with fangs. The human-like hands and gnarled fingers ended in talons as large as the big blade of his pocketknife. His pocketknife? Yes, he remembered there was one in the backpack, but it would be no use against this thing.

The scream wound down like a siren, and Adam flew across the field in the grip of a primal terror as fierce as any he had ever known. He arched his back as he ran, imagining the claws digging into his flesh, hooking into his spine, bringing him down in the field where no one would hear his dying screams.

Hu-chuff-hu-chuff-hu-chuff . . .

The thing panted after him, gaining, snorting like a bull.

Adam pushed himself harder, the wind beating back his tears. He wanted to lie down and cry but he knew there was no one to help him. If he slowed even for a minute he would be devoured. Out here in a field that seemed endless, with the indifferent stars above and the beast tracking him from behind, Adam felt condemned, stranded in a barren realm with no exit save his own death.

3

Darren searched every one of the showroom's twenty-five hundred square feet, behind the shelves, under the office desk, in the bathroom and closet, between the rows and aisles of goods. He found no trespasser.

Nothing had been stolen, either. He would have noticed immediately, the space and its contents as familiar to him as a puzzle he had been staring at for months, which in fact he had, nine of them to be precise. A single missing item would have registered to his eye as surely as a black slash of graffiti in a beautiful mural. The lights were on and the alarm had been deactivated, which could only mean he had forgotten to lock up. It seemed unlikely, but then again, he did not feel like himself these days.

The shop, the showroom, the Bike Cave – that had been Raya's cute name for it – whatever it had become, Darren always felt calmer inside its walls. Now that he had confirmed everything was in order, he was in no hurry to return to the main house. The Bike Cave potential was not the only reason he'd acquiesced to Beth's wish to buy this house, in this town he wasn't sure he ever wanted to return to, but it was the clincher.

Aesthetically it had been hideous, all that metal siding, but the dedicated space was the appeal of it, and the old-fashioned black and red checkerboard tile flooring inside – aged with grease and paint stains, chipped by decades of semi-industrial use, like some hybridization of an old school barbershop and an amateur stock car racer's garage – only helped shape his vision for the space.

He ordered the renovations before they moved, investing forty thousand to redo the exterior in eight-inch pine boards, finish the interior with new drywall blown full of insulation so that he could work year-round, add a new wood shingle roof, install new plumbing for a small bathroom, updated electrical, wireless everything for the small office. He hired a painting company to cover the exterior in dark brown with white trim and then painted the interior himself, in alternating panels of white, gold and P.K. Ripper baby blue to give it some life.

He equipped one long wall with workbenches, rolling toolboxes, a refrigerator, a CD jukebox wired into premium speakers, as well as the main stereo and turntable set-up he'd had since college, a leather couch, dartboard, and three stand-up classic arcade games – *Zaxxon*, *Defender* and *Tempest*.

Then, when he'd exhumed his collection from the seven rented storage bays in Milwaukee and had it all boxed up, along with the bike stands and glass display cabinets, he hired a second moving truck to bring it all here. Part bike store, part museum to his youth, part lab for a mad scientist with a serious Eighties bent, the shop now housed Darren's only remaining hobby, passion, and occupation:

The Totally Radical Sickness Collection.

One hundred and nine complete BMX bikes (even after the auction). Three road bikes. Two classic motorcycles. One motocross and one enduro motorcycle (the '77 Bultaco Alpina), another seventy BMX bike frames, forks, dozens of wheel sets, thousands of other vintage components. Wooden display bins for his eight hundred and counting vinyl records, twice as many CDs, and the two hundred and sixty-two pairs of vintage sneakers, most of which had never been laced. Concert tees and posters. A few signed professional sports jerseys. Rare toys from the Seventies and early Eighties. A few hundred issues of now-defunct BMX magazines. Three hundred VHS tapes – mostly terrible action, horror and sex comedy flicks. Scores of pocketknives, throwing stars, nunchakus, blowguns and other martial arts weaponry. A baker's dozen original Vision and Powell Peralta skateboard decks preserved in shrink-wrap. Baseball cards, primitive gaming cartridges and consoles, rare candy bars ...

Was this a hoarding obsession of some kind? Absolutely. Did Darren care what other people thought of an adult still fascinated by 'childish' things? Absolutely not. He had worked seventy- and eighty-hour weeks for over twenty years to secure his family's future. The house was paid off, the cars were paid off, the retirement accounts were on cruise control. Raya would be able to attend any college that offered her admission. Beth had been able to be the in-home, hands-on mother she always wanted to be, and now was free to dabble in non-profits without fear of financial failure. They did not spend lavishly or flaunt their good fortune. He had earned the right to follow his interests. Someday maybe he would sell it all and donate the proceeds to some cause, but for now it served another purpose.

There were no fires in the shop. No bad dreams. Money, politics, business contracts, sales pitches, proposals from new investors, health problems, their friends calling to announce a sudden illnesses or surprise divorce, Darren's own minor moments of marital discord with Beth, the depressing reality of his own waning sex drive, some hotshot in line at the grocery store barking into his cellphone, holding everyone up, whatever headache it is, whatever problems exist in the real world, you could keep that business out there – it wasn't allowed through this door. Here we are only interested in bikes. In cool. In the good old days.

In sanctuary.

And until tonight, that sanctuary had been untainted as a monastery in Bhutan. But now . . .

How had he missed *this*?

The shop's back door was ajar. Darren hadn't noticed it until his third pass, but he did so now. He'd been so lost in his reverie, he hadn't noticed the gap between door and frame. He walked to it, experiencing another wave of vertigo similar to what he had felt waking from the nightmares, and opened the door slowly.

The exterior screen door was wedged open, the exit out onto the cement porch blocked by a wooden crate the size of a child's coffin. Darren stepped over it, out into the grass. He searched the rear of the property, along the row of small pine trees, but there was no one out here.

He dragged the box inside. It wasn't light, but couldn't have weighed more than thirty or forty pounds. He shut the door and locked it, then rolled the crate over, checking each side, but there were no shipping labels of any kind. Darren shipped plenty of packages and took as many deliveries, through UPS, the US Postal Service and sometimes DHL for international service. He knew most of the drivers by name, and none of them would have delivered a box without the proper paperwork.

Someone with no official business had delivered this.

It was roughly the size of a bike box, but those were almost always cardboard. This was pine, nails, metal belting. More importantly, he hadn't ordered any new bikes or parts in almost two months, since before the auction.

He took a claw hammer from the pegboard of tools above his workbench and began to pry the metal straps off. Then he went at the nails, breaking the thin cover of wood in the process. Most collectors packaged bikes and their components in plastic bubble wrap or foam pipe tubing, then filled the excess space with styrofoam peanuts or wads of newspaper. This crate was filled with balls of old yellowed newspaper, but beneath the first layer of that, Darren found himself staring at thick bolts of purple velvet, dusty and dry. It made him think of antiques, a magician's cabinet of props.

Sensing he was dealing with something valuable, or at least very old, Darren removed the box's contents slowly, carefully placing each piece – still wrapped in layers of the velvet – on the shop's floor. There was no note or paperwork inside. In the office he found one of his old Mexican blankets, of the sort he kept for setting up items he could not afford to scratch. He spread the blanket on the floor and began to unwrap each purple bundle. When he had unwrapped the last piece, he knew what he was looking at, but had no more clue as to who had sent it to him, or why.

And he was too astonished to care.

Somehow, probably by accident, he had become the owner of a 1980 Cinelli CMX-1, a very rare BMX bike whose frame, fork and major components had been designed and manufactured by that Holy Trinity of Italian bicycle artisans – Cinelli, Campagnolo and Columbus. He had forgotten such a thing existed. He'd never owned one, never paid much attention to them, but he should have. The failed run of BMX equipment the famous Italian road bike manufacturers had collaborated on during the years 1980–81 was stunningly beautiful.

The oxblood-red CMX-1 frame and forks, anodized

gold Cinelli stem, brown suede buffalo hide Cinelli saddle, gold Cinelli seat post, had been partnered with Campagnolo's BMX-specific hubs, cranks, chainring and sealed bottom bracket, all in that famous Campagnolo blue. The tires, brakes, handlebars and grips were from other manufacturers, but still vintage, era-correct, and obviously chosen with an expert eye, color-matched and outfitted in a way Darren himself would have been proud of.

But he could not get over its miraculous condition.

Even with NOS (new old stock) bikes and parts that had sat gathering dust in the loft of some old geezer's bike shop in Akron, Ohio, there was almost always evidence of what the collectors referred to as shop wear. Little nicks or scuffs or other blemishes in the finish from rubbing against other parts and boxes or shelves, decals that had begun to crackle and flake.

But this Cinelli showed zero shop wear. Darren had never seen a bike so cherry. There were no scratches, dents, dings, bends or re-welds on the frame, and all of the decals appeared to be original, mint. He couldn't even find a fingerprint. If there were an *Antiques Roadshow* for BMX geeks, hosted by a guy who knew the market for such finds and who loved bikes, he would have taken one look at this Cinelli and wet himself.

Darren was disturbed by it for reasons he could not explain. It was a work of cycling art, but it was also a puzzle, or a message, and he wasn't sure he wanted to see what it revealed once it was complete.

There was something almost threatening about it.

He wondered if one of his fellow BMX junkies had it in for him, if he'd pissed someone off in a deal. He doubted it. He had 784 feedback comments on his profile at BMXMuseum.com (an online market and showroom mecca where he'd spent thousands of hours surfing, trading, researching) and he maintained a 100 per cent positive member rating, lacking even a single negative comment, and another perfect rating on eBay. Besides, people who had it in for you didn't send you bikes. They stole them.

A gift? The last thing anyone who knew him would give him was yet another bike.

It was an orphan, he decided, a term in the cycling community for a spare part without its other half or 'parent' unit, a piece with no mate, no home. You'd see the term in the classified listings online: Orphan Shimano DX pedal, needs a good home, $85 OBO. Orphan Comp III yellow label tire, used, $40. There wasn't much demand for orphan parts because the odds were low you would find the perfect match in terms of color, wear, fade, size, year, etc.

The entire Cinelli was an orphan, albeit an expensive one. It had no home or proper owner. It was just here, waiting for someone to take it in.

Later he would call some of his contacts, maybe set up a query on the forums, to find out if anyone had made a mistake. But in the meantime ...

Outside, the rain started up again, pattering the shop's roof with a comforting drone that made him want to stay inside and work on bikes all night with his father, until the a.m. radio oldies station gave it up for a religious sermon and Mom came out and told the boys to get their butts back to bed.

As he had on so many other nights, or lazy Sunday afternoons, Darren felt a pang of longing for a second child, a scabby-kneed, dirt-on-his-cheeks boy who could experience this with him. A father could ask for nothing more of a daughter than Raya had given him, but sometimes a man needs a boy around to understand the beauty of a wrench, the allure of a rusted chain.

He was not conscious of the decision to proceed, but there went his hands, unwrapping velvet. Working as carefully as a surgeon performing an open-heart procedure, he assembled the Cinelli. It took less than an hour because the brakes were already perfectly tuned. He inflated the tires. But when he reached the last of it, the pedals, he could not find them.

He searched the wads of newspaper spread around the shop's floor. His workbench. Finally he went back to the box. Inside was a smaller bundle of velvet, taped into the corner of the (coffin) crate. This had to be the pedals.

He pried the bundle from the crate, but another double strand of clear packaging tape was wound around the velvet seams, sealing the contents from view.

The Oakley clock above his office window read 3:22 a.m.

Yawning, Darren went to the workbench and found his box-cutter in one of the plastic trays where he kept rolls of packing tape, felt markers, labels and other shipping supplies. With his thumb he inched the blade forth from its steel handle, held the bundle down with his left hand, and drew the razor along the tape layers.

Two-thirds of the way through, the blade caught on something hard, jumped up and sliced into his thumb. There was a delay of numbness, then the stinging set in. He stared at the fish-white gap between his severed thumbprint whorls for a moment, dazed, until fresh dark blood flowed out in a thick stream.

In the grand tradition of self-injured mechanics since time immemorial, he cursed at himself and the tools rather colorfully, dancing to his right to reach for some paper towels to staunch the flow. The cut was deep, almost to the bone. Probably should get some stitches for that tomorrow . . . today. Later this morning.

Not now. He had to see what was inside and make sure he hadn't scratched them with the knife.

His blood continued to flow, droplets of it landing on his floor, the workbench, the toe of one shoe. He knew there was a first-aid kit out here somewhere, but he couldn't find it in the bathroom or the office. He didn't want to run back to the house. Wadding his thumb in two folded paper towels, Darren used his free hand and teeth to tear a length of duct tape from the roll hanging off the wall peg. He wrapped his thumb several times, but already more blood was seeping up through the tape seams.

Hurrying, he unrolled the last bundle on the bench. Two jagged-toothed Campagnolo BMX pedals gleamed before him, their gold cages and chrome spindles as spectacular as the rest of the bike. He studied them carefully but found no scratch.

Lucky break.

He walked the first pedal over to the bike and finger-tightened it into the crank arm. He went back for the second pedal and repeated the install on the other side. If anyone intended to ride this bike, the pedals and other parts would need further tightening, for the sake of safety. But Darren had no intention of riding this bike, or allowing anyone else near it.

That was it, then. The bike was finished. He almost expected a bolt of lightning to crash overhead, accompanied by the deep sonorous cue of a medieval film score, but the shop was silent.

He stared at the finished bird, hypnotized by its sleek poise. Something about the pedals affected him more than the other pieces. They were so clean and thoughtfully designed, the teeth canted inward to keep your foot from slipping to the outside. What a beautiful touch. Design with a purpose beyond mere beauty. Simple and functional but well crafted all the same.

Oh, how he wished he had owned a bike like this when he was a kid. No, not like this. *This* bike. It wouldn't have been much of a jumper – its oval tubing too slender, its geometry built for speed not torque – but man, it would have been a neck-breaking looker in the old neighborhood. A little cheetah back in the day, a kind of holy relic now.

It was Immaculate. An idol upon the altar of his work station.

Goosebumps rippled across Darren's skin as he adored it. He was panting, his heart thrumming, and his legs felt Tour de France strong, engorged with blood and limitless energy, and he could swear that, for just a moment, a little breeze gusted over his brow, blowing his hair back a bit. The entire bodily sensation was one of riding free on an endless summer afternoon, nowhere to go, nothing to do, just a boy and his bike.

He felt he was standing on a precipice of understanding, hypnotized by seeds of memory and love and forgotten longings, enough to populate a lifetime, by treasures the soul of this bicycle contained. What secrets might it reveal if he were to simply unlock it from the stand and take it for a long ride before dawn, following its whims and desires to a place no one knows, a mounded dirt park inaccessible by any other means except this one bike, a place lost in time. Yes, he should go for a ride now, cut the night in half with two wheels—

Or maybe not.

Darren frowned, walking around the Cinelli on the stand, noticing some paint out of place on the red frame. How could he have missed this? Damn it, look at that, the paint had run, bubbled in places, and was even now dripping on the floor.

No, it wasn't the paint.

It was blood. His blood.

Darren had forgotten about his thumb. Fondling the pedals, screwing them into the cranks, he'd gone and bled all over the damned bike. Drops of it were on the down tube, the pedal cages, the seat-post clamp. And higher, swiped along the handlebars, the right grip and brake lever, places he didn't even remember touching tonight. Jesus! Blood everywhere, a cup of it or more.

'Look at this!' he shouted, as if berating a dim-witted assistant. His anger was all-consuming, far out of proportion to the mess. This wasn't a big deal, after all. Blood wipes off. But how could he have let this happen? He'd been so careful . . .

He wrapped more paper towels around his thumb and rammed his fist into his pocket to keep from touching the bike with his bleeding hand. With the other hand he wet a wad of paper towels at the sink, squeezed out the excess water, and brought a few more dry ones to follow up with. He turned from the sink and walked back.

Halfway there he froze, his mouth falling open as a low moan issued from his gut. For a moment he thought he was going to be sick, and then, when his brain processed what his eyes were seeing, he damn near screamed.

The Cinelli's wheels were turning, and not in the way a wheel may turn half a revolution due to gravity and the angle of its position on the stand. The spokes were blurring, the treads gently whirring, the cranks and pedals going round and round in the smooth, continuous pace of someone on a lazy ride through a rolling countryside.

Darren looked at the blood soaking through his pants pocket, back up at the bike with its spinning wheels, and he thought again of what had called him out here, the possibility of an intruder. The cranks slowed and the freewheel engaged, its clicking buzz rattling while the wheels themselves continued to roll. The back of his neck went cold and his scalp bristled as if brushed by invisible fingertips. The sense that someone was in here, hiding in plain sight, was stronger than ever before.

He heard a boy's laughter. Coming in faint waves, as if the boy were standing far behind him. The laughter seemed to amplify, coming closer, crossing a great distance to find him until the child was standing right behind him—

He whirled and saw a pale blur, a bright whiteness inside a darker halo outline, a reversed shadow in the shape of a small person, a boy. But no sooner had he glimpsed it than the apparition began to disperse like gas, into black dots and thickening clouds of red, and he realized too late that he was fainting.

Darren reached for the workbench to steady himself, but he was too far away, too heavy to move. His legs buckled and he collapsed on the tile floor where his blood continued to trickle out.

4

When the seemingly endless field finally ended, Adam
had run himself dizzy and he found himself at the edge
of a plateau, the view beyond revealing an irregular
band of lights below, stretching in all directions.

Houses, street lights, a neighborhood.

Beyond those, a town.

The descent steepened. Adam's knees quaked with
the loose, out-of-control strides needed to maintain
speed without tumbling head over heels as he careened
to the bottom. Two hair-raising minutes later things leveled out and field grass gave way to rough dirt, but this
lasted only for another fifty feet or so before he crossed
a border onto planted grass, a vast lawn that had recently
been mowed.

A subdivision, the houses average size, hundreds of
them in a handful of shapes and colors. Lots of places to
hide, in the garages, behind a fence, between cars, any
shelter would do.

Adam looked back. The hill rose up behind him a
hundred feet or more, the top line of the plateau
waving and blurry with the pounding of his legs. He

saw no monster on his tail, but he felt no safer down here. His instincts warned him that the beast was not something out of a fairy tale or ordinary nature, relegated to the wilderness. It was more elusive, cunning, able to track him in the wild or in a city, able to blend into its surroundings and go unnoticed by average people.

He might have outrun it for now, but it would find him again.

He followed a smooth black road into the neighborhood and slowed his pace from a jog to a fast walk. A hundred steps later he was still nearly hyperventilating. The sidewalks in both directions were empty. No one was out walking, even though some of the lights in the houses were on. Probably it was too late for a walk. That was fine.

Adam didn't want strangers taking him in, hatching their own plans about where to put him, in some home for orphans. God only knew what would happen to him in one of those places. He was terrified of being caught by the monster, yes, but his fear of authority, even a good policeman who thought he was doing the right thing, was just as strong. He couldn't trust anyone. He was better off alone.

His clothes were no longer dripping wet but still clung to him, soaking a continuous chill into his bones. How many hours until sunlight? He couldn't find the moon in the sky. Could be an hour before dawn, or midnight, a small eternity from the warmth he so badly needed.

A car engine sounded a block or two away, coming closer, then only several houses distant. He ducked into a yard and paused. The engine tapered to silence. Someone had either reached home and parked or driven out of the neighborhood. He walked on, careful to avoid tripping over the toys and lawn furniture in the yards.

When another fence blocked his path, he was forced to edge his way up onto a sidewalk running through the interior of the neighborhood. The concrete path was too white in the darkness, and he feared he would stand out against its long flat background. He looked back. Hard to tell how far he could see in this darkness, but probably not more than a football field, if that.

He raised his head to the sky and let out a deep breath, watching the stars, and then lower, on the horizon from where he had come, to the mountains against the lighter night sky.

Mountains. Colorado. Boulder?

How do I know that name, Boulder? Is that the town I grew up in?

How old am I? Eleven or twelve, he thought, but he couldn't be sure. Tendrils of memory teased at him, the grass and the park and faceless kids on their bikes. A sunny day, free from his parents and free to get lost. There had been an outdoor mall with jugglers and fortune tellers and knife shops. He used to ride his bike halfway across town to hang out on the mall, watching the people, buying some candy, maybe an ice-cream cone, bubble-gum flavor with the blue that stained your fingers all day.

Maybe when the sun came up he would recognize more of his surroundings, remember more about what happened to him and why he was alone.

Tap tap tap slap-slap tap tap tap ...

Adam stopped, his ears signaling alarm. His heart resumed its forceful thumping with painful resentment. Movement of some kind, behind him, like distant footsteps.

He looked back, eyes tracing the sidewalk arcing and weaving deep into the darkness, and at the edge of his vision, where the white concrete darkened and faded to gray, something tall and dark was moving. The top of it was bobbing up and down, the motion of something walking fast. Or running toward him.

Who goes running at this time of night? Besides me? People who are either being chased or doing the chasing. Except this wasn't a person. It was too tall, and thin, and while the middle of its body was a solid band of darkness, the head was much paler, almost white in the night.

Adam ran, keeping low to the ground. When he had gone another hundred yards or so he looked back again, and his breath caught in his throat.

The thing was still coming toward him, but it had changed. Somehow it was wider, shorter, as if it were lowering itself in order to run faster. It mutated once more as he watched, dividing. Now two figures pursued him, each of them dark and bulky in the middle with crowns of blurry whiteness above the thick shoulders.

You knew there was more than one, he scolded

himself. Always was. Two at least, and maybe a third. They're tracking you like a pack of wild dogs.

Adam cut from the path and ran into the first yard without a fence. Immediately a severe cramp flared in his right side, twisting the muscle under his ribs. He pushed on, but a few steps later another cramp lit up his right hamstring and he was unable to find a stride. Running wasn't going to save him this time. He was going to have to be smarter, find a place to hide.

He paused beside a small wooden gazebo. At first he heard nothing, then a few quick taps like before, much closer, and then a softer scuffling as the footsteps moved off concrete into the grass. Adam took one look at the open gazebo and knew it would serve him no purpose beyond that of a cage, a feeding pen.

He darted away, around the house, through the front yard, then cut sideways running back the way he had come, ducking and leaping through more front yards. The cramps only increased but he ground his teeth and tried his best to ignore them.

Six or seven houses later he hobbled between two cars parked in a wide driveway and looked back. He couldn't see them and he hoped they were still on the other side of the houses. He limped alongside the house, between the exterior side wall and the next property's fence.

He was hoping to slip through, but halfway into the gap he ran into a wall, which turned out not to be a wall but some kind of tall wooden chute. It was warm, soothing against his cold body. A chimney, maybe. But it was humming too, vibrating slightly. More importantly, it was blocking his path of escape, the space between it and the fence next door too tight for him to squeeze through.

Somewhere beyond the house and getting closer by the second, the dull slapping footsteps returned. Rapid, then halting and spreading in different directions, trying to pinpoint his location, enclose him in their circle. If he ran back toward the street – his only avenue of escape – they would see him, catch him, slaughter him.

He crouched. The tall chute was even warmer down here, with a current of warm air blowing against his ankles. A faint mist rolled over the bald spot in the grass, and he understood. It wasn't a chimney. It was the ventilation duct to a clothes dryer. Someone was doing laundry at this hour.

How much space was there between the vent and the ground?

Adam lowered himself to his belly and estimated there were maybe six or eight inches of clearance. His body might fit, if he were to lie down and inch his way back, but not his head. If he kept his head to one side, between the duct and the fence, he could make it. Maybe.

He removed his backpack, smashed it flat and shoved it under the duct. Reclining like a mechanic about to slide under a car, he tilted his head to one side and began to drag himself, squirming and sliding, wiggling his hips, deeper under the vent. In such proximity, the warm air was almost hot on his chest. If his skin touched the metal lining, he would be burned. But as long as it didn't get any hotter than this, he could handle it. It felt good, actually. He wormed in deeper.

Problem – under the hum of the machine reverberating through this vent, he couldn't hear what was happening out on the street. They could be moving in, closing off the driveway, and he had no way to see them. Not only that, his legs were sticking out.

Using his elbows, straining his neck, Adam snaked backward, pushing into the grass with his heels, until at last he was able to straighten his head around the other side of the wooden chute. Now that his hips were inside the frame, he was able to twist onto his side. He tucked his knees but his feet were still exposed.

The monsters were close. He could feel them. They could be in the driveway, beside the house, squinting into the dark, staring at the white soles of his shoes ...

Adam closed his eyes and wished, with all his will and most fervent prayers, that he was someone else, somewhere else. A different boy, one with a family, with a loving mother and a good strong dad. In a nice warm house beside a fire, on Christmas morning, with breakfast cooking on the stove, cartoons on the big TV, and his family laughing with him, hugging him, holding him close while the lights on the tree glimmered beside the fireplace. He could see it so clearly that for one beautiful moment he was really *there*, gone from this place on the cold ground in the night, and his wet clothes had been replaced by new ones, dry and sharp like the other kids at school had. And he was different too, not a mental case on the run but a normal boy, stronger and faster, it was real, he'd escaped, and he would never have to run again.

His new father was a cool guy, the kind of guy who would help you build a model airplane or fix your bike, and his mother was beautiful, one look in her eyes enough to let you know she loved you no matter how you screwed up. Outside there was a huge yard with a pond, and bright orange fish swimming beneath emerald-green lily pads, their whiskers switching like antennae. Adam could see it all, it was so real, and he knew he was there because they could see him too.

Behind them, standing in the hallway, was a girl, his new sister, and she was older and very pretty, with dark blonde hair and sleepy green eyes. She had very strong opinions about almost everything, but she never hurt him and she liked to ask him all kinds of questions, as if he were the most interesting person she had ever met.

Home, he was home . . .

Until the dryer's timer ran out. The humming stopped. The soothing warm air faded to a whisper on his belly, replaced by colder air seeping in all around him. The silence rang in his ears like dying wind chimes.

He wasn't home. He was still lost. He would always be lost, and the return to this cold reality broke his heart. Trapped under some stranger's house, shivering, Adam cried, not caring who found him or what they did to him. He cried himself into a sleep too fragile and barren for dreams.

5

Raya Lynwood sort of wished Chad would stop texting her and go to sleep already. It was almost four in the morning and she kept dozing off, only to be jolted awake by her phone buzzing from under her pillow. She rarely tired of texting with Chad, and it was really sweet that he even bothered when he was out late with the guys, but this was turning into some kind of sleep-deprivation experiment.

Of course she could have turned off the phone, or set it on her dresser on the other side of her bedroom, but she was worried about him getting home safe. If tomorrow wasn't the last day of school, Raya would have been asleep long ago. And Chad wouldn't be out with his friends, playing poker and drinking beer until the sun came up. In the meantime he kept sending her silly things.

> I think we should take a roader to New Orleans this summer.

Have you seen that movie where the six chicks go spelunking and get eaten by those bat people in the caves? The one who lived sorta reminds me of you.

You ask your dad if we can borrow his Firebird yet?

It wasn't even a conversation. He would ask her something, she would respond, and then he'd move on to some other topic. Sometimes Raya wondered if Chad really listened to her, or paid attention to her texts. Most boys didn't listen very well, but Chad seemed different than most boys. He was polite, and patient, and when they were together he looked at her as if he had stumbled upon a pot of gold. Besides, what did it matter how she responded to such questions? Her dad wasn't going to let her go on a road trip, not with Chad or anyone else.

Chad was seventeen, two years older than Raya. Her mom seemed cool with this, but her dad was another story. No way would her dad let Chad drive the Firebird. He wouldn't even let Raya drive the Firebird (or his Acura for that matter), only her mom's wagon while she had her learner's permit. It was a Beemer but still a wagon and not even close to being as fun to drive as the Firebird.

What was her dad doing up so late again, anyway? Raya thought she'd heard someone pacing around her door earlier, and when she went to the bathroom for a glass of water about an hour ago, she noticed the living-room lights were on. Had to be her dad. Mom slept like a rock from ten or eleven until 6 a.m. sharp, and her dad had some kind of insomnia thing going lately.

How much money does your dad have, anyway? Sorry, the guys made me ask.

Go back to your poker, Chadly, was all she had to say to that.

Chad was not her first boyfriend but he was her longest relationship, or maybe the first one that could be called a relationship.

If I was there right now, would you let me kiss your legs?

That one cracked her up, and made her nervous. What did he mean by that? Raya couldn't tell if he really meant kiss your legs. Chad wasn't crass like other boys, texting pictures of his junk and sending her lascivious messages. Lots of them did that, she'd heard. The girls too. Chad had never said or sent anything of the sort to her. He was more cryptic, always framing things in a harmless way. But sometimes Raya wondered if Chad was this way because he was really being himself or if he was only refraining from raunchier stuff because he thought she would freak out.

She probably would freak out, or pretend to, just to cool him off. But another part of her wanted to know if what he really meant was, would you let me kiss that place between your legs?

Just once, he prompted, for like 10 seconds?

No, she texted back. Stop being a beast.

But the idea excited her too. Not the idea of Chad kissing her between her legs, because hell no, she wasn't letting anyone do that until she was like twenty-five, and then only if they were seriously in love. But the thought of Chad kissing her knees, the top of her thighs, for a few seconds ... yeah, that made her stomach go a little crazy.

She drifted off, then her phone buzzed again. Except, when she looked at the screen there was no new text, from Chad or anyone else. That was weird but not really a big deal. It happened kind of frequently, actually, but usually it was the other way around. Her brain knew before her phone confirmed it.

Sometimes Raya would sense an incoming text and it wouldn't be there, but seconds later one would arrive. Or she would just be thinking of Chad, smiling to herself about something sweet he did, like when he brought her flowers two weeks ago, or how he always remembered to open his car door for her – and right then one of his texts would arrive, or he would call. And he'd be all like, 'Whatcha doin', beautiful Raya?' in his mellow voice, like it was the most natural thing in the world for him to say.

What was that all about? The timing, not his voice. It seemed to happen with Chad more often than with any of her other friends or her parents. Was it because she and Chad were connected, and some part of her had a sixth sense about when he would call or text her? Or maybe (less fun to consider) everybody was so glued to their phones these days, texting like three hundred times a day, you were always in a state of anticipation, like Emma Bovary, thinking about your boyfriend, and it only seemed like intuition when another text arrived at the same time.

Because this had happened before, in other ways. Like the time her mom went to the store, said she would be right back, and two hours later Raya knew something was wrong. Her mom hadn't called or come home, and Raya immediately pictured her stranded on the side of the road shaking her cellphone because the battery was dead, the wagon's hood open while steam hissed out.

Raya was so convinced by the vision, she'd gone and found her dad in the Bike Cave and told him she thought Mom was having some car trouble. Her dad tried calling and there was no answer. Worried, he went out looking for her, starting at the Safeway parking lot where Mom usually shopped. Raya stayed home, in case her mom called or got back first.

They came home twenty minutes later and it turned out Raya had been exactly right. Well, almost exactly, which wasn't exactly at all, as her English teacher Mrs Iwerson reminded her whenever Raya accidentally used a contradictory or redundant adverb in one of her papers. Exactly the same. 'Exactly' was like that, it could fool you. And the car breakdown was like that. Not exactly like her vision but so close as to be spooky. In real life it turned out to be a flat tire, not the engine. And her cellphone battery wasn't dead. She'd simply left it in her office at Fresh Starts.

Still, it was enough to make a girl wonder.

Raya was on the verge of sleep for the fourth time in as many hours when Chad finally texted back.

Lost all my money. No more cards for me. U still awake? Wanna talk on my way home?

Too sleepy, Raya sent back, but are you OK to drive?

Chad wasn't a big drinker, usually limiting himself to a few beers. His personality didn't change when he drank, a sign her mom had warned her to watch out for.

Didn't drink tonight, Chad replied.

Raya found this unlikely, though she didn't think Chad would lie to her about having a few beers. She'd never hassled him about it, so maybe he was telling the truth.

Promise?

Swear. And I love you.

You too, Raya wrote.

That always made her happy, when he said the words. But she couldn't say the actual words back. She knew 'you too' was misleading, and she sensed he understood the difference. She didn't love Chad, *really* love Chad, like she knew she would love somebody when she was older. She cared about him a lot, and he was super-sweet to her, and what was wrong with telling someone 'you too', even if it wasn't the purest, strongest, most amazing

56

love you would ever have? Maybe nothing, except that she couldn't bring herself to do it. Maybe someday. Not tonight.

Finally she could go to sleep. Except now she had to pee again.

Raya got out of bed and walked to the bathroom attached to her bedroom suite. She was about to drop her pajama bottoms when she noticed that the toilet paper roll had only like four squares left. Probably enough, but she hated getting pee on her hand, even if it was her own pee. And she would need more in the morning anyway, so might as well get a fresh roll now. She opened the cabinet under her sink but it was empty. Great, now she had to go out to the bathroom at the front of the house to stock up. She could have put it off, but one of the things she took pride in was something her dad told her over and over when she was little, until it became a habit of her own.

Don't put off getting things done, honey. Even the little stuff, the stupid stuff. Every day there are dozens of things you could do, and should do, to make life easier, and you will be tempted to put them off until tomorrow. But don't do that, because it's a small bit of lazy, and it only gets easier and easier to be lazy. And pretty soon, after years and years, your life might still be good but there will be hundreds, thousands of little things you could have done, done so easily, but you didn't.

And the secret is this, honey. Putting off thousands of little things makes it easier to put off doing one or two of the really big things, something really special and worthwhile. If you want to build a company, write a book, travel around the world, get your PhD, you will never get there by avoiding the stupid little details that accumulate. To do the special thing, the one main thing in life, you have to sweep up the little things like dust, out of habit, without even using your brain. Because you're that smart. And your life is special, Raya, so don't do that to yourself. Don't live your whole life accomplishing less than you are capable of and making things easier on yourself when you could be onto something great. Understand?

She hadn't minded the speech because he wasn't lecturing her, and she respected her dad. He'd already built his own business by the time she was born. By the time she was three, he owned a strip mall in Milwaukee. It was totally ghetto, but he owned it. So she digested what he told her, and soon she began to notice things, little things that nagged at her when she didn't do them.

Like folding her clothes, which looked nice and made getting ready for school easier. Or writing thank-you notes after Christmas or her birthday, which felt like an obligation and a hassle until she did them, then made her feel grateful and calm. Lots of stuff got easier once she got in the habit of just doing them before she made them a big deal in her head. Which is why now, at age fifteen, even something as small as changing out the toilet-paper roll at four in the morning would drive her nuts if she put it off.

That's my Lynwood girl, she could almost hear her dad saying, *go get yourself a damn roll of toilet paper and go to bed*.

Stuffing her phone into the waistband of her pajamas, she walked into the hall. The living-room lights were still on. On the other side of the foyer, she turned into the front bathroom and flipped on the light. The cabinet was stocked, so she grabbed four rolls, making a mental note to tell her mom to buy more anyway, because she liked to have a good supply of everything in her own bathroom, and the mini-fridge, which made her suite like a boutique hotel. Carrying two rolls in each hand, her fingers hooked into the cardboard spools, Raya used one roll to turn off the bathroom light and headed back into the hall.

She had gone a few steps when her phone vibrated inside her waistband. She thought of ignoring it because her hands were full, but it might be Chad, confessing his inebriation, and she didn't want him giving up and driving home drunk. Wedging two rolls under her left arm, she pulled the phone out and looked down at the screen.

when he takes away your childhood you can never get it back

That was it. No punctuation, no context. At first she thought it must be another of Chad's non sequiturs, until she saw the number, which did not list Chad or any of her contacts and which wasn't a phone number at all, just a string of zeroes and ones.

01010100100100110 1100011

That was weird. She'd never seen a number like that as a source for an incoming message or call. She was reading the text again when it disappeared. The entire screen of her phone went black, as if in shutdown mode.

Must have been an error, a message garbled in the company's servers or something.

She hadn't liked the feel of those words, but it was gone now and she was tired.

Raya was stuffing the phone back into her waistband when it vibrated again. She held it up. The screen was still black but a new text was visible, this time in white letters.

once he takes it all away you can never go back

The white text seemed to dissolve before she could tap the screen, and then another string of crisp white words replaced it:

first he takes your childhood away

Again the letters dissolved to total blackness, but almost immediately were replaced by:

then he kills you

The four rolls of toilet paper dropped to the floor. She looked back toward the kitchen, expecting her mom or dad to be in there, hoping one of them was there to explain this. She needed to show someone. But there wasn't anyone in the kitchen, and worse, the kitchen lights were off, except for the little ones under the cabinets.

The bright white letters dissolved and she was left standing in the dark.

Instinctively Raya pivoted and looked back, past the bathroom, to where the hall angled into the laundry and mud room that connected to the garage. She felt like she was being observed by someone, or something. But it was too dark to see to the end. A draft of cold air swept by her and she decided the door to the garage must be ajar. It was always colder in the laundry room.

None of which had anything to do with her phone, but still . . .

Who was sending these messages? Chad wouldn't play a trick on her like this. The messages bore no resemblance to his tone of voice, or his sense of humor.

The phone vibrated in her hand again. Raya's entire body tensed, as if the air were alive and something around her was pulling on her skin. Her mouth was open and she felt short of breath.

once you are dead you can never come back

'Okay, stop,' she said, needing to hear a voice of sanity, even if it was her own and she did not feel sane. 'Who's doing that?'

No one answered her. The house was silent.

As if to scold her for shifting her attention, the screen flashed bright white, glowing like a bulb in a lamp for several seconds, then instantly turned black.

once you let him take it all away he will kill you kill you kill you

Raya dropped the phone on the floor and covered her mouth to keep from screaming. She felt watched, stalked, and she had the craziest idea that if she made a sound, whoever was doing this would find her, show himself, pop out of thin air. If her phone started ringing right now she would have a heart attack.

Kill you? He will *kill you? Kill you kill you kill you ...* there was something desperate, threatening, even enraged about the last one.

The hall was dark, the phone on the floor no longer glowing. Raya didn't know whether to call for her parents or run to her room. She was paralyzed by the cold around her and a growing, throbbing sting in her eyes, behind her nose, a sensation she could only describe as a hot headache.

The white glow emanated up at her once more.

the orphan is coming home

The screen went black, faster than before, and a new message surfaced.

he needs to come home

The white glow seemed blinding, then there was blackness.

his entire family is dead the family is dead

Blackness.

62

the boy is coming home soon

Blackness.

the dead boy

Blackness.

soon

'Stop it!' Raya startled herself by yelling. 'Mom! Wake up!'

The screen turned black and she heard someone crying. Not her own tears, which had come in a series of whimpers, but the crying of a lost little boy. The sound made her want to scream and she turned to the front door, certain she had felt a draft of cold air beside her, but he wasn't there either and—

Footsteps thumped to the end of the bridge, into the living room.

A shadow person stood there watching her.

'Raya? What's going on?' The shadow slowly resolved into the shape of her mother. 'Did something happen? What in God's name are you doing up at this hour?'

Raya was too shocked and relieved to speak. She was trembling, toilet-paper rolls spilled around her feet.

'Raya? What is it, honey?' her mom said, hurrying over, hugging her.

'Someone was here!' Raya blurted, though she knew

this was not strictly true. But it *felt* true. 'The boy! I heard him crying!'

'What boy? Here, in the house?'

'Someone was talking to me, sending me messages – there, on my phone!' She pointed at her phone where it had fallen in the hall.

Her mom picked up the phone. She looked at the screen, at Raya, then back to the screen.

'Do you see it? He was talking about killing, saying he will kill you, he's coming home, horrible things . . . '

Her mom clicked through, checking her messages. 'There's nothing here,' she said. 'Just texts from Chad. He's out playing poker?'

Raya continued to cry, shaking her head.

'Where's your father? Is he out in the shop again?'

'I don't know.'

A pattering sound began to drum the roof and they both looked up, holding their breath, tensed with the expectation of some terrible arrival.

'It's raining,' her mom said. 'It's just the rain.'

6

Shelter, at last. Warm, dry shelter.

But the comfort would be short-lived, because he couldn't risk staying and it was not a shelter of his own. He had not been invited in and would not be welcomed upon discovery. The longer he stayed, the greater his chances of causing trouble, for himself or for the ones who lived here. In his heart Adam did not believe he was a criminal or a bad boy. But he felt guilty for trespassing, or breaking and entering, though he hadn't done much breaking to enter.

The first few seconds after waking to cold drops of water landing on his ankles and cheeks, he hadn't remembered where he was, or why, but then it all came back and he realized he was wedged under the ventilation duct. By the time he crawled out, the rain was really coming down, reversing what little dryness he had achieved since falling in the stream.

He'd crept along the back of the house intending to move on once he was sure the coast was clear, but when he saw that the house's rear sliding glass door was open, and only a screen door separated him from the inside, he couldn't resist going up for a closer look. He expected a living room or kitchen, but what he saw looked an awful lot like a basement. Carpeted, mostly empty, with only a pool table and stacks of boxes in the long room he could see.

Garages were good. Basements were better, warmer. He'd let himself into strangers' homes before, he knew. The familiar feelings of guilt and fear and a touch of excitement that hit him as he stepped inside told him that he was not new to such survival tactics. Emboldened, seeing no beds or other furniture, he ventured deeper into the space.

There were three doors off the main room. The first led to a half-finished bathroom with a sink and a plastic shower stall and then a hole and some pipes in the concrete floor where, he assumed, the toilet would be installed. The next opened into a larger room, also unfinished, with wooden studs and a few slabs of drywall framed around a large tub sink and a deep freezer. The last room was not much larger than a closet and contained only a tall white cylinder with copper pipes running from its base – water heater or furnace.

Adam placed his hands around it, gently at first, willing the heat into his palms and the rest of his body, and before long he was hugging the unit, pressing his entire body to its smooth surface. A source of heat. Perfect.

The rest of the basement wasn't much warmer than the air outside, but at least it was dry. The boiler room was also the least likely of the rooms anyone would find a reason to enter tonight or come morning, which couldn't be more than an hour or two from now. He took off his shoes and socks, then his pants and shirt, draping them over the top of the heater in hopes they would dry. Strangely, he felt warmer after that, even though he was almost naked. There was nothing to lie down on in here, so he slipped back to the room with the sink in search of some clothing or a scrap of carpet.

Beside the big sink, folded on a gray metal shelving rack, were some thin bed sheets with what he hoped were only paint stains on them, and half a dozen raggedy towels. He took three towels and one sheet back to the boiler room, wrapped himself in the sheet and then layered the towels across the floor in the form of a crude and very thin mattress. Not great, but better than resting his bare back and legs on the concrete, and much better than sleeping outside.

With any luck, the people who lived here would prepare for their day without any need to come down into the basement, then head off to work or school or wherever they had to go, and he could rest unnoticed all morning. Maybe even into the afternoon, waking with a few hours to spare before they came home. He might even be able to scrounge some food from the fridge and pantry.

Adam leaned back against the tank for a while, wanting to soak up the heat before stretching out to sleep. His tired gaze fell on his backpack. Time to see what was inside. He dragged it closer with his foot and unfastened the small plastic buckle on the nylon strap, flipping open its cover.

The first few items were more or less what he had expected. Clothes. A plain red T-shirt, a pair of plain white briefs, two pairs of white tube socks with colored bands at the top. Something he thought was a pair of jeans, but when he unrolled the denim he discovered it was a jean jacket, faded and so beat up it was as soft as a sweatshirt. He regretted not checking the pack earlier; the jacket would have been nice to have outside.

My jean jacket, he remembered. *My only jacket. Even in winter. I was always cold because this was all I was allowed to have. But I loved it. It was mine.*

Under the clothes, packed into the bottom, were a few basic food stores. Sticks of beef jerky, half a Snickers bar, and a depleted wax sleeve of Ritz crackers. He chewed a few of the crackers and ate two sticks of beef jerky, swallowing dryly. The basement had water at the sink, but he didn't want to risk turning it on, waking the people upstairs to the rattle of pipes. What else was in the bag?

A magazine rolled up tightly. Looked very futuristic, somewhat spooky, with an illustration of a man covered in armor astride a war horse and blowing a trumpet, with a pearl-colored planet in the sky behind him. *Questar*, it was called, and its otherworldly cover took him to another time and place. This issue was well worn, creased and wrinkled, as if someone had turned its pages a hundred times. He did so again now, idly, and almost at once the magazine flopped open to a bent sheaf of pages bookmarking an advertisement for amazingly realistic masks.

Monsters, aliens, ghosts, characters he recognized from movies he could not recall. There were dozens of masks, their photos not much bigger than postage stamps, enough to fill two pages. Pretty neat stuff. But then why did he feel something sour sinking in the pit of his belly? He sensed that at one time he had loved looking at these masks, dreaming of Halloween and ways to scare his friends.

But now they served a different purpose, and he understood why he had been carrying this magazine around for so long. Among the rows and rows of different creatures depicted here, he'd been trying to find the one that most resembled the monsters that had been chasing him. Another squall of terror swirled inside him and he closed the magazine, lowering it to his side, not wanting to see the thing's face.

He leaned out of the boiler room's doorway to make sure no one was coming for him. Everything was quiet, safe as it had been before. Stop being a baby, he scolded himself. It's only a mask. Not even that, only a *picture* of a mask. Just because you look at it, doesn't mean it's going to come roaring out of the darkness, here and now.

This is important, that other, knowing voice spoke up inside him. *It might even save your life.*

Adam opened the magazine again. Flipped to the marked page. After scanning the rows of fantastic but lifelike creations for only a few seconds, his eyes darted to the bottom right corner. There it was, circled in marker ink that had faded, and he knew he'd done this to remind himself. And maybe so he could describe the thing to someone else, if he ever found someone he could trust.

It was horrible to look at, even in a silly ad for Halloween masks.

Unlike all the other monsters, with their excess facial hair, horns, fangs, gaping flesh wounds, spilling brains or forked tongues, their skin in shades of green and blue, scaled or gilled or dripping red blood, this one was disturbing for its simple, haunting intensity and terrible lack of distinguishing features.

Overall the face was pale white with small, glossy black eyes, the head shape somewhat long or oval, with a wide lipless mouth and a flat nose with two small holes in it. It had no hair, only the smallest ears, and a sharp chin. It wasn't snarling or growling or sticking out its tongue, and in many ways had no personality at all. To Adam, it looked like a pitiful, lost, utterly dead thing. Almost alien, but not an actual alien like the other alien masks with tentacles and multiple sets of eyes. There was something human yet unidentifiably evil in it. It had no feelings, no goal or clear role in the world, and he doubted it had ever appeared in a movie or comic book. Staring at it, he was sure it had no purpose but to inflict pain and cause death.

How it might take life, he did not know. Probably through some deceptively powerful psychic act, like sucking the life force out of you by sheer willpower alone.

Like all the other creatures, this one had a name. It

was printed right there above the product number, and its name was as unsettlingly plain as its looks. Adam didn't even know what it meant, but it didn't sound cool, like Wolfman, Creature From the Black Lagoon, Scarecrow or Frankenstein. Difficult to remember, a strange name whose meaning he could not quite grasp.

The Nocturnal.

Adam thought it had something do with sleeping, or the darkness. Late-night fear. The kind he had been living with for days, weeks, maybe years.

Whatever The Nocturnal meant, he didn't like it.

Adam put the magazine away, the crackers he had eaten now a dry sour mash stuck somewhere between his stomach and his throat.

He remembered his pocket knife. There was nothing else at the bottom of the pack, but his fingers hit upon a zipper, opening to a small inside pocket. Inside the pocket was a knife, but it wasn't his pocket knife. The knife Adam remembered owning was small, maybe three inches long, with a wood-grain handle and brass ends. Inside there were only two blades, and while they weren't very sharp, he trusted it, the knife had felt at home in his pocket, as if it possessed some special powers or had come to him as a gift from a benevolent source.

This wasn't a pocketknife at all. It had black steel handles with holes in them, and when he raised it, one handle fell open on a hinge, revealing a five-inch, smoke-steel blade with a tip so fine it might have been a needle. Etched into the base of the blade was a butterfly. Adam didn't like holding it. It looked like a knife made for nothing besides stabbing people. Viciously. He liked it even less when he rubbed the base of the blade with his thumb and felt something grainy and dry stuck to it, like flakes of rust. Some of it came off like powder on his fingers and when he looked closer, he knew it was dried blood.

Whose knife was this? Adam didn't think it belonged to him, but it must. Why else would he have it? But if so, whose blood was this? He didn't remember stabbing anyone, and how could you forget something like that? Maybe he had cut himself playing with it. But that felt like a lie of the sort you tell yourself to keep from freaking out. Someone had used this knife to hurt someone else and, along with the picture of The Nocturnal mask, it made him feel sick and afraid.

He put the knife back, careful to fold the blade up and latch the handles together so that he wouldn't stab himself running with it in the pack. He was done scavenging for the night, but his fingers brushed against something in the pocket, smaller, also metal. They felt like keys and made the same clinking sound.

He took them out. They were rings, three of them hooped together. Gold-colored, but probably not real gold, because they looked like ordinary hardware, something you would use to hang something on the wall, or lock something together. Each ring was about an inch in diameter, the metal surface flattened all around except for one groove at the top. The ends of each ring fastened together with a tiny screw, like the plastic rings that held the shower curtain up.

Something was engraved on the outside surface of each, in cursive script. A single word starting with a C, but he couldn't read it in the dark and he thought it might be written in another language. C-a-m ... something. He had no idea what their purpose might be or why he had kept them, but the fact that he had kept them, along with the other things in the pack, suggested they had a purpose. He would need them at some point, or they might help him remember something.

He hoped there was a purpose in all of this.

Tired and sad in ways he didn't understand, Adam closed up his pack and used it for a pillow. Stretching out on the towels, listening for any signs of movement overhead, he closed his eyes and tried to think of all the good food he would eat tomorrow. He tried to think of anything but The Nocturnal in the magazine, and the pale dead faces that were out there in the real world, hunting for him.

He slept peacefully for a couple of hours. When he woke up, the sun was rising, his long lonely night was almost over, and the people who lived here were screaming bloody murder.

7

The first few hours of morning and the last hour of night, that was all she had left.

Many years ago Geri Kavanaugh had thought it would be this way for only a few years, that when Josh grew out of his diapers and started school, she would have more of her waking hours to herself. But then the big round of layoffs came at Croswell-Anderson, their medical device division was sold off to that biotech firm in California (and no, we don't want your remaining staff, thank you), and her husband Eric lost his engineering job. She had to go back to teaching full-time sooner than she'd planned.

Teaching history to tenth- and eleventh-graders wasn't the worst job in the world, but it wasn't easy or often inspiring. Then there was the grading of homework, meetings with parents, faculty meetings, and errands, cooking dinner, cleaning up the house while Eric worked the night shift as a facilities manager in the Quartet Corporate Complex in Broomfield, making sure Josh was fed and bathed and put to bed by nine (when he was still a little boy), then making sure he wasn't out late doing bad things (when he was, well, ever since he crossed the wicked threshold of puberty).

Where had the years gone? What happened to all her happy days?

It was only a little after six in the morning and Geri had been up for nearly three hours. She had already run two loads of laundry, the only chore she didn't mind, because she couldn't stand having piles of dirty clothes laying around and the task required no mental effort. Folding everything was another story, so she left the last batch in the dryer, which had buzzed to a halt around five this morning.

Eric had just come home from his shift and was taking one of his long showers before seeing them off to work and school and then going to sleep. She was on her second 'defibrillation', Eric's name for the huge mugs of latte she brewed for herself. She was reading the *New York Times* at the kitchen table, as much for the tactile and olfactory sensations real newsprint provided as for the content.

Geri didn't dwell much on the front page, national, global, political, terrorism or financial sections. That swath of the world was too depressing to follow, and so far removed from her interests and ability to influence, it all might as well have been so much palace intrigue on Neptune. She usually skipped straight to the lifestyle, fashion, design, real estate and book review sections. She like reading the longer pieces about entrepreneurs, designers, artists, anyone who'd made the paper for the interesting life they were living, and who might inspire a few small changes in her own.

She fought the urge to look up from her paper and check the clock. She didn't want to know how many minutes she had left before Eric came down and started talking about all the crap he had to deal with last night, how much he despised his boss, Tim Wheatley, who did nothing except walk around the campus with his clip-board, guzzling energy drinks and checking off tasks on his list. Eric's morning grumpy was usually her cue to slip upstairs to begin the onerous task of rousing Josh from his vampiric slumber.

The boy was sixteen, hated school, hated mornings, loved his bed, and the twenty-minute ritual of asking, then telling, then ordering, then yelling at him to get up and get ready for school was without question the part of her day she dreaded most. Pretending to be asleep was step one. Step two was trying to hide under his pillows. Steps three through six were reserved for loathing, slander and violence. Occasionally he would throw a shoe at her standing there in his doorway, and more often than not would wind up swearing at her.

'Lee-me the fuck alone!' was one of his favorites.

'Are you seriously this stupid?' was another.

'You don't have to be such a bitch all the time,' was somehow worse.

Yes, somehow. Somehow fifteen years had gone by and she still couldn't find a moment to herself, except during the first hours of the morning, and the last hour of night, when dinner was done and she could putter around the house, listen to some music on her head-phones, read a book, watch a movie, anything so long as it was private and in some way self-nurturing.

Geri loved her husband. Eric was a reliable partner, even after twenty-seven years. And God knew she loved her son, though Josh had become a young man-child-person who seemed less like her son than some invasive, messy stranger who rarely spoke a sentence not laced with profanity. Problems in school, fights, pot smoking, depression from breaking up with that awful Melanie, who'd done a real number on him, despite Geri's warnings when she saw the emotional manipulation coming months before it started. Lately sports and girls were out. About the only thing Josh seemed to enjoy anymore was eating, scratching himself, watching unrated Korean movies, and of course sleeping in as late as possible.

Today was their last day of school, and she had half a mind to let him skip it altogether. But no, he could handle one more day. She wanted to stress the importance of finishing what you started. He could sleep in tomorrow and for the rest of the summer, at least until she convinced him to find a part-time job.

Geri looked up. 6:52.

She could hear a shower running upstairs, but she knew it was Eric, not the boy.

She should start knocking on Josh's door now. Get the ball rolling so they wouldn't be late for first period.

Geri had already showered and dressed, and applied what little make-up she needed to avoid looking to her students like the tired mother she was. She was dressed in her heather-brown twill pants, black ankle boots, and a cream blouse with a black cowl-neck sweater over it. She felt as ready for the day as she was going to get.

She carried her defib mug to the sink, rinsed it – *thud thud . . . thud thud thud* – and set it to dry on the rack. She shut the faucet off, cocking one ear.

What was that? She'd heard something while the faucet was running. Had someone knocked on the door? God, she hoped not. Who knocks on your door at seven in the morning? No one you wanted to speak with, that was for sure. She ignored it, hoping she had been mistaken. She went back to the kitchen table and raked up her paper, carrying it to the recycling bin.

Ding-dong.

Okay. The last time it had been a knock. Now they were ringing the bell.

'Take a hint,' Geri said, knowing they wouldn't.

Jehovah's Witnesses, she thought, though she hadn't seen one of those in a long time and maybe things had gotten so bad out there, they'd given up, taken their gospels to the World Wide Web of Idiocy. Was it Girl Scout Cookie season again already? Last year the Nichols family had come by with their precious tyke Sidney, hawking boxes of Thin Mints at seven-fifteen in the morning. Geri had signed up for four boxes just to get them off her porch so she could go back her coffee.

Ding-dong-ding-dong.

Two in a row. Impatient. Jesus Criminy, already. Might be an emergency of some sort. Something important.

Geri rolled her neck with a sigh and marched around the living room, down the hall, to the entryway. She thought about looking through the window to the side of the door first, but whoever was there would see her checking, and then there wouldn't be a choice, would there? She'd have to open the door no matter who it was, otherwise they would think her rude. This was such a safe neighborhood, and it was so early in the morning, caution never even crossed her mind. She unlocked and opened the door.

Too late. They were already gone. The porch was empty.

Geri looked up the sidewalk, which curved around the garage, and to the street, but there weren't any cars parked in front of her house.

Relieved, she shut the door. Probably a solicitor, some kid selling subscriptions to the *Denver Post*. Not a bad paper, but not the *New York Times*, either.

She turned and took the first three steps on the front stairway to go wake up Josh when he startled her from the top of the stairs. He was in his boxer shorts, frowning down at her, wiping the dregs of sleep from one eye.

'Who was at the door?'

'What are you doing up?' This was so rare, her son out of bed of his own volition, it unnerved her more than the prospect of solicitors. 'What's wrong?'

'I just heard something outside. Who was it?'

'No one. They were gone.'

Josh stared at her, and she couldn't read his expression. His legs looked too thin and he was developing a small belly roll. He'd never been tubby, but the kid needed exercise. Another motherly pang of sadness passed through her.

'What did you hear?'

'Don't know. But it was weird. They didn't sound like they were speaking in, like, a normal language. They sounded like ...'

Impatient, Geri gave him a look. *Like what?*

He shrugged. 'I don't know. Like idiots? It was all garbled, but loud enough to come through my window.'

'Did you see them?'

'Tried. I got up and looked out the window, 'cause it sounded so dicked up I was like, what is that? I thought my friends were playing a joke or some shit.'

'Josh. A little early for the potty mouth.'

'Sorry, they were playing a joke or *something*. But there weren't any people, just this ugly hunk-of-shit truck with a camper shell on top.'

'I didn't see that,' Geri said, thinking, And we don't get many beat-up trucks with a camper shell around here.

Josh yawned and turned away, no doubt heading for his bed.

'You're getting in the shower, yes?'

'After Dad. The hot water up in this bitch sucks.'

'Do not go back to sleep.'

Josh mumbled something and shut his bedroom door.

Geri turned and stepped down the three stairs she had climbed. A draft of cold air caught her from the side and she paused.

The front door was open, and slowly swinging open wider. She must not have pushed it hard enough to latch it. She shouldered the door until it clicked and threw the deadbolt to make sure it stayed closed.

She walked back into the kitchen and saw two people standing in her living room, in front of the fireplace, the TV morning show going on behind them.

Geri screamed shortly before her throat pinched off her voice.

Her vision went hyper-vivid.

Reality got very unreal.

Because they weren't people. Not people like she had ever seen. They looked like adult-sized babies, too awful to be real, people in costumes, but they were real, they just walked in, and here they were, hideous. Their faces. Oh my God, their faces. Both of them were hairless, with pale white skin stretched and glistening, their eyes dark and lifeless, like cold dabs of chocolate set inside cookie dough. They turned to watch her as she stumbled to one side and backed against the kitchen counter, but they made no sudden movements and didn't even raise their arms, or speak.

They just stood there.

Plaid flannel shirts of ruined color, dirty black or brown pants, hiking boots. One was shorter than the other, the small one bulky at the waist and back, the taller one lean and stooped, its shoulders folded inward.

Masks, Geri thought, they're wearing masks, they have to be, even though they look so real. This is a practical joke. Josh's friends think they're being cute but this is so not amusing, I'm going to ground his ass for the entire summer.

They stank of smoke, of old human body odor. Vinegar, or urine.

Not masks. Real. Geri was whimpering, breathing was difficult. She'd screamed, hadn't she? Where was Eric? Still in the shower? She couldn't hear. Her pulse was pounding and her ears rang with panic. Josh was awake, he must have heard. But did she want her son to come down and get caught in this?

No. Please, God, keep Josh upstairs.

They watched her, swaying stiffly, breathing through their mouths.

A robbery? Were they going to rape her? What the hell was this?

'You're in the wrong house,' Geri managed, but her voice sounded mousy. Mustering as much firmness as she could, she said, 'Please leave. Now.'

The short one moved first, taking three or four slow steps toward her.

'At-uhm?' it said, whatever that meant. Its mouth didn't work right. It sounded like a boy Geri had had in one of her classes a few years ago, the one with the speech impediment.

'At-uhm?' the small one repeated, closer now, tilting its head.

Geri could just make out a pair of low flabby rolls below chest level, maybe breasts? Dear God, was this short one a woman?

The taller one bunched his fists over his thighs and

tugged at his pants as if he were getting excited. Geri noticed his hands, the skin there pinker than the white faces, and puckered, like wrinkled newspaper. He kneeled slowly on the kitchen floor and removed something from his pants pocket, a small can about the size of a hockey puck. He groaned as he settled stiffly, and it occurred to Geri that these were not young people or young things, whatever they were. They seemed feeble, almost geriatric. The possibility of them being old and too slow to catch her was of no comfort, however. If anything, their quiet patient nature was out of synch with anything she'd imagined when she thought of home invasion, criminals, perverts. This was somehow worse.

The man unscrewed the cap from the can, produced a faded red handkerchief from another pocket, wrapped it around two or three fingers, and dabbed into the can. He reached forward and wiped the rag across her floor, smearing a band of black until he had drawn a circle.

'What are you – excuse me, you can't do that,' Geri said, but when she moved toward him, the short one stepped in front of her again. Geri stopped, gasping in disbelief as the man ignored her, dabbing more of what had to be shoe polish.

The female moved another step closer and raised one hand. The fingers at the center were fused, a cobbled single branch of flesh where there should have been two or three fingers, and it pointed at her.

'ADUM,' she repeated, and Geri realized this might be a name – Adam. But before she could think of anyone by that name, her attention shifted to the floor.

Beyond the woman, the male one was drawing a triangle inside the circle, and then more lines, and Geri's first thought was a peace sign, or maybe the Star of David. When he finished she realized it was neither of those things.

It was one of those hex thingies. A pentagram.

Geri began to tremble violently. She backed deeper into the kitchen, until she was wedged beside the fridge, at the counter's elbow.

The man stood and stared at her. The woman was an arm's length away, also staring at her.

'I don't understand,' Geri said. 'I don't know what you want. There's no one here named Adam.'

The tall one put away his shoe-shine kit and was now coming around the other side of the island, looking at the floor, the counter, the chairs, and his face was twitching. The mashed stub of nose was stretching, wiggling. Was he sniffing? Can regular people do that?

What scent was he after? Adam's?

Upstairs the shower continued to run. It seemed that her husband had been in there for hours. Geri had to make a decision now. She could scream again. She could run, try to break her way past them and make it up the stairs before they caught her. Or she could snatch up a weapon and try to beat them back. She didn't think screaming would help. And they probably wouldn't let her run through them.

She glanced toward the stove, where she kept a tall

masonry jar filled with cooking utensils, and she took a speedy inventory: wooden spoons, potato masher, a clawed pasta server made of plastic ... no knives. The knives were in the drawer over by the toaster oven, too close to the tall one for her to reach.

She tried to gauge their movements while keeping her eyes averted, for it was hard to look at them and on a subconscious level she was trying to display a manner of submission. Not provoke them.

'Mom, what the hell is—' Josh said, hurrying around the corner from the hall into the kitchen. Her son had pulled on a pair of jeans, no shirt, and his face was flushed with concern. He knew there was trouble but not how much, and he hadn't brought a weapon. He was moving fast and he wasn't a big kid and he wasn't in good shape, but he was still much leaner and faster than his mother.

'Josh, no!' she barked. 'Stay away, go get your dad—'

But her warning came too late. Josh was already standing between them, not hearing her. He was too shocked by the sight of them.

'What the fuck!' he shouted at them. 'What the fuck!'

They weren't fast, but that didn't matter, because they had prepared. The man reached into his back pocket again and coolly produced a long plastic cord looped back on itself like a lasso. He went two steps and tossed the hoop at Josh. The thin band fell around Josh's collarbones and there was a sickening *zzzzziiiii-ippp*.

Josh's hands flew to his neck but the cord was already sinking into his flesh and his face reddened in seconds.

Geri screamed and threw herself at her son, only vaguely aware that the two of them were falling into the black circle on the floor, inside the pentagram.

Upstairs, the shower turned off.

Down here, the ceremony began.

8

After recoiling from the chaos of screams and heavy concussions on the floor above, a destructive rage that seemed would never end, Adam's paralysis broke. He could no longer remain in hiding, hunched into a ball under the sheet behind the water heater, his mind furnishing itself with horrors he could hear but not see.

Trembling so violently he thought he would vomit, he pulled on his damp clothes as fast as he could, fingers slipping on the buttons of his jeans and the laces of his shoes. He didn't have time to put on his socks. He bit his lower lip to keep from crying out but he was crying anyway.

He was responsible for this. He had led them here. Because he had chosen to hide in this random house, innocent strangers had been killed, or were being killed at this very moment. But he couldn't dwell on that now. He had to escape before they got him too. Cinching the straps of his backpack tight, he slipped into the basement's rec room and considered his options.

If he stayed down here they would search the house, sniffing him out until they trapped him and killed him.

The stairway leading up to the first floor was out of the question – it would land him in the killers' path. If he exited the sliding door he had come through, he would appear somewhere in the backyard and they might see him fleeing on foot. He thought of wrapping one of the towels around his fist to punch his way through another of the basement windows, escaping through a window well or some such, but he feared the sound of shattering glass would only draw their attention.

Above him, the sound of a door slamming echoed down. Another, and then another. Adam knew they were going room to room now, searching for him.

The backyard, then. Same way he came in. He looked across the billiard table, to the rack of cue sticks on the wall. He thought of taking one to use as a spear or a club. But he discarded this option out of fear the long stick would only slow him down.

He remembered the butterfly knife and slung off his backpack, intending to carry it with him as he ran. His fingers were shaking too severely to open the drawstring top.

Lumbering footsteps sounded above, changing in pitch the way they do on stairs. For a moment they sounded like they were descending into the basement, and whether that was true or not he couldn't stay in this house another second.

Adam trusted his feet more than the knife. He donned his pack, yanked the sliding glass door open and dashed across the lawn, never looking back.

He ran for a long time.

9

Beth Lynwood pulled the blinds to dim the encroaching sunlight, then returned to her daughter's bedside. She leaned down and kissed Raya's hair, noting how it had been darkening from golden blonde to honey brown into her teens, as if the hair were trying to warn her that her daughter was changing, shedding the last light of girlhood. Even so, the scare Raya experienced earlier had temporarily reduced her in a way, offering Beth another chance to soothe her like she used to, when the girl was still just a little girl.

'I love you, Ra-rah,' Beth whispered, using Raya's name for herself when she had been too young to pronounce it correctly.

'Love you too. Wake me up soon,' Raya mumbled without opening her eyes.

'Just sleep. No one cares about the last day of school. You said so yourself.'

Raya offered her a faint smile, and Beth hoped it was a sign that she was already letting go of the ... event. She didn't know what else to call it. Between Darren's increasingly frequent late-night wanderings and Raya claiming to have received a series of threatening texts, Beth was beginning to wonder if they were coming down with a case of late spring fever. Hormones and Chad might explain part of Raya's hysteria or nightmares, but what about Darren? What was his excuse for being out of bed until sunrise?

She went into the kitchen to make coffee and thought about pregnancy, children and their parents. Raya had come early, easily, and unexpectedly, when she and Darren were still just twenty-five and living in their first house, the one he had purchased with a down payment from the trust his father had set up, which was really an early inheritance in disguise. Andrew and Eloise had borne Darren late in their own life, when Eloise was forty-two, his father in his mid-fifties. Andrew had suffered a heart attack and passed away when Darren was not yet finished with college. A meticulous man who had kept his affairs in order, and a husband who had not wanted to burden Eloise with financial management, something she'd never showed an interest in, Darren's father had established individual trusts for the two of them.

Eloise had spent the following fifteen years leading an active life, never remarrying but traveling with friends, taking dancing lessons, volunteering with the church, and all manner of other things to keep her busy until her health declined. She was still alive but Beth knew she would not be for long. She was eighty-five and succumbing to Alzheimer's.

As for Darren, Beth had been impressed when she met him. He studied without the benefit of self-mercy, rarely drank, never took drugs, and at the tender age of twenty he had big plans. Instead of blowing his inheritance on drugs and parties and cars, like so many college kids might have, he had invested it in a strip mall located in a rough but improving neighborhood on the east side of Milwaukee. Later, when he left the ad firm and struck out to launch his first company, his eighty-hour work weeks and entrepreneurial plans put their plans for a second child on hold.

They started trying again when Raya was three, and this time it became much more of a struggle. Neither Beth nor Darren had any unusual medical conditions thwarting their efforts, but after eighteen months they lost their enthusiasm. Darren was busier than ever with work and Beth was fulfilled with Raya. Darren joked about needing a son so he would have someone who would sympathize with him when Raya was a teenager and the household was ruled by girls, but Beth had never sensed any real resentment or disappointment in her husband. By the time Raya was seven, they stopped discussing the possibility of a second child and let nature take its course, or not, with respect to matters in the bedroom. Nature had declined.

But she had never stopped wondering if Darren still longed for a son, if the old jokes weren't more than jokes. Why else the bike collection? Or, more precisely, his love of his own boyhood, and childhood in general, a love which had spawned his obsessive collection. Or was it the other way around? She could never tell if The Totally Radical Sickness collection was the result of his obsession and nostalgia, or the source. The addiction or the drug itself.

Either way, his connection to his youth was almost magically pure, sometimes startlingly alive. The fact that he had built a shrine to it – the shop standing in their backyard – had rendered his past a tangible thing, even for Beth.

Poor Raya. Between the ages of nine and twelve, a period as close to a true tomboy phase as she would ever have, she'd tried to get into BMX. Going out for rides with him, spending time in the garage working on bikes, trying to learn how to lace a rim with new spokes, opening herself to the enchantment these bikes cast over her father. But, patient as Darren was with her, and grateful for her effort, he could never keep her interested for more than a few summer days when she was bored. When Raya broke her collarbone one day at the dirt park, her interest in BMX came to an end.

Well, too late now. They weren't going to try for another in hopes of having a boy this time. If that was what he needed, he'd have to find another remedy for the Radical Sickness. Perhaps he already had.

'We should take a vacation,' Beth said from the kitchen, filling a cup of coffee before joining Darren in the great room. He was slouched down in the corner of the leather sofa, a fleece jacket zipped to the throat like a child's jumper, picking at the bandage on his thumb. Was he shivering? She sat in one of the leather armchairs, sipping the hot Guatemalan blend. 'I'm serious, by the way. In case you're listening.'

'Where would you like to go?' Darren said, distracted, eyes punchy.

'Mexico. Hawaii. DIA has non-stops to Costa Rica. Did you know that?'

'What's in Costa Rica?' he said, still avoiding eye contact. She followed his gaze across the room, to the sliding glass door, and she knew he was thinking of the shop again. His damn bikes, or whatever else was out there keeping him up all night.

'Volcanoes, rainforest, beaches. Who cares? As long as we get out of the house for a week or two.'

'Raya just had spring break. She has the whole summer ahead.'

'Lotta good it did her.'

He faced her, nodding tightly. 'I'm worried about her too.'

'I'm thinking of finding someone for her to talk to.'

'She talks to us,' he said.

'But we don't know what's going on with her. That's the point.'

He seemed to consider it for a moment. 'I don't know that the problem is Raya.'

'You heard her description of those texts, the boy's laughter at the end. She said she felt watched, like someone was here. But you checked the alarm yourself and there were no texts on her phone. Why would a boy break into our house, and what else could it be if not her imagination getting the better of her?'

'It was four in the morning,' Darren said. 'Maybe she had a nightmare.' But he didn't sound like he believed that anymore than she did.

'I asked her. She wasn't sleeping. She was up texting Chad.'

'Like I said. A nightmare.'

'Oh, stop. He's a good kid. And more importantly, she's a good kid. She knows how to take care of herself.'

'Good. Glad you have that under control. I'll know who to come to when he gets drunk and cheats on her.'

Beth set down her coffee. 'Is that what's bothering you? Chad? Somehow I don't think Chad is responsible for your insomnia, or that bandage on your hand.'

Darren shot her a look of warning.

She shot him one right back. 'You think I didn't notice? At least twice last week. It used to be an hour or two. Now it's all night. I don't always hear you get up, but I always know when you come back.'

Darren sipped his coffee, winced.

'You were out there until seven in the morning, Darren. What time did you leave? Tell me the truth.'

'A little after one.'

'Six hours,' Beth said. 'Are you avoiding me?'

'No, Beth, that's not—'

'Are we girls driving you batty around the house? You've been running a company for the past fifteen years, now all the sudden you're stuck with us. You can tell me. If that's the case, I get it, I just want us to be honest here.'

He was shaking his head. He looked at her warmly.

'Honey, the fact that I've even given you reason to ask that makes me feel horrible. I love spending time with both of you. You can't even begin to understand how much I missed the two of you all those late nights, the weekends on business trips. I'm not avoiding you, okay? I promise you that.'

She believed him. 'Then what is it?'

'It sounds so stupid, but . . . '

'It's not.'

'The nightmares,' he said with a sigh. 'They're worse than ever.'

'Is it still the same version? The fire?'

When he looked at her, she almost didn't recognize his expression, it was such a rare one for him. He was genuinely scared.

'Oh, honey. Hey. You're really rattled by this thing. Okay, let's talk about it.'

'Here we go,' he said.

'Is it the dream itself or the number of them that's spooking you?'

'Both, I guess. It's the same as before. I'm trapped, I smell smoke, I can hear the flames coming closer. I don't know if it's this house but it's our house. There's just this roar all around, everything's burning, and I always know when I'm struggling, near the end, that's it's too late.'

'You're going to die in the fire? Is that—'

'No. Too late for you and Raya. It's already gotten both of you. I can hear you screaming, dying like something in a gas chamber.'

'God, that's really awful.'

'What's worse is, it doesn't feel like a dream,' Darren said.

'They never do when you're in them.'

'No, this is different. When I wake up and realize it's not real, I'm still convinced it is, or it's going to be. Almost like I can feel it coming. I realize it sounds crazy, but I believe it's going to happen. I really do.'

'Listen to me,' she said. 'It's not going to happen. You checked all the fire alarms. Now you've got me on high alert. We're careful. The house was inspected when we bought it, the guy said the electrical would last another twenty years. There isn't going to be a fire. This isn't about a fire, anyway.'

'Then what's it about?'

Beth took a moment to gather herself. She didn't want to upset him more by suggesting he was the one who needed psychological counseling. She tried to think of anything he'd been through, recent stress or some trauma that would inspire such nightmares, but nothing came to her. Not recently. But the past . . .

She looked up at him. 'Unless . . . were you ever in a fire?'

'What?'

'No, really.' She softened her tone, easing him toward the possibility. 'I mean, what if you were? In a fire. When you were young? Any close calls? Maybe someone you knew was in a fire? Lost a friend, an ex-girlfriend, anybody?'

He looked at her like she was crazy.

'Are you sure?'

'Pretty sure I would remember being in a fire, Beth.'

'Anyone in your family?'

Darren scoffed. 'You're not hearing me. No, I've never been in a fire, not like this, okay? I'm alive, sitting here with you. I'm not burned up like charcoal, am I, which is exactly what happens in the dream. There's nothing like it, you have no idea.'

'Okay, okay. Sorry. But then, what are we missing?'

He opened his mouth to say something, changed his mind and went in another direction. 'This thing tonight, it got me thinking. Have you ever noticed anything funny about Raya's little hunches?'

'What do your dreams have to do with Raya?'

'Just think about it. Our daughter gets hunches, and it seems to me, pretty often they come true, or close enough. What do you make of that?'

'Everyone has hunches. Does Raya have different hunches?'

'That thing with your car,' he said. 'When you had the flat tire, lost your phone?'

'What about it?'

'Raya sort of predicted that.'

'Coincidence,' she said too quickly, then realized she sounded defensive. 'At the time, yeah, maybe it was a little eerie, but all in all not that difficult to put together. Mom leaves, Mom's late coming back from the store, what else would she think besides I had car trouble?'

'Maybe,' Darren said. 'But there have been other incidents.'

Beth was about to argue otherwise until she remembered their first trip out to Boulder two years ago, when they decided to fly out together to spend the weekend touring the town Darren had grown up in. He'd stayed back in Milwaukee wrapping up the deal to sell Revolver, and it had been just the girls. Sitting in General Mitchell International waiting to board the Frontier flight, Raya had turned to Beth out of the blue and said, 'I betcha twenty dollars it snows while we're in Boulder.'

Colorado was famous for its snow, especially along the Foothills where severe weather changes came over the mountains with alarming lack of notice. Still, Beth had dismissed the notion because this was late August and Wisconsin, a colder state than Colorado, was at that moment basking in a heat wave. Temperatures had reached almost ninety and there hadn't been any precipitation for weeks. Their lawn at home was burned brown, dead for the season.

'No way,' Beth told her.

'Afraid you'll lose?'

'I don't want to take your money, sweetie. And since when did you become a gambler?'

'It's going to snow. I can feel it.'

Beth had refused the bet, but sure enough, that night the temperatures dropped sharply and Boulder got its first snow of the fall season. Fat wet flakes, two inches that melted as fast as it fell, but snow nonetheless. Raya nagged her about it all the next day, until Beth begrudgingly handed her a twenty just to shut her up.

'The snow thing, here, on our trip,' she said, her mind already racing for more of Raya's hunches that had proved correct. 'She was so sure, she wanted to bet on it.'

Darren said, 'She sees me storming around the house looking for my keys or my phone, she blurts it out and ninety per cent of the time she's right. My keys are right where she said they'd be.'

'She's intelligent,' Beth said. 'She notices everything.'

'She knows when Chad's about to call. You're telling me you never noticed that one? She's a regular radar dish when it comes to Chad.'

'Chad's always calling her. They're glued to their phones.'

But her conviction was falling apart. She began to open herself to the possibility, and soon remembered another event, years ago, when Raya was still in elementary school. Beth picked her up one day at three o'clock, and Raya was gloomy, non-communicative. Beth asked her what was wrong, did she have a bad day, did something happen? And Raya only shook her head and said her teacher was sad because her husband was sick. 'With what?' Beth asked her ten-year-old daughter.

'I dunno, but it's very serious,' Raya had said. 'He needs an operation.'

Beth let the topic go and didn't think much about it in the coming days. But two or three weeks later she stopped by the school to drop off a math workbook Raya had forgotten at home. She caught up with Mrs Lambert in their homeroom while the class was out to their morning musical appreciation session. Iris, as the parents were allowed to address her, seemed more downcast than usual, pale and tired, and without thinking it through first, Beth had touched the sleeve of her sweater and asked, 'How is your husband doing? Raya mentioned that he hasn't been well. I hope it's nothing serious.'

Iris Lambert, who was only in her late fifties but seemed to have aged fifteen years since the last round of parent–teacher conferences, recoiled. Her lips parted and she glared at Beth with a combination of alarm, resentment and fear.

'He's ... no, he's not well. His heart is failing.'

'I'm so sorry,' Beth said, feeling she had offended the teacher.

'But how did she know?' Iris Lambert said. 'I haven't spoken of this to anyone at all. Not here, not to the faculty, and especially not with the children.'

'Oh. Is that – are you sure?'

'We haven't even told our own children. My goodness, Robert was diagnosed just two days ago. It was a terrible shock. A terrible, terrible shock.'

This revelation silenced them both. It was unlikely in the extreme that Raya had been around Robert Lambert, ever, let alone in the past few days. Even if she had, little girls don't look at middle-aged men and sense oncoming heart failure. More importantly, the day Raya had been so sad and made the comment was more than three weeks before. If Mr Lambert had just been diagnosed two days ago, then something very strange had transpired.

'I'm sorry, I don't understand either,' Beth said, wanting to get out of the classroom and the direct line of Iris's reprimanding gaze as soon as possible. 'Kids are strange like that sometimes. They pick up on things—'

'No one knows,' Iris said, her sadness made worse for this uninvited conversation. 'No one knows, don't you see?'

At which point Beth had apologized again, then handed over the math book and hurried away, making an excuse about being late for an appointment.

She hadn't thought about that unresolved incident for years, but it seemed damning now. She looked up at Darren. He could see it in her.

He nodded. 'I bet you if we put our heads together and really pored over this, we could come up with a list. A long list. Sometimes when she—'

Beth put a hand up, warning him to slow down. She had a headache. The coffee had been a bad idea, so early and on an empty stomach.

'Even if we're prepared to believe something like that, which I am not, what does that have to do with what happened this morning? These texts? With your nightmares?'

Darren surprised her with his answer. 'I have to tell you,' he paused, raising his bandaged hand. 'This cut? I wasn't just opening a package. I didn't want to scare you earlier, but now that we're talking.'

'Oh God,' she said. *What now?*

He told her about seeing the light on in the shop, his

fear of an intruder. Then he told her of the mystery bike, the Cinelli, how it had arrived by unknown delivery, the strange spell it had cast on him.

She interrupted him. 'You think someone broke into the shop?'

'No, not now. The alarm was deactivated. I probably forgot to lock up.'

She raised an eyebrow, not trusting his memory.

Darren waved her off. 'Nothing was missing, okay? Everything was as I had left it. Don't worry about that. My point is, once I saw everything was okay, I knew I wouldn't be able to go back to sleep, so I decided to build this bike. I was opening a bundle of this cloth all taped together, holding the pedals. That's when I cut myself. But right after I finished, something happened.'

Beth did not like the look on his face. 'Something besides you cutting yourself?'

He frowned, concentrating. 'It was confusing. I wasn't really myself, like I wasn't really there. I thought I was tired, groggy. I may have lost track of time, because I remember waking up around one-fifteen, but when I came back inside it was almost seven, and I really don't think I spent six hours out there. But when I finished, the wheels began to turn. I didn't spin them. I was standing a good ten feet away, but they just started turning. And it really seemed like someone was in there with me.'

Beth felt something inside her tying itself in knots. 'What do you mean, "someone was in there with you? The wheels began to turn." What does that mean?'

'I mean, I wasn't alone. When I turned around, the shop was empty, except there was this bright white light. I could feel him. A boy. It had something to do with the bike, I think, with me assembling it. I felt him standing right behind me. I heard him laughing. And when I turned around to see him, I got this ... glimpse. And then I fainted. Come to think of it, that's probably where all the time went. I could have been conked out for hours. Didn't feel like it, but—'

'Who?' Beth said. Her skin was crawling. 'For God's sake, who are you talking about? What glimpse? Who is this boy?'

Darren looked at her as if it were obvious. 'The boy. The one Raya heard crying. The texts were talking about a boy, she said. What if he was there with me before he ... reached out to her?'

Beth couldn't speak for a moment. 'You're trying to tell me that the two of you experienced some kind of, what, event?'

Darren looked into her eyes, and she saw something in them very different than everything she was feeling right now. He didn't look scared or distracted any longer. He looked interested, almost excited.

'You're scaring me. I can't believe this. I won't.'

'I know how it sounds, but what else could it have been? I felt him there, the bike was moving. She gets these messages in her phone because, I dunno, that's the best way to "get in touch" with her. That's her point of focus, right, the phone? And you searched the house and didn't find a boy anywhere.'

'And you think because Raya gets these hunches, that sometimes she sees things that have happened or are going to happen, you think this boy texted our daughter? Why? From where? The future, or some kind of "other side" nonsense?'

'I don't know. You've seen those shows on TV. Isn't that sort of how it works?'

'That's TV. This is our home!'

'Hey.' Darren moved closer to her, took her hands in his. 'No one said he was dangerous, honey. Maybe he's just some lost kid. Maybe he used to live here.'

'Well, that's comforting. Do you realize what you're saying?'

Darren nodded. 'Yeah, I guess I do.'

For a moment, Beth wanted to slap the calm right off his face.

Instead, she stood up. 'I'm going to take a shower. I have things to do today. Please don't share your theories with our daughter. I don't want you upsetting her more than you already have.'

She turned the water on much hotter than usual, but ten minutes later, her skin turning pink from the spray, she still felt cold.

10

Raya emerged from her boutique suite a little after ten, looking rested and in good cheer, as if the texting episode really had been nothing but a bad dream, one that she had already broken down like a cardboard box and heaved into the recycling bin of her resilient mind.

'Morning, darlin',' Darren said. 'I thought you were going to sleep in.'

'Can't. Chad's on his way to pick me up.'

With this news, Darren's pride in her independence was dealt a moderate blow. 'And where is Chad taking you today?'

'Uhm, to school?' Raya went to the fridge and retrieved her morning bottle of water and a single pack of string cheese. 'Last day, remember?'

'You sure you're up for that?' her mom asked, joining them from the other side of the breakfast bar. She had just finished dressing for work.

'I want to get my yearbook signed and I can't miss the luncheon.'

Beth fidgeted with an earring and fluffed her hair out

of her collar. 'What's the luncheon again? Is this for one of your classes?'

Raya looked up at the ceiling as if maybe God was up there and could explain why her mother was so dense. 'I told you. The girls and I have a reservation at Ten-Ten?'

'Oh, right. That's cute. Do you have money?'

'Brasserie Ten-Ten?' Darren said. 'The French place on Walnut?'

'Yes,' Raya said without looking at him.

'That pretentious, overpriced little joint where all the perverted business-*men* go to drink their lunch?'

Raya ignored him and moved closer to her mother, dangling cheese into her mouth. 'You said I could use your card.'

'What's wrong with McDonald's?' Darren said. 'Hell, how about Chili's? I'd spring for that.'

Raya gaped at him in horror.

'What's wrong with Chili's? Those fajitas are darn tasty.'

'Uhm, everything?'

Beth opened her wallet and thumbed out a Visa. Raya pinched the corner of the card daintily and beamed at her mother. 'Thank you.'

'Only for you,' Darren said. 'Don't go picking up the tab for the whole damn table.'

'It's her last day, honey. Give her a break,' Beth said, but the look she gave him was the real warning: Your daughter had a rough night. If buying lunch for a dozen of her friends helps her forget about the disturbance, that's a cheap price to pay.

'Yeah, Dad, give her a break,' Raya said. She stuck the cheese in his hand and skipped off to her shower.

Darren watched her go, munching down the rest of the string cheese. 'It's like it never happened. She's coping very well, I'd say. Thanks to Chad.'

Beth heaved her bag onto her shoulder. With all her woman stuff and her laptop and files, it looked like it weighed fifty pounds. 'I'm not getting into this again.'

Darren gave her a hug, kissed her hair. 'We're fine. You, me, her.'

Beth kissed him on the neck. 'Love you.'

'Love you too.'

'What are you doing today?'

'What do I do every day?'

She looked back at him before entering the garage. 'Play with bikes?'

He nodded. 'Play with bikes.'

'Be careful.'

Darren nodded. 'I'll call you in a bit. Maybe a late lunch of our own downtown?'

Beth made a face, wrinkling her nose. *Maybe, probably not*.

'Come on,' he said. 'Look at this weather. A glass of wine on the deck at the West End. Oysters at Jax. Be good for us.'

'Send me a text.' Beth closed the door behind her.

'That sounds like a date,' Darren shouted.

The doorbell rang. *And that must be the Amazing Chad*.

'Daddy, will you get the door?' Raya called from her bathroom.

'Don't be so eager,' he yelled back. 'And close the damn door.'

Darren walked around the living room and into the foyer. He opened the door.

'Morning, Chad.'

'Oh, hey, Mr Lynwood. How are things with you?'

'You can call me Darren, Chad. Remember?'

'Oh yeah, cool. Thanks. Is, uhm, Raya here?'

'She'll be a minute. Come on in.'

Chad was a decent enough guy, seventeen going on thirteen except for his height and clothing. Kid went six-two or six-three to Darren's five-nine, but this wasn't what annoyed him. Nor was it the fact that Chad wore cuffed slacks and oxford shirts year-round, often with a blue or khaki sports coat and striped tie, for no reason at all, with calfskin driving loafers and no socks like some fraternity pledge let out for a Memorial Day barbecue with alumni donors. It wasn't Chad's prep-school hair-cut, either, with the close-cropped sides and the tuft of curls that dropped over his forehead just so.

What annoyed Darren was the way Chad always ducked his head and lowered his shoulders when speaking to his girlfriend's father. It was something between a nervous tic and a parody of the respectful bow of greeting so prevalent in Asian cultures, with an added tremor. Chad bobbed and quivered and juked and jived as if Darren had on several occasions beaten him with a bamboo cane. Darren was never quite convinced that the whole broad-smiling, apple-cheeked, yes-sir, no-sir act wasn't a kind of barely repressed rage, a subliminal

Screw you, old man, I'm taking your daughter out for a date that's gonna last all night, and it's gonna get real.

'Can I get you something to drink?' Darren said, leading the boy to the kitchen, away from anything that could be construed as in the direction of Raya's bedroom-bathroom suite.

'Oh, okay, that's very kind of you.' Chad took one of the barstools at the serving counter. He removed a pair of Persol sunglasses from his breast pocket, breath-steamed the lenses and began to nervously polish them with his tie. Today's was yellow with orange stripes.

Darren stood with the fridge door open. 'Orange juice, milk, Pellegrino, coconut water, whattya like?'

'Would you happen to have, maybe, a Diet Coke?'

Darren peered into the bottom shelf. 'We would.'

'That'd be perfect, if it's no trouble.'

Darren popped a can and filled a glass with ice.

'Would you by chance have any lemon?' Chad said, wincing theatrically.

Darren blinked at Chad as he opened the fridge for the second time. What do you know, two lemons in the door, right where Chad could see them, probably saw them the first time, gave him the idea, so, basically no way to lie and turn him down now.

'As a matter of fact.' Darren set a lemon on the cutting board, dug a knife from the drawer, and began to slice in swift strokes that clocked on the board, the entire act drawing attention to the gauze and medical tape around his thumb.

Chad didn't mention it. He said, 'Raya got me into

that. I don't know why, but it's just not the same without a lemon. I probably sound like a snob, huh?'

Darren took the opportunity to laugh. 'It's fine. Actually, this sounds good. Mind if I split this can with you?'

'Please do,' Chad said. 'I already had one this morning.'

Darren filled another glass with ice, split the soda two ways, and threw a lemon wedge in each. He carried them to Chad and raised a half-hearted toast.

'Thank you, sir. Darren, I mean.'

'You're welcome.' Well, maybe the kid wasn't full of beans. Maybe he really was this nice. He should give his daughter the benefit of the doubt, shouldn't he?

'So, last day of school,' Darren said, wishing Raya would hurry up so he didn't have to stand here and entertain Chad all morning. He wanted to go have a look at the Cinelli and clean up the blood. See if the bike had any new surprises in store for him today. 'That must be exciting. Just one more year and then it's off to the big leagues.'

Chad had a mouthful of cola and could only nod before swallowing. 'I'm glad this year's over. I'm just sorry it had to end this way.'

'This way,' Darren said.

Something in Chad's face changed. Guilt or regret pulling his mouth tight. 'Oh. I guess you didn't hear. Raya doesn't know yet either, then.'

'What doesn't Raya know?'

Chad set his cola down and wiped his lips. 'School's

110

cancelled, sort of. They're not letting anyone in. Students who were already there for first and second period are stuck. The place is in lockdown.'

Darren squared his shoulders. 'Please don't tell me another dumbass brought a gun to school. Didn't we already have a couple of those this year?'

'No, well, I don't think so. Maybe there was another threat, but that wasn't the main thing.'

'Jesus, what's the main thing?' For the first time this morning, he understood why Chad's nervousness seemed more exaggerated than usual. The kid was scared. Something had shaken him up.

'One of our teachers, Mrs Kavanaugh, she taught history.' Chad took another quick sip. 'She was ... they're saying she was killed.'

'At school?' Darren was feeling a bit shaky himself now, imagining how close they had come to sending Raya into whatever little CNN Situation Room event had gone down at Boulder High this morning. The name Kavanaugh rang a bell but he didn't have the same grip on the faculty that Beth did. 'This happened today, this morning?'

Chad shook his head. 'No, no, sorry. She was home. I don't know who it was or why or anything, really, but her husband, too. And her son. His name was Josh.'

'Someone killed them. The whole family?'

'Like one of those home invasion things,' Chad said. 'I heard, well, the rumor is, it was really bad. Gruesome. There was some kind of ritual, like Satanist stuff. Mrs Kavanaugh and Josh were found in the living room. Her husband was found in the shower, like mutilated or something.'

Darren tried to picture that. 'The cops catch who did it?'

'No, not yet. It's all over the news and the radio, but when I was on my way over they said they were still searching around town.'

'They closed the school?' Darren was trying to decide if this was normal.

'I guess her son was pretty messed up. Josh. The guys he runs with, they're being questioned. Like, maybe there was some motive to get back at his mom for something. I don't know any of those guys, so I don't have a clue, but I guess the school doesn't mess around anymore, not when there's any suspicion and the people are still on the loose.'

'People. So the police think there were more than one.'

Chad nodded, then seemed to get lost in his own mind for a minute.

'Jesus,' Darren said. 'I thought you were coming to take Raya to school.'

'Oh, no. No way, sir. I came to make sure she didn't go. And she really liked Mrs Kavanaugh. I thought I should tell her in person.'

Darren regarded Chad with a swell of gratitude and newfound respect.

'Or maybe you want to tell her?' Chad said. 'Whatever you think is best.'

Then Darren remembered. A few weeks ago. Raya

112

talking about her upcoming history final. 'Mrs Kavanaugh. She was Raya's history teacher.'

Chad's eyes brimmed and he blinked back tears.

Darren took a deep breath and walked around the counter. He put a hand on Chad's shoulder and squeezed. 'You're a good kid, Chad. I appreciate you coming here to look out for her. We'll tell her together, okay?'

Chad nodded. 'Okay.'

They had shared a breakthrough. If Beth was here to see it, she would have called this a new level of intimacy or something sensitive like that. Darren smiled to himself, thinking that, for once, he wouldn't have teased her for saying so.

'I just don't understand,' Chad said. 'I mean, what's wrong with people? How hard is it to be a decent human being?'

Darren reclaimed his position behind the bar, in the kitchen, which seemed more appropriate for the next phase. The man-to-man complaining part.

'You'd be surprised,' he said.

'My friends and I sort of joke about it, but stuff like today? It makes you wonder.'

'Yeah, what's the joke?'

Chad tossed down half his drink. 'Just, basically, the big things. No one is perfect, but how difficult is it to not be a terrible person? We always say, How hard is it to *just not do that*? Like, how hard is it to *just not* steal another man's car? How hard is it to *just not* rape a village in Africa? How hard is it to *just not* shoot a whole grocery

113

store full of people? How hard is it to *just not* throw your baby in the trash—'

'I get it,' Darren said.

Chad was red in the face, forcing himself to wind it down. 'I mean ... seriously.'

Darren nodded. 'World's full of wickedness, Chad, plain and simple.'

'People are fucking stupid!' Chad blurted, then froze, looking very much like he wished he could reel his words back in. 'I'm sorry. Excuse me, Mr Lynwood.'

'Don't worry about it,' Darren said. 'You're right. People can be shi ... a disappointment. But here's the thing, Chad. If you can remember this, and stick to it, say, ninety per cent of the time, you will pretty much pave your own way.'

Chad was gazing at Darren as if he were about to impart the meaning of life. Darren felt a little foolish, but what the hell, the moment called for such proclamations. They needed something to feel better about.

'The truth is,' he said, softening his voice, 'most people aren't stupid. Some are, no question, and they can't help it because they were born that way. We can forgive these folks, because they don't have a choice, and even dumb people can give something back to the world. The problem is, too many people – not all, not even most, but too many people – are weak. They're not strong like you, Chad. And Raya, and my wife.'

'And you,' Chad cut in. 'You're strong.'

Darren sniffed. 'Maybe. I can be when I need to be.

114

My point is, we all have weaknesses, but this is not the same thing as *being* weak. Most of the problems in the world, the real corruption, happen because too many people aren't strong enough to resist whatever will make them feel better *right now*. I'm talking about everything from petty criminals to the ones we put on a pedestal. Look at our institutions: government, the church, Wall Street, professional sports, Hollywood, you name it. It's everywhere, people grabbing for as much as they can get, by any means necessary, and when they get caught, which they always do, eventually, what do they do?

'They lie, cover it up, bend more rules, and then give a half-assed televised apology that is, without fail, one hundred-per-cent staged. Integrity is a lost concept in our culture, Chad. We're living in an age when it's winner take all, even if you have to cheat to win. Put your sin on a credit card, pay for it later, or don't. This is weakness, people caving in to their weaknesses.'

'That totally makes sense,' Chad said.

'This thing today, with your teacher? I don't know the whole story, but I promise you when this thing comes out, it's gonna be all about somebody – a parent, a kid, a family, a psychopath, whoever's involved – who took the easiest route to getting their rocks off. Cause it's easier to steal and lie and, yes, even commit murder, than it is to deal with your own problems. To take the hard road and resist whatever makes you feel better now, today, in the moment.'

Chad looked like he wished he could take notes.

'I'm sorry,' Darren said. 'I'm sermonizing here. All I'm saying is, and this is a talk I've had with Raya more than once, if you want to be good, and I'm not talking about being rich or successful, but good at something, and good to the people you love, then the single most important thing to do is resist your own weaknesses. We all have them. Some of us work at rising above them, others don't. And that's all I want you kids to remember, okay? Before you cut a corner, or do something that seems too good to be true, take a second. Stop. Think. Is this the right thing to do, or just the easy thing to do? Because, son, those two things are almost never the same thing.'

'That's awesome,' Chad said.

Darren chuckled. 'No, I probably just drank too much Coke. What's in this stuff, anyway?'

The two of them laughed.

'Whoa, someone's having way too much fun in here,' Raya said, bounding into the living room, hair still wet, but otherwise dressed and ready to go. 'What are you boys up to so early in the morning, and can I have some?'

The reality of the news they had to share with her halted their laughter. Darren was nearly cleaved by how vulnerable she appeared, how trusting she was, how brightly she approached this mess of a world.

'What?' Raya said, reacting to the somber turn. 'What's wrong?'

Chad looked to Darren for the cue. Darren eased his way around the counter and patted Chad on the back.

'This here's a good man, Raya. He was looking out for you today, and for that he will always have my gratitude. Go ahead, Chad.'

Chad told her about Mrs Kavanaugh.

Darren knew from the way her skin turned ashen and her tears rolled out spontaneously, she hadn't seen this coming. She'd been too happy this morning, and in the previous days, to have sensed such a tragedy heading toward one of her teachers.

Her hunches were just hunches, coincidence.

And thank God for that.

11

By lunchtime Adam knew he needed another mode of transport besides his own two feet. He was too small to get away with driving a car, didn't know how to drive, or steal one. Taking the bus would have been an option if he had any money, but he'd searched his pockets and the backpack twice, finding not so much as a lucky penny. Hitchhiking was out, because he didn't trust strangers or adults in general, and the last thing he needed was someone kidnapping him or handing him off to the cops.

He could think of only one viable option – a bicycle. The idea of a bike excited him. He believed he had owned one at some point, and loved to ride it. More than just a mechanism to get away from the things pursuing him, a bike would allow him to move faster, cover more ground, go almost anywhere he pleased.

As he walked toward the mountains, he scanned the porches and open garages, hoping to spot a bike someone had left unlocked. After he had gone two or three miles without seeing a single bike, he was preparing to give up. A few blocks later, though, he noticed a yellow road sign with the black shapes of children crossing a lane. Which meant he was close to a school, and every school had a bike rack, didn't it?

Adam didn't care for the idea of stealing anyone's bike, but stealing another kid's bike was exponentially worse. Take a kid's bike, you are also robbing him of his mobility, his self-esteem, probably a year or more's worth of his allowance, and ultimately his freedom. Only a truly mean scumbag of a human being would steal a kid's bike.

On the other hand, there wasn't much choice. Which would be worse, some kid losing his bike, or Adam being slaughtered by The Nocturnals? The way Adam saw it, if he had a bike and giving it up meant saving some poor kid's life, well, he could live with that. He wouldn't like it, but he could live with it. Maybe if he found a bike to steal, he'd leave a note behind explaining why, hoping the boy would forgive him.

Those people are dead. You got them killed—

But he shut off these thoughts. They were too big for him to deal with.

He walked on, the sun warming his skin and drying out his clothes. He was not as tired as he should have been after only a couple hours of fragile sleep, but he was very hungry, and thirsty. The crackers and beef jerky were not going to get him through the day. What Adam wanted more than anything right now was breakfast, a real homemade breakfast. Pancakes, scrambled eggs, six strips of bacon, a pile of biscuits and gravy, and a chocolate shake. He could not remember his last home-cooked meal.

He followed the side streets, near some houses and past a trailer park, and he knew he was on the outskirts of Boulder. On the north side. Some things looked achingly familiar, like the trailer park, with its wooden sign and the two lanes that forked around it so people driving in wouldn't crash into the people driving out. Other sections of the neighborhood seemed strange, out of place, as if portions of this Boulder had been drastically changed overnight.

Six blocks later, he reached the school. A wide, flat building made of tan brick, so short it was obviously made for elementary school kids. He could tell that much even before he saw the playground swings and climbing dome and the low-mounted basketball hoops. He might have gone to this school, but if so it was a long time ago.

Hollow, partial memories of school returned: the cafeteria smells of baked cheese pizza, steaming green beans, sour milk cartons. He remembered drinking fountains, desks bolted to chairs so you could never adjust how close or far you were sitting to the desk itself. A teacher, some man with a brown beard who always wore brown corduroys and thick-soled shoes, but he couldn't remember the teacher's name, or his face, or any of his classmates' faces, if he had ever had real classmates.

He was tempted to sneak inside and see what else was familiar, but he couldn't risk that. The last thing he needed was for some teacher or the principal to shake him by the arm, ask why he wasn't in class, who were his parents?

Good questions, but not ones he wanted to answer now.

He found the bike racks on the far southwest corner, barely visible from the classrooms on the west side. There were two rows, with only five or six bikes hooked into the spars, which meant the odds of one of them not being locked up were slim. He approached slowly, nearly tiptoeing, before realizing this would only make him appear more suspicious, then walked purposefully, like any kid who's just been let out of class early and is in a hurry to meet his mom at home for a doctor's appointment. Yes, that was it. That's what he would say if any adults came out to harass him.

The first two bikes had steel chains coated with a rubber sleeve, one of them as thick as his wrist, and he knew he would never get through those. They were dumb bikes anyway. One was a long yellow ten-speed type with flowers painted on, and a low seat. Probably a girl's bike. The other was too small, red with black plastic wheels. A bike made for a first- or second-grader, and Adam knew he would have to pedal like a maniac just to get the thing going ten miles per hour.

Engine noise. A car approaching.

Adam looked over his shoulder and saw a small white pickup truck coming toward the school. His face began to burn with shame and guilt and he was sure that if the driver looked his way as he passed, he would see everything Adam was planning as clearly as if it were painted on a sign.

The truck shifted through the gears and increased speed, nearing the school's front entrance. The driver was an older guy, wearing a trucker hat high on his head of shaggy gray hair. Adam waited for the red brake lights to glow but the truck continued on without slowing, and the man never glanced his way. Regardless, Adam's heart pounded for another minute before he was calm enough to continue his thievery.

On the next row was a BMX bike, dinged up and dirty white with silver wheels and a crooked seat, but it didn't look too bad from a distance. Adam hurried to it, but his heart sank when saw that both tires were flat and the cranks and bearings rusted all to hell. Probably been sitting here for months, in the rain and snow, left for junk by some spoiled kid whose rich parents bought him a fancy new bike.

Adam headed back, head down, so hungry and tired all over again he wanted to lie down in the next drainage ditch he saw and fill his mouth with dirt.

Until his eye caught on something black. A thick smooth tire, black forks, faded chrome handlebars – another bike! It was all he could do to keep from running for it. Every part of it except the bars was dull, matte black, so plain he hadn't noticed on his first pass, but hell if it wasn't a real BMX bike. It had no decals, no brand name, looked like someone had welded it together in their barn. Either that, or the damn thing had already been stolen and the thief spray-bombed it all black to disguise it. With its fat wheels and miniature sprocket geared to the tiny cog built into the hub, it was different than any BMX bike he'd ever seen. He couldn't remember any specific BMX bikes, come to think of it, but this one felt different than even his faintest memories would allow. Nevertheless, it spoke to him in that subtle way bikes could.

I will do right by you, my man. We could do some real damage together. Take me out for a spin and you'll never want to get off.

But no dice. A massive steel chain was looped through both wheels and the frame and terminated at a blunt, fist-sized mechanism with a combination lock built into it. Adam kicked the chain and nearly broke one of his toes. What was he going to cut this open with, his knife? He'd need a blowtorch and half an hour to break this chain.

Oh, but how he suddenly wanted to ride it. It looked like a tough bike, a bike that could handle anything. Street, dirt, rocks, ramps.

Even though he knew it was pointless, Adam found himself holding the blocky combination lock in his palm. It was not a dial lock, with numbered notches on the colored face. This one had a row of black switches, like teeth, with six numbered settings per tooth. The lock felt hot in his hand. He touched one of the hanging loops on the rack to see if it was hot too, but that dark steel was much cooler than the lock. Weird.

He couldn't bring himself to let go. Not only was it warm, it was almost humming, as if some deep vibration were channeling its way up from the ground, through the long beam of the bike rack, into the combination lock.

Without wondering why he should bother, Adam closed his eyes and tried to imagine the boy who owned it. Soon he heard distant noises, like faint breathing, and the rhythmic hum of tires rolling on smooth asphalt. The breathing grew heavier, and the music of a well-oiled bike chain making its way around the sprocket filled his ears.

There was no flash, no startling vision, only the soft susurrations of young legs pushing force into smooth revolutions, the clean ticking of spinning cogs and the growing hum of tires. He could *feel* the bike working under his own legs now, the steam-engine labor of his own lungs, and the gummy rubber grips under his sweating palms. He was riding, and it was another boy he was riding along with, or perhaps inside of, and this boy was bigger than Adam, a tough kid from a rough home where he lived with only his dad because his mom left them, couldn't stand the smell of horse manure, or the drinking, and they lived on a farm with a barn and rows of junked cars, and he liked to hide things out in the trunk of one of the cars, little plastic baggies filled with grass, the *kind grass*, which always made the boy laugh, and something that belonged to his best friend Kurt, they called it the *otter bong* ...

Emerald-green light flared behind Adam's eyes and the taste of metal spread over his tongue, like he'd swallowed a mouthful of pencil lead. The green light was some kind of electrical pulse in his brain, making his nose hurt and his eyes water, stinging like he'd just jumped into a swimming pool and forgot to hold his breath—

The boy took a notebook from his backpack, flipped through it, and there they were. The numbers, scribbled on a sheet of blue-lined paper in soft pencil.

5-1-5-2-2

Adam opened his eyes and all sense of motion ceased. His sinuses were stinging, but the lock no longer seemed to be humming. He flicked the little black teeth in the same sequence he had seen in the notebook.

5-1-5-2-2

The metal key slipped from its cage as gravity dragged the heavy chain through the wheels, cling cling cling, until it fell to the ground, coiled and limp as a dead snake.

All he had to do now was take it.

Adam shivered, looking in all directions. He would never know if someone was watching from behind the school windows, waiting for him to commit the actual crime before coming out to holler at him.

He was stunned by what had just happened. No, it hadn't just happened. He did it. It was like he had performed a magic trick without even trying. But what was it?

Something bad had happened to him, he knew. He might have amnesia, he might be a psycho who lost his mind from one day to the next – but this was different. Something buried inside his hollow mind knew he had done this before, or other things like it. He had touched things and learned things about the people who owned them before today, and this must be one reason he'd found himself in so much trouble. It might even be the big problem, the one that angered the beasts and sent him on the run.

I have something, almost like a power, but it's not a good thing. It causes more problems than it solves. And it's responsible for hurting people, the people who used to be close to me but are gone now, all gone.

Heart racing, legs jittery, Adam felt detached from himself, a boy standing idly by as the other boy took the bike by its black rubber grips. In one fluid motion he heaved the bike up and turned it one hundred and eighty degrees to chuck it under his legs like a miniature stallion. He held on tight and pedaled as hard as he could.

By the time the front tire leaped out of the gravel and bit into the street ahead, he was moving almost as fast as a car, and he felt saved. The bike was the magic, not him. The bike took the town, the roads, the neighborhoods and the world that only minutes ago seemed so vast and pitiless – and most of all *huge* – and shrank it all down to a manageable size, made it his world. Adam wasn't afraid now. He could go wherever he wanted, as fast as he dared, and the monsters would never catch him.

He ducked in and out of neighborhoods, and soon he was careening down the steep hill on Broadway, the sidewalk seams blipping faster and faster beneath his wheels, the wind blowing back his hair, setting his thoughts free.

What if it wasn't magic or some special power? Maybe this was my bike all along and I just happened to forget the combination. Today I remembered, and if I can remember that, I can remember anything. Maybe I found my school and then I found my bike, and pretty soon I might just find my way home.

Now that he was riding again, anything seemed possible.

12

There was another kind of magic, one she called the Reliving. She was lost inside it now, back inside Pete Sampson, and he inside of her, where he had come to dwell.

Pete Sampson worked as a sales representative at Gebhardt Audi-BMW in Boulder, and he was good at his job, but not good enough to earn the kind of commissions that would allow him to live in Boulder. In the meantime he lived in an apartment in Lafayette, a small but growing town approximately eight miles east of Boulder. His commute each morning led him through a series of paved roads zigzagging across rural east Boulder County, and because he didn't begin his weekday shifts until 10 a.m., morning traffic was almost always thin. It was a stress-free drive, one Pete could enjoy at a leisurely clip, sipping a coffee and listening to sports talk radio. He drove an older BMW, one of the first 5-series, with over a hundred and seventy thousand miles on it, but it was still a fun car to push through the turns coming in on Valmont, the winding road that took him to the dealership's front door.

There were large houses and some small farms along the way, long split-rail and barbed-wire fences keeping small herds of cattle or a few horses back from the road. Heading into town meant aiming west, and the view of the mountains rising above Boulder was always something to appreciate.

It was an average Thursday morning that spring when Pete came down 95th, made the left turn onto Valmont, and began to crest that first small hill when he saw the woman in distress. She seemed to come running at the road, at him, as if she were going to leap in front of his car. Parked on the gravel shoulder perhaps fifty feet behind her was an old yellow hatchback, the hood up, and the woman was waving one hand, flagging urgently. The situation presented itself quickly, not leaving him much time to make a decision.

Pete didn't own a cellphone, and he wasn't the sort of guy to pick up a hitchhiker, but she was a long walk from town, and the good guy thing to do was at least pull over and make sure it wasn't an emergency. The woman wore a nice dress and heels and she looked respectable. He wasn't scheduled to start his shift on the lot for another twenty minutes, and even if he was a few minutes late, hey, who knew? This gal might need a new car. This could be his next commission. And it was the right thing to do.

All of which passed through Pete's brain in the time it took him to swerve into the oncoming lane to avoid striking her with his car, set down his coffee between the driver's seat and the emergency brake, and downshift as he nosed ahead of her and checked his rearview mirror.

She was already hurrying up along his passenger side, leaning down to the window. Pete reached over the seat and rolled the window down. Wind blew strands of sandy blonde hair inside the car and then the neckline of her dress was there, the pale top bone-nubs of her sternum visible in the V of purple and gold fabric. She was already talking before he saw her mouth, and then her face was filling the window, eyes behind gold-framed sunglasses with smoke-tinted lenses.

'Thank you, thank you, oh, I can't believe this morning,' she was saying, talking fast but not quite in a tone of panic. Flustered, was his first impression. Her forearms and bony elbows jackknifed across his windowsill as she set her chin on the backs of her hands. 'Can you help me out? Are you going into Boulder? I'm in a bit of a pinch here.'

A part of Pete knew already he was not going to be able to say no, but he wasn't eager to have a passenger, either. He had the weirdest feeling he should ask a few questions first, slow this down – not because he was unnerved by her, but almost to protect her, since she seemed ready to hop into the car with any creep who would have her. Maybe it was simply happening too fast.

'What's the trouble? Your car break down?' Pete said, looking back over his shoulder, to the open hood of the yellow hatchback.

'I had a terrible night,' she said, grimacing in a kind of apology. 'My car is screwed. I have to make a phone call.

I have to get out of here. Can you drop me at the next gas station or some place like that? It would be a huge help.'

She appeared dressed for work in an office of some sort. She was somewhere between twenty-five and thirty-five.

'Yeah, all right, hop in,' Pete said.

She did just that and then some, opening the door and somehow crumbling into the seat and slamming the door and juggling the mess of her purse and a little black notebook all in a flurry he hadn't expected for a woman in a dress and heels.

'You are a life saver,' she said. 'Seriously, thank you so much.'

There was the scent of candy, sweet cheap perfume, something like grape soda and old flowers. Pete's nostrils wrinkled against the potency of it and he notched his own window down a couple of inches. He checked both the side mirror and the rearview before pulling back onto Valmont, shifting the BMW up toward forty.

She babbled about the horrible night she had just made it through, something about a girlfriend who had left her at the bar, then her boyfriend, who was an asshole and no longer, as of this morning, her boyfriend at all, and then something about running out of gas, her boss, all of it out of order and coming too fast for Pete to really follow the sequential narrative, if there was one.

While she prattled, sometimes giggling, other times groaning with self-disgust ('How do I get myself into these stupid situations?'), Pete noticed certain things about her that put him on a nervous edge. Such as, her dress was the kind with a silk belt below the buttons, and the belt was loose, the knot unraveling, as if the dress were on the verge of flying apart. Also, her legs were pale, gangly, bruised at one knee and inside the left thigh. Her hair looked a bit unwashed, slept on, and her shoes – the white wedge heels – were dirtier than could be attributed to a little road dust from this recent car trouble.

This lady's a desperate mess, was what it came down to. She doesn't have car trouble. She's got life trouble. Bars, bad boyfriends, and the way she's talking over herself, she's on some kind of drugs, or coming off them. Bottom line: this is not someone you want in your car. Get her out as soon as possible.

'Where did you come from?' Pete heard himself asking. He was thinking of the way she had come running at the road, not like she had been on the shoulder to begin with, but as though she had come scurrying out of the field or some small patch of woods he might have missed. 'Looked like you were running back there.'

'Did you see that house? The red one?' she said, not looking at him. She was digging into her purse, flipping through the pages of her little black notebook. She would focus on one page for a moment, shake her head or bite her lip, then tear through more pages. 'That's where I was staying. At my friend's place. But she split, left me all the way out here in the middle of nowhere.'

'But what about your car?'

'Which one?' she said, ripping another page out and

crumpling it into a ball before stuffing it back in her purse. Her knuckles were chapped.

'The yellow hatchback with the hood up?' Pete suggested.

'Oh, that's not mine. I lost my car yesterday, at the bowling alley. Long story.' She smiled, laughed, and he saw her large eyes behind the smoked lenses, checking him out as he drove. Her eyes were twitchy.

Pete steered through the first of the long S-turns on Valmont. He had to concentrate to keep his eyes on the road. The curves here could sneak up on you.

'You seem nice,' she said, as if he had just offered to buy her a drink and now she was the one sitting in judgment. 'What do you do?'

'I work at Gebhardt Motors,' Pete said. 'The dealership. You need a new car? I can help you with that.'

'What kind of cars do you sell?'

'Audi, BMW, used European imports mostly. But we get a little of everything.'

'Out of my league,' she said. 'I bet you're good at your job.'

Pete wondered if he had just insulted her. Or offended her. He was only twenty-eight. He made just over thirty-two thousand last year. He hadn't thought of them as being in wildly differing income brackets – hadn't thought of her income bracket at all – but the comment gave him the impression that she existed in a pocket of life that did not bother with income brackets.

'It's really good of you to help me,' she said, touching his right arm, allowing her hand to linger there, long enough for him to feel the cold of her palm and fingers through his dress shirt. 'What's your name, sweetie?'

'Pete,' he said.

'I'm Sheila. Nice to meet you, Pete.' She smiled at him. She was leaning over in her seat, too close for a stranger.

'Okay,' he said, nervous in ways he could not explain. Or maybe it was this – she was making him feel pervy, though he had no such intentions.

'She took all my money, Pete. My friend did. I have to find a new place to stay. I'm really at a loss here.'

'I'm sorry to hear that.'

'Am I making you late for work?' Sheila said.

'No.' Pete checked his watch. A Casio G-Shock too thick for his lean limbs. It had been a gift from his dad. 'I have a few minutes. Our shifts are a bit flexible anyway. I work on commission, so if I'm a little late or whatever, it just comes out of my pocket.'

Sheila seemed to find this very funny. She laughed too loudly and her teeth were large. The longer he was in the car with her, the less attractive she became. Not that he had been thinking it mattered.

Pete exited the second S-turn on Valmont and followed the straight lane into a cluster of more houses lining the two-lane country road. He reduced his speed, knowing that cops sometimes tucked themselves in here to radar people taking advantage of the country roads. He imagined being pulled over right now with her in the car and something about that unsettled him. He felt like he was up to something risky here, he did not know what.

'So,' he said, clearing his throat. 'What do you need? A phone? A service station? Where should I take you?'

Sheila turned on her seat, facing him. She snapped her little black notebook closed. Her tongue poked out at the corner of her mouth and wet her top lip.

'That depends on how much you're willing to help me,' she said. 'I'm up for anything, you know? Is there a bar around here? I could use a drink.'

Pete laughed. He looked at her. She was smiling.

'Or whatever,' she said, facing the windshield again. 'I need a shower too.'

Well, okay, this was wrong. She was proposing something here, something like prostitution, he knew, and this was part of her scheme, wasn't it? The speech about car trouble, the bad boyfriend, the bad night. It was all some sort of sales pitch. Maybe she wasn't, like, officially a prostitute, but there was some kind of game happening here.

Pete was not flattered or interested. He was scared. He did not have a girlfriend, but he had dates, friends, a life. He had goals. He was a decent-looking guy. He neither wanted nor needed any of this. His stomach was acidic. Her candy perfume was making him feel sick.

And that was what made it all so strange, why he couldn't explain how twenty minutes later, after letting her use a pay phone at the gas station on the corner of 75th and Arapahoe, then crossing Valmont again to drop her off at the Residence Inn hotel suites, he found himself walking into the room with her. He couldn't even remember who had paid for the room, how they wound up with a key. His thoughts had turned thin, slippery. Speaking had become difficult and his limbs felt weak.

At the gas station, she'd said something about him not looking too good, and then he sort of blanked out for a few minutes, and when he returned to a state resembling normal alertness, he was in the passenger seat of his own car. Sheila was driving the BMW. He felt very tired, and still scared, but he could not pinpoint the exact nature of his fear. Checking into the hotel, he couldn't remember the last time he had spoken, or what he had said to her. She seemed to have stopped talking too.

And yet he could hear her, or follow her drift. Little prompts in his mind. Simple hand gestures, her pink chipped-polish fingernails cueing him this way and that. He felt as though he were under arrest. Being followed by a secret camera crew. Several times he thought of running away, but every time he considered this his knees locked up and his back stiffened.

Maybe I need a day off, he thought as Sheila opened the door to the room and waited for him to enter. He couldn't move.

'What's the matter, Pete?' she said, though he was looking right at her and he could swear that her lips did not move. 'Don't you want to come inside?'

He looked away. Looking directly at her was difficult. He would focus on the room. That would help. There was the couch, a small end table with a lamp, the Guest Services card standing next to it like a little teepee.

She locked the door behind him. They were in a

Residence Inn suite, the kind with the kitchenette, living room and loft bedroom on the second floor. There was a fireplace. It was like being in someone's house. He felt like he used to when he ditched class in high school, the guilt poisoning every bit of fun he thought he'd have. Had he thought at some point this would be fun?

What was happening here? Whose idea was this?

He was sitting on the couch, staring at the blank gray TV screen. He wanted to turn it on but he could not see the remote control. He tried to stand up but his legs and body felt enormously heavy. Had she drugged him? No, that was not possible. He had not ingested anything since she got into his car. His coffee had gone cold and he was sure he hadn't touched it after meeting her.

Seeing her running from the field into the road, that felt like something that had happened yesterday, a week ago. What time was it? He attempted to check his Casio but his wrist felt tied to the couch. He looked down. It wasn't.

'I'm just going to make a few phone calls,' Sheila said from behind him. Her cold fingers were at his neck, then digging into his hair, climbing the back of his head like a large spider. She caressed his scalp, making his skin tingle.

Pete looked up to see her but she was on the other side of the room now, sitting in the chair at the desk, where the phone was plugged in. She was over there, at least ten feet away, but he could still feel her fingers massaging his scalp. Pete turned on the sofa and looked where she had been standing, because maybe someone else had followed them in?

But no, there was no one in the room with them.

Spiders in the thick of his hair. Tingling.

His tongue felt dead.

Sheila held the phone to her cheek. She listened. He did not see her fingers push the buttons to dial. She nodded a few times, glanced at him with another of her weird smiles, and set the phone back on its cradle.

'There's no one home,' she said. 'I guess we're stuck here for a while.'

Pete nodded, thinking, I know you're lying. He wanted to get up and run but he couldn't. He could move his feet, his legs and arms, turn his head. But his will was gone. She had done something inside his mind. The willpower to take action had been snipped like a piece of string, and Sheila was the scissors.

'I'm going to take a shower, Pete,' she said.

He nodded. He began to hum.

A long time later, she reappeared. He was still staring at the blank TV screen when she stepped in front of it. She was naked. There were scars up and down her torso, her belly, around her thighs. Long sleek scars like burn marks, or lashes from a whip. Her breasts were small, flat, oddly muscular. Her pubic region was a small riot of jungle. Her hips were bruised purple and yellow. She stood before him dripping wet from her shower and he could not look up into her eyes. He knew that if he looked at her face, he would see that it had changed. He could feel that her smile was gone. He could feel her bared teeth. One of her fingernails had crusts of red near the cuticle.

'Oh, Pete,' she said. 'Poor Pete.'

She walked behind him, into the kitchenette. A drawer opened. Utensils clinked. She walked back into the living room and in her left hand was a dull steel butter knife. She shook the handle so that the flat blade slapped against her thigh, pat pat pat, over and over. It's just a butter knife, he thought. Literally the thing you use to spread butter across a roll. She can't possibly think she's going to get anywhere with that.

Pete giggled a little and leaned forward to sit up. When he did, a cold belt of force tightened against his chest and slammed him back into the couch cushions. The force was so distinct, he looked down to see the strap, but there was nothing there around his dress shirt.

His hands were on his thighs. 'What are you doing?' he tried to say.

Sheila's mouth did not open as he distinctly heard the words, 'We're going to experience murder now. Together. Wait until you try this. You've never felt anything like it. Are you ready?'

'No,' Pete Sampson said, hearing his own yes echoed back at him.

'Good. That echo you hear? That's me inside your head. I'm going to bring you into me now, and I will be inside of you. It's called sympathetic murder. Have you ever heard of that, Pete?'

'No.'

'It's really magical,' Sheila said, and still he could not look up at her. He could see her naked body. Her scar tissue. The flat seam of her belly button. 'This way, the chosen and the devourer get to share each other's experience, in effect erasing the whole concept of murder completely. There is no suffering. My will is your will. Your will is mine. I'm sort of controlling the whole show now, but you get to come along for the ride, and you will attain immortality within my temple.'

Pete was aware of hot tears streaming down his cheeks. They tickled and he wished he could wipe them away.

'All right,' the woman said. 'Here we go.'

Inside of Pete, something pulled hard, and he felt himself yanked from the couch, above the floor, flying like a child who has been grabbed by a very angry father, and he was slamming into the woman without resistance or impact. His vision went blurry pink and flesh-toned, with veins of red like closing your eyes to look at the sun, and then he was looking back down at himself on the couch. There was Pete Sampson, sitting on the couch in the hotel room, looking up with stark terror in his eyes. His cheeks were wet. His pants were wet around the crotch. His fingers were clenched around his work slacks. His mouth was open, saliva dripping down his chin. He looked like a patient in a hospital, one who had suffered a severe stroke.

Inside her, here in the other one, his perception of himself was sustained but only dimly. He felt enveloped in something stronger, feminine, fiercely on edge. A

140

woman re-conceptualized as a razor blade, or maybe a starving alley cat. Seething hatred boiled in her blood, his blood. Dark, horrifying memories flash-flooded in and out of his mind, blinding him to the hotel room for seconds at a time: a bloodstained bedroom floor, a little girl's bed, black candles lighted and melting in every direction, a leather belt stripping itself from a pair of dirty brown work pants, black symbols smeared across the walls, on his skin, her skin, the little girl's skin, a mother watching with black eyes . . .

The young man on the couch started to scream and the female fury controlling Pete locked his every muscle with her own and together they sprang forward, straddling the young man on the couch. He bucked and thrashed. Her thighs were shower wet astride him and the butter knife slipped in her fist. He felt her fingers aching with tension. She used him to bring it down with terrible force. The dull rounded tip stabbed into the neck four times before the skin broke. The side of her hand stuffed itself into his mouth and he felt her hand going into his mouth even as he brought the knife down again into the soft hollow of the young man's throat. Bite marks. First on his hand, which was her hand in his mouth, then on the young man's ears from her teeth. The pain was exquisite and immeasurable. It was a fire and a rage, hot agony, a self-demolition.

Pete Sampson stopped screaming. He collapsed inside the woman, his spirit shriveling as he ceased struggling and became a hanged but not yet dead man inside the closet of the woman killing him.

The knife went up and down more than seventy times, but the last thirty or forty slashes were Sheila's and Sheila's alone and Pete Sampson did not feel them.

He turned away inside her, into darkness, receding from the windows of her eyes and the light of the hotel room down into a hall of many rooms, through a door, inside an empty bedroom with nothing on the floor, and he knew the other rooms were also occupied and he was not alone.

When she finished, out of breath, she felt clean again. She felt safe, protected, and as comfortably sated as a serpent who has ingested meal enough to last three months.

She walked into the bathroom, to look at herself in the mirror. Dots and splashes of blood speckled and striped her naked form, but she hardly noticed these. She was staring into the eyes, her own dark eyes, looking for him. She knew he was in there somewhere, probably cowering in shock. She leaned closer to the mirror, inspecting her dilated pupils. The circles of green around them had taken on a filigree of gold.

He had been a sweet boy, Pete Sampson. She would never forget him. He would always be with her, inside of her, a forever friend who had come to her aid in a time of need with his sympathy. He would follow her everywhere, experience all she experienced, and grow old with her. A loving companion and kindred soul, like the other twenty-seven she had swallowed.

'Don't worry, Pete. I'll take good care of you.'

The mirror blurred and darkened around her beautiful

countenance, but Sheila held her own gaze, and that of the others, as long as possible, until the Residence Inn and Hotel Room was but a memory.

Then she was looking into a different mirror, a smaller oval mirror on a stand. The stand was perched on a glass top, one lined with bottles of perfume at its bottom and a cash register to one side. She was not standing in a bathroom, but behind a glass display counter. Bright lights overhead, plastic mannequins arranged across the gleaming white floor in front of her. A cacophony of female voices and the soft, insinuating drone of muzak filled the air.

'She's not even listening,' someone said. 'What is she staring at in that mirror?'

Sheila blinked, realizing she was at work, in Nordstrom Rack. Worse, she was no longer twenty-seven and in her prime, at the peak of her powers. Within seconds the face in the mirror aged (fifteen? eighteen?) too many years, and Sheila was forced to look away, to a pair of impatient old women standing just a few feet away. One was staring at her, drumming her red nails on the glass.

'Excuse me, ma'am? Can I have some service down here? Isn't there someone who can help me?'

Sheila turned on her high heels and click-clocked to the woman. That the woman was hideously aged beyond Sheila's years did not alleviate the drill of rage that shot forth inside her upon hearing herself referred to as 'ma'am'. But then, when was the last time any of these old goats called her 'miss'?

Sheila located a mood mask somewhere below the gift packs of perfume and skin toner and anti-aging creams and pasted it across her lips, transforming a snarl into a bright smile.

'I can help you, dear,' she said. 'What are we shopping for today?'

The old goat began to babble and Sheila was grateful for the Reliving with Pete Sampson. It had lasted longer than any she had been able to achieve in the past six months, but it was getting harder to stay there, in touch with her collection of the devoured. Which could only mean one thing.

She was going to have to find some sympathy again.

Soon.

Part 2

OLD FRIENDS

13

The sun arced across the cloudless sky and swung the shade of one particularly large maple tree in North Boulder Park around like the minute hand on a giant watch with a face of lush green grass. The sun crawled over his sneakers, up his legs and shirt, until it reached his pale cheeks and fluttering eyelids and sprung fresh dew sweat from his brow, making him dizzy with heat and dehydration. He sat up, blinking until the blinding brightness receded and the park was revealed.

Only a couple kids remained on the playground, near the swings and the teeter-totters, their parents cleaning up after the birthday party that had thronged the clubhouse earlier. Behind him, the riotous game of flag football had ended and now there were only a few college-aged guys sitting around a red cooler, sipping beers. There had been a man with a pair of black Labradors, but that Frisbee-playing trio was gone too. The diminished numbers left him uneasy, but it was still daylight and he didn't think The Nocturnals would risk coming for him out here, not while there were at least a few regular people in the area.

He counted himself lucky he hadn't slept all day under this tree, waking after darkfall. The bike was laid over in the grass beside him, the heavy chain tangled in the spokes to serve as an alarm should someone try to steal it.

Adam reached into the plastic grocery sack and took out another bottle of water and drank half its contents in one go. He caught his breath, finished it, and put the bottle with the rest of the trash: two empty potato chips bags, the wrapper to a ham and swiss sandwich, three granola bar wrappers, and two banana peels. All that was left were the two apples, the can of beef stew he was saving for dinner, a bottle of macadamia nuts, and the last bottle of water. He removed these and shoved them in his backpack.

Stealing his meals had been easier than he imagined. After so much desperation, he kicked himself for not heading directly to the nearest grocery store weeks or months ago. There wasn't any secret to it. He didn't cram things into his pack when no one was looking, scurrying out the back in a terrified dash. He'd simply ridden by the giant Safeway store on 28th Street, taken one look inside at all the people going in and out, the few employees working, let alone paying attention, while half the people in the store used the new self-checkout lanes, and the strategy became clear.

He found a discarded receipt in one of the carts at the front of the store, took a plastic bag from one of the checkout lanes, then wandered the aisles, adding foods that would travel well to his bag. On his way out, he kept the receipt displayed for anyone watching him. The bike was chained to a parking sign ten feet from the door and within seconds he was cruising across the parking lot, then behind two strip malls, back into a neighborhood of apartment buildings, vanishing into the town.

He'd taken to riding at night, sleeping here and at other parks during the days, near groups of people. It seemed to be working. He had not been chased in three days.

Adam got to his feet and stretched, then pulled on his backpack. After disposing of his trash, he walked his bike down the center of the big park, loosening his legs. He passed two small baseball diamonds where some kids were warming up for Little League, though it must have been practice because they weren't wearing jerseys and there were hardly any parents in the risers. The sight of baseball mitts and bats and chalked baselines failed to stir any longing in him. To Adam the boys looked to be engaged in a stupid, meaningless game. He resented the way they chattered and chased after the baseballs their studly-dudley coach was plinking at them, clueless to the ugliness and danger lurking behind the curtain of this sunny play land.

Adam didn't care about sports, unless riding bikes was a sport, in which case he cared about that a lot. Teamwork, the coach shouted at them. Teamwork! A bike wasn't a team, it was for him, a team of one, and it was survival, and that was fine because a team couldn't save you from anything that happened off the field. A team wasn't going to be there in the middle of the night when the ghastly things came to drink your blood.

But where the hell was he going?

A goal or plan of some kind seemed to have seized him during the delirium of his binge eating. Something to do with a theory about Boulder and all the changes he kept noticing. Like the big Safeway store, which was twice the size of any grocery store he remembered, and nicer, with wooden floors in the produce section, and two whole aisles dedicated to health-food items (none of which had looked remotely tasty to him). The self-checkout lanes were another weird development. He hadn't even known what he was looking at until he saw the other customers swiping their credit cards in the machines and heard the robotic female voice walking them through each step, telling them to 'PUT THE SCANNED ITEM IN THE BAGGING AREA' and 'PLEASE CONTINUE SCANNING YOUR ITEMS' and 'PLEASE SELECT YOUR METHOD OF PAYMENT'.

That had been a shock, almost like he had stepped into one of those movies about the future. Except, Adam knew this wasn't the future, because in those movies, and in his *Questar* magazine, there were always flying cars and the people wore clothes made of tinfoil and there were robots and aliens everywhere. The fancy grocery store and the new houses and the other things that seemed out of place weren't like that. A lot of the cars looked newer than he remembered, but they weren't spaceships.

150

He was pretty sure he had lived here, before the thing that messed up his memory came along and changed him. And he was still a kid, so whatever happened, it couldn't have been that long ago. Who does a kid live with? His family.

What happened to his parents? Somebody had to be responsible for bringing him into this world. But when he searched his mind and heart for them, there was only a cold emptiness. If he'd had a family at one time, shouldn't he miss them? Or, if they were bad people, the kind you're better off running away from, wouldn't you feel sad about that?

Angry? Hurt? Confused?

He was nearing the south end of the park, where a large triangular flower bed stood in one corner, made of stacked railroad ties, containing at least a hundred or more yellow and orange flowers. Those looked familiar, as did the small brown apartment building at the end of the park, and the huge drooping trees lining the other corner. Weeping willows, they were called.

He stopped in his tracks.

He was only a couple hundred feet from the end of the park, but something was standing in the shade of two massive willow trees. A big brown truck with a dirty white camper shell on the back, parked horizontally, one whole flank facing him. The camper windows were dark, either from tinting or lack of sunlight, though he thought he could detect curtains behind one of them.

The sight of the truck and that camper shell made the hair at the back of his neck come alive. He knew it from somewhere. A quiver of fear slid down his gullet, twisting through him until his entire body felt numb, stuck.

No, it can't be. They're not human, so they can't drive. It's just a truck sitting by the park. Some family passing through town on a vacation. That's all it is.

But he didn't believe this.

The truck should have been obvious sooner, but it was so brown and dirty and close to the apartment building and the trees, it was almost hiding in plain sight, like whoever owned the truck had chosen that precise spot because they knew it would be camouflaged.

Nothing had happened yet, and no one had come for him in the park, so maybe they weren't even in there. Maybe the camper shell was empty. The truck might belong to someone else. Part of him wanted to walk right up to it, to have himself a good look just to prove there was nothing to be afraid of. If something happened, he could scream for help, or ride away. If nothing happened, he might learn something by peering inside.

He might remember something that would later save his life.

Adam continued walking his bike toward the truck, veering slightly left, angling ahead of its front end. If he could read the license plate, memorize it, that could be useful. That would mean going to the police or a private detective at least, but he might need the police sooner or later.

He was perhaps fifty feet away when he realized no

one was using this end of the park. No couples sitting on a blanket, no kids playing, not even a student reading a book. It was probably crazy to think such a thing was possible, but right now it felt like the truck and its big fiberglass camper shell were giving off a dark energy, dangerous vibes, a sense of wrongness that repelled people who probably hadn't even noticed it here. It was just part of the background, something you subconsciously avoid, like the mouth of a dark alleyway in a crime-infested city.

Thirty feet away. Adam slowed.

He could feel the rotten spirit within it now, like toxins in the air, nausea building inside him. He could almost see the cramped, cluttered seats and the tiny table inside piled with trash, the shabby brown curtains hanging limply over the grease-smudged windows, and it would never be bright and fresh in there, no matter where it was parked, no matter how much sunlight shined upon it. The smell. Inside, the camper smelled like dirty socks and raw onions, and something else, something wet and muddy but not dirt, like the blood you find in the bottom of a foam tray of spoiled hamburger. The scent of animals left on the highway, baking in the sun, the organs rotting until the gases burst through the skin.

Twenty feet away.

The tires were huge but worn down, the hood split at one corner like a busted lip. A thick white antenna reached up from the right side like a crooked branch of bone, a dirty tennis ball stuck to the top.

It wasn't a camper. It was a den, the den of animals pretending to be human. Ghastly things lived in there, this was their home, and they used it to roam around in search of children, boys like him, or maybe *only* him, and when they couldn't find him, they killed other people and took cups filled with blood inside and drank them like milkshakes, spilling it on themselves, eating peeled patches of human skin, wallowing in flesh the way most families would consume a fried chicken dinner.

Adam was shivering in the sunlight on a day that had to be at least seventy-five degrees. He stopped, but he could not tear his eyes away from the truck.

Somewhere inside, maybe up high in the top bunk overhanging the truck's cabin, nestled deep under blankets that hadn't been washed in years, burrowed between pillows grimed with sweat and blood and saliva and sex messes, something monstrous was dozing. Sleeping away the day. Rebuilding itself and digesting its last meal in deep slumber, building up stores of energy for tonight's hunt.

'Like me,' Adam whispered.

That's how he knew, because what had he done today?

Travelled. Fed. Found a patch of shade.

And slept.

The things inside the camper were keeping the same schedule. He'd lost them at the house because they stayed behind to feed. Eventually they'd followed him here, or felt his presence in the vicinity, but were too tired to track him further. They'd come as close as they were able, going by sense or smell or some kind of intuition (an intuition not so different from the bizarre trance that gripped him now), and when they couldn't go another step, they collapsed with exhaustion.

And if this were true, if he could sense them from out here, then it must also be true they could sense *him* from in there. The presence of so many people might have spared him from their attack, but each step closer to their hideaway was one step closer to rousing them with his presence.

But he'd come this far. He had to know. He might never get so close again.

He took a step, then another, bringing the rest of the chipped chrome bumper into view. FORD, the grill said. The other headlight was broken, its steel cone and smashed bulb visible behind jagged glass teeth. But the license plate was bent, curled at one corner and nearly torn off, probably from the same accident that had mangled the bumper and hood.

One more step, two at most, and he would see it.

Hurry, they're going to wake up any moment now.

He took three quick steps and it was there, the green Colorado plate with its mountain-shaped background and white lettering.

MP-3515.

Say it, say it three times in your mind, so you don't forget.

MP-3515. MP-3515. MP-3515.

Got it. Now get the hell out of here.

Adam shuddered, forcing himself to look away. All at

once he felt insane for coming so close, and he wanted to hop on his bike and ride like a demon.

But he couldn't. It was almost like he was inside the camper with them, tiptoeing over the trash and junk on the floor, and any sudden movement or the slightest crinkle of paper would snap them awake. Somehow they had found themselves in a fragile peace, a time out from the hunt due to their mutual need for sleep. If he bolted now, he might sever the connection too abruptly, like tearing the bandage off one of his scraped knees before the scab had time to heal.

He didn't run. He walked until he was out of the shade, back into the harsh glare of sunlight, and then casually lifted one leg over the bike and kicked himself along the grass, afraid to pedal.

He thought of looking back one final time, but somehow even that small gesture seemed it would doom him. They would slither down from their filthy bunk, rip open the camper's back door and come bounding after him like a pair of man-eating lions. Drag him back to their lair. The blood-soaked interior of the camper would be the last thing he ever saw.

When his bike rolled onto clean sidewalk, he began to pedal, dipping through the crosswalk, watching for oncoming cars. He bunny-hopped the next curb, found his stride, and passed a hospital's emergency room entrance. Three blocks later, when he finally looked back, the brown Ford truck was nowhere to be seen.

Only the mountains watched over him, and this place he once called home.

14

By Saturday, life around the Lynwood residence seemed to have stabilized. Darren hadn't mentioned any additional nightmares, and he'd promised Beth he would tell her if the fire dream visited him again. Raya had not received any new cryptic texts. The three of them – four, counting Chad, who had been spending more and more time around the house with Raya – seemed to be relaxing into summer. Maybe it was Chad's presence, Beth thought. Maybe he's the fourth leg under our family table, the lost older brother Raya never had and the son Darren wished he had all along.

The four of them took a late lunch at the West End Tavern downtown, and somehow even their seating arrangement resembled a family – the two teens on opposite sides of the table, Raya with Beth, Chad on Darren's side. Darren kept making immature jokes and murmuring things to Chad, the two of them cracking up every few minutes. Have another chicken wing, dude! Thanks, Darren! My God, Beth thought, if this keeps up they'll be riding bikes together by the end of the week.

Raya had noticed it too. 'Look at you two over there. What do you think, Mom? Is it a man crush?'

Chad laughed nervously.

Darren said, 'We're just making sure we get the best view.'

'The Flatirons are behind you,' Beth said.

'The prettiest part of this town has nothing on our girls. Right, Chad?'

'Absolutely.'

'You're my little chicken wing,' her husband said, winking.

Beth and Raya collectively rolled their eyes and pretended to be sick, though she knew Raya appreciated her father's renewed effort to bond with her boyfriend. Still, Beth couldn't help wondering how far this could go before someone wound up disappointed, or embarrassed.

By the time the burgers arrived, Darren was on his second beer, one arm thrown around Chad's seat back, acting as if they owned the place.

'You know, if you two kids are nice to me and promise not to stay out past nine o'clock,' Darren said, peering intently at Raya. 'I might let Chad here take you out for a drive in the Firebird. But if you get caught speeding, I'll tell the cops you stole my car.'

'Dad! I haven't even gotten to drive the Firebird yet. How dare you.'

Chad's cheeks were turning red, but he was grinning.

'That's because you don't have a license yet, sweetheart, and Chad does.'

'I'll let you drive it when you're seventeen,' Chad said.

Raya gasped at the both of them.

Beth said, 'See what you've started?'

Darren and Chad laughed like a couple of howler monkeys, and Beth looked down into her lap, lost in thought for a moment, and when she looked up again, Darren was watching her with concern. She put on a smile.

'So, what do you kids want to do this afternoon?' she said. 'We could walk down the mall, look for some sandals, grab a coffee and some ice cream?'

Raya looked to her father, then back to Beth. 'I think we should visit Gremme. That would be nice, right?'

'Really?' Beth said, surprised and then feeling guilty she hadn't been the one to mention Gremme.

'It's been a while,' Raya said. 'Like, months.'

Darren frowned. 'Not months. Your mother and I saw her a few weeks ago.'

'A month anyway,' Beth corrected. 'I think that's a really sweet idea.'

'Don't you want to, Dad?'

'Of course. That just wasn't what I expected to hear on your first weekend of the summer. You kids are supposed to be out partying and behaving irresponsibly, not visiting your grandma. What made you think of Gremme?'

Raya shrugged. 'Chad's been wanting to meet her and, I don't know, I was just thinking about her this morning for some reason. I think she wants us to come visit, that's all.'

Beth looked to Darren, wondering if he was reading anything odd into this declaration, but he was only nodding. 'Okay. I'm sure she'll appreciate it.'

Hunches, Beth thought as they paid the tab. Either something's wrong with Gremme and Raya's having another one of her hunches, or we somehow managed to raise a really good kid.

Grandma Eloise Lynwood – Gremme, as Raya had called her throughout infancy – lived in the Atrium, an assisted living facility on the northeast corner of Boulder, near the Diagonal Highway. True to its name, the condominium-style building featured an impressive glass roof and six floors of interior walkways encircling a respectably large and lovingly cared for garden-courtyard at its center, with real trees and a variety of flowers and the accompanying humid vegetation and fertilizer aromas of a greenhouse.

Residents of the Atrium enjoyed various levels of assistance. A few were hardly more than paying tenants, taking advantage of the upscale standards and guest services but otherwise enjoying nearly total independent lifestyle like anyone else living in an apartment building or hotel, one that just so happened to have a medical staff on hand. Others were plugged into plans that included meal service, weekly or daily health check-ups and in-home visits from the nursing staff, but not much more. While still another category of residents, the ones who had lost all ability to care for themselves, were fed, bathed, and tended to in all the ways a full-time care facility was required to do so.

Darren's mother had been in the earliest stages of Alzheimer's Disease when they began planning the move back to Boulder, and there had been some discussion about whether to move Eloise out west along with them. Not because they didn't want to keep her close, but because the woman was still of sound mind and did not wish to leave Mequon, the small city in the Milwaukee metro area she had called home for more than forty years. She had been living a vigorous life in a quality retirement community there, with plenty of mobility and a private nurse who spent three days a week in her unit. But that was last spring.

By the time Beth and Darren's moving plans turned into moving boxes and real estate contracts, the erosion of Eloise's faculties had accelerated. She had begun leaving the unit without notifying anyone, taking walks at odd hours, getting lost. Physically she had been strong, but the other common symptoms were worsening monthly. Friendships she had enjoyed with other residents in Mequon suffered or unraveled. Darren had been their only child, and now he and Beth and Raya were all Gremme had.

Darren had been torn about what to do. On the one hand, he didn't want to disturb her anymore by moving her from a familiar environment. On the other, it was obvious that soon enough Gremme would not know the difference between her place in Wisconsin and a nice room in Colorado with all the same belongings. Money for her care was not an issue, and being out of the corporate world had freed up plenty of time for Darren to fly to and from Milwaukee to visit her. But Colorado enjoyed a milder climate, and ultimately Darren felt that if he did not move her to Boulder, he would regret having missed a few more days with her, even if she no longer remembered him on those days.

The move had gone better than expected and the change of environment actually seemed to rouse Gremme's once-sharp wit for a winter renaissance of good spirits and general awareness, but spring had seen her regressing. They used to say Gremme had good days and bad, but in the past few months most of her days fell into the categories of not-terrible and heart-breaking. Vulgarity and profanity had seeped into her conversations, ugly racial slurs of the sort Eloise had never expressed and had not seemed capable of before the disease struck.

The last time Beth and Darren had visited her, she had recognized them both only briefly before referring to Beth as Raya a number of times and then lost track of them altogether, until she was unable to respond to any visitors. As recently as winter she had still been referring to Darren as 'my son' or 'my boy', but lately the best she could do was, 'him' or 'you know, that one'.

The four of them checked in at the reception area, then took the elevator to the third floor. Gremme had a corner unit at the end of the hall, with just under a thousand square feet of living space: one bedroom, living room, kitchenette and a full bath, plus a small nook with a desk and a view of the Flatirons. From the outside it looked like a Hilton hotel. Inside, a wealthy old woman's small but upscale apartment.

Gremme's door was open a few inches and Beth heard voices, which meant a staff visit or cleaning services were present, but they knocked politely anyway.

'Come in,' a young woman said.

Darren pushed the door open and they all shuffled into the entryway beside the kitchenette to watch a young Latino attendant in pale pink scrubs and a black cardigan sweater finish making Gremme's bed with fresh sheets and duvet cover. Beth recognized the employee but did not remember her name.

'Hello, how's everyone doing?' the attendant said, trying to cue Eloise.

Gremme was sitting upright in her reclining armchair, dressed in gray slacks, a loose burgundy blouse and her bright red flats. She was watching a talk show on the small TV set wall-mounted above her dresser. Her hair had been cut recently, so short it did not cover her ears, and Beth wished they had let it go. Gremme's hair seemed to have stopped growing altogether and she found herself wondering what was the point. She didn't think Gremme would have asked for this near-crew cut, but it was possible.

'Hi, how are you?' Beth said.

'Just finishing up in here,' the woman said. Then to Gremme, 'Eloise, you have some company. Your family is here.'

'Oh really?' Gremme said, but she did not turn to see them.

Darren went ahead first and Beth stepped aside to allow Raya and Chad to follow before she brought up the rear. They circled the Lynwood matriarch, delivering hugs and hellos, until Raya plopped down on the couch to Gremme's right. Chad sat with her, a warm smile on his face as he studied the room, the family photos on the walls, the fresh flowers on the breakfast bar. Darren stood to his mother's left, hands in his pockets, trying to look more comfortable, Beth knew, than he felt.

'Hi, Gremme!' Raya belted once more. 'How are you today?'

'There you are,' Gremme said, beaming at the two kids. 'Isn't she beautiful?'

'Yes,' Chad said. 'It's nice to meet you, Mrs Lynwood.'

'It rained last night,' Gremme said, turning her attention back to the TV. 'Did you see it? They said it was gonna happen.'

'Yes,' Raya answered. 'I like your hair. Did you get your hair styled recently?'

Gremme looked over to Darren with mild alarm. Sized him up from feet to head and back again. Beth watched her closely to see if she would recognize her son. 'Do you want to sit down?' Gremme asked him. 'All this standing is making me tired.'

'I'm good, Mom,' Darren said, then crouched beside her chair and held her arm, patting her hand. 'How are things? You look good. You feelin' good?'

'Have you seen this show?' she said, gesturing at the

TV. They all turned to look. It was a political round table of some sort. 'This is really something. These people ...'

'What's new in here?' Darren said. 'Any new hot dates we should know about?'

'Darren,' Beth said.

'Oh? What did he do this time?' Gremme said, arching from the chair to find Beth. 'Come in here, you.'

Beth moved in front of Darren. 'Hi, Eloise. You look well. Have you eaten today? Can we bring you anything?'

Gremme's eyes widened. 'I'm stuffed! They're always making you eat. I wish they'd leave me alone.'

To die, Beth couldn't help thinking. Sometimes you heard the residents saying that. *Please just let me die!*

Raya spent a few minutes telling her about school, asking Gremme if she was ready for summer. Gremme said she didn't trust the lake, which Beth interpreted as memories of Lake Michigan.

'Who's that one?' Gremme said, pointing at Chad.

'This is my friend Chad,' Raya said. 'Chad, this is Grandma Lynwood.'

'Nice to meet you, ma'am,' Chad said for the second time.

'Where's the other one?' Gremme asked Raya.

'Which other one?' Raya said, smiling.

'Your little friend.'

Raya looked at Chad, her parents, then shrugged. 'Just Chad.'

'You *know*,' Gremme said, impatiently waving her hand in a wobbly circle. 'The one who used to follow you around all the time.'

'Chad, I think your girl's got another boyfriend,' Darren said, winking at the kids as he stood. Beth heard his knees pop.

Gremme turned in her chair and looked at Darren. 'You know who I mean. The little one. Your friend.'

Darren blinked down at his mother. 'I don't know who you mean, Mom. My friend or Raya's friend?'

'Raya?'

Darren pointed. 'That's Raya, your granddaughter, and her boyfriend Chad.'

Gremme waved her hand again, her mouth puckering, the thin remains of her eyebrows inching together like silkworms.

'Not him, the other one, the little one followed you.'

'Followed me?' Darren said.

'Yes, that one. Adam.'

'Adam?' Raya said, looking to her parents.

'Who's Adam?' Beth said.

Gremme pointed to Darren and laughed bitterly. A small string of saliva dripped from the corner of her mouth to her chin. 'He knows. He knows.'

'I don't know who she means,' Darren said. 'Who's Adam, Mom?'

Gremme took hold of the TV's remote control and smashed it against the pad of her armchair several times. 'Adam. Adam. Adam!'

'Okay,' Darren said. 'That's all right. Easy. What about him?'

'He was just here, didn't you see him? The little boy?' Gremme looked at Raya as she said this, but her tone, Beth thought, was meant for Darren. As if she were scolding her son some twenty years ago. 'He follows you everywhere and look what you did to him. Cruel. Very cruel.'

Beth saw Raya's eyes widening and she knew what her daughter was thinking. *Stop it*, Beth wanted to say, *stop encouraging her right now*. But she didn't know who she wanted to say it to, Gremme or Raya.

Raya was staring at Gremme, taking her by the hand. 'You know him, Gremme? The boy who came to visit you?'

'Every day,' Gremme said, leaning forward and speaking gravely to Raya. 'For years. He was always a very dedicated boy, you know. Very dedicated.'

The old woman's sudden, disproportionate clarity around this subject unnerved Beth.

'What's he look like?' Raya said.

'Honey, please,' Beth interrupted.

'Just a little itty bitty thing,' Gremme said. She turned to Darren once more. 'And you were so mean to him. Shame on you.'

'Okay, Mom,' Darren said with a distracted sigh. Beth thought he was being too dismissive. Hiding his own discomfort. 'Do you need anything else? Do you have enough of the licorice?'

Gremme loved black licorice. Twists, Nibs, ropes.

Didn't matter what kind. She couldn't get enough black licorice. They should have brought her some more, Beth thought, but there was a bowl full of twists on the kitchen counter.

'He'll be back,' Gremme said to Darren, her eyes shrunken, dark with old resentment. 'He'll find you. You're a bad kid.'

'I am?' Darren said.

'Mom? Mom!' Raya was on her feet, waving Beth over. Chad looked confused. Beth stayed where she was.

'Bad kid,' Gremme repeated, staring at the TV. 'Rotten little fucker.'

'Okay,' Beth said.

'She knows,' Raya said.

'Cool it, Raya,' Darren said, then to his mother, 'We'll come back soon, all right?'

'Oh, you're not going to trick me with that one,' Gremme said. 'Not this time. You know what you did to him.'

'No. What did I do to Adam, Mom?'

'Terrible things. Terrible things.'

Gremme started to laugh, cackling to herself.

Beth felt cold air running itself up along her bare arms, beneath her clothes, as if the unit's air-conditioning were running on HI.

'We're upsetting her,' she said, taking Darren by the arm. He was red in the face, staring down at his mother, tongue-tied. Beth whispered. 'Come on, kids.'

A tired glaze fell over Gremme's features. She leaned

back in her chair, head pushing into the cushion, and set
the remote control down. They hugged and kissed her
goodbye, but she did not respond in kind. Beth held the
door while the others filed out, then told Darren she
would catch up with them down in the lobby.

'Leave it, Beth,' he said. 'Enough for one day.'

'Just give me a minute. I won't upset her.'

Darren shook his head and walked off.

Beth let herself in, shut the door and returned to
Gremme's side. She kneeled and took Gremme by the
arm, rubbing her sleeve.

'Gremme? Eloise? Honey, can you talk to me a
second?'

Gremme's head lolled to the side as if her neck had
been turned to rubber. Her eyes were moist, vacant,
roaming around Beth without landing on any one
point.

'The others left us alone. Can you tell me?'

Gremme's lips pursed and rolled against each other.

'Did he come for a visit?' Beth said. 'When was Adam
here, Gremme? Do you want to tell me?'

Gremme blinked, nodding almost imperceptibly.

Beth smiled gently, to encourage her. 'That's nice. I
don't remember him. Who is he? Can you tell me who
he is? How do you know him?'

Gremme's eyes wandered to the side, then up, high
toward the ceiling. She said nothing.

'When was he here?' Beth said. 'Can you tell me the
last time you saw him?'

Gremme's hand lifted from the padded arm of her

chair, her frail hand clutching the remote. She aimed the remote over Beth's shoulder.

'There,' Gremme said softly. 'He's there, in the corner.'

Beth's smile disappeared.

Gremme smiled and patted her lap. 'Come here, little one. He won't hurt you. Come say hello, Adam.'

15

Sheila resisted the urge until Saturday evening.

She told herself on the way over that this was not her reason for coming to Dillinger's, the seedy little oddity of a sports bar in the strip mall less than a mile from her home. She would never hunt so close to the safe haven she had finally established after so many years of sleepless nights on the move. Told herself she was only in the mood for a drink, a place to unwind, somewhere unpretentious and not too crowded, where she would be the best-looking thing in the bar. She had watched the bar's clientele from time to time, whenever she stopped at the gas station at the other end of the strip mall, and she was confident her wattage would prevail among such an assortment of dim creatures.

Sheila had not bantered for many moons. If some man pretending to be a gentleman decided to chat her up, that might make for some harmless fun. It would be a distraction from the dull white noise in her head and the even duller silence that had seeped into every facet of her life these past eighteen months she had gone clean. The white noise had gotten so bad it had even begun to wash out the communications she typically enjoyed with her cats. A break in the routine was good for everybody, even Sheila, who, as one of her teachers once remarked, needed routine like a prisoner needs cell walls.

So, okay, a little harmless flirting. Nothing more.

But after spending only half an hour in Dillinger's, watching the contractors who'd skipped out on work early, wasting their lives playing air hockey, deer-hunting video games, and swilling shots of Jim Beam along with their cheap draft beers, Sheila knew she was going to have to unlock some sympathy. Sap another pig. She felt neither guilt nor the rush of excitement she had known so long ago. She didn't feel very much at all, which was the whole point.

She needed a little taste of that old black magic. The Speaking and Listening had been two forms of the black art, the Crawling another. There were a dozen other ways to get there, methods that did not require intimate contact or the threat of weapons, but she'd lost her gifts years ago, thanks to The One Who Disappeared, as they used to refer to him, hating his name so much they had put a ban on speaking it. Now there was only the lonely nights, and the boring days at the department store that made her want to stick a plastic fast-food knife in her own eyes, or the customers'.

Just a little sympathy. I deserve it.

She sat with her elbows on the bar, palms cupping her delicate chin. The jukebox was playing a horrendous country rap song about God and the U.S. of A. In her

172

Kate Spade shoulder bag was a short-barreled .38, the one she had taken from the cop, who was also a pig. Sheila had nothing against police per se, but all the men who used to love her had turned into pigs, and he'd proven as much that night when he tried to put it in her Exit Only. Sometimes she wished she could remember his name, but so many of the devoured had stopped speaking to her. Pete Sampson returning the other day, that had been a surprise visit from within the hotel of many rooms. She longed to find another Pete – someone so open and giving – but people had grown cautious in the past fifteen years. She was out of practice.

The bartender was the only other woman in here. Tall, much bigger-boned than Sheila, and not nearly as pretty. She wore a satin bowling jacket with a sports team logo on the back and Shelia noticed the woman hadn't smiled as widely at her as she did to all the other customers. Probably thought she wasn't going to get much of a tip from a woman, so why bother being nice? Talk about a self-defeating attitude. Well, the bartender was right about that. Slut would be lucky if Sheila left her two dollars for the five or six Myers Rum and Cokes she intended to drink.

The two young swine playing air hockey were interesting, the way they balanced on their toes, buttocks clenched, legs shivering as they leaned over the table to smash the puck around, jumping up and down and shouting at one another when one of them scored a goal. Sheila could smell the epoxy resin stains on their tattered sweatshirts, the mud caked into the cuffs of their jeans, the wet sock mildew seeping from their construction worker boots. When they finished their game they high-fived their way to the same side of the wobbly little table, inching their stools close to one another, ostensibly to better view the baseball game on the TV across the center parlor, but Sheila knew they were secretly homos who screwed each other in their Exit Onlys.

She would not choose either of them, even if that had been her style, but Sheila never chose. They always chose her, unless fate chose for them both. That was her rule, and part of what made the sapping such a gamble, a little mystery every time out.

Sheila caught herself nibbling on the corner of a bar napkin, mentally reprimanded herself, and put it back under her drink. She was craving a cigarette, but she could wait. If no one chose her by ten, she would go home and smoke a whole pack of Newport 100s while practicing her symbols.

She fingered the inside of the Kate Spade hooked over the back of her stool, caressed the textured grip, tapped a nail on the barrel. Maybe she wouldn't use the gun tonight. Maybe she would find a way to go old school, like Daddy'd taught her. Rope around the throat. A knife in the kidney. Handcuffs, Drano down the throat, though that one had been extremely messy and prolonged.

One she'd strangled herself – *Can you still hear me in there, Jason? Jonathan? RickTomBrianJamesAlex?* – with nothing but her own two hands, taking the risk and going for a little more intimacy because he had been small and because her more intuitive tools had been rusty and the sympathy had been reluctant. One of those little Napoleon pigs with stubby little hands and small shoes, the regrettably short man tool between his legs, so small she'd hardly even felt it in her Enter Here. Where was he now? Where had they all gone?

Poor Pete. I miss you ...

The bar's front door clattered. He came in wiping his blond hair forward to minimize his baldness, tugging the knot of tie loose from his throat. She saw him in the bar mirror and resisted the urge to turn. A lady never turns or makes first eye contact. He was in a dull gray suit not of department-store quality, but he was handsome, or had been once, even though his cheeks were flushed in a way that did not bespeak plumb health. Sheila had read that phrase in a book once and it stuck with her. Bespoke plumb health. And he looked clean. A Bob or a Jeff or a Tim, something safe.

He sat two stools away from her, shrugging off his jacket, eyes sporting around as he waited for the bartender. Nice; he thought he was being subtle, taking a stool close to her when there were nine or ten empty ones further along the square bar, but leaving one between them so as not to come off aggressive.

'Hey, Nancy,' he said when the bartender slopped her way over to him. 'Bud Light, when you feel generous.'

Nancy the bartender smiled warmly. 'You got it, Steven. Good week?'

Steven inched a twenty from his leather wallet and

set it on the rubber gutter mat. 'Hell, no. Still in the slump. Friday sales meeting from two to five to motivate the pimps. I said, Thanks but no thanks.'

'Good for you.' Nancy set the beer before him, broke the twenty, left the change on the gripper. She glanced at Sheila. 'How you doin' there, hon? Another rum and Coke for ya?'

'In a moment,' Shelia demurred. 'It's still a little early.'

'Take your time.' Nancy winked and went back to the kitchen counter to ferry two cheeseburgers and a basket of fried mushrooms to the Village People.

I'll break him in ten minutes, Sheila thought. No more than fifteen.

But ten minutes passed, twenty, and nearly half an hour later – though Steven had checked her out once or twice, his eyes never lingering – he hadn't said a thing to her. Sheila was intrigued, a little confused, but definitely not offended. This did not mean her talent had abandoned her. He looked like he had something on his mind. He kept frowning at his phone, which he'd set on the bar and spun like a top from time to time. He wasn't wearing a wedding band. He was probably checking his email on the phone to make sure his boss hadn't ordered him back to the office.

Sheila signaled Nancy for another Myers and headed for the bathroom, wanting him to get a look at the goods coming and going. She passed a couple of inches behind his back and had a good sniff. No cologne. Maybe a hint of something athletic, probably too much of one of those action hero deodorant bars they used now, with a scent named Recharge or Power Blast or Clean Energy. She could live with that.

In the disgusting grimy potty she layered a four-ply of toilet paper around the seat, urinated ferociously, wiped three times, used the arch of her high heel to pump the flush lever, and washed her hands. Her eyeliner should have been a little thicker for the lighting in this dump, but her make-up was nice, softening her sharp nose and bringing some color into her flat pale cheeks. She shook out her hair, ratting it up a little, so it would look like she might have just come in here and masturbated for a few minutes, then applied a thick coat of the red lipstick she had debated using before she left her apartment but had saved for that extra push to put her over the top.

Her lips peeled back and she imagined biting his ear off while she inspected her teeth. Very nice. The whitening strips were finally working.

All she needed was an opening to penetrate, loosing the charm within him so that sympathy would bloom.

'Eleven even, hon,' Nancy said, sliding her new drink into place as she returned.

'Oh, I thought I paid for the first one,' Sheila said.

'Nope. I can run a tab if you want?'

'I'm sorry.' Sheila reached for her Kate Spade, clunking it onto the bar. She fidgeted in its depths, rubbing the gun, the pepper spray. How funny would it be if I took those out instead of my wallet and sprayed everything all over Nancy and Steven at the same time? 'Sorry, it's in here somewhere, I promise.'

177

'I'll take care of that,' Steven said, nudging some of his bills at Nancy.

Nancy looked to Sheila for approval. 'Nice fella, here.'

'Hm? Oh, wow. Thank you,' Sheila said, convincingly surprised and mildly flattered. 'You dih'n't have to do that.'

'Sure. What's that dark rum all about, anyway? It looks rich.'

'It is,' Sheila said. 'I call it my vacation.'

Steven snorted. 'I could use a vacation.'

'Wanna try it?' She offered the glass, but he was too far away to lean over. He would have to come to her.

He gazed at the glass of dark fluid and ice chips, calculating.

'It's all right,' Sheila said. 'I don't put the roofie in until the third around.'

The Steven pig tittered. 'Yeah? Okay.'

He stood, shuffled a few steps, and she raised the glass for him, letting him know it was okay to let her nurse him with it. He stiffened, bobbed for it, missed.

'Here,' he said, taking it from her hand. He gave it a swirl, sipped, and handed it back, avoiding hand contact. 'A little strong for me, but I can see the appeal. Thanks.'

He returned to his seat. Looked up at the TV. Spun his phone nervously.

Sheila stared at him. What was wrong with this goddamn dork? Was it the gray in her hair? Maybe she should have used another box of the Clairol this morning to deepen the auburn cover. But he couldn't have seen that. Or her smoking wrinkles. Not in this light. He was just shy, that was all. She was going to have to lead him to it, like yanking the dog's leash to let him know where it was OK to piss.

If you still had the power, he'd already be sapped by now. Resorting to guns and knives? You're an amateur. Give it up, you sad delusional brat. You're not up for this. You'll get sloppy, like you did that time in Glenwood Springs, at the pool. The lifeguard saw what you were trying to do to that boy, the one who looked like Adam. You want to wind up in prison?

Shut up! Sheila hissed to herself. She willed him to look at her, pushing with all she had, but he only stared up at the TV.

I'm only forty-six, Steven, and pretty sure I could suck your cock until you cried.

'Sorry, what?' he said, turning to her with alarm.

'What?'

He looked at her. 'Did you say something?'

Oh. Had she said that aloud?

'I don't think so.' She giggled, smiled at him.

'No, you said my name. And maybe something else that wasn't too nice.'

'I'm sorry. I forget that I mumble. People tell me that all the time.'

He glared at her, took a hurried sip of his beer.

She leaned toward him. 'All right, you busted me. What I said was, "What line of work are you in, Steven? I'm pretty sure we're off the clock now that it's five."'

He relaxed somewhat. 'Ha. All right. I sell corporate cleaning services. But where'd you get my name?'

Sheila nodded toward the bartender. 'Nancy said it. Sorry, I didn't mean to pry.' She made a sad face and stared down at her drink. 'Or bother you.'

Steven finished his Bud Light. 'No, that's OK. Hey, my bad. I misunderstood you, guess I'm just a little wound up. Hard week, you know?'

Sheila brightened. Let him see her eyes go from his face down to his lap, up again. 'Everyone's wound up these days. Maybe we need to find a better way to unwind.'

His smile was warm, kind, and she could see some of the boy in him, before he had lost his sympathy and become a true pig. Oh, damn it, now she wanted him. Really wanted him. She didn't have to sap anyone today. There would be other pigs. There always were.

Suddenly she saw herself and Steven stumbling tipsy and laughing gaily to his beige Ford Taurus, a safe car. He would open the door for her, and he'd place his hand on her leg as they drove to her apartment. Once inside, she would insist on making him a snack while he waltzed around her living room looking at her beautiful paintings, asking if she had really done all these herself. She would say yes, not having to act shy, because she really was shy and modest, especially about her artwork, and he would say, these are really something, truly original, while she defrosted his lasagne that she made back in February. She would let him open the wine. They would share the lasagne on the couch and he would kiss her, getting her homemade red sauce on her lips and nose, and she would scold him playfully and make him lick it off. She would invite him into her bedroom, where no one except her cats, Teddy and Alanis, was allowed. Steven would undress her slowly and she would undress him and they would make love. He would be sensitive and patient and not try to put it in her Exit Only. After, Steven would ask permission to stay the night and she would consent. They would dream together and in the morning he would take her to breakfast at that little cafe in Louisville and she would have whipped cream on her latte. It could be this way. She could control herself, she didn't have to be the way they made her, the way her little brat shit brother made her, and her dearly departed zoo animal parents, the drugs and the séances and her ape father grubbing in her child loins all those years, all that could be over, she could love this man and feel loved and it would all get better. She would never have to sap again, for their new love would be a balm upon her soul.

'You think so?' Steven said. 'Got any ideas how to go about that?'

'I do. But first you're going to have to buy me another drink, cutie pie.'

Steven laughed briefly, but his smile was gone. He stood.

'You bet,' he said, and flipped another ten on the bar. 'Nance. Another Myers and Coke for the lady.'

'Thank you,' Sheila said through her teeth.

Steven took his jacket from the back of the barstool,

filling its sleeves with his arms before snapping the collar down. 'Enjoy that.'

'You're leaving?'

''Fraid so. Lotta work to do tonight.'

'On Friday?' Sheila said. 'I don't believe you.'

Then she saw the little silver band on his left ring finger. It had been there all along, but it was a symbol, and you couldn't always see the symbols coming.

Steven gave Nancy the bartender a look. They exchanged something with their eyes. One of them was embarrassed and the other was sympathizing, but Sheila could not tell which was which because they were both clever pigs.

'Catch you later, Nancy. Nice meeting you,' he said to Sheila.

But they hadn't met. He didn't even know her name. He never asked, even though she'd used his. She sauntered over to the jukebox to spot his car through the front windows.

He got into a small gray Audi, the smug pig. Sheila watched it exit the parking lot, turning south onto South Boulder Road. She went back to the bar, grabbed her Kate Spade with the pistol and the pepper spray and amyl nitrates and then shoved her way outside, wheeling off in her Pontiac.

She watched him go into Sprouts, the healthy food grocer, and emerge ten minutes later with a single sack of what appeared to be a free-range roasted chicken and a fresh baguette. From there it was only five minutes to his house in a Waneka Lake subdivision, where he parked in the driveway and did not notice her one block back. She waited until he was inside plus ten minutes, then walked around back, into the yard. Peering through the windows off the deck, she saw why he had forced himself to resist her even though he wanted to hump her brains out like all the other pigs.

Enter Here Exit Only Enter Here Exit Only Enter Here Exit Enter Exit—

His wife was young, almost pretty, even though she was pregnant. The filthy pig bastard. Leading her on, flirting with her, sticking his tongue in her drink. But, all considered, this was fine. This was better. Sheila could forgive him. He'd led her to a gift here, a world of possibilities. Sheila hadn't sapped a pig in eighteen months, but Lordy, she hadn't raped and killed a woman since 2003. The preggo thing threw her off a bit. She didn't know what that meant, but there could be a lot of power in it. Too bad she was rusty on her symbols. There must be a special one for the unborn. Well, she would figure that little situation out when she got there. As always, it would be part of the mystery. She would create her own black magic, sympathy be damned.

– Enter Here.

She took the gun from her Kate Spade and held it at her side as she walked to the back door and let herself into their living room.

'Hi, Steven.'

His wife looked across the room, eyes widening, then to her husband.

'Hey, whoa, what the hell?' He jumped from the

couch. 'No, no, no way. In my house? You better get the hell out of here!'

Sheila smiled at the wife. 'It's okay, we're old friends.'

The wife looked to Steven pig. 'You know this person?'

'I absolutely do not. She was at the bar. Something's wrong with her. She's unstable.' Talking about her as if she weren't standing right here, stable as pig-fucking Abel. 'Not happening, OK, got it? I tried to ignore you and be polite about it, now will you get the hell out before I have to throw you out?'

Her nostrils flared but she forced herself to present calmly. 'You shouldn't have screwed me and left me in the bathroom like that, Steven. That wasn't nice.'

The wife reacted in an amusing fashion.

Steven looked at her, really looked at her, as if he were finally seeing Sheila for the first time. She gave him one more chance, but it was clear from his expression that he was not going to choose her. Times had changed, and time had been cruel. She was going to have to break her rule and choose for him. The three of them would find sympathy together in the moment. It would all come back.

Sheila broke one of the amyls and inhaled hard. She raised the gun. The room went underwater and their screams weren't very loud at all.

Oh, how she wished her parents were still alive to see this.

16

Darren had been trying to fall asleep for almost three hours. Normally, he would have gotten up by this time, slipped on his sweats and sneakers and headed for the shop, but he didn't want to work on the bikes right now. He didn't even want to see them, especially the Cinelli. He did not know if all these experiences they'd had concerning the boy were somehow connected to the Cinelli, but there was bad juju around that bike. He couldn't explain it, but he knew it was there.

'Are you still thinking about that bike?' Beth said, rolling to face him in the dark.

'No. Maybe. Not the bike but ... I mean, Jesus.'

Beth rested her hand on his chest and draped one leg over his lap. 'I'm sorry. I should have dropped the whole thing.'

'First me, then Raya, now my mother.'

'She has no idea what she's talking about,' Beth said. 'It was a coincidence. Chad was new to her. Raya was putting ideas into her head.'

'You really believe that? After what she said to you

after we left? Come on, Beth. That was scary. You said so yourself.'

'In the moment,' Beth said. 'But what did she really say, when you get down to it? She barely recognizes us anymore. She could have been talking about anybody.'

'Adam. She said his name.'

'Do you know anyone named Adam?' Beth said.

Darren sighed.

'Of course not. And there was no one there. I knew that before I even turned around. No one at the reception desk had any record of a little boy visiting her, I told you that. No Adams in the logbook.'

'Then how do you explain it?' he said.

'She gets that way when too many people see her at once. Please don't turn this into a thing.' She kissed the hollow of his throat, thick bands of her hair pushing up against his chin. She kissed his chest and thigh-nudged his hips.

Darren coughed dryly. 'She said I did terrible things.'

Beth took a deep breath. 'Honey, really. It's an awful disease. My Great Aunt Polly had it and you would not believe the things that came out of her mouth if I told you. You need to let this go.'

'I'm trying.'

Beth pushed herself up and sat astride him. 'Try harder.'

Darren looked at her, taking the clue as Beth pressed against him, grinding her hips back and forth.

'Is Chad still here?' he said. 'I didn't hear his car going the other way.'

'They're watching movies.' Beth leaned down to kiss him. She met his lips delicately, then firmer with her tongue, entering into a routine that was elaborate for them at this point in their marriage.

But he couldn't let go yet. 'And you're okay with that? At this time of night?'

'Stop it. Chad's your new best friend, remember?'

'That doesn't mean he's allowed to sleep over.'

Beth sat up and removed her tank top. He took in the sight of her bare shoulders and breasts, her fleshy hips, all this roundness suddenly before him. Beth was still inspiring to him. She was short, full and soft in all the places he wanted her to be. Her legs were strong. He had an eye for design, loved good design, the aesthetic and the tactile. Her smooth knees, the grace of her thin fingers, the taut cords behind her knees, the tightening brown skin of her nipples and the pale white around them. The lines where the final garment met hip bone and navel, soft, wet.

'What are you laughing at?' she said.

'You. You are inspired design.'

'Stop.'

But he knew she liked it, was happy to feel him sinking into the moment with her. They kissed for a while and Beth sat up again, peering down into his eyes, questioning.

'What?'

'Do you blame me?' she said.

'For what?'

'You always wanted a boy. Do you blame me for giving up?'

'You didn't give up. We had other plans. We already made a family.'

'Do you regret it?'

'How could I regret Raya?'

'But what if we're not enough?'

'Don't ever think that,' he whispered into her hair.

She scaled down, held him in her mouth. There was a slow, spacious pressure, the faint edge of her teeth. He reached the verge too soon and closed his eyes, thinking of the bike. The red bike. His blood on it, the boy in white shadow outline.

'Stay with me,' Beth said.

He opened his eyes. She sat back above him, holding her breasts, rolling her nipples between her fingers, watching him watch. He knew what she was doing, reminding him to think about her, them, their family, not the past. Just this, now.

Beth leaned forward and slipped one knee up through her underwear, turning them aside with urgency, and then she was onto him, sinking, then connected in near-total stillness. She wouldn't release him. She wasn't even moving now, and her tightening paralysis triggered it for him, made it like breaking into pieces. Beth moaned, her hand moving to finish herself while his vision went black. She fell upon him panting in the warm room, their muscles releasing stores of tension. Her lower back dappled with sweat. She clung to him like a koala and fell asleep in minutes.

Darren listened to her breathing for a long time.

Close to an hour later he heard Chad leave through the front door, his car rumbling off into the night.

Darren didn't feel tired, but eventually he heard his mother's voice, her frail but knowing voice, and he slipped into something that might have been sleep, but if so, was unlike any he had ever known.

He was a very dedicated boy, you know. Very dedicated.

Terrible things. Terrible things.

Rotten little fucker.

Adam. Adam. Adam!

17

His name is Adam, and today is the day he is sent into exile.

All summer he's been shadowing the five members of the Wonderland Hills Gang. He doesn't know all their names, but he knows three of the five and he remembers them all by their bikes. Wonderland Hills is where all the rich kids with the hottest bikes in North Boulder live, but today he's followed them to Palo Park, a mile or two east, to the dirt park between housing developments, where the cool kids come to ride.

Tommy Berkley is the chubby one on the baby blue P.K. Ripper. He's a good rider, not scared to go after the big jumps, but he's even better at sitting back with his fat butt hanging over his Uni seat as he holds a wheelie for blocks, sometimes one-handed. Tommy is mellow and funny and Adam isn't afraid of him. He's even said hi once or twice at the bike racks when they are locking up before class starts, though Adam doubts Tommy knows his name.

Ryan Triguay is the thinner athletic one who always wears soccer shorts and sweatshirts with the names of

European soccer teams on them. He has two bikes, today's the beautiful white JMC with red components. Ryan rides fast, never jumping high but taking triples and doubles in one go, crossing up his bars and doing crazy tailwhips before landing as quietly as a glider. Some weekends he races out at the track in Brighton. Adam's seen his trophies, that day Ryan brought them to school for show and tell. Racing is how Ryan won his second bike, a brand-new Hutch Pro Racer, with all-chrome Hutch parts. Ryan has feathered-back hair and piercing blue eyes, with the sleek face of a hawk. He's confident but quiet. The one time Adam said hi in the hall, Ryan only nodded and kept walking.

The third boy Adam knows by name is Darren Lynwood. He's the most bad-ass rider of the whole gang, in the whole school, maybe in all of Boulder. He doesn't race because he doesn't have anything to prove and he prefers to free ride, concocting his own jam sessions. He is fearless on a bike. His parents are loaded, so he has five or six bikes and a garage full of parts. Today at Palo Park he's flying around on one of his two Pattersons, the chrome on yellow gold, Zeronine racing plate #1.

Darren is their leader, you can tell by the way the others wait for him to jump first, or last, when he's setting up for some massive air or a new trick he learned. He's not big but he's got a lot of muscle and he's tougher than the rest of them. He has dozens of scars from BMX. Rumor is, when he broke his arm tabletopping a six-foot berm last summer, he didn't even cry. Just picked up his bike, told them his arm was broken, and rode all the way home, where he waited for his mom to come home from work and take him to the hospital.

The other two guys are kind of wimps compared to Darren, Tommy and Ryan, not very good riders but still better than Adam. They get to tag along with the gang because they have sweet bikes. The tall kid is from special ed class, clumsy, silent, and his name might be Greg, but Adam isn't sure.

The last kid lives outside of Wonderland Hills but he's still part of the gang. He's got one of the rarest bikes, a Diamondback Harry Leary Turbo signature model, the one in smoke-black chrome. For this reason Adam thinks of him as Harry Leary, even though he knows the real Harry Leary is a grown-up pro racer dude with a blond mustache, not this kid, who's short and squat, a member of the city's wrestling league.

The five of them are all in fifth or sixth grade, though some of them look older. They are all popular. Sometimes they even talk to the girls. Each kid in the Wonderland Hills Gang owns at least one bike worth over four hundred dollars, or more, because they have been tricked out with custom parts.

The bikes are everything, their identities, it is tribal.

Adam is in fifth grade but he's the size of a third-grader. He has the lean frame of a swimmer, or a track star, and it's true he can run fast, but when it comes to riding, he's a disaster on wheels. Just practicing a few minor tricks in the cul-de-sacs of his trailer park, he's already broken two teeth and fractured his wrist. But he's proud of his injuries and, besides, his dad's done a lot worse to him than the bike ever will.

Adam's bike is a yellow and blue Huffy, a gift he received for Christmas three years ago, when he was still too small to ride it. He is pretty sure his mom made his dad buy it for him with the check they got for his dad's back injury, and Adam knows a Huffy only cost eighty-nine bucks at K-Mart. But that's new. Adam's Huffy was used when he got it, he knows, after he overheard his mom saying something about a yard sale while she argued with his dad about thirty dollars.

Now that he is almost eleven, and big enough to ride it, the Huffy is falling apart because his folks make him keep it outside the trailer, year-round. The bearings are rusted, prone to locking up. One of the five spars in his front mag wheel is cracked. It's a slow, heavy bike made of cheap steel, and even when Adam pedals as hard as he can, he feels like he is pedaling in a swamp. Just riding here today wore him halfway out.

Adam is ashamed of his bike, but he wants to learn how to *ride*. Get good at curb tricks, bunny-hop one-eighties, learn how to hold a wheelie, and most of all how to get big air like the other guys. He comes down here to Palo Park once or twice a week, but he never rides the dirt trails and jumps when the other guys are here, only when he is alone. He is afraid they will run him over, that he will block traffic on the hills and jumps, and he is even more afraid they will laugh at him, or laugh at his bike, which would amount to the same thing.

But today something amazing happens. They invite him to join in.

He's been so hypnotized by the sight of the Wonderland Hills Gang running their rotation – one guy spotting for traffic while the next guy takes the long downhill run through four jumps and then up the final embankment for huge air to land in the street, taking spot position after he lands so the next guy can go, the last guy racing to the back of the line, so that they continue this circuit in something of a team relay, a unit of friends working together – he couldn't help himself from getting closer. He's managed to walk his Huffy within hollering distance of their acrobatic flow.

Harry Leary and the big dude Greg take one last turn and then beg off for the day, leaving only the core threesome. Ryan Triguay is on at the back of the line, waiting his turn. He waves Adam over.

Adam experiences an endorphin rush, followed by a quiver of fear. It could be a trick, they might want to mess with him. But even if they don't tease him, he's too afraid to ride with them. He will lose control and try something stupid, yanking his handlebars too hard on one of the small jumps, flipping himself onto his back. He will be humiliated, permanently barred from their gang. So he sits, paralyzed.

But Ryan won't leave him alone. He keeps waving.

'Come on!' he calls across the ravine separating the good jumps from the wide patch of weeds where Adam has been lurking. 'Quit watching and get a ride in here!'

Then Tommy joins in, cupping his hands to shout, 'Give it a go! We won't bite!'

Well, Tommy's all right. Maybe this is cool. It's not like they own the park. Lots of kids ride here and Adam's never seen a fight or anything bad like that.

The desire has built up so long, Adam cannot resist. He nods at them and turns around in the weeds and pedals his skinny ass back to the road, around the ravine, using the street bridge to cross over because the ravine is twenty feet deep, extremely steep and nothing but rough dirt clods and sharp rocks all the way down. Only a maniac would try to ride in and out of that.

By the time he is pedaling into their midst, Tommy and Ryan are sitting on their bikes in a semicircle, front tires turned sideways, practicing that trick of balancing with your feet out on the treads, rolling side to side. Adam has practiced this simple trick many times but he can never keep his feet off the ground for more than five seconds.

He approaches them on his mount, easing up cautiously.

Darren Lynwood is standing over his Patterson, his feet flat on the ground, wearing a Patterson Racing jersey and a pair of new Haro gloves that look incredibly cool and tough. He's checking out Adam's bike, blinking as if the sun got in his eyes.

Darren chins in Adam's direction and then looks at Tommy and Ryan. 'Guess it's just us three and the runt now.'

Adam is about twenty feet away, but at this remark he feels his coaster brake engage, skidding his rear tire in the loose dirt.

'He's cool,' Tommy says. 'I see him riding all over the place. He goes to Crest View.' Tommy turns to Adam. 'Aren't you in Mrs Fletcher's class?'

'Yeah,' Adam says.

'I'm just screwing with ya,' Darren says to Adam. 'Come on over, let's get a look at your rig. What is that, a Murray?'

'Huffy,' Adam says, swallowing his embarrassment.

'Those mags are all right,' Ryan says. 'My first bike was a Huffy and I rode the shit out of those wheels.'

For this small endorsement, Adam is immensely grateful.

'I tried riding Tuffs,' Darren says. 'But I can't get on board with mags. Too heavy.'

'One of them is cracked,' Adam says. 'To tell you the truth, the whole bike's a piece of shit.'

He didn't mean this as a joke, but all three of the guys laugh heartily. Adam understands that he has placed a small bit of his own humiliation before them as an offering, a way to say, *I know I'm a loser and not even in your league, but don't worry, I am aware of my limitations and wouldn't dream of threatening your hierarchy.* He hopes this will endear him to them in some small way, giving him just enough room for them to allow him to hang around for a little while.

Darren steps off his Patterson and lets it fall to the ground with a clatter, something Adam cannot imagine ever doing if he owned a bike that nice. He walks toward Adam, sizing up the Huffy.

'Don't mess with the guy's bike, Darren,' Ryan says. 'It's in bad enough shape already.'

'I'm not gonna hurt his bike,' Darren says, as if Adam weren't even here. 'I'm trying to help him with it.'

Adam doesn't know if he is allowed to respond.

'Some new wheels would be the first thing,' Darren says. 'Any aluminum rims would be better than these mags. They're slowing you down. You need three-piece cranks, too. Those one-piece set-ups are strong as hell but way too slow. Probably a new headset, bottom bracket, and a plastic seat. That alone would save you six or eight pounds. Roll a lot smoother too.'

'Yeah, I know,' Adam says. 'I'm saving for a new bike.'

'Cool.' Darren nods. 'What do you have your eye on?'

Adam feels like a liar even before he answers. He is saving for a new bike, but he has only managed to save thirty-one dollars, a long way from the kind of bike Adam would like to own, so far away that he hasn't really allowed himself to get specific. So he lies some more, naming the first bike that comes to mind, but one that he hopes doesn't sound too presumptuous or absurdly out of his league.

'Kuwahara KZ-1.'

Darren nods approvingly. 'Kuwahara's a good bike, for Japanese. Some of them are crap but the new KZ-1 is bitchin'. The test ride review in *BMX Action* was hot.'

Adam grins. Congratulations, grasshopper. You have chosen wisely.

'But you can't ride this dog in the meantime,' Darren says, frowning. 'Better to get some decent parts on it so you can learn how to throw a bike around, then strip it down and keep the parts when you can afford a new frame.'

This has never occurred to Adam, but it makes all kinds of sense. No way will his parents help him spring for a new bike. They have a lot of problems lately, and money is only one of them, and not the worst. It will take him another whole year to save for even a decent bike, but he could mow enough lawns this summer to upgrade his wheels.

'Good idea,' he says brightly, his mind racing with visions of Darren and the guys helping him pick out new bike parts, tuning up his ride in Tommy's garage until it doesn't look so much like a Huffy anymore. 'I'll remember that.'

'Can I take it for a spin?' Darren says.

'Oh no,' Tommy says.

'I won't hurt it, I promise.' Darren looks Adam in the eye for the first time, sincere, mellow. 'If you want, you can take my Patty for a spin just to be safe.'

'No, that's okay.' Adam steps off his Huffy and leans the handlebars toward Darren, his mind reeling. How crazy is this that Darren Lynwood wants to ride his bike? And did he really just offer Adam the chance to ride his Patterson? Adam must have heard that wrong. But even if he didn't, there's no way Adam will get on the Patterson. That'd be like the world's worst driver getting behind the wheel of a Lamborghini.

Darren wraps one of his Haro gloves around the hard-ened vinyl of Adam's peeling grip. 'You sure it's cool?'

'Of course.' Adam is compelled to add, 'I don't care if you wreck it. It's a jalopy, man. Do whatever you want.'

Darren mounts the Huffy. 'Really? You don't care?'

'Ghost it!' Tommy suddenly barks. 'Ghost that sucker!'

'Yeah, ghost it, D!' Ryan says.

'Shut up,' Darren says. 'I'm not going to ghost the kid's bike. What did you say your name was? Aaron?'

'Adam.' He doesn't have any idea what 'ghost it' means, but it sounds like a trick, some cool jumping move, and if that's true, it would be rad to see Darren pull it off on his bike. Darren Lynwood nailing some awesome move off on his crappy little Huffy would, in some way, instantly make his bike a lot less lame.

There is an awkward moment with the three of them watching him, with weird expressions on their faces, waiting for him to say something more.

Adam can't think of anything except, 'Go ahead, ghost it, man. I don't mind.'

Darren looks away for a moment, then laughs. 'Okay, little bro. Whatever.'

He rides off, cruising in a slow circle, getting a feel for the inferior bike as he yanks on the bars a few times, popping small wheelies, then gets up a little speed and kicks the rear end out. He pedals directly at a two-foot high tumbleweed stuck to the grass and bunny-hops all the way over it. Adam is a bit awed, thinking how strong and coordinated Darren has to be to yank his Huffy two feet straight up in the air, both wheels clearing the brush like that.

'Adam,' Tommy says, in a solemn voice. 'You know he's going to ghost your bike, right? He'll fucking do it. He's an animal.'

Adam can only nod, confused, playing along. He senses he is missing something here, but he doesn't want to admit it now and look like a fool. And, anyway, who is he to tell Darren Lynwood how to ride a bike? If he tells Darren to stop now, he will look like a pussy and they will never let him ride with them again.

'Look, look at him go,' Ryan says, pointing.

They all turn to watch as Darren pedals the Huffy hard down the long slope of the main trail, into a four-foot dip that shoots him a good three feet high on the other side, sailing him another fifteen feet across the track before the balding cheap blue tires touch down. He pedals hard again, then makes a sharp left turn and climbs another hill, six or eight feet tall, and Adam thinks he's going to soar out of the top and disappear over the other side.

Instead, Darren reaches the top and plants one foot, as if he were riding a bowl or a half-pipe, and kicks the bike up in a tabletop while keeping the tip of his right toe on the ground. The Huffy swings horizontal and holds itself outside of gravity for a moment before swooping back down under Darren's legs with effortless grace.

'Are you gonna ghost it?' Ryan hollers across the field as Darren speeds back toward them.

Darren shrugs, looks at Adam.

Adam is thrilled to see Darren Lynwood shredding it up on his bike and he waves his hand in a circle, go go go!

Darren's face sharpens with concentration, he pushes the bike up to high speed, crouching as he comes barreling at them. The angle of his approach shifts slightly to Adam's right, and then all of a sudden he jumps up, legs spread, releasing the bike. For a moment he seems to hover like a boy bouncing on a trampoline, limbs thrown in all directions, and the bike flies away from him, rolling in a perfect straight line.

Darren brings his legs together and lands at a trot, jogging down the trail as if all the fun is over and he's not even really interested in what happens now.

Adam's Huffy cruises along without a rider, centrifugal force holding it upright, even as it bumps over small rocks and dirt clods, and at last Adam understands the meaning of a ghost ride. Because it really does look that way, like a ghost is riding his bike. The pedals continue to rotate a few times before the freewheel kicks in, and the surprise of it, his bike, it could be any bike, whistling along the trail with nobody on it, is pretty damn funny.

They're all laughing, including Adam, though the weird rush of it is winding up inside his belly like he is falling, and his laughter subsides before everyone else's.

Adam runs a few steps after his errant bicycle, then slows knowing he won't get there in time to stop what's happening.

The handlebars jerk this way and that as the front wheel meets various forms of resistance, but it is still moving at running speed when it reaches the edge of the ravine, the wheels turn in midair, and the bike flies like it is part of a ghost Evel Knievel stunt over the Snake River Canyon.

Adam wonders if it might make it to the other side.

The Huffy tips sharply, going hard endo into the ravine, the front wheel snagging on a larger rock before it somersaults crazily and smashes its way down to a spectacularly hairy wipeout. The other guys are laughing like maniacs, and Adam understands why, it was funny, seeing his hunk of junk bike wreck itself, because you could imagine some clown kid going down with it, getting all mangled like Wile E. Coyote, and wipeouts like that are hilarious on TV.

But by the time Adam slips and slides his way to the bottom of the ravine, gashing his palm on a jagged rock and skinning both knees as he collapses at the bottom, when he sees that the front end of his frame has snapped off at the head tube and one of his wheels is shaped like a taco, he is no longer laughing. He is crying.

He doesn't care about the Huffy. He hated the bike anyway.

Adam is crying because he is already picturing his father's red screaming face as he drags the bike up his driveway. He can hear his dad yelling, spittle flying from his thick scarred lips. He can already feel the whiplash at being yanked off his feet, the pummel of his father's fists for being so careless with his bike. He cries because he will not get another bike for a long time, and that is all he will think about while he sits at home in his bedroom for the next six weeks, taken out of school because his mom won't let his teachers see his broken collarbone and his two black eyes.

But more than any of that, Adam cries because his dad will be right. This is not Darren Lynwood's fault, or Tommy's or Ryan's.

It's his own fault. For being a stupid loser of a kid who thought he could be cool for a day and obviously didn't know any better.

18

Beth waited until seven-thirty before going to look for Darren. Actually, she knew damn well where he was. She'd heard him slip from bed at around two in the morning, which meant he had been in the shop for going on eight hours. She wanted to give him the benefit of her patience, but enough was enough.

Until the past few weeks, she had never resented his bike collection or the money and space he dedicated to it. But there was no denying it now. He was hiding, running away, becoming someone she knew less and less each day. His moods had become exaggerated, feeling on top of the world with the family on the mall, concerned about nothing during the day, then plunging into a funk every night. Whatever was happening out there in the shop, it was unhealthy. Bad for him, for her, for all of them.

She went out the back door, across the patio and over the acre of grass in need of mowing, half expecting to find the door to his little hideout locked. She imagined him lost in the corner of the shop, covered in bicycle grease, having a nervous breakdown. Or maybe just gone, vanished, his altar to youth grown powerful enough to have sucked him back to the 80s, the way Neverland had summoned Peter and Wendy.

The door was unlocked, however. Inside, she was surprised to find the music on, tuned to Darren's favorite satellite station, First Wave, playing The Police's 'Driven to Tears'. She called to him.

'Hello? Honey? Darren?'

But he didn't answer and she couldn't see him through the office wall's glass window. She entered the showroom and still couldn't locate him. Annoyed, she marched over to the shelf holding his stack of audio equipment and turned the power off. Silence cut across the room like a slap, but still he did not reveal himself.

'Darren, are you in here?'

Well, obviously not. But then why had he left the music on, the lights on, and – she noticed as she made her way to end of the showroom – left the back door open? He was usually obsessive about locking the door, setting the alarm, even if he was returning to the house for half an hour to make himself lunch.

Beth experienced a wave of cold apprehension. Her senses heightened and reality seemed to warp at the edges the way it could on the verge of a terrible discovery. She pushed the screen door open with a creak and stepped onto the concrete porch, scanning the very end of the yard.

He wasn't out here, either.

Her anger was mostly gone now, replaced by outright fear. Something awful had happened to him, she was certain. She turned back, intending to call his cellphone from the shop's extension, and pulled the screen door shut with a bang that set her nerves a little higher on edge, if that were possible.

'Oh, God!'

Darren was in the corner of one of the aisles, between shelves. She hadn't seen him on her first pass because she had been staring at the open back door to her left, not this aisle on the right. And because he was curled into a ball on the floor, beside an open cardboard box filled with plastic bicycle seats. He looked like a child nestled in his crib, one hand under his head, and she was surprised he wasn't sucking his thumb.

'Darren?' she said. What if he's . . . no, he's not dead. But this wasn't really something as simple as sleeping, was it? 'Darren! Honey, wake up!'

He didn't move.

She hurried over and kneeled at his side. He was dressed in his fleece jacket, a filthy pair of Levi's jeans, and his old blue canvas Vans. The shoes were muddy, the jeans wet in places, and torn at the knees, the skin inside the torn fabric bloody and dirty. His was not the face of a man at rest, sleeping peacefully. His jaw was clenched, his eyes tight, and when she placed a hand on his shoulder she realized he was trembling in rigid little spasms. Not from cold, but fear.

'Darren, wake up. Wake up, honey,' she repeated, shaking him by the shoulder. 'Darren, come on—'

Then she smelled it. His wet jeans. A darkened oval

around the crotch and along the lower thigh. He'd wet himself. Oh, Jesus. This was not okay. What could have done this to him? The word 'seizure' popped into her mind. His nostrils were flaring, his breathing was labored, as if someone had clamped a hand over his mouth. He could be swallowing his tongue right now.

'Darren!' she yelled, shaking him harder. 'Darren! Goddamnit, talk to me!'

His body went perfectly still. His eyes opened and continued to stare beyond her, vacant, unresponsive. He did not 'snap awake' or bolt upright, but gradually he came back, his pupils shrinking. He blinked a few times, raised his head from the floor, had a quick look around to ascertain his surroundings. Finally, he smiled at her rather innocently. This was not the expression of a man waking from a nightmare.

'Hey,' he said, then swallowed. 'Hi, is everything all right?'

'No! Are you hurt? What happened?'

He sat up with ease, blinking, and stood. 'Did I scare you?'

Beth gaped at him.

'I'm sorry,' he said, wiping his hands over his thighs. He noticed the wet spot at his crotch, then looked up quickly at her like a child who'd been caught being naughty.

'Honey,' she said. 'What's happening to you?'

Darren walked past her, all the way to the fridge to retrieve a bottle of water. He offered her one and she declined. He moved tiredly to one of the barstools beside his workbench and sat, brushing at the scrapes along his knees.

'I met the kid,' he said.

He took her through the whole story, or what he promised was the whole story. Adam, a ten-year-old loner of a boy. Darren and his friends at the bike park. He spoke clearly, in vivid detail, so much so that she could almost see it too. The inadvertent bullying that led them to trash the kid's bike. It was a sad story, and when he got to the end, his voice cracked with guilt and shame.

'That's a terrible dream,' she said. 'I can see why you're upset.'

'It wasn't a dream. I'm absolutely sure of that.'

'All right. What was it?'

He looked her in the eyes, speaking evenly. 'It was awful, one of the most uncomfortable, freakish, terrifying things I've ever felt. I was wide awake the whole time. After we fooled around, you fell asleep immediately, but I didn't sleep all night, Beth. I'm sure of it. One minute I was lying there with you on top of me, the next I was gone. Somewhere else. In daylight. I wasn't myself anymore. I was inside him. Or he was inside me.'

He looked down, perhaps in shame or embarrassment to admit such a thing.

'Inside who?' she said.

'Adam. The boy.'

'I see.'

'No, you don't. Beth, I'm telling you, it was an out-of-body experience. I was not there, I had no awareness of myself, the way we do in a dream. I was literally inside this kid, except that's not even right, because I didn't know I was there and he didn't know I was there. I saw everything he saw, felt everything he felt, all of it.'

'So, you dreamed you were someone else—'

'It wasn't a dream.'

'Okay, you imagined you were someone else.'

'Look at my pants!' he shouted, pulling at the holes in his jeans, exposing his scraped knees. He turned his hands over, revealing another gash inside his palm. 'My body hurts. My legs feel like I rode ten miles. I was gone, Beth. Gone.'

'I don't understand,' she said. 'This is some form of sleepwalking?'

He slumped. 'I don't know. But here's the hellish part. I was there too, Darren Lynwood was there, but my awareness of him was . . . bound up inside of Adam. The other Darren, he was as real as you are now, and he was me at age twelve. I saw everything that happened. What I did. Twelve-year-old Darren ruined Adam's life.'

'You were just a kid,' she said. 'You didn't know any better. You couldn't have known what would – no, you don't know what happened to him after that day, when he went home.'

'I think I do know,' he said. 'I had everything. A spoiled rich kid with six bikes by the time I was twelve. The only child. My parents bought me whatever I wanted. Adam had nothing. Adam Burkett, that was his name. I haven't thought about him in thirty years, but I remember now. We treated him like a punching bag. He followed us everywhere. He worshipped us. He tried to fit in and we trashed his bike and his father beat the grease out of him for it. Put him in the hospital, or worse. What kind of person does that make me?'

Beth walked to him and held his face in her hands. 'It doesn't make you anything. It didn't make you anything besides who you are. It was a horrible thing to do and a mistake, but you couldn't have known how his father would react. You didn't assault him. You were screwing around, it got out of hand, and you probably spent the next five years trying to make up for it.'

'I don't know about that,' he said.

'You were twelve! Kids are awful, honey. From the time I was thirteen to sixteen, I was a royal bitch. My friends and I inflicted more psychological damage gossiping and calling each other fat sluts than ruining some kid's bike ever could.'

'It's more than the bike. More than some broken bones. This kid, something bad happened to him, Beth. Something very bad. I know it.'

'Here's what I know,' Beth said, stepping back to cross her arms. 'I know the man I married, and he has a conscience. You've obviously carried this around for decades, and for whatever reason' – she paused, gesturing at the bikes on every side of her – 'maybe because of these bikes, something reminded you of him. You have all the bikes, don't you? Because you have been successful and you've earned it and you're passionate about bikes. But now all you can think about is the kid who didn't have it so good. All of a sudden this . . . this tumor of guilt swells up inside you and you're eating yourself up because of something that happened thirty years ago. You still feel bad, but Darren, honey? It's ancient history. It's not who you are.'

He seemed to sway on the barstool for a moment. 'The dreams about the fire, the feeling I got when I finished building the Cinelli, the cut on my thumb. It's all part of something bigger. Has to be.'

Beth nodded. 'Was that his bike? Did Adam own a Cinelli?'

Darren shook his head. 'He was poor. He lived in a trailer park. His father beat him senseless over the loss of a worthless K-Mart bike. Even back in 1981, that Cinelli would have cost over five hundred dollars. No way.'

Exasperated, Beth threw her hands up. 'What do you want me to say? You've been sinking into despair ever since we moved back to Boulder. Maybe it's being here that's opened this all up for you. If that's the case, I'm sorry, maybe I shouldn't have pushed so hard for us to move here. And I'm sorry about the nightmares, the bad memories, I really am. But we're here. We have a life, and it's a good life. I need you to be a part of it. Raya needs you to be a part of it. You have a family here and it's not a gang of twelve-year-olds running around town on bikes.'

'He's doing it to all of us . . . ' he mumbled.

'What?'

'Raya's texts. And my mom. He's doing it to all of us.'

'It? What's "it"?'

'Don't you see?'

'No, I don't see. Why don't you tell me what you see?'

'His father didn't abuse him. He didn't just go to the hospital that day. His father . . . I got him killed that day, Beth. Adam's dead.'

'You don't know that.'

'Oh, but I do.'

'Fine, why don't you call the pol—'

'Mom? Mom!' Raya called from outside. She appeared in the office, swinging around the corner and sizing them up, taking in the vibe between them. 'Oh. Sorry. Is this a bad time?'

'Yes,' Darren said.

'No,' Beth said. 'I'm coming. Wait for me in the car.'

'Oooo-kay.' Raya gave her dad a small wave and disappeared.

Darren stood and hitched up his pee-stained pants. 'Where are you two headed today?'

'I have some work to do down at the center. They need me all day, so I'm dropping Raya at yoga. Chad's going to pick her up and she'll call you later to let you know where they are, what time she's coming back.'

'I'll check in with her,' he said.

'And I'll check in on you,' Beth said.

'I'm sorry I gave you such a scare.' He moved to hug her but she put a hand up to stop him.

'I want you to talk to somebody. Today, if possible.'

He hesitated, then nodded. 'Probably for the best. Be nice to understand. There's gotta be something I can do about this before you have to start strapping me to the bed.'

'Will you make some calls or do you need me to do it?'

'I'm not afraid of doctors.'

She rewarded him with a quick hug. 'Maybe this is a bad idea. Going to work. I should stay home with you.'

'No. Raya's waiting on you and I don't want her thinking this is turning into something serious, because it isn't.'

'Are you sure?'

'I'm sure.'

She wasn't, but she left him for the day anyway.

19

Adam realized he was going in circles, closing in on his destination as if drawn by long-buried memory, preternatural instinct, or a higher power guiding him on a mission whose purpose could not be revealed until he had passed the ultimate test.

Namely, survival.

He had been riding all night and all morning, afraid to stop moving or close his eyes until daylight returned. He had napped under some trees at a corporate office park on the east side of Boulder for a few hours after dawn, until a security guard roused him and told him to move on. After that, he was so tired he didn't know which direction he was going, and he fell into a mindless dozing on the bike, pedaling robotically as he stared at the ground unspooling before his front tire.

He revived to find himself coasting downhill, along a winding road that bent its way around a middle school, through side streets protected by mature trees, until he emerged on the back side of a large white building with a broad, wood-shingled crown that made him think of what his memory knew to be a Pizza Hut, though this was much too large for any restaurant. From the parking lot he could make out a high-dive and broad concrete patio on the other side of a chain-link fence, the prospect of a swimming pool and the concession stands tantalizing him on another hot day.

But when he rode up for a closer look, he saw that the pool was empty, its pale green walls stained brown, with a ruined tarp sagging down inside the deep end. There were no chairs or umbrellas, and if there had ever been a snack bar, it had been closed for a long time. Curious to know what this place was – it tickled at his memory like so many other places he had passed – he rode around the building's irregular parking lot until he reached the front side.

There wasn't a sign on the building, but near the main entrance was an old wooden sign with metallic gold letters that said ELKS B.P.O.E.! Adam couldn't remember what B.P.OE. stood for, but he knew this was an Elks' clubhouse. Come to think of it, he didn't know what the Elks were either, but the name called to mind visions of old people in a bingo parlor, costume balls with lots of men in funny hats drinking cocktails and dancing to old show tunes, and vast picnics with softball games, the swimming pool, a pig roast. Associations he couldn't possibly be making right now if he had not attended some of these events with parents, grandparents, or another family.

Burkett.

The name just came to him, clicking in his memory the way it sounded, like something low, broken.

Adam Burkett. I am Adam Burkett. I had a family and our family name was Burkett. We went to guest day at the Elks' once, many summers ago, and I had fun swimming with the other kids from school. Tommy and Ryan and Darren were there, because they were some of the B.P.O.E.s.

'Best People On Earth,' he said to himself, turning to stare once more at the pool beyond the fence.

But he couldn't picture the boys named Tommy and Ryan and Darren. He couldn't picture his own mother and father's face, his siblings, if he had any. Only their names floated in his mind, tethered to the sense of wrongdoing.

Best People On Earth. Somehow it didn't feel that way. Staring at the mossy tarp and the empty pool, Adam began to feel sick. He found it difficult to breathe. He saw himself splashing into the deep end, the other boys calling to him, *Come on, come over here! What's a matter? Don't you know how to swim? Three of them, treading water around him, splashing him, throwing water in his face. And he kept turning in circles, trying to keep an eye on each one, but he was getting tired. He didn't know how to swim very well, and they kept dunking him, filling his mouth with water, making it hard to breathe. And then one of them, the strongest one, was leaping onto his shoulders, shoving him down, and he was choking, their legs thrashing around him, the sunlight fragmented, their voices dulled, and he started to cry and choke, swallowing more water, and he knew they were trying to drown him, he was drowning . . . and then a lifeguard whistle. Choking for air, being dragged from the pool. The boys hated him after that. Because he cried.*

216

Because he scared the other parents. Because he caused a scene at the Elks' Club.

Adam shuddered and turned away from the pool.

Leaving the Elks' Club parking lot, he crossed 28th Street, riding into another familiar housing development. The houses and townhomes were neither new nor old, but average, clean, in shades of tan and pink and blue. The sign at the entrance said Palo Park. Reading it, Adam's arms went loose, his right foot slipped off the pedal, and he forgot how to operate the handbrake. Staring at the sign as if it were coming alive, morphing into a three-headed dragon, he was jolted when his front wheel hit the curb and he toppled into the narrow strip of grass between street and sidewalk.

Palo Park. Palo Park. Palo Park.

The name flashed like a red emergency sign in his mind. He'd been here. Something bad had happened. Something that changed everything. It was right there, on the tip of his tongue, or the cliff of his memory. He saw bicycles, kids riding . . .

The dirt park! This is where he used to ride, when he had his own bike.

Behind him, a block away, an engine revved. He didn't think much of it until it revved again, harder, and then several cars honked. Adam looked back, to 28th Street, where he had just crossed.

The big brown Ford truck, with its camper shell sitting atop it like a rotted tooth, was swerving through traffic on 28th, leaving the forked entrance to the Elks' Club.

Coming for him.

'Oh shit.'

Adam jumped on the bike and cranked up to speed. The bike swayed as he pumped furiously, and he quickly realized as long as he was in the street, they would have a clear path to plow him over.

He swerved right and hopped the curb, onto the sidewalk. He took the first right turn, hoping the street would not dead-end anytime soon. He needed to stick to the sidewalks, slipping between houses where the truck could not follow. Or, better yet, find the dirt park, if it still existed, where he could lose them on the rough terrain. The Ford was off-road capable, but with that camper shell on the back, there was no way it would be able to keep up with him through the smaller trails, down the steepest hills and between the trees.

The truck's big V-8 engine roared as it closed in.

Parked cars flashed by on either side of him, a newspaper machine, a fire hydrant. He hooked left onto another street, eyes scanning ahead for loose gravel, puddles, potholes – anything that might cause his tires to slip, wiping him out just before the Ford smeared his carcass into the road.

Damn it, where was the dirt park?

Just before the lane ended, another street opened to his right. He shook the bike left to fake out the truck, then darted right, pedaling through the sharp turn.

The truck tires squealed, swerving to stay on his tail.

Adam looked back over his shoulder. The truck was less than a hundred feet behind him but the windshield was a flat gray shadow, revealing nothing of the driver or passengers. It seemed inhuman, a machine come to life, a rolling box of death.

Adam followed the sidewalks, weaving between parked cars, hoping to make the truck crash, but it didn't. When he reached the next turn, he found himself in a long curving cul-de-sac. Mistake. He would be trapped, unless he took to the yards.

The truck was pacing him from the street, coming up on his left side. It swerved closer, its front fender close enough for him to reach out and touch.

Adam looked to the passenger window and behind the dirty tinted glass he saw faces. For just a moment, two old waxen faces like the ones in the magazine, in his nightmares, the driver's leaning forward, the passenger's nearly pressed to the glass.

Their mouths were open, their black eyes wide.

Adam yelped and swerved away, focusing on the ground ahead. He estimated the length of the sidewalk curving around the edge of the cul-de-sac, and his speed versus the truck's. Only two choices, then. He could pull the brakes, screech to a halt, turn around and try to outrun them the way he had come in. Or he could follow the sidewalk all the way around, hoping to maintain enough speed to sweep around the front of the truck before it reached the end. Of course, if he timed it wrong, the truck would broadside him at the top of the circle, killing him instantly.

His fingers extended from the grip, hovering over the brake lever.

The truck downshifted, its driver seeing his predicament.

Adam ignored the brake and crouched, heading into the turn, pedaling as fast as his legs would allow.

The Ford shifted again, swerving to head him off.

He was rounding its right flank, then directly ahead of it. If he looked up now, he would crash. The turn was too sharp and he was moving too fast to do anything but lean in and pray the bike's tires did not lose their grip on the sidewalk.

The truck tires screeched loudly.

Adam passed the top of the circle, coming around the other side, all but heading toward the truck as it slid sideways in the cul-de-sac.

The engine roared, the truck lurched after him, aiming for his inside flank, and the houses on the outside ring.

Adam tucked, leaned closer to the ground, and his inside pedal snagged on the sidewalk, jogging the entire rear end of the bike out from under him. For a moment the bike was hovering, then the tires caught, biting into concrete at the grass's edge with a second jolt that threw him like a bucking horse. He almost flipped to his outside, then swerved, nearly lost control of the bike, but saved it. His speed dropped severely but he managed to hold on.

The truck's banged-up chrome grill filled his left field of vision, close enough for him to feel the warmth of the engine and catch the scent of radiator steam.

Adam yanked the bars and pedaled for his life.

His front end rose in a surge.

Less than a second later, a massive gust of air whistled behind him as the truck jumped the sidewalk, missed his back tire by inches, and slammed into a car parked in a driveway. A gigantic crash of metal sent beads of glass into the air like a swarm of bees. Adam caught the sting of glass fragments along his bare left arm and the back of his neck, but he was clear.

He looked back in time to see the Ford's grill mangled and stuck to the smaller car, which was now pitched halfway into the garage door. Steam billowed from under the Ford's tented hood, but the truck was already grinding its gears, lurching back and forth as the driver attempted to free it from the smashed compact.

Adam pedaled out the way he had come in, seizing the opportunity to build a small lead, knowing it wouldn't last more than a few minutes.

After Beth and Raya left, Darren had taken a hot shower and let the water work on his sore muscles. He tried to get dressed, but found himself closing his eyes for long intervals even while pulling on his socks. He gave up and reclined on the bed, drifting, trying to recall where he had gone last night. The only thing that came to him was the dream-vision at Palo Park, but he had no memory of traveling there by means of sleepwalking or sleep-riding, if that's what he had done.

It was like a light switch. One minute he was in bed with Beth. The next he was there, in the past, remembering or seeing through Adam, and he wondered if he was in some way possessed by the kid. Then the switch flipped the other way and he woke up in the shop, Beth crouching beside him, scared out of her mind.

He was so tired now, and had been for days. His skinned knees and other cuts still felt raw from the shower, but he fell asleep anyway.

When he woke up, only an hour or two had passed, and he knew what he was supposed to do. Last night's vision had shown him, hadn't it? Wasn't that the point? His memory was trying to show him where the answers lay.

He needed to return to the scene of Adam's tragedy, to Palo Park.

Darren had not bothered to visit the old dirt park since returning to Boulder nine months ago. Driving there now, he wondered if he had been subconsciously avoiding the site of so many memories. Memories that, until last night, seemed to be nothing but good, but which he now knew were laced with poison.

He considered taking the Firebird, but the engine could be fussy and he couldn't remember the last time he'd put in the fuel additive needed to keep it from running too hot, so he opted for the Acura instead. He eased down Linden and turned right on Folsom, then took another left on the short section of Kalmia, which popped him out minutes later at 28th Street, at the corner of what had once been his dirt park.

Not even half a mile. More like six or eight blocks. He shouldn't have been surprised it was so close, but in his mind it had seemed much farther, probably because he had always ventured here as a kid on his bike, not by car. Most of Boulder was like that for him, the neighborhoods and quaint streets that stretched on and on back in the day now seemed shrunken down to 1/4 scale, as if he had become a giant rather than simply grown up.

The dirt park was gone.

In its place stood a uniformly ugly complex of attached abodes. Townhomes or condos, plus one section that looked to be an assisted living 'resort'.

Darren waited for traffic on 28th to clear, then stomped the gas pedal. The Acura shot over four lanes and onto the last section of Kalmia and he felt a deep stab of longing as he neared their old spot. He could almost see the narrow path through the trees and the naturally formed, almost vertical dirt ramp he had ridden hundreds of times, now obliterated by a flat patch of perfectly manicured grass, a clean sidewalk, and a ridiculously cramped parking lot for the tenants who lived there.

He slowed, distracted by the cruel hands of time and real estate. All this progress. Development. Goodbye to the wilderness and wildness of youth.

Darren couldn't help thinking it was the perfect symbol of the broader evolution his home town had undergone. Instead of valuing a stretch of wild terrain no one could claim as their own – where boys and girls could frolic free of parental supervision, where they could laugh and test themselves and fall down and bleed and get back up and ride away stronger, in a small corner of the town with no real designated bike tracks, no entry fees or lifeguards, in this place where kids could be kids and play, get some natural exercise without ever feeling like they were exercising – the town had allowed another developer to turn their magic kingdom into a generic cluster of turd-brown apartments surrounded by more chemically fed, water supply-draining, inoffensive lawn. Darren was disgusted by it.

The Acura had come to a halt.

He should have known better, after twenty-six years, and he was angry with himself for getting his hopes up. What had he been expecting? That the dirt park would still be here, full of kids riding and jumping, performing death-defying stunts like the old days? Get serious. Today's parents wouldn't let their ten-year-old ride a bike to the end of the driveway without strapping on a helmet, elbow and knee pads, a mouthguard. It was over, and it had been over for a while.

Which means I couldn't have come here last night. It was only a dream. Adam's influence, his vision, not real, even though it seemed like it happened yesterday ...

A car honked behind him.

Darren raised a hand in apology, but before he could shift into drive, the car – a Range Rover with a vanity license plate that said RENDER – sped past, its wake wind rocking the Acura, the Rover's brush guard inches from sheering off his side mirror. Darren watched the bastard race ahead, saw that it was a redhead babe with her hair in a ponytail, her thin arm extending to flip him off. She was not content with the standard, one-time bird, however. Apparently, stopping on a nearly dead calm street was enough of a violation to earn a truly vengeful, thrice-repeated jamming up and down of the extended middle digit: *fuck you fuck you fuck you!* As if she wanted to jab him with it, stick it up his nose.

He was already in a sour mood. The woman jack-hammering her finger at him made Darren's blood boil.

Not knowing what his intentions were, maybe to tail the psycho and scare her for a mile or two, maybe just to get the hell out of here, Darren pressed the pedal to the floor. The front-wheel drive engaged with a good dose of torque steer, pulling him left and then right before he got the car under control, and the speedometer climbed to thirty, then forty, in no time.

He passed the attached-housing development and a thick line of woods cutting through the land revealed itself on his left. Darren vaguely recalled a stream or culvert inside these trees, something too dense for him and his friends to ride through, and he turned his head in that direction as he ascended the rise on Kalmia.

We used to wet our T-shirts down in there on hot days ...

The blur came out of the trees some fifty feet ahead, a blue and black insectile figure with spinning disc wings spread above its central mass, hurling itself from Darren's left field of vision and instantly hovering just ahead of the Acura's front end. Darren's adrenaline went berserk, dilating time, hauling the world into focus, and the figure resolved into something altogether simpler and more terrifying than a UFO.

Wheels, jeans, sneakers and a hump of backpack – it

was a boy on a BMX bike. The bicycle itself was laid out pancake-flat, as were the boy's legs, while his upper body remained vertical. Darren instantly recognized the move as a tabletop, the planning and execution and speed of which could not have factored in the presence of a car and therefore qualified it as death-defying. The handlebars were crossed-up, the blurring chrome spokes aimed skyward, and above the small model of planetary rotation Darren caught a glimpse of the face: open-mouthed, wide-eyed, sweating as if caught in the midst of a ferocious gym workout.

The superb control and exertion required to pull off this trick gave way to raw fear as the kid realized he was about to collide with a speeding car. He straightened the bars, righting the bike, and Darren saw the rear tire touch down at the dead center of his windshield with a dull plump. The windshield splintered and spider-webbed, bowing inward. Darren's foot mashed the brake pedal as the kid's rear tire dipped preciously close to the dash, and then the anti-lock brakes bit hard.

Darren would never know if the bike's rear tire caught the lip of his right-side A-pillar or if the Acura's grind to a halt and the still-intact windshield were enough, but in either case the boy rebounded up and away, catapulted down the road and over the shoulder, soaring at least seven feet above the ground. Darren caught sight of the two-wheeled steed flipping freely, then a flash of the body itself tumbling down into the weeds that seemed to engulf him like an airbag collapsing around a stuntman.

The Acura skewed sideways across the double-yellow lines and rocked to a halt, but for nearly half a minute Darren continued to feel as though he were careening around a race track. His hands were white around the steering wheel. His ears popped. He expected to hear screaming, bystanders rushing in, ambulances to follow shortly, but there was only quiet, a stillness punctuated by his own heavy breathing.

Trembling, blinking away visions of carnage and lawsuits and grieving parents, he inched the Acura onto the gravel shoulder. He pushed the shifter into park, turned off the motor, opened his door, and stepped out to discover whether death was merely imminent or already here.

20

The boy was on his back, arms and legs outstretched, a snow angel in weeds. His backpack was shoved up under one shoulder and beside his head, and Darren wondered if the pack had saved his skull from bursting open. He didn't see any blood. No road burn on the boy's arms or face. Luckily he seemed to have fallen on a downward slope with few rocks in the vicinity. The fact that he had come through unscathed on the outside was of no comfort, however. Darren knew there could be large amounts of blood pooling inside, around broken bones and ruptured organs. His eyes were wide open and his chest was still heaving from the hard riding he'd been doing leading up to this.

Darren stepped closer and the kid put up a hand in warning – don't come any closer, don't touch me. He had the strangest feeling that if he made one sudden move or said the wrong thing, the kid would leap to his feet and dart off like a wounded rabbit, finding a hole in the ground where it would be safe to die.

'Hey,' Darren said, unsure where to begin. 'Can you

hear me? Can you move? Where does it hurt? Say any-thing, my man, talk to me.'

'I'm okay.' The boy paused for breath. 'I rolled.'

Darren noticed the T-shirt. On the chest was a faded iron-on of The Creature From the Black Lagoon, with a thought bubble that read, 'Who peed in the pool?' He remembered seeing this years ago, when he was a kid, back when those iron-on T-shirt shops were all the rage. A quiver of recognition swam through him, the first tingle of realization that something about this situation was extremely . . . odd. But like the boy, he was in shock, not able – or not yet willing – to process much more than the basic questions he was supposed to ask now. Assess the damage. Worry about the rest later.

'Did my car hit you, your body I mean? All I saw was your tires.'

The boy shook his head an inch or so. 'Bounced off you.'

'That was one hell of a tabletop,' Darren said.

The boy frowned. 'How do you know what a tabletop is?'

'I used to ride BMX. Still do. Well, these days I col-lect a lot more than I ride, but I try to get out now and then.' Darren looked back but saw no sign of the bike. 'Your bike is probably ruined. I guess I owe you a new one.'

'Wasn't mine,' the boy said, sitting up.

'Whoa, easy, don't move. You need to lie still while I call an ambulance.'

'I said I'm not hurt.' As if to prove this, the boy

pushed himself upright and stood. He immediately looked to the road, both ways, as if expecting company.

'You're in shock,' Darren said. 'You might feel fine, but we have to get you checked out. I don't want you walking around only to find out you have a severed vertebra or a brain injury.'

'Not possible,' the kid said, wiping his jeans and straightening his backpack. 'No doctors, no cops, no nothing. I gotta get out of here.'

'That's insane. No way I'm letting you walk away from this.'

Ambulatory, looking tired but otherwise fine, the kid walked past Darren in search of his bike. 'You don't have a choice.'

Darren glanced around for help, wanting to wave a witness over, wishing for an expert to intervene. But this was a seldom-used section of Kalmia. The nearest condos were in front of them, facing southwest to take in the sun and the mountain views. There were only trees to the north, and no one had come running out to offer help.

They were alone.

'What's your name?' Darren said, following him. 'We need to contact your parents at the very least.'

Combing the weeds, the kid said, 'Don't have any.'

He found the bike, lifted it to inspect the damage. The handlebars were snapped at the crossbar, the rear wheel bent, one of the crank arms was gone. The kid chucked the bike back into the weeds. He turned and looked at Darren.

'Nothing left to do. You can go now.'

'All right. Hey, I'm not trying to hassle you. Just hold on a second. What's your name? Can you at least tell me that?'

The boy only stared at him, and suddenly Darren knew. It had to do with the boy's size, his thin build, his sweat-flopped hair, certain facial features. But more than anything it was the look in the kid's eyes. The sadness, the forlorn look of someone who is utterly lost. There are coincidences, and then there are things too rare to be a coincidence. It had to be him.

But also, *it could not be him*. There was just no way. No explanation.

'Patrick,' the kid said, looking at the ground. 'Patrick Robinson.'

See? It's not *him*. And only an insane person would even consider otherwise.

'Okay, Patrick. I'm Darren. What do you mean you don't have parents? You don't live around here? Did you run away?'

'Something like that,' Patrick said, but he no longer appeared calm or resigned. He was staring at Darren with a caution that hadn't been there before.

'What's the matter?'

'Your name's Darren?'

'Lynwood, yes. Darren Lynwood.'

The boy looked away quickly, then back at him with a flash of . . . what? Anger? Repulsion? Fear? Maybe all three. Then he trudged away, up toward the road.

Darren followed him. 'Hey. Patrick, you okay?'

'I gotta get going. Sorry about your car.' Patrick turned east, walking faster.

'Wait,' Darren called after him. 'Hold up, man.'

Patrick stopped, looked back.

If I can just get him in the car, get to my phone, I can call 9-1-1, or drive him straight to the hospital. Or home first. Maybe if I set him up with a new bike, he'll tell me what the story with his parents is and I can call them … Hell, Beth will know what to do. She deals with runaways and troubled kids. This one fits the bill. Then we'll get to the bottom of this. All of this.

'At least let me hook you up with a new bike,' Darren said. 'I mean, if there's one thing I have, it's bikes. Come on. I live close by.'

Patrick watched Darren with increasing suspicion. His eyes widened and his entire body went rigid just before he ducked, throwing himself to the weeds.

'What's wrong?' Darren said.

'I knew it. They found me! Get out of here!' Patrick was scurrying deeper into the weeds, keeping low. 'Did you do this? You lead them here? They're with you, aren't they?'

'I don't know what you're talking about.'

Darren turned to look back up the road.

Two blocks away, at the intersection of Kalmia and 28th, there was a big brown truck with a mangled front end, steam rising from under the hood, and a white camper shell on top. It was idling on the opposite side of the road and he could not see anyone inside from such distance.

'Who is it?' Darren said. 'Your parents?' Another wave

232

of premonition passed through him, with no specific details attached to it, only the sense that something bad was about to happen. That this meeting was not a coincidence, but had been imminent for days, maybe weeks.

He turned back to the kid. 'Who's in the truck, Patrick?'

'Yeah, I bet you don't. Trying to kill me. All of you. They almost ran me over about fifteen minutes ago, right before you did.'

'I've never seen that truck in my life,' Darren said. 'I have no idea who's inside it. I swear.' When Patrick did not respond, he added, 'I can't help you unless you tell me who they are. What's going on.'

'I don't know, but I can't stay here. They don't care. They'll kill you to get to me.'

Darren turned and faced toward the truck. He wasn't afraid. He believed the kid, but the introduction of this third element aroused his protective instincts in a way he could not define. He walked into the middle of the road and waved.

'Don't do that!' Patrick said.

Darren ignored the boy and raised his arms with bravado, taunting the truck. *You want something? Come get it!*

The Ford's engine revved twice, the big camper shell rocked back and forth, and then the truck lurched forward in a tight U-turn, away from them. It paused at the stop sign, turned right onto 28th Street and disappeared.

Darren lowered his arms, turned to Patrick. 'They're gone. Now, do you want that ride or not?'

Patrick got to his feet. He said nothing for a long time. He seemed impressed, then only tired and sad.

'Come on, you need a new bike,' Darren prodded. 'What do you say?'

'You promise no hospitals? No police?'

Darren nodded. 'Yeah, of course.'

Patrick took one last look down the road and Darren could see him calculating the choice of risks. Get in this car with this stranger, or take your chances out there alone, no bike, with whatever was in the truck looking for him.

'All I want is a bike,' Patrick said. 'Then I'm gone.'

'Fair enough.'

They got into the car, Patrick sinking down with his backpack clutched in his lap. The windshield was ruined but Darren pushed a hole through the left side, enough to get them the six blocks home. He started the engine and turned back the way he had come.

Patrick didn't say a word, only stared straight ahead, worn out.

He's lying to you, Darren thought. *His name's not Patrick Robinson. It's Adam Burkett and you know it. He should be your age by now, or dead, but he's not either of those things. He's a lost soul in a warm body. That's why he's not injured. He's real but ... not natural. He is Adam. It's impossible but it's true. He knows it. And he senses that you know it.*

This was meant to happen today. Even though this is true

234

and right, whatever happens next is going to cause a lot of problems for everyone involved.

'I know,' Darren mumbled.

'What?' Patrick said beside him.

'Nothing. Tell you later. After we get you back on a bike.'

Patrick tightened his grip on his backpack, as if it contained his entire world.

21

Darren was relieved to see that Beth's wagon was not in the driveway. Chad's used gray Saab wasn't here either, which meant Raya and he were still out. Good. He needed some time to prepare for them to meet 'Patrick' and, he supposed, for the boy to meet them. It was a little after 2 p.m. Beth said she'd be down at Fresh Starts all day, but Raya could be home at any moment. He'd worry about that when the time came.

He nudged the Acura into the garage, beside the Firebird, hoping to conceal the damage to his car, though of course he would have to explain that to Beth sooner or later. He would have to explain it all, though he had no explanations.

Darren led him inside, to the kitchen, where Patrick shucked off his backpack and set it on the counter.

'I need to use your bathroom.'

'Down that hall, by the front door.'

Patrick headed that way, then paused, looking back. 'Are you sure we're safe?'

'Whoever's chasing you can't get to you here,' Darren said.

'You don't know what they're capable of.'

Darren wondered what that could mean, other than that the kid was paranoid. 'Well, I have a gun in my office safe. It's not like we're at war here. It's just another sunny Saturday afternoon, okay?'

Patrick frowned and shut himself in the bathroom.

While he was in there, Darren opened the backpack. A few clothes. A grocery bag with a bottle of water and some granola bar wrappers. Beneath the bag he unearthed a well-worn magazine with the title, *Questar*. Looked to be a science fiction & fantasy rag, long defunct. Darren remembered this too, a mildly cheesy version of *OMNI* for the fanboy set, back when *Star Wars* was new and comics featuring intergalactic babes with huge boobs and long, silver-booted thighs were as close as a boy could legally get to *Playboy* on the news-stand. He couldn't be sure, but he thought he had a few copies of this magazine out in the shop, among the issues of *BMX Plus!* and *MAD Magazine* he had saved. Or maybe he just remembered it now because he had seen the magazine when he was a kid.

That was one of the weird things about collecting vintage goods. Sometimes what you had really owned back in the day got confused with stuff you had only seen. And sometimes the things you remembered weren't really memories, but the hunger to claim more of your forgotten past, even the portions of it that belonged to someone else.

Darren flipped the pages, then checked the cover again for the newsstand date. November, 1980. What year had he ruined Adam's bike? Later than 1980, but no later than '83, when Darren was twelve and Adam would have been closer to eleven. How old was this boy using his bathroom? He looked eleven, acted a little older, but he could be twelve or thirteen. He had been carrying this magazine for two years. Or, in another way, for thirty.

Patrick. Adam. Patrick. Adam. Patrick. Adam . . .

He looked up to make sure Patrick was still in the bathroom, then quickly rifled through the rest of the pack. In one of the hidden pockets he felt a slender shank of metal with hollowed grooves, and when he took it out, he knew without opening it that it was a butterfly knife. A street knife, illegal in many states. Darren remembered being fascinated by these things when he was a kid, along with all the other martial arts stuff. Nunchakus, throwing stars. He had a few weapons of this sort boxed up somewhere in the shop's attic, maybe even a butterfly knife or two.

He flipped the latch at the base of the handles and let the knife fall open. The smoke-steel blade swung down and dangled back and forth like a pendulum. Darren stared at the dried crust on one side. Blood? It sure looked like blood.

Jesus Christ. The kid's been in some kind of trouble. What if he used this thing on someone? Whose blood is this, anyway?

The toilet at the front of the house flushed.

Darren shoved everything back into the pack and closed the top flap. He went to the kitchen and ran the faucet, filling two glasses of water. He was taking ice from the freezer when Patrick appeared, looking from Darren to the backpack and back to Darren with obvious suspicion.

'Thirsty?' Darren said.

Patrick nodded.

Darren set the water before him and the boy drank the entire glass in one long pull. Darren refilled it, and he drained another half-pint before setting the glass down with a gasp.

'Hungry?'

'Why are you doing this?' Patrick said.

'Offering you food and drink? You're a guest. That's what you do when people come over.'

'Can I just get that bike and get out of here?'

'Absolutely. Can I ask you one question first? You don't have to answer if you don't want to, but I need to ask.'

'Sure.'

'Do you know who you're running from? The truck? What's that all about?'

'Why do you want to know?'

'Maybe I can help.'

'I don't think so,' Patrick said. 'Safer for you if you don't.'

Darren sighed, ran his hands through his hair. 'Look, I don't know how to say this, and maybe we don't need to talk about it, but this is all just a little too ... I'm just as confused as you are, okay? I don't think it's an accident I ran into you. You look familiar to me, and I think

239

I look familiar to you. I don't know how this is even . . .
but we have to start somewhere, right?'

Patrick neither agreed nor disagreed.

'Whatever you tell me will stay between us,' Darren
said. 'I won't tell a soul.'

'You'll laugh.'

'No, I won't. I've been experiencing my own little . . .
problems, things I can't explain and . . . whatever it is, I
won't laugh.'

The boy looked away. When he spoke, his words
were all but mumbled. 'Most people don't believe in
monsters.'

'I know,' Darren said. 'I won't lie to you. I don't
either, not in the literal sense. But I know people see
things differently, and give different names to bad
things. More importantly, you know what I do believe?
I believe you, Patrick. So if you tell me you saw something, hey, I will take you seriously.'

Patrick opened his backpack and dug out the issue of
Questar. He immediately turned to a bent-eared section
in the middle and rotated the two-page spread so that
Darren could read it from his side of the counter. He
stepped away, flicking his hands as if he had come into
contact with germs.

It was an ad for masks, dozens of them. Darren
remembered these ads from back in the day. They were
high-quality masks, not cheap toys. Priced from $29.99
to $59.99, even in 1980. He wondered how much they
would be worth now. He should hunt down a few
online, see if they were still in demand.

Patrick stabbed one finger down, to a picture of a mask that had been circled in faded marker. The Nocturnal. Something about its flat stare and human-but-wrong features sent a tingle of discord through Darren. He almost flinched, and he could not look at it for more than a few seconds.

'They look like that,' Patrick said. 'There's at least two of them, maybe three, and they already killed a bunch of people. Some not far from here.'

The calm conviction in the boy's voice was unsettling.

Darren was careful with his response. 'How do you know they killed people?'

Patrick looked him in the eyes. 'I was there. A few days ago. I don't know because my sense of time is all messed up. But it was real early.'

'You saw it happen? Where was this?'

'At their house. Some random house. I was hiding in the basement. Didn't see it, but I heard it all.' Again, the cold certainty with which he spoke gave Darren the chills. 'Screams, the sound of their heads getting smashed on the floor. I think it was a family.'

'What makes you think that?'

Patrick swallowed hard. His eyes glassed and shimmered but no tears rolled out. 'I could hear the mom screaming. "Josh, no, Josh." I think he was her son.'

Josh. Darren knew this name. He'd heard it recently. Who mentioned it to him? Chad. When they were talking about the school being locked down. Mrs Kavanaugh ...

'What?' Patrick said, noticing Darren's change of

241

expression from puzzlement to what must have been pale shock.

'One of my daughter's teachers was killed Wednesday morning. At home. Her family members too. She had a son named Josh.'

Patrick's lips trembled. His arms began to shake and he looked around as if searching for the nearest escape route.

'Patrick?'

'I have to go. What am I doing here?' the boy wailed. 'They're gonna come for me again. They'll get you, and your family.'

'Then shouldn't we call the police? If you're so worried?'

Patrick stiffened. Did not answer.

'Why are you afraid of the police?' Darren prodded.

Patrick only blinked at him and looked away.

Either the boy had done something wrong and was guilty of something, or he was lying. Darren tried a different approach. He pointed to the magazine. 'I understand you're scared. I would be too. But whatever happened over there, it wasn't your fault.'

'Yes, it was.'

'How could it be?'

'They were after me. Everywhere I go, they find me. Don't you get it?'

'Why? I mean, no offense, but what's so special about you?'

Patrick looked down at his hands. He clenched them into fists again and again.

'I won't call the police if you tell me,' Darren said softly. 'But if you won't, then what choice do I have?'

Patrick grabbed the water and sipped, spilling on his shirt. His hands were shaking. 'All I know is, something bad happened to me. Somebody cut off my past. I'm sure of that. I remember a few details, other things are familiar. Like your name. Things around town. But if I have a home somewhere, there is no family in it. No parents. No brothers or sisters. Whatever happened to me, it happened to them too, only they're all gone. It's like I'm an orphan, and I did something to piss those things off, and now they're coming for me.'

'But—'

'I'm not like other kids. I touch things and I can tell things about the people who owned them. Something's wrong with me, and I think that's part of why they're after me. They want to use it, use me, or kill me so I don't find out.'

'Find out what?'

'I don't want to talk anymore!' Patrick shouted. 'You owe me a bike, Darren. Are you going to give me a bike or not?'

Darren's thoughts were reeling. He should call the police right now. If this kid knew something about what happened to the Kavanaughs . . . and then he thought of the knife in the backpack, the butterfly knife with dried blood on the blade. What did he know about this kid? Who was he really? What was more likely, that he was somehow a reincarnation of Adam Burkett, the boy from

243

1982, or some psychopath roaming around town worming his way into people's lives and homes?

This could all be a set-up. A hoax, like the Cinelli. Someone had sent an anonymous kid here to mess with Darren, just like they had sent an anonymous bike. There was a connection here, there had to be. He could not let the kid slip away yet, not until he figured this out.

But it didn't feel like a scam, and Patrick didn't look like a killer. He believed everything he was saying. The kid needed help. Something had brought him into Darren's life. He felt like he owed this kid a real debt, something more than a new bike. He wanted to help him, not turn him over to the police.

Be careful, a voice inside him warned. *You are playing with fire here, the kind that can burn a house down.*

'Sure, we don't have to talk about that other stuff. Come out back,' Darren said, leading the boy out the sliding glass door, into the yard. 'I think I have the perfect ride for you. We can see how it fits, and if you don't like it, you can pick out something else.'

Patrick put the magazine away and followed Darren to the shop.

22

Sheila had not slept in almost four days. She did not know whether it was day or night. The blinds of her apartment had been drawn since Wednesday night, the doors locked. Every now and then, when the itch became unbearable, she pried one of the plastic vertical slats aside an inch or two. She did so now, and confirmed (in order of importance) that yes, the door was still locked, the police were not here, it was daytime, and no one had stolen her orange plastic Adirondack chairs, the ones she had bought on sale at Home Depot to spruce up her patio.

Satisfied, but still feeling like a death row inmate with about three hours to go, she closed the blind and examined the rest of the window to make sure no one could see in. Of course, she could no longer see out, either. This would be a problem if someone came creepin' around, but she needed privacy, a sense of being hidden, until she could set this new jumble of reality planes in order and find her path forward.

Alanis and Teddy had become extremely agitated by her, but Sheila couldn't help stomping around, looking at her face in the bathroom mirrors, chewing her nails, brewing cup after cup of her medicinal tea. She was very angry with herself. Losing control like that, waving a gun around in those idiots' home like she'd been having a nervous breakdown, like she was some kind of thwarted duchess.

Then leaving them alive. That was not one bit smart.

Not to mention how many people had seen her talking to Steven pig at the bar before she went after him. If he had called the police – oh please, no ifs about this one, one look at that tight-assed wife of his, you damn well knew she had made him call the police – to file a report about an unstable woman who'd stalked him into his living room, pressed the barrel of a gun to his wife's nose and promised her husband would join her in Hell soon enough, well, then Sheila was going to be in a real patch of trouble. Or was already. She would have to leave this place. Her home. Her apartment in Prana.

Any moment now she would go. Soon as she got her thoughts in order. But she had been telling herself this for three and a half days and she couldn't bring herself to abandon the comfy nest she had made after so many years of strife.

She should have emptied the gun into the wife, reloaded, and emptied it again into Steven pig. Even after she received the signal. Even though the signal had hit her like a charging bull, paralyzing her for ten or twenty seconds that felt like an hour. There was no excuse for such a slip, no matter what the signal told her. She was losing her edge. In the old days, even as recent as two years ago, she would have never left a witness behind. Losing her edge, getting sloppy, yes, yes. But not soft, she had not gone soft. She hadn't refrained from opening their skulls out of pity, because God knew she had wanted to. She had been furious with them, with the wife and her pregnant belly maybe more than Steven pig.

She was still furious, with them and with herself.

But there was nothing to do about it now, except think of a plan. She couldn't go back and kill them. The real pigs in blue would have been all over the neighborhood by now, and probably were running security patrols in case she was dumb enough to come back. Lafayette was by no means a hotbed of criminal activity with the seasoned police force to respond to it, but it wasn't a total sleeper like some of the ones she'd done her sapping in. Halfway between Boulder and Denver, surrounded by other towns of ten, twenty and thirty thousand, they'd have all the backup they needed once word went around the wagon train there was a raving hot bitch on the loose with a pistol.

Sheila opened her iPad mini and logged into WellsFargo.com. She was not surprised to see that she had only $1,743 in her checking account and $52.00 in her savings account, but the numbers looked much smaller now than they had three days ago. She wasn't going to be able to go back to her job ever again, so there went her carefully scheduled direct deposits of $1,645 and change every two weeks. She would no longer be able to afford her car or the apartment (and the pool, spa, gym membership, coffee bar and other amenities that came with the Prana living experience) or her Nordstrom Rack charge card, with or without the 25 per cent employee discount.

She would have to burn everything, burn it all down, including her identity. She had nothing now. Nothing but the clothes she could pack into one bag, the remains of her bank accounts, and the pussies.

She looked at Teddy on the couch. His hind leg was aimed straight at the ceiling and he was bathing the inside of his thigh. He stopped and looked at her with his golden eyes and she wanted to skin him right now and take his pelt on the road with her, to save him the misery of living with someone else, complete strangers with some mongrel child who would pull his tail and shove Crayons up his butt.

The indignity of it all.

Four days of pent-up rage swept over her and (for the sixth or seven time in three days) Sheila could not contain a scream, which turned into a lot of screaming.

'You worthless idiot! You stupid cow bitch! How could you do this to us!' she wailed, screeching at the walls, not caring if her neighbors heard. She almost hoped one of them would come over and complain, so she could vent the black doom on somebody. She beseeched herself, shrieking until her throat felt torn to ribbons. 'I hate you you stupid useless monster bitch, why don't you kill yourself right now, you cowardly whore! Trash doll worthless trash doll whore!'

She took the coffee pot from the maker and swung it

across the room, sending it into the wall where four of her beautiful precious paintings were hung. The coffee pot did not shatter but it did smash through the canvas of one of her favorite acrylics, the one with the coyotes gathered around the camp fire with the cactus and prairie sunset in the background. Four months she had spent on that painting. She hated it, she realized. It was not art but the work of a delusional mind too feeble to call itself an amateur. The coyotes looked about as realistic as fur-covered baked potatoes with button eyes.

Sheila went to the wall and tore down the other paintings and broke them over her knees, puncturing the canvas with her nails, imagining they were her brother's eyes, his precious baby-skin face. She crumpled the torn canvases into balls and kicked them across the floor, stomping the gilt wood frames with her heels, chanting obscenities until she saw red and black and fell on the floor sobbing, breathing uncontrollably. If she had not thrown the gun out the window of her car on the way home, she would have stuffed it into her mouth right now and blow the top of her head off.

She cried herself out for almost fifteen minutes. Alanis found her on the floor and hunched over her belly, purring. Sheila petted the animal's neck, tugging at the fur, thinking of the bones inside, the needle teeth.

But damn it, the signal had derailed her. Derailed everything. Not just the moment, ruining her concentration and taking any possible pleasure away from the double sapping she was about to serve up (two and a half if you counted the lump in the wife's belly). The signal had ruined her whole life, or her entire ... what was the word? Conception of life. Perception of it. It had royally pooched her entire place in the universe. Of course, that's what signals did, especially when they were sent by a powerful force.

Adam is alive. Adam is close.

We almost had him, but he got away. We're coming to bring you home.

Prepare to take all possible steps and serve the original order.

That's what the signal said, though of course not in words. The signals never came in words, they arrived in colors, shapes, images, splinters of fierce emotion. It had been so long since she'd gotten one, she almost didn't trust it. But it had come on strong, the green light in her sinuses making her eyes water and making her sneeze almost orgasmically, better than the rebound off a proper hoof of the amyl. A stab of pain between her eyes, behind her nose, and for a moment she had been blinded. His face, his life force, the cloud of their horrid past roiling into a cross-hatched symbol for now, today, here.

Adam is close. Adam is alive.

Sheila had nearly soiled herself as its meaning unfurled across her frontal lobes. How could it be possible? What could it mean? Adam had been gone for thirty years. Gone, forgotten. He was dead to them before he disappeared and all indications were that he was literally dead, dead as could be.

Her parents were dead along with him, Gaia rest their animal souls.

So then, who could have sent the signal? And where the hell was the next one?

'There must be some mistake,' she said to Alanis, who had left her and was scaling the chairs to the kitchen island, tail held high, purring gutturally. Hungry or just aroused by her mistress's emanations? Was she emanating yet? If not, she would be soon.

Something had awoken in Sheila the moment the signal arrived, something she hadn't felt in a long time, not even when she was finishing a particularly satisfying sap. Could be the cats sensed it now. They knew feline power when it was close.

She wished she could take the pussies with her, to help her find her brother.

To let them lap his artery blood from a saucer like so much milk.

Sheila ran to her walk-in closet, stripped out of her clothes, suddenly certain she needed to run, get out, right now. The question was, where to? To do what? They hadn't sent instructions with the signal. Only, *Prepare to take all possible steps and serve the original order.* That could mean a lot of things.

She dressed in her preferred Crawling attire: black jeans, black long-sleeved shirt, her black hiking boots. Scooted into the bathroom and tied her hair up in a ponytail. Wiped away all traces of the make-up, which was frowned upon by her kind in general. She unclasped her bra and threw it in the laundry basket.

The original order, The Family of Many. Were any of them really still alive? If so, where? In Colorado? But Sheila would have felt that by now. Unless her powers had diminished so much she could no longer sense her own kind right under her nose.

Adam is close.

Oh, God, she hoped so. She would give anything to see him again, to touch him, to hold him, to finish what he started thirty years ago. She would break his ribs with a hammer. Turn his lungs and intestines into a symbol, the real art she was capable of.

She wanted to leave now, withdraw as much cash as possible until the bank opened tomorrow morning, drive far away, steal another car, and wait for the next signal. But she didn't dare leave yet. She couldn't risk waking up in Nebraska, alone, out of reach, like some sad old black and white TV with a rabbit-ear antenna.

She picked up her car keys, set them down. She went to the cupboard and dug two scoops of cat food from the bag and set the bowls out. This could be Teddy and Alanis's last meal. The clan would never allow them on the trip. She would have to drown them soon. She should get it over with now, in the tub, the way Momma had done to her first kitten Jezzie ... She almost burst into tears again, stroking the feeding animals, but stopped herself. Be strong. Playtime, the waiting, is almost over.

There was a tapping at her door.

Not the front door. On the glass, at the patio's sliding glass door.

Sheila turned and stared at the blinds, wishing she had not shut them. Now she had no idea who was there. Could be the police, or it could be her people.

Tap tap tap. Tap tap tap.

For a moment the thought of actually seeing them face to face after so much time filled her with such dread, she almost hoped it was the police.

What would she see when she twisted the blinds open? What did they look like now? If they had been without the power and resources, time would not have been kind to them. Who was she kidding? Time had never been kind to them.

Scrape scrape screeeeeeeeeeeccchhhh . . .

Nails now, squeaking and dragging against the glass.

It wasn't the police.

But if it was them, shouldn't she have felt them by now? Maybe they were still weak, weaker than she was. Maybe the signal they had sent had taken everything from them. They would need rest, shelter, sustenance. She would have to provide for them, to make them all strong again.

Sheila watched her cats feeding. This was her last chance to send them her love. She emanated for them with all she had, and said her goodbyes.

Then she crossed the living room and twisted the plastic stick.

And tried not to scream.

23

The Cinelli was still hidden in the shop's attic/storage loft. He'd moved it there last night, when he could no longer look at it without feeling as though he were staring at someone's headstone. He had intended to lead Patrick directly to it, to provoke a response, an explanation, if there was to be one. But moments after entering the shop, he forgot about the Cinelli. He was captivated by the boy.

If Patrick maintained the capacity for speech over the next ten minutes, he chose not to exercise it. He entered cautiously but soon walked ahead of Darren, gazing in all directions, pausing every few steps to adjust to the space, then standing motionless. He gazed down the rows of restored bikes as if he had walked into a funhouse optical illusion, mutely mesmerized by candy-colored alloys and castles of gleaming chrome. He seemed very small now, vulnerable, no longer the rambunctious kid who'd pulled a tabletop across the road, but a fragile boy with lint in his pockets suddenly thrust into a Willy Wonka world of bicycle cool.

Darren had been prepared to give Patrick a whole

spiel, a deluxe guided tour, but almost immediately decided it would be better to let Patrick absorb it on his own. If Patrick was really Adam, then he recognized most of this stuff, from the BMX magazines he had salivated over from the top of his American flag bedspread, dreaming of each gooseneck and seat clamp while his broken bones healed.

Then something changed. Without asking or even looking back, as if he had tunneled into some other realm where Darren did not exist, Patrick began to touch the bikes. He moved with intent, placing a hand on a grip here, a wheel there, squeezing as if taking its measure, then moved ahead to the next bike. When he reached the red, white and blue 1982 Robinson R Gusset, he flinched.

Robinson bike, Darren thought. *Patrick Robinson.*

Of course. I asked his name and he had to make up one quickly, and what he came up with was a bike. This isn't mere curiosity, admiration. Seeing all this stuff is wounding him, probably on a physical level.

But something else was happening here. Patrick moved faster, cupping a tangle of brake cables in a bin, tapping a file of number plates, racing his fingers down the cardboard display panel of finned Mathauser brake pads the way a one-time pianist traces the keys at a cocktail party . . .

I'm not like other kids. I touch things and I can tell things about the people who owned them. Something's wrong with me, and I think that's part of why they're after me. They want to use it, use me, or kill me so I don't find out.

If this was true, then what could Patrick be taking from the bikes now? Was he reading their histories, or Darren's? Whatever the purpose of all this touching might be – and Darren was sure it was no longer browsing – it was making Darren dizzy.

When he finally stopped and looked across the showroom at Darren, his face had reddened, he was panting, and his eyes had narrowed, darkened somehow.

'You okay?' Darren asked.

'You have all the bikes,' Patrick said in a soft voice. 'You got them all.'

Darren leaned against the workbench, where the roll of duct tape and a wad of paper towels with some of his blood on them still sat in disarray.

'I guess I did.'

'Why? How? How does someone do this?'

What could Darren say to help him understand? How could he explain to a kid who had not lived forty years that it was about reclaiming that spark, the spark you got from seeing a new bike come into the bike shop, some new part you'd seen in the magazines but had never held. The way the supple leather of Haro racing gloves felt better now than it had then, the way you were transported by the smell of injection-molded grips and your mom's hairspray you used to mount them on your chrome Hutch bars, how a set of mint-condition Bullseye cranks were more appealing to this man of forty-three than art or pornography or bank-fresh $100 bills.

What would Patrick/Adam know about the hunt, the

seeking of the next rare find? We are hard-wired for hunting, seeking, sorting, and in this regard collecting vintage goods in the internet age is like serving cocaine to tired rats in a cage. The late-night web browser searches triggering endorphins in his brain as he jumps from thread to thread, because you never knew when some dude in Mountain View, California, or Seattle or Houston or Huntsville or Scranton or Malaysia or Sydney might roll his grail out of his bedroom. The car needs repairing, his wife is pissed, and now he has to sell his dream bike – the one he kept for thirty years or spent six grand assembling just last year – for $4,000. Except not too many of these collectors had four grand to drop on a bike with six hours' notice, so the bikes usually got parted out, and you didn't want the whole thing anyway, but you've been looking for that perfect pair of Bob Reedy pedals for four years because you had them on your first Torker and now here they are. Back in the day they retailed for sixty bucks, not cheap in 1978 dollars, but now you are more than happy to drop $700 on a show-quality pair, you call DIBS on the forum, Paypal automated, sold, and they're in your mailbox four days later.

How could he explain what this has become?

What he has become?

And that is when he understands for the first time, Darren does, that he has become a monster. He is addicted to the high of collecting, the *find*, and he is always jonesing for more. He's worked hard to earn his security, but this does not change the simple fact that he is a taker, a keeper, a rich man who has never given back to those who have made possible his ascent to paterfamilias and CEO apparel mogul. He has never atoned for the things he did to this boy, and to who knows how many others, and it's too late now, the kid is here, in a bad way, and words are meaningless.

'Because I could,' Darren said at last. 'Because something in me needed it, or thought I did. I can't really remember.'

Patrick scoffed.

'Yes.' Darren walked down the row, gesturing. 'Any one you want, Patrick. Take your pick. Any bike in here, it's yours.'

Patrick glared. 'You know that's not my name.'

Darren nodded.

'Say it, then.'

Even now Darren was unable to say the name. In front of this kid. To do so would be a form of consent, agreement to participate in insanity.

'Are you afraid?'

'Maybe.'

'Of me, or what you'll find out?'

'The touching,' Darren said. 'What did you get from the bikes?'

'They're not bikes. Not for you, are they?'

'No? What are they?'

'Memories.' The boy looked to the bikes. 'Must be nice. Having so many good ones.'

'Wait here.'

Darren walked to the back of the shop, to a crude,

uncarpeted stairway made of plywood. He climbed it to the attic, which was really more of a short, open, unfinished loft. He used it mainly to store extra boxes, a few of the uglier bikes he hadn't gotten to yet, goods he was intending to sell. He had the strangest feeling as he neared the top of the stairs that the Cinelli would be gone, now that the boy was here, as if one was real and the other was not and the two could not exist on the same plane of reality.

But it was there, balanced on the small center stand where he had set it after cleaning off the blood. He lifted it, marveling once more at its light weight and sleek design. Was he really going to give this kid the Cinelli? He didn't want to. He wanted to keep it for himself, even if he never looked at it again. But he knew that he must give it to the boy, or at least offer it. He didn't know what it would change or how it would help, but deep down he felt that if he did not make this offering – to this boy who could not exist in the present day, in the state he was in, age eleven – more bad things would happen, like they had happened to the Kavanaughs, only this time it would happen to him, to Beth and Raya. And as disturbed as he was about what was transpiring, as afraid as he was to learn the truth, he would not risk his wife and daughter's lives over this bike.

He carried it down the stairs, careful to avoid bumping it against the wall or railing. He had been tasked with delivering it in perfect shape and he intended to fulfill this mission.

When Darren returned, Patrick was staring into the Zaxxon arcade machine. Maybe they would plug some quarters in later and play a few games. He carried the Cinelli to the bike stand, almost locked it in, and instead decided to leave it on the floor, one end of the handlebars leaning against the workbench so that the kid could approach it at his level. Not as a holy artifact but as a bike.

Patrick turned and glanced at Darren for a second before his eyes flew to the bright spot of color between them. The red CMX-1 in all its Italian glory, red and gold and Campagnolo blue. Bicycle candy. The boy stood immobile, his teeth and lips locked in a grimace of pain. His shoulders began to tremble, one of his knees went limp, but he managed to keep himself upright. Eventually he approached the Cinelli with his hands balled together at his belly, taking small furtive steps, and gradually the rictus relaxed into pure, beatific awe.

Darren crossed his arms and waited.

The boy reached out and touched the frame's top tube with his index finger, drawing it back along the bike's flank, to the built-in seat-post clamp, the winged letter C molded into the brake bridge, and up to the suede buffalo hide Unicanitor saddle. He sunk to the floor, crossing his legs and closing his eyes as he leaned into the bike, pressing his forehead against the seat tube. His right hand found the front tire, a mint-condition, never ridden Mitsuboshi Comp II Silver Star skinwall, arguably the rarest tire in the BMX world, gummy blue and still dusted with white release powder. Tears rolled down his cheeks in perfect silence. The Cinelli shone, and the boy wept silently and as intensely as anyone Darren had ever seen.

He felt like an intruder. He should not be here. No more than a stranger should be in the delivery room when the doctor hands the father his stillborn son.

After a time he looked up, his small brown eyes gleaming.

'This is the one.'

Darren nodded. 'I thought it must be.'

'It can't be,' the boy said. 'It's too perfect.'

'It's a collector's item, the best I've ever seen. Worth over six thousand dollars, I would guess. Maybe more. But, you know, it's also just a bicycle. It's never been ridden, not by anyone. Maybe it was waiting for you.'

'I don't understand,' the boy said.

'That's your bike now, Adam—' He stopped, realizing what he had said.

Adam blinked. 'I wondered if you could admit it. Do you know the rest?'

What did it matter now? 'Adam Burkett.'

'Yes. Adam Burkett and Darren Lynwood. Old friends.'

Something in Darren protested. To admit it seemed like another irrevocable step down a bad path. His mind felt like it was melting. 'No.'

'No, we're not friends?'

'No, I mean, we could be. Could have been. But this isn't possible. Someone must have put you up to this. Who was it? Why are you doing this?'

Adam smiled again. 'I told you, I don't know. Maybe you?'

Darren shook his head. 'But you're real. How can that be?'

'You're real, aren't you?'

'But I'm old. Grown up. You're still . . .'

'A boy.'

'Yes.'

Adam turned his attention back to the Cinelli. Maybe, Darren thought again, if I can get him to accept it, he will leave us in peace.

'I want you to have it,' Darren said. 'It belongs to you. I think it has always belonged to you.'

But the boy was shaking his head.

'Why not?'

'I didn't remember until I saw it, but I'm sure. This was the bike I dreamed about for a whole year. The man at the store held it for me. He had a big bushy mustache. We had a contract. But when I went to the store . . . it was the last day of school, I remember that now. Someone didn't want me to have it. I never made it that day. Later I went back, but someone else had stolen it.'

Darren was frowning. 'I don't understand. Someone else stole it, or bought it?'

'The man, the manager . . .'

'Arnie?' Darren said. 'Arnie was the manager at Dick's bike shop. He would never sell someone else's bike, not if he'd signed the hold slip. You must be mistaken.'

Adam kept shaking his head. 'Someone got to it. This bike was my life. It was going to change everything. I went through hell for it and . . . and it was just gone. Was it you? Or one of the other guys? Was it Tommy? Or Ryan? Who took it from me? Who did this?' He stared at Darren, pleading for an explanation.

'I honestly don't know,' Darren said. 'I don't even know how it got here. Someone sent it to me five weeks ago, no paperwork. Nothing.'

Adam's eyes widened, peering through Darren, beyond him, far away from here, back in time. 'I walked home. I should have been on my new bike, but I had to walk. That's when it happened. When it ended.'

'When what ended?'

Adam stood and faced him, the Cinelli no longer of interest. His eyes darkened and his mouth set itself into a hateful seam. Darren caught himself taking a step back, then another. He could not hold the boy's penetrating gaze much longer.

'Whoever took this bike from me is the one who did it,' Adam said. His eyes seemed to darken and recede inside their small sockets. 'Don't you get it? It was never just a bike. It was murder.'

Darren only stared at the boy, unable to speak. Guilt hardened inside him, filling his joints, leaving a taste of rust and decay in the back of his mouth.

Something chirped, breaking the silence building between them. Vibration inside of Darren's pants pocket.

Adam scowled, suddenly on edge.

Darren removed his cellphone from his pocket. 'It's just my phone. My wife, Beth.'

Adam retreated several steps, looking around in slow building panic.

'I was supposed to check in with her,' Darren said. The phone continued to chirp. 'I'll be just a minute.'

'I can't stay here,' Adam said. He ran to the workbench and took up his backpack. 'They'll come for me. They'll kill your family.'

Darren thumbed the screen and held the phone to his ear. 'Beth? Hold on a second, would you?'

Adam ran past him, heading for the back door.

'Wait!'

'Forget it,' Adam said over his shoulder. 'I don't want your help!'

The boy pushed through the back door and Darren chased after him.

'Darren? Are you all right?' He could hear Beth speaking. He put the phone to his ear as he caught the rebounding screen door and stepped out onto the porch. 'Who's there with you?'

'Hold on, honey.'

He ran into grass at the back of the yard, glimpsing a flash of the kid's blue shirt and the backpack slipping around the corner. Darren darted right, rounding the shop.

Adam was sprinting across the yard, into the neighbor's grass, faster than Darren would have imagined an eleven-year-old boy capable of moving.

'Adam! Wait! I'm trying to help you!' he shouted across the yard. 'Come back here!'

The boy did not look back before disappearing behind the Nehrer residence.

'Beth, I have to call you back,' Darren panted into the phone.

'Did you say Adam? Is he there?'

'I gotta go,' Darren said, clicking his phone off.

He shoved it into his pocket and took off running in search of the lost kid.

24

Beth arrived home twenty minutes later, but Darren didn't join her until almost 6 p.m. He drove around the neighborhood, returning to Palo Park in search of Adam. There was no sign of the boy, and the ruined BMX bike was nowhere to be found in the weeds. The kid must have taken it with him, in hopes of repairing it. Either that, or someone else had found it and taken it for scrap parts.

Beth kept ringing his phone and he knew she was freaking out, so finally he returned home. He told her about the accident and bringing Adam home, his reaction to the Cinelli. He told her that the boy was convinced that 'monsters' were chasing him, and that the person responsible for taking his bike away was also the person responsible for his 'murder'.

He could see that she was finding all of this difficult to digest, so he walked her into the garage and showed her the car.

Beth stared at the Acura's milky-webbed windshield for a moment, then moved around the front, he supposed to look for blood. He joined her. They did not find any.

Beth turned and looked at him. 'We need to call the police, right now.'

Darren felt himself reaching for an excuse not to, recalling Adam's repeated warnings not to contact any authorities. 'I promised him I wouldn't,' he said.

'Do you think you have a choice?' Beth said. 'You hit a little boy with your car!'

'But he wasn't hurt. Someone is after him. He's a runaway, from what or who I don't know. What if the police find him and return him to his parents and they wind up hurting him?'

'Then the police will sort it out and social services will get involved. But if you don't report it now, you're putting us all in a bad situation. He could be injured in ways you don't know.'

'But how do you explain the rest?' he said. He had not eaten all day and felt exhausted beyond the capacity of rational thought. 'The warnings we got about his arrival. I mean, it was him, Beth. It was Adam Burkett.'

'How can it be?' Beth nearly shouted. 'You met a boy. You hit him with your car. He was sweating, breathing, he broke your windshield. He was eleven years old. Whoever he is, he's not the same boy, Darren. For God's sake, listen to yourself!'

Darren stomped back into the house. In the kitchen he ripped open a loaf of bread and took a handful of lunch meat from the refrigerator, a slice of Raya's Velveeta, slapping it all together and wolfing it as if the

267

food would ease his anger. He was pissed at Beth, at himself, at Adam. The whole mess made him want to break something.

Beth came in a moment later. She picked her cell-phone up from inside her purse and set it on the counter where his crumbs were falling.

'If you won't call them, I will.'

'Fine,' Darren said through a mouthful of dough and bologna. 'Let me finish my lunch first.'

He washed down the last bite with a slug of milk direct from the bottle, then picked up her phone.

'Wait,' she said.

'What?'

'Don't tell them you brought him here.'

'Oh, now you want me to lie?'

'No, maybe. I don't know. I'm just thinking there's no need to tell them all the rest just yet. We want to avoid liability if possible and what difference does it make if he ran away right after the accident or – how long was he with you before he ran off?'

Darren thought it over. 'No more than an hour.'

Beth flexed her hands at her sides. 'Okay, tell them about the accident, and that he ran away before you could get him to a doctor. We live close by, and you had to get him out of the road. He tried to run at first – isn't that what you said anyway?'

Darren nodded.

'Right. So you had to calm him down first. Once he was here, you went to call 9-1-1, and that's when he ran off.'

'But now three hours have passed and we're finally calling now because ...?'

Beth frowned. 'Because you went looking for him and ... shit, maybe you should just tell them the truth.'

'But not all of it. Not the part about the bike, the dreams, Raya's texts. Or else they'll think we're out of our minds, yes?'

'Right,' Beth said. She was breathing hard.

'It's going to be okay,' he said. 'One step at a time.'

He dialed information to get the non-emergency number, and was patched through to the police.

It must have been a slow evening for crime in Boulder. Less than an hour later, Officer Sewell was handing over his business card, reminding Darren and Beth to call if the boy turned up again or if they had anything else to add to the report. Sewell was a polite cop, one who spoke little and listened carefully as Darren took him through it, showed him the car, and gave a description of Adam Burkett, who might also be using the name Patrick Robinson.

The officer was tall, in his late thirties or early forties, and obviously a body builder, his thighs, shoulders and arms all but ripping his uniform apart at the seams. Above all this sculpting was an oddly small head, short brown hair, pink ears and lips. He drove them the six blocks to Palo Park and Darren showed him where it had happened, but there was no new evidence to be found.

On the way home, Darren and Beth sitting behind

the plexiglas partition like a couple of criminals, Darren asked Sewell what this was going to be filed as.

'What do you mean?' the officer said.

'Is it like a hit and run, a missing persons thing, or what?' Darren said, sitting forward to speak through the ventilation holes.

Beth pinched his leg, warning him not invite charges pressed against them.

'Well, it's not strictly a hit and run, seeing as how you called us,' Officer Sewell said after a moment. 'We'll run a search for his parents, any family, and see if there have been any other inquiries. My guess is he's a runaway, so it will go down as missing persons, most likely.'

'Oh, right, that makes sense.' Darren experienced mild relief.

Officer Sewell cleared his throat. 'But if we locate him and it turns out he's injured, and there are parents, they might file charges. You should be prepared for that. Sounds like a lawsuit any asshole lawyer would love to take.'

Darren could only nod. He sat back in the cruiser's bench seat until they turned onto Linden. He was thinking how glad he was that he had not told Beth about the boy claiming to have been in the Kavanaugh house when the murders happened. It seemed too far-fetched even now, and as long as he had reported Adam out there somewhere on the run, what did it matter?

Because there's a difference between searching for a runaway kid and searching for a suspect in a multiple homicide, you idiot. If you tell them about that little piece of the puzzle, they'll tear the town apart looking for the kid with the butterfly knife with, oh yes, let's not forget, dried blood on the blade.

Looking at it this way, Darren thought he really had to tell the cop about that now. But the next question would be, why didn't you provide this information sooner? And any link between Darren's report and the town's most famous recent murder case would be bad for them, no matter how well-intentioned. Things would turn serious in a hurry. He would have to explain things he could not explain, and their lives would be under a microscope.

Even so . . . we're talking about murder. Can you live with that?

And then the cruiser was halting in the driveway and there was Raya, standing on the porch with Chad. They must have just come home. The door was open and they were about to step inside, but paused to watch as her parents emerged from the back of a police car. Officer Sewell got out with them.

'Do you need me for anything else?' Beth said.

Sewell handed her a copy of the report. 'No, we're pretty much done here. For now.'

She hurried up the walk to usher the kids inside.

Darren waved to Raya. 'Be there in a minute, honey.'

Seeing the concern in his daughter's eyes, he knew he would not mention the Kavanaugh link, if such a thing existed. Adam Burkett was not a killer, Darren was certain of that. But what about the others? The ones chasing him? At least give him that much. What could be the harm in that?

271

'One more thing I forgot to mention,' he said to the officer.

'Yeah, what's that?'

'Adam said he was being chased by someone. Right after the accident, we saw something, and he seemed pretty afraid of it.'

'You saw something, or he did?'

'Both of us,' Darren said, and gave a description of the brown Ford with the camper shell on top. The broken-up front end.

'Did you get a license plate?'

'No,' Darren said. 'It was too far away.'

'Any idea who was in it? Who owns a truck like that?'

MP-3515.

The tag popped into Darren's mind. He could see the plate now.

'MP-3515,' he said to Officer Sewell.

'That's the plate?'

'I just remembered it. The kid must have told me. He'd seen it before.'

'Well, this could help us. This is good.' Officer Sewell made a few more notes and closed his notepad.

'What happens next?' Darren said.

'I'll be in touch soon,' Sewell said, betraying no emotion. Then, with just the right amount of strained politeness, 'Please continue to make yourself available as we investigate. We would appreciate any updates on your summer travel plans.'

Something isn't sitting right with him, Darren thought. He smells something rotten in this situation.

'Thank you for coming out,' he said.

'It's what we do.'

'Appreciated.'

Sewell walked around the open driver's side door. He looked over the top of his sunglasses. 'Drive carefully, Mr Lynwood. You're lucky that boy isn't dead.'

'Yes, sir. I will.'

Darren went inside and tried to hold a conversation with the kids, reassuring them everything was all right, but Beth waved him off and he knew she wanted to handle it. She would decide what to tell Raya, how much and when.

He could barely keep his eyes open. He told them he wasn't feeling well and needed to lie down for a while. He took off his shoes and leaned back on the bed, where he slept for twelve hours without interruption.

Officer Sewell called early the next afternoon to report that he had no real breaks in the case. They had not found a boy fitting Adam Burkett's description, and their databases had not turned up any missing boys by either name. The license plate had been stolen off another vehicle months ago and was of no use. Local families with the matching surnames had been contacted; none had reported a lost son. The police would expand their search state- and nationwide, Sewell said, to see if any connections turned up.

'One interesting thing,' Sewell added, in a tone more convivial than any he had displayed previously. 'A woman who lives in the area, Palo Park, reported a truck like the one you described fleeing the scene earlier that day, after she discovered her Nissan plowed into her garage door. Sounds like they were chasing him, your runaway kid. So we have an APB on the Ford, but so far no hits.'

Darren felt vindicated in some way. The truck was real. Everything that had happened was real. And yet he knew they would find no trace of the boy.

They spent the next forty-eight hours in a state of high anxiety, puttering around the house, pretending everything was all right.

Adam stayed away for two days and two nights, returning on the third morning, a Tuesday, June 12th.

The day all the bad things happened.

25

The large Ford truck with its yellowing eggshell topper rolled east on Highway 7 out of Lafayette, to Interstate 25, where it turned north, carrying three occupants who in their silence agreed that north felt true, the best bet. Not quite five miles later the driver decided to exit, onto Highway 52 east for another twelve minutes into Fort Lupton, a small town with no action but enough amenities for them to do what needed to be done before they resumed the hunt for Adam.

The town offered plenty of other, more upscale choices for the required facilities, but Sheila chose La Paloma Motel, located on the northern edge of town. The short single-story building was white with green trim, and only two of the dozen parking spaces in front of the rooms were occupied by a vehicle. She parked one block ahead, on the street, to make sure the check-in process went smoothly.

The desk clerk, a young Hispanic woman named Griselda, wearing a button-down white blouse with a puffy collar and a beaded necklace featuring Jesus on the cross, accepted cash payment. She did not linger over Sheila's fake Minnesota driver's license, which showed an eleven-year-old photo of her (back when she was a blonde) and the name Lisa Campbell. When Griselda asked for the make of her vehicle and license plate number to note on the guest form, Sheila told her it was a white Honda Civic, plate number TFL-644, from a car she knew from the parking lot where she had worked, before the emanation storm hit and their collective Adam doppler had begun to spin.

Once she had the room key and Griselda finished explaining where the soda and ice machines were located, and that she recommended Wholly Stromboli for dinner if they liked Italian, Sheila walked to room 7, a corner unit, as she had requested. It was not far from the front office, but the best she could hope for here. She inspected the room, the views, the bathroom, and then returned to the front desk.

'Yes?' Griselda braced herself for a complaint or request for a different room.

'I forgot to mention I've been traveling for business,' Shelia told her. 'On the road for two days without a break. Do you think you could spare me some extra soap and towels, maybe some shampoo and conditioner if you have it?'

'Absolutely.' Griselda dipped into a storage closet at one end of the counter and returned with a stack of clean white towels, two miniature bars of soap, and two bottles each of a miniature shampoo and conditioner called Outer Beauty. Sheila was tempted to ask for ten more, but she did not want to arouse suspicion.

'Will that do it for you?' Griselda said.

'Perfect, thank you.'

Sheila walked all the way around the building, to the truck parked up the street. Her passengers mumbled from inside the camper, something about being hot and hungry and tired of being left in the dark, and Sheila told them to shut the fuck up, they had one more stop. The reunion had been a little bumpy, notably when Ethan suggested taking the cats with them. For dinner. Teddy and Alanis would have been a step up from their usual roadkill, but Sheila drew the line at pets. She'd been forced to beat him back with a broomstick. Only a few hours together and already she wanted to sap them both.

In town she found a grocery store and parked in the far corner of the lot.

'Do not exit the vehicle. If you set one foot outside, we're in big trouble,' she called through the cab's port-hole. 'I'm amazed you aren't in jail already. You disgust me.'

They grunted and mumbled some more and Sheila thought she heard the phrase 'spoiled bitch' somewhere in there.

'You want me to use the mace again?'

They quieted.

She found the toiletries aisle and loaded a handcart with a large bottle of Head & Shoulders, three bars of Dial anti-bacterial soap, a family-size tube of Colgate with Professional Whitening (because every little bit helped), four toothbrushes, a liter of Listerine, nail clippers, two loofa exfoliating sponges mounted to wooden hand-paddles, a box of Q-Tips, a pair of grooming scissors, a pack of men's Gillette triple-blade razors, a can of aloe shaving gel, a stick of Arm & Hammer antiperspirant, and since she was feeling generous and might want some herself, a bottle of Lubriderm moisturizer.

On her way out, she paused in the dish-soap and kitchen-cleaning section and threw a box of Brillo pads and a pair of rubber dishwashing gloves in the basket.

She paid cash.

Crossing the parking lot the thought hit her, they'll be clean, but then what?

Fort Lupton did not have a mall with department stores or any boutiques, but it did have an Everything 5, which Sheila was given to understand meant nothing in the store cost over $5. Perfect. Thirty bucks later she emerged with clean socks, underwear, a big brown bra, two pairs of green polyester sweatpants, two black sweatshirts, a six-pack of colored bandannas, and two pairs of squared-off Total Blocker sunglasses of the style favored by Florida retirees with damaged retinas. In the checkout aisle she couldn't resist the 3-for-1 special on Miracle-Lips Lip Balm.

Back at the motel, she parked on the street and waited another hour for dusk to settle in, when the street was as clear as it was likely to get without her waiting till ten at night. She masked them in bandannas and the Blockers as best she could, then helped them down from the camper's loft bunk, out the back door, around the motel and into the room. They were severely weakened from their last hunt and she had to walk them in one at a time. Dehydrated, malnourished, bacterial infections of one sort or another, bruises, sprains, and possibly coming down with summer colds, on top of the generally feeble mental state they lived with except during those precious moments when the target was near and their powers were at their apogee.

Sheila did not like to look them in the eyes, which were the lizard-flat slits of coldblooded killers. Some things had not changed.

Before she even finished getting them locked inside the room, curtains drawn, Sheila wanted to scour herself with bleach. She did not have to ask how long it had been. She knew from experience they would not have bathed in three to six months, and then only in a lake.

'Miriam goes first, so come with me, honey,' she said. The old bastard tried to heave himself from the bed anyway. 'Ethan, no, you stay here till we're through. Have a rest – on top of the covers – until we get this doll all spiced up for ya. There, thank you.'

For someone's decency, she couldn't imagine whose, Sheila shut the bathroom door. She donned the rubber gloves. She helped the woman undress, turning the fan on before the first shirt came off. The socks had to be peeled from the feet blackened with grime. Sheila tried not to look or breathe, but it was impossible. Miriam had lesions on her thighs, buttocks, and under her arms. She had not shaved in years. The flesh of her belly and breasts was mottled like the face, in some places the skin appearing to run in long rivers, pucker into membrane-like spirals in others, and the long mark across her back reminded Sheila nothing so much as the zipper to an actual monster suit. The bones were in no better condition; Miriam's humpback had doubled in size since Sheila had last seen it. Oh, but if only they could remove these hideous costumes.

Miriam whined and mewled through the inspection, and screeched when Sheila turned the shower head on and set the water to full hot. That's right, almost forgot. They hate the spray. Feels like needles on their delicate skin. They only like calm bodies of water, warm and still. Well, tough cookies. She let the old woman tenderize in there for a good five minutes while she undressed herself, folded her clothes neatly, and set the stack outside the bathroom door.

Carrying the bag of toiletries, she stepped into the shower and went to work. It took forty minutes. There was no hair on top, of course, but she needed the shampoo to soften everything else, and to loosen the dirt, which streamed down in gray tides. There was a terrible smell for the first fifteen minutes, one whose source Sheila would never have identified as a human being if she were not witnessing it, but it got better with each head-to-toe scrub with the soap and loofa. When she got to the part where she had to wash between the cheeks and under the remnants of the sex organs, she averted her eyes and told herself it was no different than when she was a girl, feeding the billy goats at the petting zoo. Sheila used the rough wooden paddles to scour the skin, the nails, between the toes. Two times Miriam urinated uncontrollably, then cackled at her ability to serve some measure of revenge, and Sheila berated her for it.

Once the dirt was mostly gone, she tilted the spray to one side and lathered Miriam's legs and 'bikini area' and armpits. Two razors later she had to unclog the drain. She used one of the motel-provided wash rags to scrub the face, behind the ears, and pretty much everywhere else once more for good measure, then allowed the woman to rinse. Miriam rejected the toothbrush at first, biting the top and jerking her head from side to side, but Sheila continued the campaign until the old woman gave up and allowed her to pass the bristles around the clamped teeth, which eventually slackened. The gums drained in loops of pink foam.

By the time it was over, Miriam was shuddering, crying helplessly, her legs weak from standing, her head resting against the tile wall. Sheila took some pity and massaged the poor creature's shoulders, arms, legs, and lower back, until the sobbing turned into a gentle cooing of pleasure.

She turned off the water and helped Miriam step out of the tub.

She toweled her down gently, like brushing an old stable nag, and then applied two layers of the Lubriderm to the legs, feet, back, breasts, especially around the chapped and peeling nipples, the shellfish hands. She massaged more lotion into the sensitive scalp and added a third layer to the worst of the scars.

She filled a cup of cold water and allowed Miriam to drink while she clipped the toenails, fingernails, and groomed the wild eyebrows and ear tufts.

She wrapped the woman in two towels and sent her back to the room.

'Lay down and have a nap, old gal. And send the bugger in.'

Ethan would be worse in some ways, better in others. Worse because he would get excited, couldn't help himself. Better because once he shot his sap he would not resist her ministrations toward the hygienic.

This was Sheila's burden, the price of so many years of neglect. But she did what she had to do. To get them into shape for the coming fight, and because it was the right thing to do. Someone had to look after them, despite what they had become.

They were her parents, after all.

26

Beth, Raya and Chad left the house around eleven for a day of shopping and lunch down in Cherry Creek, Denver's most affluent suburb and shopping mecca, an hour's drive south of Boulder. They had invited Dad along but the thought of a shopping mall, all that browsing and waiting for Raya to try stuff on, wore him out just thinking about it, and he wanted to stay home in case the police checked in. He kissed them both goodbye.

'You're a stronger man than I am,' he told Chad. 'Have fun and bring me a surprise. I need a new hat.'

'What kind of hat? Chad said.

'He's joking, Chad,' Beth said. 'The last thing he needs is a new hat. He has forty or fifty old ones in the shop.'

After they were gone, Darren went out to the Bike Cave, thinking it was time to make some calls about the Cinelli. He could reach out to bike shops nationally, try to track down the Cinelli dealers who had been around a long time, see if there was a way to get in touch with the company headquarters and find out if the serial number could be traced to its original shipping date and destination here in the U.S.

The bike was where he had left it on the main floor. He pulled the serial number from under the bottom bracket shell, then decided to stash the bike in the attic. Thinking about it was enough. Looking at it was too much of a distraction and led to bad things. He carried the Cinelli back up the stairs to the attic space above the showroom. A bundled form in the darkened corner rolled over and stared up at Darren from twenty feet away with the expressionless face of a corpse.

'Oh Jesus!' Darren said, hair standing on end, so surprised he nearly dropped the bike. His heart felt like it was going to burst through his sternum and his mouth went dry. He set the bike down with shaking hands and wiped his face. 'God damn you, you scared the shit out of me.'

'Sorry,' Adam said, sitting up. His backpack was on the floor where he had been using it for a pillow. 'I had nowhere else to go.'

'You've been here? All this time?' Darren was incredulous.

'Just since last night. I thought of something important.'

'Do you have any idea—' But he stopped himself. If he told Adam the police were after him, the kid would only bolt again and that wouldn't solve anything. 'What's so important you had to come back?'

Adam got to his feet. He looked tired, worn out, his

same old clothes dirtier than ever. He picked up his backpack and pulled it over his shoulders.

'Tommy Berkley,' he said. 'Remember the Wonderland Hills Gang?'

Darren sighed. 'What about him?'

'We have to find him. He knows things about my family. I think he can tell us what happened to me. Have you talked to him? Do you know where he is?'

'How did you get in here?' Darren said. 'I set the alarm every night.'

'I told you, I can learn things by touching them. I picked up your code the other day, when we first came inside. Or Ryan Triguay, we could check on him too. But I think we should start with Tommy. He was the one who was nicest to me.'

Until he heard Adam use that term for their old riding crew, it had never occurred to Darren that the former members of the Wonderland Hills Gang might still live in or near Boulder. He turned away from Adam and went down the stairs, into the office.

'I have no idea where those guys are,' Darren said.

Adam followed, asking, 'You moved back here almost a year ago and haven't bothered to look up any of your old friends?'

'It wasn't a conscious thing. I've been busy moving, unpacking, remodeling the shop, settling in. For the past twenty years Beth's been the one to maintain our social calendar.'

'Sounds like a lot of excuses to me. How hard is it to call some friends?'

'I haven't talked to any of those guys since junior high. The odds of them being in Boulder are slim. People move away all the time, Adam.'

'And sometimes they come back,' Adam said. 'You did.'

'Maybe they're on Facebook.'

'What's Facebook?'

Darren frowned. 'This is so messed up, you know that? You scare me.'

The first number they retrieved from information belonged to a college-aged Thomas Berkley, according to his roommate, a young woman who informed Darren that "Tom" had moved back east, to Rhode Island. Wrong Tommy.

The second number rang seven or eight times.

'No one's answering,' Darren said, preparing to disconnect.

'Wait!'

Darren frowned. On the tenth or eleventh ring, a man answered. He sounded too old, his voice raspy but light, pleasant.

'Hi, I'm looking for Tom Berkley. Tommy, as I knew him back in school.'

'Oh yeah? And who's calling?'

'My name's Darren Lynwood.'

Delayed silence. The man on the other end cleared his throat. 'Darren Lynwood? Mr BMX Darren Lynwood?'

'Oh, man,' Darren said. 'Is that you, Tommy?'

Adam was grinning like a fool.

'Saw you in the paper a month or so ago,' Tommy said. 'Didn't even know you were back in town. Kinda never expected to hear from you again.'

'I know. Sorry to call you out of the blue like this. I was hoping we could catch up on a few things.'

'Is that right? And what would that be about?'

'I have a bike story for you,' Darren said. 'A crazy one. I could use your help.'

'Hm.'

'It's important, Tommy. Extremely.'

'Oh, well, I guess you could swing out to the farm. I'm none too busy these days.'

Tommy gave him directions. They took the Firebird, not wanting to drive the Acura with its busted windshield. Twenty-five minutes later, east of Boulder, they found the dirt drive off County Line Road, out in a rural patch between newer housing developments that had sprung up all around Erie, a small town that had been a sleepy little place when Darren was a kid but which had since become another suburban bedroom community feeding into Boulder and Denver. Darren parked close to the road, on the side of a small barn, hoping to keep Adam out of sight.

The kid reached for the door.

'I think you better wait in the car,' Darren said to his passenger.

'Why?'

'Because we don't want to give him a heart attack.'

'Tell him I'm your cousin. Your son. Whatever. I won't give it away.'

'I think ... no.'

'He'll see me, anyway,' Adam whined.

'Stay put. I can't think straight with you. If he asks who you are, I'll make something up, but don't screw around, you got it?'

Adam fumed for a moment, then sunk down into the seat.

Darren got out and approached the main house, a three-story white Craftsman farmhouse in decent repair, plus a smaller guest house across the dirt turnaround. A hundred feet to the north stood three rows of horse stables and what appeared to be an indoor training arena. In between, there wasn't much of a yard, just a wide swath of packed dirt and weeds. A giant cottonwood threw shade over a picnic table, a plastic kiddie pool filled with wet leaves and muck, and the largest home-made barbecue Darren had ever seen. It looked like two oil drums split open and mated to a small train engine.

A blond-bearded man in green Carhartt coveralls waddled out from the shade of an open garage, his duck boots squeaking. He must have weighed three-twenty or three-fifty, he stood at least four or five inches taller than Darren, and he had the good-natured smile of a ten-year-old boy holding an ice-cream cone. His eyes were buried behind two rosy hills of cherubic flesh. A pair of black glacier glasses hung from an orange nylon lanyard around his neck, but he did not put them on, despite the sun glare.

'You don't look like Darren Lynwood,' Tommy said before he got close enough to shake hands.

Darren felt his intestines cramping from nervous tension. The sun was very bright, even though he was wearing one of his twenty-four pairs of Oakley Frogskins. This was a bad idea. He knew already it was going to turn out bad. The only question was how bad and over what.

'But I guess I don't look much like I used to either,' Tommy added. 'I'm too damned big to get on a BMX bike, that's for sure. What the hell are you doing still monkeying around with those things? Aren't you ever gonna grow up?'

Darren chuckled. Oh, where to begin?

They had made the usual small talk for about fifteen minutes. Where you been? Where are you now? Married? Kids? What brought you back to Boulder? Darren told his side of it as quickly as he could.

Tommy told a longer tale involving a lot of juvenile delinquency, drug abuse, an alcoholic father who earned a fortune in stock from IBM and took an early buy-out to retire on the farm to raise horses, screw as many bad women as he could, and drink himself to death. The old man had been renting out horse stalls and the living quarters attached to the arena to some fellows who turned out to be part of a Mexican drug cartel with a gambling interest in horse doping. Tommy's mother had died of bone cancer when Tommy was still in high school. During what should have been the college years, Tommy and his younger brother Nate had got into crystal meth and the dog tracks, but since then Tommy had found love and religion and sobered up while Nathan was still on the loose somewhere down in Albuquerque.

Darren recalled none of this. The more Tommy talked, the more Darren realized he had no memory of the kid beyond age twelve.

After Tommy's father bequeathed him the farm, Tommy had sent the Mexican dopers packing and nowadays he rented the stalls to decent people. He rented the guest house to three lesbians who were trying to make a go of organic farming. Tommy performed repairs and updates around the farm and fed and cleaned the horses for some of his clients. On weekends he liked to walk out to the pond on the back hundred acres and shoot his guns. 'I have a lot of guns. Mostly for target practice and the occasional coyote or nosy coon.' He was waiting for the farm to reach two-point-five million in value, at which point he would sell it, pay off his brother's debts, and downsize to a regular house, smooth retirement. He seemed to have found peace out here.

Eventually they got around to Adam, by way of talking bikes and the rest of the Wonderland Hills Gang. Darren told him about the Cinelli, how it had come to him with no shipping labels. Tommy hadn't sent the bike – 'Why the heck would I send you a six-thousand-dollar bike, you nitwit?' – and he didn't remember a Cinelli. They talked of other bikes, naturally linking them to the other guys from the gang.

'Whatever happened to Ryan?' Darren said. 'Any idea?'

'He's dead,' Tommy said. 'Suicide. About, what?

Fifteen years ago? Somethin' like that. Parked his car in the garage, ate the fumes, left a wife and daughter behind.'

'Jesus. Sorry to hear that. What was the problem?'

'Who knows?' Tommy said. His jovial demeanor dialed way down, the way it happens when old friends recall the loss of one who did not make it into adulthood. 'Depression, alcoholism, money problems. I saw him at the five-year reunion. He looked like he was dead already. Could hardly put together two sentences. You didn't make it to that one, did you?'

'The reunion? No. I missed all of them.'

Tommy nodded, as if this confirmed something damning about Darren. Maybe it did. Darren opened his mouth to raise the subject, but Tommy said it first.

'Adam Burkett. You remember that sorry case?'

Darren decided to play it loose, see what Tommy recalled without prompting. 'Adam, right. The kid with the Huffy. Yeah, vaguely.'

'We were vicious to that kid,' Tommy said. 'Unbelievably cruel. Ruining his bike wasn't the half of it. Dunking him that day at the pool about drowned him. Things we did, we oughta gone to jail. I carried that guilt for fifteen years. Only thing got me past it was meeting Charlotte, and the church. Do you go to church, Darren?'

'No, we don't. Maybe I should.'

'There's forgiveness to be had. Forgiveness is real, if you believe in it.'

Darren chuckled again. He couldn't seem to stop

291

chuckling, though there was no heart in it. Tommy had not invited him inside and Darren had the feeling his old friend was playing nice but wanted to keep his distance.

'Social Outcast,' Tommy said. 'That's what we called him. And sometimes just shithead.'

'To tell you the truth,' Darren lied, 'I remember that day we wrecked his bike in Palo Park, but not much after that. I sort of recall something bad happened to him, there was more, but it's been so long. You were friendlier with him. Anything else you can tell me about him? His family?'

Tommy studied Darren with what appeared to be real skepticism, or contempt.

'I wasn't his friend, but I knew a kid who lived in his neighborhood, Brad Cader. Up there in that trailer park just north of Crest View. Brad and I used to ride sometimes, he had an old Mongoose Motomag, I think. He told me some real morsels about the Burkett clan. You really don't remember any of this?'

Darren shook his head. 'What can I tell ya? I was an asshole rich kid from the other side of the tracks.'

Tommy laughed. 'You were quite the asshole. That's true.'

Darren sighed. 'I hardly remember anything between the ages of twelve and eighteen, after we moved away. Things were different in Wisconsin. A lot of my memories of growing up out here sort of vanished.'

Tommy looked down at his boots, stomped something into the dirt, and went on with his story. 'Cader used to dink around the trailer park with Adam from time to time. Maybe he played in that house on one or two occasions, Adam's trailer. He was a softie like me. He didn't have anything against kids like Adam. Back then you'd play with whoever was free. But Adam's pop was a real mean old bastard. Drunk all the time, running drugs, driving around late at night picking up hitchhikers just to mess with them. He carried a baseball bat in the truck and used to go downtown and sweep up the hippies for fun. Me and Cader, we'd see his truck at the BustTop sometimes, three o'clock in the afternoon.'

Darren recalled that the BustTop had been Boulder's only topless bar, and not a ritzy one at that. He wondered if it was still in business.

'The mom was no better,' Tommy continued. 'I saw her a few times at school, picking Adam up for this or that. She was a dark lady.'

'What does that mean?' Darren said. 'Dark how?'

Tommy's cheeks bunched up again. 'I don't know, exactly, you just saw it. She was short, built like a brick shithouse, big boobs and hips, and she was wild-looking, with dark black hair and dark eyes, but there was something else. She dressed in these weird outfits, vests and skirts, a lot of dark eye shadow. Everyone said she had a way of turning fate on people she didn't like. Making people sick. The family was into occult stuff, bad stuff.'

'What, you mean like Ouija boards?'

Tommy didn't smile. 'No, I mean like rituals. Satanism The real deal, if there is such a thing. Remember

293

this stuff, though? This was the late Seventies. In Boulder, it was like the Sixties never ended. Town was full of drugs, ski bums, rich kids playing bad. Alternative living was standard. Still is. But the Burketts were ... well, whatever they were, they were different. Mrs Burkett wore moccasins and homemade tattoos, sometimes on her face. Brad Cader asked Adam about those once and he said they were symbols. "Whattya mean?" Brad asks, and Adam says, "You know, symbols, for calling on spirits and channeling energies." Like this was normal, everyone did it. He had been raised in a household where this stuff was normal.'

'That's interesting,' Darren said. He did not want to know more.

'There were other things. Rumors of séances, curses. One time, I guess another family had a birthday party there at the clubhouse, in the trailer park, and all the parents went bananas because Adam's parents showed up loaded and started teaching the kids how to put spells on each other. Telling them Satan was real, he wore human masks, and he would be their friend if they would open their hearts to him. I'm sure there's more I don't remember, but you get the idea.'

'Satanism and drugs,' Darren said. 'Nice.'

'And abuse. Physical, probably sexual. Or definitely sexual.'

Neither man spoke for moment.

Darren said, 'Anything else worth knowing about this wonderful tribe?'

Tommy licked his lips. 'Sure, if you really wanna

know. I guess I could tell you about the scariest thing I ever saw. And I do mean in my entire life.'

Darren thought about leaving then. He wished he would not have come out here. But he was here now, so: 'I probably better hear it.'

Tommy wiped sweat from his face and began to tell it.

27

'You remember Adam's sister?'

'That doesn't ring any bells,' Darren said.

'I forget her name, but she was a little creep. Thin as a stick, skin that malnourished pale color, so white it's almost gray. Ratty blonde hair. She hardly ever came to school, used to pee her pants on the playground all the time. Adam didn't attend much either. They were those kids who always had a broken wrist, pink eye, some kind of problem. Seemed like Mrs Burkett was always dragging one of them out of class. One thing that I never forgot, she always wore these little rainbow barrettes in her hair. Same ones every damn day, year around, like they were the only ones she ever had. Something beyond sad about those rainbows in her unwashed hair.'

'She was older or younger than Adam?'

'Two grades ahead, but three or four years older,' Tommy said. 'Underdeveloped, stunted. She hated her brother, but she hated everybody. She was a mean girl, like they were training her to be nasty. After she made it out of Crest View, they tried her at Casey Junior High, but that didn't last more than a few months. She was "home schooled" from then on. She freaked me out, man. Shannon? Was that her name? Sissy? No . . . '

'What was scary about her?' Darren said. 'What was the thing?'

'Right. So, Cader takes me by their place one Saturday night. This would have been sixth grade, fall, after we ruined his bike. Adam would have been a fifth-grader, which would've put his sister around fourteen, but like I said she was stunted. Looked three years younger and rumor was she was still wetting herself in public.

'Anyway, this night we went up there, I remember it was Halloween or a few days before. Maybe it just felt like Halloween. We were out riding bikes after dark. I knew I was supposed to be home two hours ago but Brad talked me into going up there. "You gotta see this," he told me. "You gotta see Adam's sister."

'I remember riding up there curious but not really afraid, because I'd never been to their place and I didn't know if everything we'd heard about them was true. By the time we get up there it's dark dark, and the trailer court had those streetlights, but not much lighting in some of the smaller cul-de-sacs. We ride around for a few minutes, until we find the Burkett place. And maybe it's just my memory working too hard, but soon as I saw it, I knew something was wrong with it. All the other trailers, they were pretty much clean, some of them with little yards, a fountain, the grass mowed. Adam mowed lawns to save for his bike, come to think of it. He probably mowed fifty yards in that little dump to make a hundred bucks, but the point is, these were decent people, most of 'em. You know Boulder. The worst part of town, even back then, wasn't like some kind of ghetto. The other trailers were homey, quaint. Not the Burkett place.'

Darren was beginning to feel a little queasy himself. He pointed to the picnic table in the shade. 'You want to sit down? Get out of the sun?'

'Yeah, I think so.' Tommy lumbered over, straddled one of the picnic benches and plopped down with a sigh.

Darren sat on the other side, turned sideways to keep one eye on the car. What the hell was Adam doing in there?

'It was a double-wide, with dark brown siding, nothing odd really, except that it looked darker and dirtier than all the others,' Tommy continued. 'The front windows had newspaper for curtains. I'm telling you I got the worst headache of my life within sixty seconds of sitting outside their trailer. Felt fine all day and minutes before we got there, but sitting there on our bikes, no more than thirty feet from that place, my head felt like someone had pounded a couple of four-inch nails into each temple. The front of the trailer was dark, no lights on, and you think, okay, nobody's home. But he swore they were. Brad just knew it. Said you could always tell 'cause of the headaches, like that was a normal occurrence for visitors.

'"We shouldn't be here," I says to Brad. '"Let's get the hell out. My mom's gonna be pissed."

'"Won't take long," Brad says, "Leave your bike here a minute."

'So we laid the bikes down on the sidewalk, real quiet. Brad goes first, telling me we're going to look in her bedroom window, the sister's. Why can't I remember her damn name? Sabrina? Sadie? It's right there on the tip of my tongue. I asked him what the big deal was, were we gonna see her naked or something?

'"No, it's crazier than that," Brad says, but he's excited like a kid who's just found a stash of nudie books, and I admit I got kind of excited too. Rumors of cult shit, the mean dad, and the creepy mom, all that was there, but I wanted to see her, whether she was naked or not. We had our bikes close by and you remember how it was, we'd spy on people all the time. We knew if they saw us we could get away fast.

'Brad creeps along the side of the trailer, down the little sidewalk, to the back side, and I was a few steps behind him. There was a little chain-link fence about two feet high, made to keep toddlers in the backyard, which was really only a square of dead grass about six feet in either direction. One big cat litter box. That family had all kinds of cats. And Brad finds a milk crate or something along the way, so when we get near the window all the way at the end of one side, he sets that down and steps up, takes a quick look. He was only up there for a few seconds, but he came down and looked at me and he was grinning, but he looked like he was gonna be sick too. "Your turn."

'"Tell me what it is," I says, because maybe I didn't

want to see. But Brad shakes his head, no. "You gotta see for yourself," he whispers. "I can't explain it."

'"Is she in there?"

'He just walked on behind me to wait on the sidewalk. So, I took a deep breath, tiptoed over to the crate, and stepped up to have a peep. I was shorter than Brad so I had to balance on my toes. My fingertips were hanging on the windowsill. At first I couldn't see anything through the window. There was a screen on the outside and it was dark inside, but not too dark, because I could see shapes, like in a bedroom, with a small bed and a dresser on one side. I pressed my nose up to the screen and focused. I didn't see anything else, except then I did, and realized I'd been lookin' at it all along.

'She was on the bed. Laid out stiff as a board. I couldn't see her at first because she was covered in black. Not black clothes or a robe. She was black on her skin, like tattoos all over. Only her face and a few streaks along her belly and legs were white, pale between the black marks. Her dark blonde hair was down, straight and long to her shoulders, and those pretty little rainbow barrettes were gone. She was naked, I realized, but you couldn't see anything because they had drawn these black symbols on just about every inch of her skin. Circles, spirals, upside-down crosses, arrows, and a bunch of wacko stuff I didn't recognize. It was like looking at an Egyptian tomb painting, except on a fourteen-year-old girl. Her eyes were closed. She didn't move. I thought she might have been dead.

Maybe they were preparing her for burial or some damn thing.

'I can't imagine I was able to look at her for more'n ten seconds, but it felt like ten minutes, or longer. Even as weird as the symbols were, I didn't feel scared at first. She looked so peaceful, like she was resting. No expression on her face. Hair down around her shoulders, and as crummy as this might sound, she looked prettier than I'd recalled, probably because she was always scowling or crying over some incident. But right then, she looked real blissed out. So it wasn't so bad, until I saw what was really happening.

'She wasn't lying on the bed. There was no bed. The floor was empty, there was only the dresser on the opposite wall. Adam's sister wasn't lying on the floor, either. It just looked like she was on a bed because she was floating two feet off the floor. Nothing between her back and the carpet but empty space.'

'Come on,' Darren said. 'That's not possible. You must have been mistaken.'

Tommy glared at him. 'I know what I'm talking about, pal. I saw it. That girl was floating, perfectly still and level as a beam, and whatever was holding her up, it was alive, a force, real and dangerous as electricity. I kept looking for ropes or wires or something that could explain it, but there wasn't anything. And here's how I know.

'About two seconds before I stepped down, when I was already imagining myself running away but still too scared to move, two things happened very fast. Wham, the bedroom door flies open, and then the lights flick on. And for a second that girl was bathed in light. There wasn't anything under her, or around her except air. She was floating, hovering, and those black symbols all over body? They were moving, crawlin' over her skin, writhin' like snakes, and I'll take that to my grave. Word of God. Also, there wasn't anything or anybody at the door.'

'What do you mean?' Darren said.

'I mean, the doorway was empty. The hall behind the doorway, empty. No one in the bedroom with her. And soon as that door ripped itself open and the light came on, she fell down. Dropped to the floor like someone had cut the wires. I heard her hit, and she immediately started bawling, crying like something attacked her. She thrashed her arms and kicked out her legs. Her eyes opened, and I could swear she knew I was there, but she didn't look at me. She was wailing and looking around like she didn't know where she was. That's when I just about lost my dirt.

'Jumped down and ran for my life, convinced her parents were gonna come out with a butcher knife and kill me right there. I hurdled that little fence and Brad was already on his bike, pedaling away, because he'd heard her screaming. I grabbed my bike, threw my leg over, and pedaled so hard I slipped the cage and gashed my shin open. Still got the scar.'

Tommy lifted one leg, pulled down his boot, rucked up his pant leg, revealing a long white scar down the front of his shin. To Darren it looked like a fat white worm.

'I had those Lightning pedals, the ones with the jagged teeth, and they tore the hell out of me. Cut right down to the bone. I didn't care. I rode as fast as I could, all the way home. I don't think I slept for three days after that.'

He waited for Tommy to catch his breath. The man really did not look well.

'And it wasn't over,' Tommy said. 'That girl ... she wouldn't leave me alone. Not for weeks and weeks.'

Darren braced himself.

'See, the thing is, that night after I saw, when I got home and it was time to get ready for bed, I was taking off my jeans and ... damned if one of those rainbow barrettes didn't fall out of my pocket, onto my bedroom floor. Never got near her, never set foot in that trailer, but sure enough, there it was, with a couple strands of her dark blonde hair stuck inside the clip. Part of that girl found its way into my pocket, see. They made sure of that. Made sure I took her home.

'I took that barrette straight out to the garage and I was about to throw it in the trash cans when I realized my mom might find it. I didn't want it near me and I didn't want to have to explain it, because I had no idea how to explain it. What I did was, I walked down the driveway to the street, and I followed the sidewalk until I came to the next drain to the sewer. One of those wide cuts in the gutter, under the sidewalk, and I chucked her little barrette in there. I saw it go down and I believe I heard the plop in the water. So that was that.

'The weeks passed. Even when I calmed down

enough to sleep a little, I had terrible nightmares, the most realistic experiences, and I kept waking up in the middle of the night not knowing where I was. Sometimes I dreamed I was back at her place, peeping into the trailer, only this time she'd be covered in blood instead of ink, and when I tried to run away my legs wouldn't work. I'd be concentrating on running as fast as I could but it was like I was stuck in a world made of gelatin, and they'd be coming after me, kicking the door of the trailer open, her dad first, then mom, both of them wearing black hoods with eyeholes cut in them, chasing me with butcher knives. I couldn't eat much, not for weeks. I felt like I was coming down with a nasty flu all the time. I was edgy, looking over my shoulder everywhere I went.

'Then it all tapered off, right before Christmas. Maybe I was finally able to let it go, thanks to Christmas, being all excited for break from school and decorating the tree with Mom, all that. So, Christmas came and went and then we had a week left till school started again. Nate and me was getting kind of stir-crazy in the house. This was back when we still had the place on Poplar, the old house up in Wonderland Hills. We'd built enough snowmen and done enough ice skating out there on Wonderland pond, and we were driving our parents crazy. They had a New Year's Eve party to go to, and even though I was only twelve, Nate would have been eight or nine, they had no problem leaving us home to ourselves for the night.

'We watched some movies, ate popcorn, and stayed

up to watch the New Year's ball drop. Nate fell asleep on the couch just after midnight, but I wasn't tired yet, and I guess I didn't want to leave him downstairs by himself in case he woke up and got into some trouble. Mom and Dad were younger then. They might have stayed out until one or two. I switched the TV off and was about to hook up the Atari when I heard footsteps above me, upstairs on the second floor.

'The living room was at the back of the house, the stairway right there at the front entrance. I thought I must not have heard Mom and Dad come in, so without thinking too much about it, I hopped up from the couch and went upstairs to see them and say goodnight. But when I got up there, they weren't in their bedroom, or the bathroom. The hallway was empty. I got a little restless but I wasn't too scared. When you're a kid, sometimes you hear stuff or your mind runs away from you. Maybe I didn't hear footsteps. Maybe I was just expecting Mom and Dad to come home. I decided to go to bed then because I was already upstairs and I was bored. I had some books beside my bed, some *Boy's Life* magazines my ma kept making me read for Scouts, so I thought I'd sit in bed with the lamp on and read myself to sleep.

'In my bedroom, I took off my jeans and shoes, and I was about to hop in the sack when I saw it. Sitting there on my pillow, resting in the middle like a hotel mint. A little rainbow barrette, with three long dark blonde hairs stuck in it. I hope I don't need to tell you I about jumped out of my skin seeing that.

'I had to get rid of it, but I was afraid to touch it. No one had seen me throw it in the sewer, I hadn't seen it since, but here it was, back in my possession. I looked around my room, thinking maybe she got in here, but how would she have known where I lived? Maybe she'd followed me, broken into the house, but I guess I knew then the truth was something simpler and far worse than that. She'd sent it back to me another way, same way she'd slipped it in my pocket the first time. She was cursing me or something, and that barrette was like the key. Didn't matter if there were miles between our houses, or walls. She wanted it there, so she put it there.

'I was too scared to go outside in the cold and the dark, so what I did was, I opened my bedroom window up there on the second floor, and I flung it out across the backyard, aiming for the neighbor's fence. Tomorrow I could see if it was in the yard and if so, I'd smash it, burn it, flush it down the toilet or something. But right then I just had to get it out of the house.

'Feeling a little better, I hopped in the sack. I don't remember what I ended up trying to read, but I was only at it for maybe ten or fifteen minutes, unable to concentrate on anything, and then it started. I heard her whispering to me. The girl. I hadn't thought of her in at least a week or two, well before Christmas, but now all the sudden I could hear her voice.

'"*Tommy Berkley*," she said, whispering. "*Toooooommmmyyyy.*" Like she was teasing me, being playful. Her voice was clear and soft, but I couldn't tell where it was coming from. I figured it was just my imagination again. I tried to ignore it.

'"Were you spying on *me*?" she said, even softer now. "Were you watching me through the window, Tommy Berkley? Did you like what you saw? Don't you think my barrettes are pretty? I wanted you to have it so you could remember me."'

'I sat up in bed, my skin all goosed out. It sounded like she was in the room with me, right there in my bedroom, but I couldn't see her anywhere. She sounded so close, I thought maybe she was hiding under my bed. I remembered the footsteps and I couldn't help thinking maybe she had snuck over and slipped her way inside while Nate and me was downstairs watching the ball drop.

'I didn't want to look, but I had to know. I couldn't stand the thought of her lying there under my bed. What if she started making me levitate? What if she tried to possess me? All I could think of was that stuff we'd seen in all the movies, like *Amityville Horror* and *The Exorcist*, except this was worse because she was real, a real girl we went to school with, and I'd really seen something I knew wasn't normal. Now what if she was in my house? Under my bed?

'I counted to three and then fast as I could I leaned over and looked beneath it. My lamp was still on, right there on my nightstand, so I could see plenty good. And she wasn't there, of course. Nothing under the bed except a couple of lost socks, an old baseball, and a bunch of dust.

'"If you want to see me again," she says in the same playful voice, "you have to open the door, Tommy. Come in here and let's look at each other. Fair's fair. You got to see me but I didn't get to see you."

'So then I knew. She was in the closet. My bedroom closet, just about ten feet away, across from the foot of my bed. But by then I was sort of tired of all these nightmares and thinking about her, and I wanted to prove to myself this was all a bunch of bullcrap. You know, twelve years old is old enough to know the difference between real and make-believe. I was determined to prove her wrong, straighten myself out.

'I got out of bed and marched straight over to my closet door. I hesitated for a second or two but not much longer. I opened it. There were my clothes, my shoes, some toys piled in the corner, stuff I never played with anymore. That's all I saw. Until I looked down at the floor, right in front of my feet, and there it was again, sitting on the carpet. The little rainbow barrette. The same one. With the same three dirty blonde hairs sticking out of it.

'I was scared, and then almost furious. I bent down to pick it up, pinching it between two fingers, and that's when her hand came out. I just saw a pale blur from the left side of the closet, just inside the door, and then her fingers were clutching my wrist. Her fingers were ice-cold. I cried out but she wouldn't let go, and when I looked left, following that arm into the dark, there was Sheila Burkett lying on the floor, staring up at me. Her face so white it was gray, gray like a dead person's skin, and her eyes were wide open, black inside. She was on her back, naked from the waist up, which is all I could see. Her mouth was open wide. Her little hands was still clutching my wrist but nothing moved, she wasn't moving, and her other hand was curled into a claw at her throat as if she was trying to pull away a rope that was strangling her. But there wasn't any rope. Her lips were chapped white, they looked like dried clay. She didn't make a sound, and I knew she was dead, that's why she'd been haunting me all this time. She'd been in my closet for weeks. Dead, whispering to me from the other side.

'I started screaming and pulling away but her fingers were frozen around me. I screamed and pulled until I slipped free and fell back on my ass, and then I got the hell outta there. I ran downstairs screaming my head off, and ran right into my old man as he was coming through the front door, snow on his coat, skunked to high hell. Mom too. They both drank in those days. I collapsed between them, raving like a madman. I didn't want them to know anything about Sheila, I was afraid they'd find out I spied on her, and in that state, I probably would have confessed everything once they started asking. I just said there was a dead girl in my closet. My mom stayed with me while my dad went up to have a look.'

Tommy paused again, catching his breath and blinking himself back to the here and now. Darren waited for him to finish, but he already knew the rest.

'My pop didn't see any girl in my closet,' Tommy

said, embarrassed, as if he had forgotten he was an adult and was still foolish for believing what he'd seen. 'But I wouldn't sleep in there for a month. I never saw the barrette again, not in the room or in the yard or anywhere else. I slept on the couch, or sometimes on the floor of Nate's room. What a sucker. Big brother sleeping on his baby brother's bedroom floor. Well, whatever I shouldn't a done to her, I guess she showed me.'

Darren waited a minute before speaking, but that seemed to be the end of it. 'Sounds like she really got to you, Tommy. I'm glad I never peeped in her window.'

Tommy scowled at him. 'Lucky you.'

If you only knew, Darren wanted to say. He was thinking of objects, the need to possess, the power of holding on to things. Rainbow barrettes and knives and magazines and a certain red bicycle.

28

Tommy looked spent, irritated. Darren understood that his old friend was ready for him to leave, but he had to know the last piece.

'What happened after we trashed his bike? He missed some school, if I remember. Sort of disappeared. My memory tells me his father beat his ass for letting his bike get ruined, being bullied by us. Is that right?'

'The bike wasn't the end of it, no,' Tommy said. 'Adam was in and out of school for the next year. He told everybody who'd listen he was saving for a new bike. That would have been his fifth-grade year, sixth for you and me and Ryan.'

'But somehow he never got the bike,' Darren said. 'Do you know why?'

Tommy shook his head. 'I don't know nothing about the bike. What I do know is, the last day of school was always a half-day, which is how I remember when this happened. That was the day the Burkett trailer burned to the ground. His parents and his sister were inside. They burned to death. The firemen and police or whoever, they found the bodies. Three of them. Not four.'

'Not Adam,' Darren said.

'Adam disappeared. They never found his body, dead or alive. He didn't come back to school the following fall. Police searched everywhere for him, but as far as I know, they never did find Adam Burkett. He just disappeared.'

Darren looked Tommy in the eyes. 'You're telling me Adam did it. Adam set the fire. Burned his own house down. Killed his whole family.'

'I probably would have too, the way that kid suffered,' Tommy said. 'You really don't remember any of this? It was big news in school.'

Deep black smoke of burning wood and charred insulation coiling inside his nostrils. His eyes opened to a stinging furnace of orange, red and black phantoms feeding their way toward him. Streams of tears immediately blurred his vision and wet his cheeks. The skin of his arms and neck were coated in a veneer of hot panic sweat. He thrashed in bed, tangled as if his limbs were in the grip of invisible forces who wanted him to surrender to the billowing layer of dusty ceiling smoke and the flames licking up his bedroom walls.

He tried to scream but his throat was dry, rough, constricted. His lungs heaved and ached for fresh oxygen. A lattice of fire snaked across the floor, igniting the bedding, and flash-fried his hair to oily ash in seconds. His skin blistered and bled in rivers, but still he could not scream.

My nightmares, Darren realized, feeling invaded. Those weren't just nightmares. They were Adam's life, visions, the way he showed me what happened at Palo Park. The kid's been infecting me with his lost memories, his trauma. I'm remembering what he can't. The more I remember, the more real he becomes.

'Something wrong?' Tommy said.

Darren removed his sunglasses to wipe the sting from his eyes. He shook his head, trying to focus. Tommy was staring at him like he wished Darren had never come to the farm. He couldn't stand this one moment longer.

'Tommy, I have to show you something. In my car.'

Tommy shifted in his seat. 'What would that be?'

'I met him. He's here. I don't know what happened to him back then, but he found me a few days ago. Maybe longer.'

'Who? What are you talking about?'

'Adam's real. Come on. I'll show you.' He stood and headed off toward the car.

Tommy stood but did not follow. 'Hey. What is this?'

'You remember what he looked like,' Darren said. 'I want you to see this . . .' he almost said 'kid' but stopped himself. He wanted Tommy to see the boy before deciding Darren was flat-out nuts. 'Come on, it will just take a minute.'

'Is this supposed to be funny?'

'No, it's not. Just trust me on this, would you?'

Reluctantly, Tommy followed him to the car. 'I got work to do, Lynwood. Whatever you're up to, make it quick.'

They rounded the small barn. At once Darren could see that Adam was not in the front seat. He leaned into the open driver's side window. Adam was not in the back seat, either. Alarmed, he withdrew from the car and scanned the front yard, the weeds behind the barn.

Tommy waited a few paces back. 'So?'

'He was here,' Darren said. 'Waiting in the car.'

Tommy said nothing.

'He came to see me, Tommy. That's why I needed to talk to you. You don't understand. This kid, he knows things only Adam could know.'

'Whose kid?'

'No one's. It's Adam.'

'Adam would be our age,' Tommy said. 'If he's even alive.'

Darren nodded distractedly. 'He must have gotten out. I told him to wait in the car. Did you see him? Maybe he's screwing around in the barn.'

'You aren't making one bit of sense,' Tommy said.

Darren trotted to the front of the barn and began to pry at one of the large wooden doors. It was heavy, the hinges rusted. The planks were dry, splintery. Darren heaved the door, jerking it outward, and one of the boards cracked.

Tommy stomped over and took him by the arm. 'There's nobody in my barn, you flake. Knock it off.'

Darren ignored the larger man and wedged his body between the doors. 'Adam! Are you in here? Adam, god-damnit! I told you to wait in the car!'

The kid did not respond.

Tommy seized the back of Darren's shirt and yanked him from the barn.

Darren staggered back, nearly falling as Tommy

released him. He was out of breath. 'I'm telling you, he was here. He's real, Tommy. I don't know how, but I'm not lying to you. Why would I?'

'I think it's time for you to leave,' Tommy said.

'Just wait—'

'Now. I want you off my property, Lynwood. There's something wrong with you. Always was. And I don't like it. Now, go.'

Darren struggled for the words, something that would help Tommy understand. And he couldn't leave Adam here, could he? Not now, not after what he had learned.

Tommy came at him, one fist raised. 'I said—'

Darren backed off, hands up in surrender. 'Okay, okay. I'm going. I'm sorry, Tommy. I didn't plan any of this.'

He opened the Firebird's door. Adam's backpack was on the front seat. See, he wanted to cry, there's his backpack! And everything in it is from 1982, just like him. But he'd lost Tommy, that much was clear. He wouldn't believe anything Darren said now.

He got in and started the car. 'Tommy, listen. If you see a kid out here, you might want to stay away from him. Call the police.'

'Asshole, in ten seconds I'm going to call the police on you.'

Darren waved him off. 'Fine. Good. I tried to warn you. You deal with it.'

Tommy was still watching as he backed the Firebird into the turnaround and spun a cloud of straw dust into the dry summer air.

29

Sheila walked the pastures, in the fields and across the country roads. The sun was going past four o'clock now and she was sweating, her skin running with clean fury. The time was coming, and she could feel her body preparing itself, cleansing itself of mercy, her senses opening to the call. She walked over barbed-wire fences, down through drainage ditches, stepping on soft rows of tilled soil sprouting baby crops, waiting for the signal.

For two days the family had done little more than eat, sleep, practice their invocations, and try not to squander their emanations. They kindled reserves of spite and prayed to their victims, remembering the dead. Sheila slept little, her brief dreams populated with the faceless pigs she had ceremonied and sapped.

The parents were recovering quickly, now that their threesome had been reunited. Physically they were a wreck, but their faculties quickened, confusion giving way to clarity, purpose, unity in their hatred. Sheila made several trips back into town to fetch other medicines for them – Ibuprofen for their aches and pains, ginger and ginkgo for vigor and alertness, sage and lavender to burn in the room and awaken their channels. She also brought meals high in clean protein, rich in amino acids and iron: salmon, broccoli, farm-fresh eggs, cottage cheese, brown rice, haddock, kale, chard. She hand-fed them until their appetites had been primed but not sated. On the second day they were able to bathe themselves, and she rewarded them with better sets of clothing and another round of massages. They slept sixteen of every twenty-four hours.

She had been a good soldier, and a smart one, ditching the Ford and its befouled camper in a grove of trees in the middle of public land, fifteen miles east. She did not bother wiping the interior for prints, at least not beyond the steering wheel and cabin surfaces she herself had touched. Torturing that young district attorney two decades ago had ensured there were no public records of her family; besides, Miriam and Ethan literally had no fingerprints, only scars. It was a relief to be rid of their disgusting living quarters, their pathetic and rancid mobile home. It had only reminded her of childhood, the stink of the trailer, life in the mobile-home park, where every loser, twat and pig was up in each other's business.

She had walked the fifteen miles back to town her-self, to a used car lot in need of some easy cash. After twenty minutes of frustrating banter with the salesman, she negotiated for an inconspicuous and sad but serv-iceable little Toyota Tercel, melon-green with gray cloth interior. It would not be much help in a getaway or a hostage situation, but it ran smoothly and it was all she could afford. The car cost eleven hundred, leaving her just under four hundred. Miriam and Ethan had not carried money for over a decade, siphoning gas and stealing food to sustain the vermin existence, living on trash like trash.

Once they had the boy, their fortunes would turn around.

Sheila took walks, usually close to midnight and just before dawn, but sometimes in the middle of the day, clearing her mind of conflict and misgivings and resentment toward her parents. Strolling around the town, and outside the community, down the long country roads and in the fields, she felt her primal instincts returning with renewed ferocity.

She practiced The Crawling near two of the farmhouses, keeping to her belly and channeling the serpent for silence, as she had been taught. The first house had been empty and she spent nearly an hour inside, scenting the rooms until she had developed a picture of their lives, the useless toil and numb misery.

The second house, she arrived at sunrise and the family was just beginning their morning rituals. She got as close as the front screened-in porch, where she perched on a bench seat and kept still as Mom brewed coffee, Dad watched the weather report on TV while shaving with an electric razor, and eventually a little girl, six or eight years old, a freckled Irish lass Ethan would have drowned had Miriam birthed it to him, came out in her pajamas to bundle up on the sofa, snuggling with the family Labrador.

The door from the porch to the kitchen and dining area was unlocked and Sheila knew she could Crawl past them with ease, finding a safe zone to hide until one of them separated from the unit. She had brought along the straight-edge and six feet of cord, and twice she was tempted to use them, the fevered itch for murder unbearable. Instead, she tamped the black down inside herself, savoring it, letting it coil and build. She needed to store up as much animosity as was possible in such a short time. The couple she mercifully excused after Dillinger's had added precious fuel to the cause, but she needed more.

Sheila walked on, saving her wrath for her brother, The One Who Got Away. They did not speak of him; they needn't. But she could feel the anticipation gathering between them, even miles away on her walks, and like Miriam and Ethan, she hoped that he had retained his own talents after all these years. If they could bring him home for a proper ceremony, they would reap great improvements in their own abilities. Adam had always been the strongest, both in his latent abilities, like The Reading and the Touching, and in his will not to use them. Sheila knew that's why he had run away, and that was why she had grown to hate him. He thought he was superior to them, but he would discover his true purpose soon enough.

She meditated a great deal on his parting gift to them – burning their home to the ground. Sheila had always wondered if he had intended to kill them, or if in his fury he had simply lost control. Perhaps he had wanted only to take away their shelter, scatter them from sanctuary. He had been only a child, after all, and one who had abhorred violence as much as Sheila and Mother and Father craved it. Hard to imagine him torching the place with murder in his heart.

She had always wondered if he knew of their escape, her awakening just before the flames reached her in the closet and her heroic rescue of Miriam and Ethan. What had he been doing in those first few days during the aftermath, while she had been busy nursing the third-degree burns at their parents' bedside in the camper? Had he followed the newspaper accounts? If so, what had he made of the reports? The bone-charred remains of two adults and one adolescent female discovered in the wreckage. He would have been convinced his family was gone by his own hand, as had the police and firemen and other investigators.

He would have had no way of guessing that Sheila, age fourteen, had been forced to return to the burn site and exhume the other three half-consumed bodies beneath the trailer's foundation stilts. It was a kind of miracle, a stroke of dark Fate working in their favor, the family's full sextet of victims had not been discovered on the first day. Otherwise the police would have been forced to conclude something beyond a small family perishing in an accidental fire had been at work in that rathole trailer park.

Sheila didn't think her young brother had ever come to terms with, or ever admitted to himself, what Mother and Father had been up to on those late nights, coming home with large, carpet-wrapped parcels. Digging into the back end of the trailer, storing the homeless ones and that couple and the two teen runaways where they belonged, in their new home, where in death they would continue to feed the Family's darkly blooming auras as surely as they fed the worms below.

But he must have suspected something, felt the black mass gathering that spring as their business escalated. Maybe that's what drove him away. The ticking of his internal clock as it counted down to the final choice, join the cause or defy them and die.

Many times, when he was too young to understand the Family's true purpose, he had come to Sheila for guidance, for protection and solidarity, none of which she could provide. The way he used to whine about being tied up in the shed for two or three days at a time. The way he refused to help them pick the winning numbers out at the dog track. Or that time he refused to help them deal with the homeless couple they brought home for Thanksgiving one year. Always such a baby.

Sheila had always teased him along, sometimes walking him to the park at night and then ditching him to walk home alone, or taking him to the shed to show him her blossoming womanhood, but what she really missed was torturing him. Binding his wrists and ankles while he slept, prodding him awake with pencils or a kitchen fork, covering his mouth with a wet rag and pinching his nose until he screamed from his ears. And the symbols, of course. Maybe, when she caught him, she would spend a few days inscribing him in symbols and removing his fingernails with pliers, just for old times' sake.

I wish I was the one, Sheila thought, walking as the moon guided her across another cow pasture. *I should have been the one to burn the house down*. Because wasn't it true that, in trying to kill them or at least send them packing, Adam had also earned their ... well, not respect, but their esteem. Awe, maybe. That he would dare to take it all away, what little they had, and cast himself out into the world, left to fend for himself. Whatever it had done to them, it also changed their estimation of him.

I hate him, I hate him, hate his shit-lined guts.

But if he was back, mightn't that mean he had run out of luck? Perhaps he needed them now as much as they needed him.

Did he have murder in his heart that afternoon? Had he really been capable of burning them all?

Was he now?

But it didn't matter much, she supposed. What was done was done. No matter what he had intended to inflict, he had hurt them. In many ways sentencing them to a fate worse than death, for in his disappearance after the cleansing fire, he had condemned them to walk the earth as freaks, their private scars made visible, the Family business worn like a mask that could never be removed. At least it was so for Mother and Father. Sheila had been lucky in matters of physical presentation, only because she had felt the approaching heat of his anger as well as the flames, waking from her sleep ritual even as the smoke filled the trailer. Even so, she almost left them to burn. Maybe she should have.

Miriam and Ethan had blamed her anyway, furious she had not come for them sooner. Without the boy around to blame, they punished her instead. They let her tag along through puberty, for the obvious reasons, but as soon as she developed a will of her own and reached eighteen, demanding rights, a fair share of the food and drugs, they cut her loose. From nineteen till now she had been forced to become her own woman. Sometimes she felt she should thank them for that. Other times she wanted to gas them.

All of this speculation and nostalgia was a fine way to pass the night hours, walking, waiting, but she needed to focus on the task ahead. The big question.

Would the three of them be strong enough to see it through?

To fight Adam when he resisted?

To harness his goods?

Sheila was ready, but Miriam and Ethan were weak. They weren't emanating much of anything yet, and this concerned her. How much help would they really be able to provide, when the moment of truth arrived? It was a miracle they had been able to drive in from Wyoming, stalking Adam around Boulder for nearly a week before getting close enough to kill. That was a source of hope, that they had been able to kill at all. It proved Adam had been close, and they to him, for how else would they have found the strength to sap the

Kavanaugh family? Not without Adam's help, that was for sure. And yet the ceremonies had depleted them severely.

They could also be bluffing, faking their arthritic movements. What if they wanted him for themselves? When it was all over, they might turn on her, trap her in a ceremony, sap her once and for all.

Of course, she could do the same to them. Use them until they had fed on Adam, then get rid of them so that she could spend all they reaped from him across the rest of her days, alone, in peace, without having to care for them like the couple of geriatric chimpanzees they were. Not much loss there. Regardless of what they were able to take from Adam, Miriam and Ethan were not going to enjoy any sort of golden retirement.

Yes, that was the plan, then. Sheila would have to treat whatever came next as though she were a team of one. Miriam and Ethan might help with scouting, playing lookout, or driving short distances. Beyond that, they were simply batteries to her, fuel cells to her psychic flashlight. Until they had Adam in their custody, the parents would be, essentially, useless. She would keep them in the game until Adam had been ceremonied, then put them out of their misery.

I'm not afraid of him, Sheila told herself. He was always stronger, but I've had more practice in the real world. He has a soft heart. I have the instincts and morals of a lioness. I have nothing to lose.

She was in the middle of a cornfield, two or three miles from the motel, when the signal found her:

>>>>>>>>>>>>!!!!!!!!!!!!!!!!!!!!!!!!!!<<<<<<<<<<<<

There were no words, only color, emotion. The exclamatory yellow energy, a hazard warning. Meaning now: alert, wake up, beware.

And then simply:

♄

The astronomical symbol for Saturn, which had been one of their codes for him, the baby of the family, the wonder boy. God's little sickle, Miriam used to say, and one day he will cut a wide path, reaping riches for the family. The first night she brought him home from the hospital, Miriam had drawn it on his forehead in her rarest unguent of eucalyptus ash, three generations of family blood, and albino goat horn marrow.

Sheila knew this had not been sent intentionally. It had not come from the parents. It was the blip of a beacon at sea, a warning light produced by her own keen senses. Immediately she turned back toward the road and broke into a run. To wake Mother and Father. If they hadn't recuperated enough to take him tonight, she would find him on her own.

Sheila could almost taste his spit.

30

On the way home from Cherry Creek, Beth and the kids stopped at Safeway to pick something for dinner. The wagon's cargo bay was loaded with shopping bags containing the goods Beth had allowed Raya to splurge on: summer clothes, sandals, two new swimsuits, a watch, hair product. Beth had bought herself a summer dress and a new pair of Dansko clogs. At the Sunglass Hut, Raya somehow had managed to make Beth feel bad for Chad and she bought him a new pair of Ray-Bans. She knew the shopping was a distraction, one she needed as much as the children, probably more so, but she regretted it. She was guilty of avoidance. Hadn't stopped worrying about Darren. Now she only wanted to find something to throw on the grill, then get home to make sure he was okay.

Entering the store, she tried his cell again, for the third time today. Chad looked wrung out from being dragged from one store to another by his girlfriend, and he and Raya split off to buy a round of frozen Frappuccinos at the built-in Starbucks.

'You want something, Mom?'

'A bottle of water,' Beth said, automatically reaching for her wallet.

'My treat,' Raya said. 'We'll find you.'

Beth took a cart from the bay and wandered into the produce section as Darren's phone rang. And rang. And rang. Where the hell was he? Why wasn't he picking up? It wasn't like him to avoid her calls. Even when he did not answer right away, he usually called her back within half an hour.

Something was wrong. Well, yes. She had found her husband on the shop's floor this morning, shuddering in a pair of pee-stained pants. No kidding something was wrong. But something else had happened while they had been out shopping. Something worse. She could feel it. She didn't bother leaving another voicemail.

Well, they were only ten minutes from home. Somebody had to make dinner.

Beth hurried, picking out a head of lettuce, fresh garlic, tomatoes, a bottle of balsamic, then moved on to the bread aisle. She would make sweet sausage and white bean salad, something easy. They would sit down like a family tonight, at the table on the back patio, and after Raya and Chad went off to do whatever they had planned, something about an end-of-school party, she would have another talk with Darren, without the rancor. She would keep a close eye on him tonight, especially after bedtime.

In the meat department, she found the sweet sausage and threw two packs into the basket. Ten sausages, too much food, but then again if Chad was staying, the kid would probably eat three himself. What else did she need?

'Bethany?' a woman said.

Beth turned in a circle, disoriented, unable to detect the source. The store was always crowded, especially at dinnertime.

'Here, honey, right behind you.' A gentle tugging at her blouse.

Beth spun once more and found Rachel Needham standing within kissing distance. 'Oh God, I didn't even see you there. Rachel, how are you?'

Rachel was a tiny little woman with dynamite in her blood, and she was a hugger. If she had gone to school with you or knew you even peripherally from work, friends of friends, or any other source, she gave you a hug and acted as though you were long-lost sisters in the cause. Beth fell somewhere in the middle, being an old friend but not a close one, and only through a string of school connections that went from the University of Colorado to Chicago and back to Boulder. Beth returned the hug and put on a smile.

'Hey, girl, so good to see you,' Rachel said. 'You were supposed to call me. When are we going to get that lunch?'

They had run into each other at a Christmas party six months ago and vowed to meet soon. 'I know, I'm sorry,' Beth said. 'Spring was a blur. We've been so focused on school you'd think we're the ones in tenth grade.'

'Tell me about it,' Rachel said. 'Caleb just finished

sixth and now we get to spend the summer playing chauffeur. How's Raya doing?'

Beth reminded herself not to brag, failed anyway. 'Perfect grades again, yay. Volunteered for SAT prep courses. Testing the water with a boy, one who's going to be a senior next year. We've been lucky so far.'

Rachel dipped her handcart in a curtsy. 'Woo-woo. Good for her. How's work? I saw the piece in the *Camera* a few weeks ago. How did that go over?'

'Great. We met our target for the campaign and I finally convinced Darren to let go of some of his bikes.'

'I'm sorry I couldn't be there. Work has been just – I should be in a neck brace.'

'I want to hear about it. Let's get that drink. Or lunch.'

'Lunch drinks. Yes,' Rachel said, smiling broadly.

'I'll call you, promise.'

Rachel did not appear ready to say goodbye. She lingered, her smile shrinking as she glanced around the store. 'Is it just you?'

'Hm?'

'In the store? Now? Is Darren with you?'

'Raya and her little friend are getting coffee up front. What's up?' Beth tensed, bracing herself for a confession, gossip, something she did not want to hear right now.

'How is Darren, by the way?' Rachel said.

'Good, same as always,' Beth lied. Why was Rachel asking this with an expression of pity on her face?

'Yeah? That's good. I was just, it's probably nothing, but if you ever want to talk.'

'I'm sorry,' Beth said. 'Is something wrong? I feel like I missed something.'

'Maybe it's none of my business,' Rachel said, switching her handcart to her other hip as shoppers swerved around them.

'Okay, now I have to know. What? Tell me what's wrong.'

Rachel moved a little closer, lowering her voice. 'I don't know, exactly. I debated even mentioning it, but I was going to call you the other day. When I saw him.'

'Saw Darren?'

'Yeah.'

Oh, boy. This is something, Beth realized. Another thing. 'Okay. Where was this?'

'Here,' Rachel nodded. 'In the store.'

'And?'

Just then, Raya and Chad approached from the frozen foods aisle to join them. Raya had a frozen coffee the size of a building in one hand, Beth's bottle of water in the other. Chad was sipping from a small cup with a tea string dangling over the lip.

Rachel saw them, cleared her throat. 'You know what? Let's catch up later.'

Beth turned to her in a daze. 'You can tell me,' she said. 'Right?'

Rachel's eyes darted to the kids and back. 'Call me. Anytime. I'm sure it was nothing. It just made me think of you.'

Beth opened her mouth to demand the woman explain what she had seen her husband doing, but

Rachel turned her mega-smile on the kids, cutting her off.

'Hey, Raya, how are you?'

'Hi,' Raya said, and Beth knew she did not remember who this was.

'Congratulations on finishing number ten.' Rachel slipped around Beth to make her exit. 'Bye, honey.'

'I will, definitely,' Beth stammered. *Call you tonight*, she meant to say. Right after she confronted her husband and asked what the hell all that had been about.

She sent Raya and Chad to get the northern white beans, then tried to find Rachel before she left the store. She spotted her in the checkout line, but there were too many people clogging the lane. Beth used her cellphone to call Darren again. He did not answer. She tried the home number, which none of them used. He didn't answer that one, either.

'Why are you speeding?' Raya asked her on the way home.

'I don't know,' Beth told her. 'I guess I'm hungry.'

When she pulled into the driveway, the Acura was in the garage and the Firebird was gone. Beth parked and the kids began unloading the shopping bags. The day of the police visit, Beth hadn't wanted to scare Raya with a story about her father hitting a boy, the boy from their collective nightmares and other unexplained episodes, so she had told the kids that Dad had been driving down Kalmia when someone threw a rock at the car. She knew the girl had not believed her, but Raya had sensed something else was going on and now was not the time to pry into it.

Seeing the Acura's windshield in the garage, her father's other car missing, prompted a new round of concern.

'Did you talk to him?' Raya said. 'Mom? Hello?'

'Not yet.'

Inside, she tried him again, the kids watching her with not-so-subtle interest. No answer. She thought about calling the hospital, but that seemed like the next step. Irrationally, she felt that if she took *the next step*, then it would come true. He would be in the hospital, injured, maybe dead.

'Mom?' Raya prompted. 'Where is he?'

'He'll be home soon,' Beth said. 'You two go put away your things while I get started on dinner.'

Her instincts, which were really hope and a prayer, turned out to be true. He came home not an hour later, uninjured and in no need of medical attention.

That part happened after bedtime, when Beth finally got to meet Adam.

31

Darren came home just before the sun went down. He had been driving around Erie, foolishly looking for the kid he knew he would not find again until the kid wanted to be found. He knew Beth would be angry that he hadn't returned her calls all afternoon, and when he stepped inside and saw them – Beth, Raya and the ever-present Chad – all staring at him from the dinner table as if he had been missing for weeks, not a few hours, he knew he was in trouble. Not in the sense that his wife was upset. More like he needed serious help.

'Where in God's name have you been?' Beth said.

He made himself a plate of grilled sweet sausage, beans, salad and bread, then took a cold can of Upslope brown ale from the fridge and sat at the head of the table.

'I'm sorry I worried you.'

Raya stared at him with sympathy. Chad politely focused on his food.

Beth was still scowling. 'Do you know I almost called the hospital looking for you?'

Darren threw back a third of the beer and swallowed. He felt drunk almost immediately, realizing that, once again, he hadn't eaten all day.

'Adam came back today. He was sleeping in the shop's attic.'

They all waited for the punchline.

Darren swallowed a forkful of garlic-laced beans. 'We decided to look up Tommy Berkley, a kid we used to ride with.' He splashed more balsamic on his sausage. 'He lives out in Erie, so we paid him a visit. I learned a bunch more bad stuff about his childhood. Then, when I got back to the car, Adam was gone.'

Darren took another swig of beer and looked to each of them. 'He's not here, is he? No, I guess he wouldn't have made it back here yet. Unless he steals a car. But I'm sure he'll turn up again soon. He won't let this go until it's over.'

No one spoke for a moment.

Finally Raya said, 'He's real? The boy Gremme knows?'

'Raya—' Beth began.

'Oh, he's real, honey,' Darren said. 'He's ten, maybe eleven years old. Same as when I knew him from elementary school. I hit him with the car a few days ago. That's the story with the windshield. The reason the police were here. But they can't find him either. His family were part of a cult, like Satan worshippers, or maybe just mean white trash. They used to do things to his sister—'

'All right,' Beth snapped. 'Enough. Raya, Chad, will

you excuse us for a while? Please. Take your dinner into your room.'

'It's okay,' Darren said. 'I'm not hiding anything. They should hear this.'

'You be quiet,' Beth told him. She turned to Raya. 'Honey? Chad? Would you?'

They got up. Raya looked to Chad. 'Are we still going to that party?'

'Up to you,' Chad answered.

Raya looked to her mom. 'Maybe we'll just step out for a couple hours.'

'Be safe,' Darren said. 'No drinking and driving.'

Beth waved them away. 'Fine, yes, go. But you better answer your phone when I call you.'

'I will,' Raya said. They carried their plates to the kitchen. Chad took an extra sausage and ate it with his fingers as they found their jackets and headed for the door.

Darren drained the rest of his beer.

When they had gone, Beth pushed her plate away and stared at him. 'What is this? Explain it to me. Everything. Don't tell me about nightmares and dreams and visions. Tell me what the hell is going on, right now, or so help me God, I will throw you into the Atrium with your mother.'

'Outside,' he said. 'So I can keep an eye on the shop.'

They sat on the back patio and had another beer together while he told her about visiting Tommy, and the story of Adam's childhood as Tommy had relayed it. The sister. The abuse. The fire that echoed in his dreams.

'I am being sucked in, haunted, invaded somehow,' he said to her with a straight face. 'By Adam Burkett, this kid who never grew up. He's not finished, Beth, I'm sure of it. He will be back.'

Beth did not argue or interrupt, and he knew she was humoring him in some way, waiting for him to get it all out before she passed her judgment. She asked no questions, at least not until he finished.

'What does he want? What is the end of this? Darren, can you tell me that?'

'He wants me to find out who killed him. Or what severed his life and memories. Maybe that's the same thing as death. Maybe he never died. Maybe this kid is someone else and Adam got inside him. I don't know how or why, Beth, but if we don't find out who kept him from that bike and whatever happened on that last day of school, why he set the fire, what he did after that, he will continue to cause problems for us. Us and others. I know that. I feel that.'

Beth set her beer down. He had been talking for over an hour and she looked as exhausted as he felt. 'I see. So, what's the plan? What are you going to do? Look up more old friends on Facebook? Build another bike?'

'I don't know,' Darren said. 'I can't do anything more tonight. I'm spent.'

'I'm sure you are,' she said. 'But since you don't have a plan, I'm going to share one of my own. I hope you're good with it, because there really isn't another choice.'

'Fire away,' he said.

'We're going to sleep now, because we're both drunk.'

336

'Okay.'

'And when we wake up, first thing in the morning, and I do mean the very first thing, before we brush our teeth, we are going to call Officer Sewell back and tell him everything we left out the first time, along with everything else you've learned since. You will tell them everything you just told me, and then they will do their jobs. If you refuse, if you hold anything back from me or them—'

'I agree,' he said. 'I'm not arguing.'

She pressed him with her eyes.

'I mean it,' he said. 'We have an obligation at this point. We need help.'

'Thank you for admitting that,' Beth said.

Darren began to rise.

'One more thing,' she said.

'Yep?'

'What happened at Safeway?'

'Come again?'

'What did you do at the grocery store a few days ago? I ran into Rachel Needham today, in the same store. She was trying to tell me but she didn't get to it before Raya and Chad showed up. Obviously it was something sensitive and not good. She asked how you were doing, the way someone asks about a sick relative. Can you tell me what she was referring to?'

Darren rocked back on his heels, shook his head.

Beth picked up their plates. 'You don't know what she's talking about?'

'No idea,' he said. 'I would tell you.'

'Do you swear?'

'Beth, I just told you everything. What else is there?'

'I don't know, but she seemed to think it was something. You didn't see her?'

'When was this?'

'A few days ago, I think. Recently.'

Darren thought about it, but no, he was sure. 'I haven't seen Rachel since we saw her together at the Christmas party last year. She didn't say what it was?'

'I'm going to call her.' Beth looked at her watch. 'Now, in fact. I can't go to bed with this hanging over us.'

Darren didn't like the thought of anyone in their social circle getting involved in their private affairs. But he knew there was no way around it. He had scared his wife enough tonight. She deserved to handle things as she saw fit.

He yawned. 'I'm going to hop in the shower. Then bed. Let me know what she says.'

'Oh, I will.'

He leaned to kiss her as she passed, but she ducked out of the way and gave him a sour look. He watched her put away the dishes for a moment, then did as he was told.

Beth found Rachel's number in her paper address book, made sure Darren was in the shower, then took her cellphone out onto the patio. Rachel didn't answer, so Beth left a voicemail.

'Rachel, hi, it's Beth. I'm sorry we were interrupted.

I'd like to continue our conversation from earlier today. Please call me back anytime. I'll be up. Thanks.'

It was only a little after nine. Beth decided to wait up for at least an hour. She went back inside, filled a glass with wine, snuck a cigarette from the stale pack she kept in one of the drawers in the bill-paying alcove, plus the lighter. She carried her mini-survivalist kit back out to the patio and took up her vigil, wishing she had brought a jacket. The air was still warm, the breeze gentle, but she couldn't stop shivering. Just as well. She needed to keep awake, alert.

She looked at her phone every few minutes. 'Come on, come on.'

What if he did come back, this boy Adam? What if she saw him? Having heard Darren's outrageous story about it all, how would she react? She didn't want to find out. Have faith, she reminded herself. Somewhere in this mess there is an explanation that makes total sense. And it has nothing to do with reincarnation, ghosts.

She shivered again.

Ten minutes later she went back inside for another cigarette. As she was lighting up, her phone vibrated. Beth recognized the number.

'Rachel?' She tried not to sound desperate, but failed.

'Hi, sweetie,' Rachel said, a cacophony of ambient noise nearly drowning her words. 'Sorry I didn't call you back right away. We're just finishing dinner downtown.'

'No problem,' Beth said. 'If this is a bad time ...'

'Not at all. I didn't want to leave you hanging earlier

today. I just thought you would want to hear it first, without, you know, Raya.'

'Oh God. Do I want to hear this?'

Rachel didn't say anything for a moment. The noise on her end quieted, as if she had stepped outside or gotten into a car. 'I would. If it was my husband. But if you haven't guessed by now, it's probably not what you're thinking.'

Beth inhaled, closed her eyes. 'Please, tell me. This is making me sick.'

Rachel told her what she had seen in the grocery store. It wasn't a long story, or anything Beth had expected. Darren walked out with a bag of food, without paying. It wasn't the worst thing she had ever heard, but she did not know what it meant in the larger scheme of things.

'You're sure it was Darren? Because, honestly, it makes no sense. It had to be an accident.'

'I'm sure.'

'He hasn't been himself lately,' Beth said. 'He's been overstressed about a few things. I'm sure it was a simple mistake.'

'Hm, maybe, but there was something else, too,' Rachel said. 'A different sort of episode. This I got from Jessica Harkins. Do you know her?'

'The name is vaguely familiar,' Beth said. 'She went to CU?'

'Colorado State. But they live here now. Her husband Brian works at a software company in the Valmont Office Park, out there right off 55th. You know the one?'

'I know the area,' Beth said, wondering what the hell this could be about.

'There's a new bike park out there, I guess,' Rachel said. 'Next to the airport. But the office complex is right beside it. Brian said he sees kids out there riding all the time, adults too. Fathers with their sons.'

'Darren was there,' Beth concluded.

'Right.'

'And?'

'Well this is the funny part, or not so funny. I don't know.'

'It's not, but go on. What did Brian Harkins see?'

'Brian went in really early for something, to prepare some project for a morning meeting, so we're talking like 6:30 a.m. Anyway, this was in the parking lot, which was empty, and I guess there's a bunch of trees and grass medians and all the rest, you know how they landscape these things.'

'Yes.' Beth could picture it, like any office park, everything groomed, the parking lot clean pitch black, perfect lane paint, the grass mowed every Friday morning.

'Well, apparently Brian pulls up and there's somebody sleeping in the grass, under a tree. The guy didn't look homeless or anything, so Brian was worried he was hurt. He went over and—'

'It was my husband,' Beth said. 'My husband was sleeping on the lawn in front of an office building. That's what you're telling me?'

'That's what I heard from Jessica, so it's not like one

hundred per cent confirmed. Brian doesn't know Darren except from the paper and the one time they met at the party, so he could have been mistaken. But when she told me, I put it together with the other thing, and it . . . well, it concerned me, and I thought you should know.'

'No, yeah, definitely,' Beth said. She felt as though she had been diagnosed with a tumor. 'I'm glad you did. Tell me. I have to . . . I need to talk with him.'

'Any idea what it might be? Is there anything I can do?'

Beth got up and paced the yard. 'I can't talk about it right now. But this is, oh, I don't know, maybe it's not a total shock. That's all I can say.'

Rachel offered more consolation, sympathy, told her to call anytime.

Beth was thinking about the knife Darren had shown her. The one that came from Adam's backpack. She was thinking about the Kavanaughs. Raya's dead teacher and her dead husband and their dead son Josh.

She was thinking, maybe we won't call the police tomorrow morning. Until we can be sure. What's the next step when you suspect your husband might have turned into a monster?

'Thank you, Rachel. I have to go now.'

Beth disconnected the line. Finished her cigarette and stubbed it out on the patio. Inside, she walked the bridge, to their master bedroom. The shower was off, along with the bedroom lights, though he had left the bathroom light on. It cast a blade of yellow across the foot of their bed, where Darren's bare toes stood upright, making her think of a body in the morgue.

'Darren?' she said softly.

He did not respond.

'Darren, honey? Are you awake?'

He breathed raggedly and rolled onto his side, facing away from her. She shook his leg, but he did not awaken. He was exhausted, she told herself. He had a very long day. Better to let him sleep.

Something he hadn't been doing a whole lot of these days.

32

Tommy Berkley's father's suicide weapon of choice had been J&B Rare scotch, which claimed to be a blend of forty-two whiskies, roughly the number of years old Randall Berkley drank at least three glasses – and sometimes as much as a bottle and half – of the stuff per day. He ordered it by the case, delivered from a wholesaler in Denver, and then would transfer the bottles to a series of wooden crates once used for antique soda pop.

He kept some of these crates in the kitchen, others in the barn, a few in his bedroom closet, one under each bathroom sink, and half a dozen more in the horse stables. He wasn't hiding them, except perhaps from himself, so that when he ran out of one supply, he could almost always count on stumbling into a reserve stash, if he was willing and able to search long enough.

Four days after the funeral, Tommy took an inventory of everything his father owned and noted it in a spiral notebook of the sort he had used in junior high, a three-subject job with manila dividers, college-ruled. He counted everything from socks to cans of oil in the barn to farming equipment to Mason jars of jam in the pantry his mother had canned years ago, and of course the J&B Rare. He searched every room, cupboard, closet, desk drawer, file cabinet, laundry basket and hidey-hole on the property, and while not every bottle was full or sealed, he found more than he had expected, which had been quite a lot.

A hundred and sixteen bottles of J&B Rare, all of them green with the famous yellow and red J&B label that had become as familiar to child Tommy as Tony the Tiger on a box of Frosted Flakes.

Tommy himself had been an alcoholic for many years, and he guessed he still was, even after he met Charlotte and found strength in wife and church. But he didn't crave the stuff like he used to, and went off on a bender only once every two or three years. Even then he stuck to beer, original Budweiser, twenty or thirty cans of it when the occasion called.

The day he rounded up the scotch, he had been grieving, heavy with the burden of taking over the farm, the good old days of shootin' and fishin' and talking about gals with his old man gone for good. He spent over two hours staring at the hundred and sixteen bottles all lined up in the barn, imagining the absolute rocket-fuel burn he could set off inside himself by wading into them non-stop. When the one sixteen were gone, he'd be on the other side of a lot of what he felt now. His lips dripped with want of the brown booze. His belly grumbled. The immediate damage would be offset by other benefits: he'd cut back on all the food and probably end up losing over a hundred pounds within the year. Might save his heart. His wife might want to sex him up again, the way she used to. He'd be closer to his old man one way or another, in spirit or beside him in the graveyard.

In the end he poured the sauce into the dirt, out behind the barn, hoping the stuff would kill off the weeds thickening up back there. He said a prayer for his pop every time another bottle gurgled dry, and then dropped the empties into one of three oil drums where he broke them up with a broomstick. A dozen crates of booze, thousands of dollars worth, enough to make Christmas presents to friends for years to come. He got rid of it all.

Except for one bottle.

One green glass beauty, its red seal unmolested by the sweaty hands of his father's disease.

This last he kept not as a warning against temptation or a test of his willpower, the way a man who has kicked smoking will keep a single butt on his desk for the next twenty years. He kept it as a symbol of his pop's presence, a sort of headstone in the house, or in lieu of ashes. It even looked like an urn, sitting up there on the mantle. Some mornings as Tommy passed it on the way to get his coffee he'd quip, 'Morning, Pop,' or 'How the ladies treating you up there today, you old coot?' and start his day with a smile.

For all that history, not one day had passed since Tommy found the old man – face-down in the third horse stall, blood leaking from his mouth, literally dead drunk – with the mantle of temptation hanging over the son. Tommy never craved a sip of that final bottle, and it had been six years since he'd let himself do a Bud blowout. He had kicked the juice for good.

Until tonight, the night that followed Darren Lynwood's visit to his farm.

After midnight now, and Tommy couldn't sleep. He wasn't used to being alone in the house, no women about. Charlotte was visiting her mom and sister down in Colorado Springs till Sunday. Trisha, Dawn and Renee – the organic farmers who rented the smaller house – were especially quiet tonight. Sometimes one of them would stop by and see if he wanted dinner, invite him over for a bit of dessert. But only one of the two cars they shared was parked in the round, and only one light was on in their place, so he guessed they were out with friends. They stayed in Boulder quite a bit, or up in Nederland. With other lesbians or members of the gay community, he assumed but never asked.

Tommy licked his lips, thirsty again. The tap water tasted flat tonight, too many minerals in the well. He began to sweat, though he wasn't warm.

It had been a hot day, but he was trying to hold off on using the air-conditioning until the real heat patch hit in July. The house should be baking by now, but he felt chilly, maybe coming down with a bug. A couple of hours ago he actually caught himself thinking about putting together a fire, and that was the first time his eyes had darted up to the mantle where the green bottle with its yellow and red label stood centerpiece, throwing off a touch of the come hither.

'No thanks, Pop,' he'd said, and went back to his dinner of leftover meatloaf pasted with horseradish and smashed between a baguette.

God bless it. He never should have agreed to let that suckhead onto his property. Lynwood. Was a jerk back then, even more so now. With his money and his bikes. Of course he was back in Boulder. All the rich bastards were.

There was no good reason to open up all that stuff about the Burkett family. Tommy had made his peace with it twenty years ago. As surely as he'd helped lower his old man's casket into the dirt, Tommy had bedded his guilt for the role he had played in tormenting an already tormented kid and spying on the sister as if she were a carnival freak show. He was only twelve when all that stuff happened, and wasn't the one who'd trashed the runt's bike anyway – Lynwood had set it all in motion.

So, why was he still alert as a bat going on one in the morning? He was upstairs in the large bedroom his parents had shared until the drinking got out of hand and Doris made her husband move into the guest house. Tommy had splurged on a new mattress but it was the same bed frame and headboard, a family heirloom that creaked like a pioneer cart on the wagon trail every time Tommy rolled his three hundred pounds over or elbowed his pillow. Tonight that was a lot of creaking, because he couldn't get comfortable, not in any position.

One drink would put an end to this bullcrap. Three fingers

348

straight and down the slide you go, Tommy John Berkley.
Sleep, and no bad dreams.

But why should he lose sleep over whatever happened to Adam Burkett thirty years ago? To any of them?

It wasn't just Adam, that was why.

Something was wrong with Darren Lynwood too. Tommy hadn't seen it at first, but he'd sensed it. Soon as Darren rolled up in his vintage Firebird, the '79 with the two-tone black on yellow paint, Tommy knew something was off. It was in the way he walked, the way he carried himself, and the way he never took off his sunglasses except once to wipe his eyes near the end. Like he was hiding something.

The man didn't look like anyone who'd built a successful business and sold it off for millions. To Tommy he looked like a strung-out midlife crisis on wheels, clinging to the glory days twenty years after the party had ended.

His speech had been off too. Not in the inebriated sense, but timing-wise. He spoke lucidly but his cadence was all over the place. Rambling like he was on speed as he filled Tommy in on what he'd been doing the past twenty years, like he couldn't get through it fast enough. Then slow and awkward, distracted as he responded to Tommy's recap of the Adam years. He had smiled at the wrong times, like when Tommy was telling of the night he spied on Adam's sister, which wasn't funny then or now. And it had not been a natural smile, Tommy thought. More like a politician's.

The girl in the trailer, pushing womanhood despite her stunted size. Her pale skin streaked black all over. Breasts encircled in spirals, stars down her belly, chains of symbols woven around her waist like a belt. Black slashes along her ribs like tiger stripes. The thick growth of pubic hair filling out, blending into the perverted symbolism of the black-tentacled vines.

Oh, Tommy wished he'd never seen that business. Because you couldn't wash that from your mind. It had been bad enough at age twelve, thrilling though frightening and wrong. To recall such things now made him feel like a pedophile. And damn it, he was a good man. He took care of his wife and lived a righteous life, or tried to best he knew how. And then the way her eyes had opened at the end, lost and searching. She'd looked like a baby raccoon who'd been drugged and then slapped awake in a strange forest, abandoned by its momma.

Wished he'd not followed Brad Cader to see it then, wished like hell he hadn't let that asshole Lynwood pry it out again today. Because tellin' the story, which he thought was so far in the past its potency had been watered down, like a glass of J&B Rare his daddy had lost and left sitting on ice all night, brought it all back in vivid detail. Some things you don't think about for so long, you assume they're harmless. Tommy had wandered into that little funhouse of his boyhood self like a man recalling a prank from high school, something that'd happened to someone else.

By the time he finished with it, his skin felt like it

350

was being tunneled by a couple hundred red ants. His heart goin' like it was countin' down from a hundred, and when it hit zero it was gonna stop. Or explode.

He couldn't get her out of his mind.

Sheila.

That was it. He finally remembered her name. Wished he didn't. It seemed to confirm something dire about himself.

One thing he'd left out in the telling, something he probably could have admitted, because such things happen to kids whether they mean for them to or not. And even that creep Lynwood would have gotten the mechanics of it. But he hadn't been able to say it aloud because he had been ashamed to remember it, was still ashamed, and now this wouldn't leave him alone either.

Seeing her there, Adam's sister naked as a Greek statue and vandalized by adult wickedness, Tommy had experienced the most fearsome erection of his young life. He wasn't sure he'd had one like it since. The hell of it was, he knew he hadn't been up there on the milk crate for more than twenty, thirty seconds, hardly enough time for his blood to start surging, let alone make him ache that way. But in the midst of his fear and the urge to run away, his little pecker had jumped up like a stepped-on rake. Five seconds later, ten at most – just about a blink before the girl dropped to the floor and started yowling – Tommy had spurted into his pants.

God sakes, that was unnatural. Like something delirious and toxic and way, way too adult had been shot into his bloodstream, triggering a physical reaction that had been at once an ecstasy and something like rape. Of her, and him. Seeing her in that trance had been a violation of both of them. The girl cuz of whatever her parents had done to her and cuz of Tommy spying. Himself for whatever black art had gotten inside him, wrenching the nut from him like a dentist pulling a tooth.

Running away he felt *assaulted*, like it was her fault.

Goddamned little rainbow barrette in his pocket. God-damned Brad Cader, Darren Lynwood, all of them, to Hell with all of them.

Tommy sat up in bed, disgusted with himself because – and this was no surprise – it was back. Well, not *it*, not the *one*. But another steamboat willy. Nearing up on two in the morning and the poison was in his loins, his brain. He got up to use the bathroom again, this time to throw some cold water on his face and down his shorts.

He was halfway across the second floor hall, on the staircase landing, when he heard the front screen door creak open and then click shut.

He froze near the top of the stairs, scalp itching, nut-sack tightening. He listened, afraid to take another step. Charlotte wouldn't have driven all the way back from Colorado Springs at this hour unless it was an emergency, in which case she would have called ahead (and he would have heard her car pulling in). Wouldn't be the organics, either. For while they frequently let themselves into the main house, they never did so after dark, respecting his privacy as much as he did theirs.

Footsteps patted across the wooden floors below. Slowly. A few at a time, then a pause. A few more, another pause. Definitely footsteps, delicate ones, but not the footsteps of someone going out of their way not to be heard at all.

In the sixteen years since Tommy had moved back to the farm, he'd never once locked the doors. *We don't live like that out here*, his pop had told him many times, when Tommy asked why his friends in town all locked their houses but their own family never did. *This is the country. Our neighbors are welcome anytime. And people who aren't our neighbors, your criminal sort, they know to leave well enough alone around a farm unless they want to get their head blown off.*

That's when Tommy thought about going back to the bedroom for his shotgun. He might have gotten there too, if the sound of girlish laughter hadn't reached up the stairs and found him first.

33

Beth heard voices.

Or was it one voice talking over itself, overlapping in streams? Either way, she couldn't tell whether the voices were coming from inside her dream or if she was still awake. She did not recognize her surroundings. Wherever she was, it was dark, perhaps inside a house, a small room at the bottom of a narrow corridor. It might have been a stairway she found herself looking up.

The voice was young, a boy's, and this alarmed her.

Murmuring in a monotone, like incantations.

Darren, she thought in sleepy panic, I have to check on Darren. Something's wrong with him. I knew it all these past couple weeks, and after what Rachel told me, there's no question. Where is he? Where is my husband?

She was lying on a floor, hard against her belly, made of wood. She turned her head sideways and peered up the corridor, eyes counting stairs going up, up, up. A big man was standing at the top, with a huge belly, looking down at her in either terror or rage. She didn't recognize him but felt as though she should. He had one hand braced against the wall.

Wake up! You were supposed to stay awake, looking after him! You fell asleep, idiot, now wake up!

The big man backed away from the stairs, shaking his head, no, no, one hand out to stop whatever was coming for him. From Beth's point of view, he looked frightened of her, warning her off.

Where is Darren?!?!?!?!

Beth bolted awake.

She was in bed, her own bed, at home. The room was dark. She could still hear the voice, the talking, murmuring, but the words remained just out of reach. She squinted, turning her head. The voice sounded like it was coming from the living room, at the end of the bridge.

. . . he has no past no past no past my childhood it's gone he took it away dead now I'm dead and I want my life back he has no past it's a lie Darren has no childhood I want it back he took it away Darren has no past he took my childhood . . .

Darren, it was Darren's voice. He was the one talking, but in a little boy's voice. And suddenly she knew this was the voice that had come texting through Raya's phone, and the voice of laughter she had heard after. There hadn't been any boy here in the house, only Darren, talking like a crazy person. A child. And maybe he had sent her the texts, or she had picked up something from his mind using the same conduit responsible for her hunches. In most ways, this was scarier than the idea of a boy visitor, even a ghost.

She couldn't stand it anymore. He must be having a nightmare, another episode.

She turned to wake him up, frightened and angry, but when her hand reached out it landed on a cool spread of sheet.

Darren was gone.

She pushed herself off the bed to go find him. She turned toward the hall and nearly ran into the bathroom door. Wrong way. She was disoriented. Too dark in here. She reached back for the lamp on her nightstand, under the shade, fingers searching around the socket. She found the plastic dial switch and turned it once – click.

The light did not come on.

That's right, you had to twist it two clicks to go on and two more to turn it off.

She started to turn the dial a second time and a small cold hand grabbed her by the wrist.

34

Tommy was afraid to move, afraid she would hear his footsteps. He wanted to go back for the shotgun, but he couldn't bring himself to do it. It couldn't be her, not the little girl. It was a spirit, a demonic presence, using her to get to him. The thing making the voice was right below him, in the kitchen where this back stairway ended. Just out of sight, but close. She giggled again.

Tommy . . . the little girl's voice said. *Toooooommy, I see you up there, Tommy Berkley. Are you spying on me again?*

Tommy began to sweat. His legs felt numb, locked in place. His feet hurt. He had grown used to never feeling light, not at three hundred and seventeen pounds according to his last physical, but right now he felt as though he weighed a thousand pounds.

Did you like seeing me that way? I know you still think about me, Tommy. My young body purified in the ceremony of womanhood. Is that what you think about when you jack yourself off on those hot nights when your wife won't let you touch her?

Do you want to see me again, Tommy Berkley? Do you want to touch my little rainbow barrettes?

Lord, help me. No. No, I do not.

But this was all a trick, because Sheila had died in the fire. Even if she'd lived, Adam's sister would be in her mid-forties by now.

And it wasn't even a real voice, like someone talking. It was in his head. This was all in his head, the footsteps too. It was two in the morning. That bastard Darren's visit today and all this talk of Adam had screwed with Tommy's head. How in the world would she have found him? Why would she bother? He'd never done anything to her except peep through her window.

The refrigerator door suctioned open, then closed.

'Enough of this,' Tommy mumbled. He gathered his breath and shouted down the stairs. 'Somebody there? Huh? You want some trouble? I got trouble for you!'

He waited a few seconds for an answer. Got nothing. Marched back to the bedroom, to the closet where his mother used to hang her dresses, and took the Remington out. He checked the chamber for shells, saw it was full, and marched back down the hall to the top of the stairs. He banged the barrel of the gun against one wall.

'Whoever you are, you're in the wrong house,' he said. 'I'm coming down, and if I find you in here, I'm gonna blow your ugly head off.'

No one spoke or giggled. But was there ... something?

Breathing, maybe?

Hard to tell from up here. It felt like someone was down there. The house no longer had that empty energy. Might just be his nerves.

Tommy hooked a finger around the trigger and cradled the shotgun barrel-upward as he descended the stairs, not attempting to do so quietly. He was in no shape to trot down, or tiptoe. He took his time. Five, six steps down ...

When he got to eight he paused for breath and a floorboard creaked behind him, above. He turned, bringing the shotgun around in the tight stairway, aiming it up at the landing. His breathing stopped.

A small ... person ... stood there in the darkness, quite possibly the outline of a girl. Short, thin, the face pale. A frame of lighter hair hanging to the shoulders. She could be no more than twelve years old.

She was stunted, small for her age.

But it couldn't be Sheila because Sheila wasn't a kid anymore, couldn't be this young, and Sheila was dead.

Tommy pointed the shotgun. 'Who that?' he barked. 'Don't move!'

The girlish shadow stepped forward to the edge of the stairs and leaped, seeming to float down at Tommy, arms spreading, the face coming into focus, legs moving in a walking motion that was too slow, underwater movement, not touching the stairs at all. She looked like an angel without wings, a pale specter with dark designs on her face, falling through space and time in cold silence.

Tommy screamed and fired the shotgun. The flash of fire blinded him in the stairway for a moment and he flinched backward, expecting the girl to slam into him. He staggered down two stairs and caught a heel on the last stair, falling to his ass in the kitchen, which caused an obscene racket and scared him so bad he fired another blast. A rain of ceiling plaster fell around him.

Nothing hit him from the stairway.

His eyes adjusted to the darkness, recovering from the barrel-flash. There was no one in front of him. Whatever it had been, it was gone.

The girl giggled again, from his right side, somewhere close.

Tommy heaved himself to his feet and backed across the kitchen until his butt hit the oven door handle. He swept the shotgun in every direction, toward the living room, the laundry room, the small open bathroom. He heard himself gasping.

He didn't see her.

But golly Christ almighty he'd heard the little fiend. What the hell was this? Either his mind was playing tricks on him or someone from that Burkett clan was here, trying to use their black art on him. Maybe the whole damn clan, their wicked spirits. Was it possible Darren had led them here? He'd said he brought Adam out, the kid was waiting in the car, and when they went to have a look, the kid was gone. Tommy had thought that was just proof Lynwood had a screw loose, but he had to admit his old friend had looked convinced.

Maybe they were all haunted by the Burketts. Maybe that's what got Ryan Triguay. To hell with depression and alcoholism. Maybe when you got down to it, all suicides were just a way to shut off the past, past and present, because without the one you didn't have to deal with the other. It got Ryan, was eating a hole in Lynwood, and now it was coming for him too.

Tommy kept the shotgun raised as he walked to the front door. It was closed, the screen door too, though he'd heard it creaking just minutes ago. So, this told him nothing new. They could be in here. She could be in here.

He scanned the front yard, threw the porch light on. No cars other than his own Dodge truck and the Jetta hatchback the girls in the guest house shared. Their Subaru was gone. What about them – Trisha, Dawn, Renee? He didn't think more than one of them was home, but shouldn't he go check on them? What if the creepers got them first?

No, he had to sort out the situation here in the main house before he wandered out into the dark. And the girls would have come running if they'd heard the gun go off, so they must be out.

Tommy locked the front door.

He moved across the kitchen, checking the small bathroom, the mud room, the closet, and had another gander up the stairs. All clear. He turned the living-room light on, the brightness a nice dose of relief, but not enough to lower the shotgun. There was his TV, his couch, the armchair recliner. He walked around the back of the furniture, checking the side yard through the windows. Nothing.

Nothing but his dearly departed old man's last bottle of J&B Rare, its yellow label and red lettering stark in the otherwise boring room.

That would go down like nectar of the Gods right about now.

'Nope,' Tommy whispered. 'Not tonight, Pop.'

The dining room was empty, and the rear parlor with its framed pictures of Tommy and his brother and some old family portraits hanging on the walls. Tommy's heart was slowing and he wasn't sweating so badly now. The downstairs was cooler. He carried the shotgun back into the living room, to the screened-in porch turned sunroom, a wide narrow space that had become a storage room for stuff he had been intending to auction off or give away to the Veterans. The room was choked full of boxes, nowhere to hide or walk except under the short coffee table, itself stacked high with boxes containing everything from old kitchenware to farm tools and rusted horseshoes. All clear in the sunroom.

Tommy headed back through the living room, intending to go to the kitchen for a glass of water. He was thirsty again.

You're imagining it, all of it. Thinking about that girl naked in her tattoos, that's what got you jumpy. Shouldn't dwell on bad things like—

He stopped. Something caught his eye. Over by the mantle.

The J&B Rare bottle had been moved.

It was standing in the same spot, but its label was facing the wall now. For over a decade it had been facing the couch, the center of the room, the red letters visible from just about every angle. Charlotte knew better than to move it, even dusted around it.

He'd just looked at that damn bottle not two minutes ago, but between then and now someone had turned it around. To send him a message. Not someone.

Her. That little fiend Sheila.

Tommy stomped across the living room and snatched the bottle from the mantle. It was hot in his hand, hot like it had been sitting in the sun all afternoon. When his fingers wrapped around its neck, a jarring tingle shot up his arm, vibrating, almost electrical, but he could not let go. Sweat sprang from under his arms, down his back, and Tommy saw his father face-down in the horse stable.

A single stalk of hay stuck in one ear, blood dried around his mouth like a clown's smile. His eyes were purple, his throat hard full of white vomit, the reek of piss and faeces emanating above the everyday manure smell. And Tommy had set his hand on his daddy's cheek, knowing he was dead, and tenderly wiped some of the blood from the old man's chin. Morning sun already hot in the horse stall, and when he caressed his daddy's chin, the old man's eyes opened, bloodshot and dark, and his hands flew up and seized Tommy by the neck.

'No!' Tommy cried, spinning around in the living room, searching for her. Without thought, without even noticing what he was doing, he released the shotgun and used his left hand to twist the bottle's screw top, breaking the seal. Whisky fumes stabbed into his nostrils as the bottle came up fast, the green top clinking against his front teeth. His mouth filled with a huge wash of the J&B and the swallow sprang tears from his eyes. Felt like someone ramming a fist down his throat. Then the heat was spreading through his gut, swirling around his dinner, seeping through the lining of his stomach walls. A long string of saliva dangled from his lips and stuck to his shirt.

Tommy looked down at the bottle in his hand, wondering how he had done it, how he had waited so long. He was suddenly calm, not drunk but marvelously light on his feet and – best of all – fearless.

He took another magnificent belt of the whisky and roared. 'Hoo-yeah! There you go, Pop. That one's for you.'

Trembling, laughing and crying at the same time, he set the bottle down and picked up the shotgun. He strode back toward the kitchen and swung the barrel around in all directions.

'Come on, honey,' he said, already slurring. 'Come on out and play, you rotten little creep. I've seen you before and I ain't afraid of you.'

She didn't answer, and in his warm, billowing buzz he grew confident she had never been here. He'd let himself get spooked and there was nothing more to it than that. He laughed at himself. Decided he would take the rest of the bottle to bed and knock himself out for the night.

Back into the living room. The bottle was where he had left it on the mantle, open, leaking its heavenly fumes. He snatched it by the neck and upended the bottle and guzzled, taking the shotgun in his left hand. He hit the bottle three or four times on his way back to brave the stairs. He was wheezing sourly by the time he reached the top, but he got there in one piece. Tommy did not feel drunk, only loose and warm, whatever bug he had been catching now poisoned dead.

He walked down the hall, into the master bedroom, and the bottle slipped from his fingers. It hit the floor with a clank and the liquor spilled over the carpet.

His father was sitting on the bed, sideways to Tommy, bare feet dangling a few inches from the floor. He was leaning forward, swaying a bit, head hanging low as if staring at his open bathrobe and boxer shorts the way Tommy had seen him on so many mornings, caught between the last hours of a barn-burner drunk and the onset of a head-splitting hangover.

Tommy's brain ceased all thought. For a long spell that could have been five seconds or five minutes, all he could do was stand at the threshold and stare at his old man. His matted gray hair, the overgrown ears, his gray stubbly chin.

Gradually, very slowly, Randall Berkley sensed his presence and his chin lifted from between the open rolls of terrycloth. He turned his head and looked at his son. His eyes were darkly wet in the darker room, and Tommy could smell the old man's horse stall and sweat scents from eight feet away. His lips were shiny, smeared.

'Tommy?' the old man said in a meek, saddened voice. 'That you, son?'

'Daddy?' Tommy said. 'You okay, Daddy?'

The old man looked away for a moment and sighed. 'Not feeling too good today, my boy. I get so tired, you know. The work never stops. Is your momma home?'

'No, sir.'

The old man looked at Tommy again. His eyes weren't as dark as before. There seemed to be clouds of white in them, cataracts maybe. His mouth was pulled down at the corners. His lips trembled. His father was in need. He looked so sad, so tired.

'We're in a bit of trouble, Tommy,' the old man said. 'I need you to come on in here and help sort this out.'

Tommy moved a few steps closer. He was within arm's reach now. He wanted to sit on the bed beside his father and hug him, hold him close, squeeze him to his chest and tell him not to give up, everything was going to be okay. There was still time. They could get help. They could do it together.

But he was afraid to sit down, to touch the old man, for fear of sending him away again, back to wherever he'd been gone so long.

'What is it, Daddy? Anything. Tell me what to do.'

The old man looked toward the closet door and exhaled all the way out, pausing before he drew another breath. Slowly he raised his right arm, the hand closed in a frail little fist, the skin gray in the dark room, the knuckles misshapen, knotted.

'Tommy ...' his father said with another disappointed sigh. 'Didn't I tell you to get rid of this?'

The fingers opened slowly, twitching arthritically. Something was perched there on his daddy's palm like a bug. Tommy took another step and sat down on the bed beside him, the springs creaking, his father's bony shoulder and the soft meat of his leg nudging against his larger son. The leg was cold.

'What you got there, Daddy?' Tommy whispered.

His father raised his cupped palm in the dark, up at Tommy, holding it there in front of his belly, and there were colors, pretty colors . . .

It was the rainbow barrette, the clip sprung open, three little strands of blonde hair stuck in the teeth.

Tommy's heart stopped cold. He couldn't move or make a sound. His mouth dried up and he couldn't look away.

'Tommy,' his father said, and there was a draft on Tommy's ear, sour breath, the smell of rotten J&B and vomit and decay. 'I been holding onto this for so long. The pain. I'm in so much pain, Tommy. You gotta tell her what she wants to know. If you don't tell her the truth, we ain't never gonna be rid of this. She won't let me settle down until you do it, son.'

Tommy knew his father was staring at him from only inches away, but he could not bring himself to look up into the old man's eyes. His heart felt broken and he was struggling not to cry.

'I'm sorry, Daddy. I shouldn't have done it. It's my fault.'

'Never mind that now, just tell her what she wants to know. Tell her where the boy is. Adam. Where did he go?'

Tommy felt relief. He saw the path out, the means by which to set his father free. 'He's with Darren Lynwood. Darren Lynwood has him. In Boulder. Darren knows everything about Adam.'

'Is that the truth?' his father said.

'Yes, sir.' Tommy nodded quickly. 'I promise.'

'Good boy,' his father said, and the bed began to creak with a series of small tremors. Tommy realized his father was chuckling silently.

His father's hand turned over, the knuckles facing upward, and the hand came up and passed over Tommy's cheek, cupping his chin for a moment. The old man's hand was very cold, and stiff, the skin at his fingertips rough. When the hand retreated the rainbow barrette fell in Tommy's lap.

Tommy leaped from the bed, staggering away.

His father watched him, black eyes shining in the dark, and his laughter sounded through the house.

'No, no, nooo ...' Tommy moaned.

His father faded like the last shot of a black and white film. The bathrobe was gone, his gray hair turned to mere streaks of dimming light, his stubbled cheek was swallowed, and then there was only darkness, rich black darkness, and swimming out of it a pale face, her face.

Sheila Burkett was on the bed, sitting where his father had been, facing him with a horrible smile. She was naked. She wasn't a girl anymore, but he knew it was her, and not just because the symbols were all over her skin, in stars and spirals and calligraphy, some of which looked ancient, others like swastikas. Her eyes were only partway open, rolled back so that he could see only the two slitted white moons of them.

Near the top of the bed, on either side of the family heirloom headboard, pillars of shadow slipped from the walls, solidifying into columns of black, then white above, their shapes coming into focus. Her parents, and he knew they had been there all along, watching, waiting. They were dressed in black, their bald heads pruned with scar tissue, and they faced him like a couple of sentries. One of them, or all three, smelled like baby powder.

'Adam is with Darren Lynwood,' Sheila said in her little girl's voice, though her mouth did not open and Tommy never saw her lips move. 'In Boulder. You promise, Tommy? Do you swear on your father's soul?'

He nodded, stepping away from her, into the doorway. He was bending to reach for the shotgun and she did not react. Her parents did not react. He found the barrel propped against the doorframe and raised it as fast he could. His fingers found the trigger and he set his left hand on the barrel's grip. Oh, sweet lord he was going to paint the bedroom with all three of these freaks.

Sheila's eyes were still white, lost, rolled back. The black symbols and lines began to writhe on her skin, swirling and shifting like a den of baby snakes, like smoke.

Don't you like me, Tommy? said the little girl. *Don't you want to play with my rainbow barrettes?*

Once it was in motion, there was no stopping it. He had Sheila's chest and head dead to rights. His arms were shaking but he did not hesitate, even when he noticed that the brown stock was at the far end and the barrel was slipping upward, toward his mouth. The steel pushed past his teeth and the taste of gun oil filled his mouth. He tried to close his eyes but they were stuck open.

Don't forget about me, Tommy Berkley. Don't you forget about me . . .

His thumb hooked the trigger, the pressure went away, and this time the barrel flash of fire was not visible, to Tommy or anyone else.

35

Click.

The bedroom filled with light and Beth shrieked, snatching her hand away from the lamp. She looked down at her feet, to the bed, behind her.

No one was in here with her. No small cold hand encircled her wrist.

The boy she had seen in her mind's eye the second before the light came on was not here. She looked under the bed, too, half-expecting him to be hiding there, but she saw only lint and dust accumulated on the carpet.

She was starting to lose her mind. Darren's delusions were becoming her own. She had to find her husband. She pulled a pair of jeans over her pajama bottoms, a loose sweater over her T-shirt, and slipped into her running shoes. She hurried through the bridge, into the living room, out the sliding glass door and into the backyard. She ran to the shop and reached the door in less than a minute. The door was unlocked. The lights were on.

Inside, she called out to him as she searched, expecting a replay of the scene from yesterday. Finding him on the floor, nearly catatonic. She checked everywhere, under the desk in the office, between the shelves, but he wasn't in here.

She pushed the rear door open and surveyed the back end of the property. Nothing. She went back inside, trying to think of someone to call.

Her gaze swept across the rows of bikes, to the plywood stairway at the back. The stairs made her think of the ones she had seen in her dream, the heavy man at the top, terrified of her ... or whatever had been at the bottom. She did not understand the connection between her dream and what was happening now, if there was one, but she knew something bad had happened and she needed to find her husband.

She climbed the stairs to his storage space above the shop.

Darker up here, and she had no idea if he had installed a light switch or where to find it. Turned out she didn't need one.

When she reached the top, he was there, seated on the bare plywood floor. He was not asleep. He was sitting cross-legged, upright, leaning his forehead against a bicycle, one hand clutching the front wheel, his fingers laced through the spokes.

It was the Cinelli. The one he said was connected to the boy.

'Honey, what is it? What are you doing out here?'

At the sound of her voice, he did not turn to her. He was in another trance of some sort.

'Darren!' she snapped. 'Talk to me!'

After a very long minute, in a voice that sounded an awful lot like the one she had heard murmuring in the bedroom, a child's voice, he spoke.

'They're not monsters. I know who they are, the ones chasing Adam. I know why he's so afraid of them.'

Beth remembered the magazine he had showed her, the masked things Adam said were chasing him.

'They pushed him to do it,' Darren continued. 'I know the truth now. He's dead. He's really dead and he can never come back. Not in this world.'

'What happened?' Beth said. 'Where are you right now?'

He finally looked at her, his eyes dull, unfocused. 'It's my fault. It's all my fault.'

Suddenly he looked away from her, down into his lap. He shuddered, crying.

Beth moved carefully, drawing close until she could kneel beside him. She put her arms around him. He cried harder and tried to pull away but she held on.

'It's not your fault,' she said. 'None of this is your fault.'

'Yes, it is,' he said.

'No. You didn't hurt anybody. I know it. I love you. Come back to me.'

He sniffed. His eyes were wet but they fixed on her. She felt him returning, not lost in some vision, but finding his way back to here and now.

'His parents burned in the fire. Adam didn't know they were home. He was trying to run away. The bike was going to set him free, not just for days but for ever.

373

He tried to run, he almost got away, but someone else caught him.'

'Who?'

'Me. I killed him,' Darren said, in his own voice. 'I cut him with the knife and put him away, deep underground.'

'No. I don't believe that.'

'It's true. I can show you where, but we have to go tonight. Before it's too late.'

He was already up and walking toward the stairs.

Beth followed him. 'Too late for what?'

'Tommy. Adam. For all of us.'

Part 3

THE BOY WHO CAME TO STAY

36

Adam wakes beside the stream, surrounded by darkness, his legs stuck in mud and wet leaves. For the first few minutes he cannot remember his name, where he has come from, or why his muscles are sore. He sits up, chilled and stiff, and sees that he is in a wood. He has been resting behind a large fallen log, with ground cover piled up on one side to conceal him. He's been on the run, something has been chasing him. At first he cannot remember his last name or his family or any of his friends. They are all blurred creatures, their features melted like pale wax, their eyes black as the sky above him.

Then he remembers the awful horror of it, everything that happened yesterday, or the day before, whichever was the last day of school. It all floods back into him like gallons of cold water, and he wants to run away from it all, but there is no running now because it has already happened.

Yesterday he lost the only thing that mattered to him, and then lost everything else, including his mind.

*

The last day of school.

He is in Mrs Fletcher's fifth-grade class, watching the black hands of the clock above the chalkboard moving slower than creation. The students grow restless, waiting for noon. It is painful for all of them, but for Adam it is the most deliciously excruciating hour of his short life. He has big plans come noon, the culmination of fourteen months' worth of pain.

Soon as the final bell rings and they all hug Mrs Fletcher goodbye, he will run home as fast as his feet will carry him. Once he is sure his family aren't home, he'll sneak into his bedroom. Brace the door with his sister's twirling baton. He will reach under the mattress, into the hole he cut into the box spring last summer, where he has hidden the old brown and orange-striped tube sock holding his savings.

Five-dollar bills, mostly, one from each lawn he has mowed. This has been his flat rate, his secret to making sure they never say no. Doesn't matter if the lawn is tiny like the ones in his trailer park or half an acre like the ones the rich people have up in Wonderland Hills – he never charges more than five dollars. Some of them offer to pay more, but he refuses. It is policy. And it has worked beautifully.

Fourteen months he's been saving, ever since Darren Lynwood crashed his Huffy into the ravine. It wasn't a tragedy, it was a blessing. Best thing that ever happened to him, even counting the whupping his father gave him for letting the other kids trick him. It has hardened him. Gave him a mission:

Saving for the best bike he could find, one that would shame all others, including Darren Lynwood's stable of elite bikes. It seems like a decade has passed since the fall, when Adam had made a Sunday habit of walking all the way down to Dave's Bike Shop (three miles each way), looking for the one.

Usually he is standing at the door by the time Arnie the manager arrives to open up. Arnie is always surly on Sunday mornings, his friendly nature and gleaming eyes dulled from the weekend. He has come to expect Adam and always points him to the newest bikes.

Adam is tempted by the Kuwahara KZ-1, the JMC Black Shadow, the Hutch Pro Racers, and even the Quadangle. But he cannot commit to any of these bikes. He needs to fall all the way in love before he commits his labor, his future, his heart. He comes to the shop, he studies, he talks with Arnie, wearing on the man's patience, but always he leaves without a bike.

Then one Sunday in February Arnie opens the doors for him and when Adam asks if there is anything new, Arnie says, 'Probably not for you.' This piques Adam's interest, because it implies there is something new and it must be different if Arnie is brushing it off. Normally Arnie gives him a cursory sales pitch, then leaves him to ogle the bikes, but not this time. Arnie heads straight back into the mechanics' bay and turns on the music and places his usual Sunday order from the New York Delicatessen. Two pastramis on rye, half a dozen knishes, three Cokes.

Adam wanders to the BMX section, past the rows of

familiar bikes, and he doesn't see it right away. Then a flash of red catches his eye, up on a special racing stand, not on the floor. The red bike is displayed at the back of the store, above all the other BMX bikes, Adam understands immediately, because it is superior. Arnie has set it out of reach to keep the kids from monkeying with it. Adam stares at it for nearly twenty minutes, trying to digest what he is seeing. The oval tubing, the smooth orb of a stem, the elegant dropouts, the clean purity of its color finishes, its exotic name.

When Arnie comes out to Windex the glass display cases, Adam asks if he can take 'this new one' for a test ride. Without hesitation Arnie says, 'Nope. No one rides that bike. Not before they buy it.'

$579.00, the price tag reads. Adam is aghast, and more or less condemned.

Why so much, he asks. Adam has never seen anything like the Cinelli, or even heard of the brand. Never seen it in a bike magazine, never heard any of the other guys talk about it. He doesn't even know how to pronounce it.

'Of course you haven't seen one,' Arnie tells him. 'This is the only one in the state. One of twenty in the whole country as of now. They ship the kit with the Campy parts. I picked out the rest and assembled it myself. This is a true Arnie bike, and there won't be another one like it, in this shop or any others. And it's "Chih-nelly", not "Sin-eely". Italian goods, my friend, hotter than a Playboy model.'

Adam asks more questions and Arnie fills him in on

the history of Cinelli road bikes, Italian craftsmanship, the Campagnolo partnership, the beauty of Columbus tubing. Over the course of three weeks, Adam gets a crash course in all things Italian cycling, frame geometry, manufacturing. Why this bike has these rims, these tires, these brakes, and a special Campagnolo road headset whose cups Arnie has machined to fit BMX because otherwise it wouldn't exist and this bike deserves nothing less.

Adam knows this is the one. It is the fastest-looking BMX bike he has ever seen. It is small, sleek, almost as if it has been made just for him. Best of all, none of the other guys' bikes even compare, not in terms of originality. This is a work of art, the Ferrari of BMX bikes. Adam will be the only kid in the state with a Cinelli.

When he says he is going to buy it, Arnie looks at him with a combination of annoyance and pity. Adam knows what Arnie is thinking. This poor worn-out kid who comes in every damn week for the past three years, holes in his T-shirts and sneakers, never enough money to buy so much as a new brake lever or a new pair of grips, suddenly he wants to buy the most expensive BMX bike the store has ever carried.

Adam pulls out fifty bucks, a wad of fives he always brings to the shop for just this occasion, the day he sees the one. He plops the mashed pile of bills on the glass display case beside Arnie's styrofoam take-out box.

'That don't look like five-seventy-nine to me,' Arnie says, gnawing pastrami.

Adam has prepared for this too. 'You do layaway, don't you? I seen you doing it for the other kids. All I'm asking is you hold it for me for ninety days, and I'll come back with the rest. I promise.'

'Son, I see your money there,' Arnie says, dabbing a smear of Thousand Island from his mustache. 'And I appreciate your business, your dedication. But even after that pile there, you got over five hundred to go. I never seen your folks in here. Where you gonna get that kind of money?'

Adam doesn't blink. 'I'm working for it. I work every single day.'

'Okay, that's something. Who's your employer?'

'Me. I work for myself.'

'Paper route? No, you don't even have a bike. I can't imagine what you kids do for money these days, but let's hear it.'

Adam explains how many lawns he's mowed, his five-dollar rule, his schedule, customer base, and everything that has happened in the past year (except for the part about his dad beating on him, because he doesn't want the pity and his family affairs are private). He sees recognition in Arnie's eyes when he mentions Darren Lynwood and Tommy Berkley and Ryan Tiguay. He casts no blame, but he senses Arnie can read enough into his telling to get the gist.

When Adam finishes his speech, Arnie leans over the counter and looks down at his sneakers, the Puma Baskets he bought for himself three months ago, white as teeth in a toothpaste commercial back then, now stained permanently, the grass clippings and juice having literally dyed the leather green. Arnie sighs and takes a layaway slip from under the counter. He pushes Adam's money back at him and writes 'SOLD!!! – see Arnie' across the invoice. He tears off the pink copy and hands it to Adam, then walks to the end of the store and hangs the slip on the Cinelli's gold v-bars.

'But what about my deposit?' Adam says, feeling tricked.

'I trust you,' Arnie says. 'And I don't want part of your money. I want it all. You go finish your lawns now. Save it up, kiddo, because with this bike, it's all or nothing. Never mind that ninety days business. You come back to me when and only when you have $579.00 in your pocket, I'll pay the tax myself, and the Cinelli is yours. Deal?'

Adam is scared. He trusts Arnie, but something about it all unnerves him.

'Are you sure you won't—'

'No one's gonna sell your bike, champ. You have my word. I'll tell all the guys. Believe me, it will be here.'

Adam's eyes fill with tears on the way out. Arnie slaps him on the back.

'Get back to work, son. Summer's gonna be here before you know it.'

How many nights has Adam lain awake in his bed, trembling with desire, dreaming of the last day of school? Turns out to be over a hundred, because the ninety days come and go and he is still sixty bucks short. For the first few weeks after striking the deal, he walks down to the bike shop every Sunday morning to make sure it is still there. 'Aren't you supposed to be working?' Arnie asks. But he had to see it. He couldn't stay away. After about six weeks of this, Arnie thinks it will be funny to trick him, hiding the bike in the back to make him think it has been sold, until he sees the terrified look in Adam's eyes, the way his face turns red and his breathing goes out of control. Arnie apologizes, says he's just trying to get the kid to lighten up.

'We made a deal, Adam. Your Cinelli isn't going anywhere until you're ready to take it home.'

After this point, it becomes too painful, visiting the Cinelli. Better to put it out of his mind and focus on work, one lawn at a time. It is only about thirty or forty lawns later that it dawns on Adam why Arnie hadn't accepted his deposit, why he'd said all or none. Because he believes in what Adam is doing, the work, the plan, the goal. Refusing Adam's fifty bucks down payment was Arnie's way of saying, I believe in you.

Arnie's faith in him – something he has never gotten from his parents or teachers or anyone in his life – pushes him harder, gives him confidence, makes him feel in charge of his own destiny. Nevertheless, when the ninety-day mark arrives, Adam is so wound up he has to visit the shop and ask Arnie three times if he is sure it's not going to be a problem exceeding the usual layaway limit.

Arnie is filling out an order form on the counter, flipping through a Schwinn catalog. When Adam finishes his paranoid rant, Arnie raises his chin and shouts back into the mechanic's bay. 'Is anybody in here allowed to sell the Cinelli?'

In unison, half a dozen employees holler back. 'Hell, no!'

Arnie shouts again. 'Who's the only person allowed to buy the Cinelli?'

'ADAM!' they hoo-rah.

Adam blushes, speechless.

'How close are you?' Arnie says. Adam opens his mouth and Arnie puts a hand up. 'No, don't tell me. I can tell by the look on your face you're close. We're talking days, aren't we?'

Adam nods.

'Then get the hell out of here.'

And so it goes. Ninety lawns on he is nearing five hundred and he knows he is not going to make it before the end of the school year, which is when he stumbles upon Mr Gerald Wimbley's chicken coops out in the pastures beyond north Boulder. Adam has ridden his bike out here on the dirt farm roads when he wants to escape his parents and the wickedness they get up to, sometimes in the middle of the night. He has seen the short, stubby farmer cursing his chickens and Adam can smell the coop from a hundred feet away. He makes his inquiry. Gerald grins like a pirate.

This turns out to be worse than all the lawns combined, the chicken coop. Over two hundred chickens in there, a reeking sauna, and it hasn't been cleaned in years. Adam scrapes every board from ceiling to floor with paint knives until his hands bleed and his lungs choke with chickenshit dust and he throws up at least six times over the course of the four weekends it takes him to strip it down. He shovels wheelbarrows full of guano paste, sweeping it all out, hauling the mess across the property to the burning ditch where Gerald showed him to dump it.

When he finishes, the grinning farmer refuses to pay him unless he paints it too. Fifty bucks they had agreed, and now Adam must renegotiate. Gerald tries to deduct the cost of the paint, until Adam threatens to call the cops and turn him in for child abuse. Seventy-five they agree, Gerald pays for the paint, but only after two coats. It will take two more weeks, plus a few more odd jobs, and then Adam will cross the finish line.

He will have the bike he's been dreaming of for almost five months and, in another way, the bike he's been dreaming of since he learned what a bicycle is. This is not only his dream bike, it is his dreams incarnate. All of them.

Adam finishes painting the coop the last weekend of the school year, and Gerald hems and haws come payday, but Adam badgers him so hard, he finally gives in, paying the agreed-upon seventy-five. That should have done it, but there have been expenses along the way. Gas for the mower, a new spark plug, blade sharpening, and more often than not, his own dinner. He's been skipping lunch at school to save a little extra, but by dinnertime he is usually shaking, palsied from labor, and his parents don't cook or keep much groceries at home.

Sunday night, the week school is to end, Adam waits until his parents are passed out and his sister is sleeping before counting up his money. This is the scariest part of the whole routine, because he hasn't told anyone what he's been up to. His folks know he is mowing lawns, of course, and he's had to buy them off a few times with a five- or ten-dollar loan. But he's convinced them that, after paying for the lawnmower repairs and tune-up and gas, he isn't earning more than five or ten bucks per week, and he tells them most of that is going for lunch at school. They believe him.

He hasn't told any of the other guys. He rarely speaks to Tommy anymore, and none of the others since last spring, when they ruined his bike at Palo Park. He isn't mad at Tommy, but the few times he's tried to tell Tommy so, the bigger kid looks away, and Adam knows he is ashamed, even though Tommy wasn't the main one who did it. Darren Lynwood has remained above it all, aloof, his same old cock-of-the-walk self. The word around school is that Darren Lynwood's family is moving away, going to Alabama or Arkansas or some other place because his dad got a new job. Darren Lynwood's leaving Boulder, but it doesn't matter anyway. Him and Tommy and the rest of them are sixth-graders. Even if he stayed, the Wonderland Hills Gang are moving on to junior high while Adam's got one more year at Crest View.

More importantly, as more time has passed, Adam comes to believe that keeping his Cinelli project under-cover, a secret inside himself, is a source of power.

Near the end of the school year, his sister has seen the changes in him and started asking questions. Sheila has always been closer to their parents, and the three of them constantly warn him not to tell anyone about the family's personal business, their rituals and beliefs. Just as often they ignore him, pretend he doesn't exist, and he wonders if they secretly know he hates them. Or maybe hate isn't the right word. Because to hate you have to care, to feel strongly, and Adam doesn't feel enough for his family to call it love or hate. Until he can run away at age sixteen, they are just people in his way.

'Where do you go all the time now, dickless?' Sheila asks him from time to time. 'What do you do with that money? Why'n't you buy me some candy?'

'What money?' he always answers, hiding his alarm. 'I don't go anywhere except to stay away from here.'

'You're lying,' Sheila says, crawling on him tickling him trying to make him tell. Sometimes she is too touchy, rubbing herself on him in ways he knew a sister shouldn't, especially now that she is becoming developed. 'Tell me, Adam, I can keep a secret. I promise not to tell. Maybe when you save enough, we can run away together.'

The thought of this makes his skin crawl. He doesn't want to go anywhere with Sheila. She is already ruined, like their parents. She seems to enjoy the sick things they do, practicing on her, calling her their Venus medium. Allowing her to lounge around the house in the nude. This spring he has noticed a foulness filling the trailer, too, a sweet rotten stench, one that seeps up through the floor. Adam doesn't know what it is, but they are all in on it together and he cannot trust Sheila with anything he suspects or plans. She doesn't know anything, he tells himself. She is bluffing.

But still, it scares him. The closer he gets to $579, the more afraid he becomes. He is sure something bad is going to happen, that someone will find a way to convince Arnie to sell the Cinelli out from under him. Or that he will get crippled in some random accident, like getting hit by a car walking home from school. The bike shop might burn down. Adam has nightmares about that, the Cinelli burning to molten steel and rubber, turning to ash.

So he always waits until the middle of the night to count his funds. And this last Sunday of the school year, when he is sure everyone is out cold, he slides his mattress as quietly as he can, taking the sock from inside the box spring and then hiding in his closet to count it. Using a flashlight to see the stacks, he arrives at $568.

Eleven bucks short of his goal.

Arnie will probably let him take the bike with that much, if he promises to bring the rest in a week or two. But this doesn't feel right. A deal is a deal. Arnie is already picking up the tax. Adam wants to stand tall and see the look in Arnie's eyes when he plunks down $579, not one dollar less.

Not to mention, the second he rides the Cinelli out of the store, he plans to live on his new bike for days and days at a time. He doesn't want to take it home and park it in his bedroom while he goes back to work. Once summer is on and the Cinelli is his for keeps, Adam will not mow another lawn or scrape another inch of chicken shit as long as he lives. Or at least until next summer, when he might need a new set of tires.

School ends this Wednesday and this is the deadline he has subconsciously set for himself. It is the official start of summer, and to cross into real summer without his new bike, well, in some way he cannot explain, that would be to miss the whole point. Of course one or two days won't matter, not in the long run. But he is determined to find the last eleven dollars by Wednesday at noon.

Adam traverses the neighborhoods with his lawn-mower on Monday and Tuesday afternoon, knocking on his clients' doors, but he already caught up this past weekend and no one wants their lawn mowed again so soon.

Any odd jobs, no matter how small? He begs them, and eventually a few take pity. He cleans out a garden for two bucks, rakes last fall's wet leaves from under a porch for a few more. One old lady pays him fifty cents to carry her trash to the end of the driveway. Another guy, Mr Richardson, who lives on Sumac near the school and carries a Buck knife strapped to his leather belt, pays him two dollars to wash his Ford Bronco.

Three bucks to go.

His parents have more than that in the change jar in their bedroom, and they are always so hungover or cooked up, they wouldn't miss it. But no. It is not their bike. The Cinelli will only, ever and always be his bike.

The one that puts him over the top comes Wednesday morning, on his way to school. He is walking the three short blocks to Crest View, practically skipping with nervous tension, when he sees a pretty young woman out in her front yard with a pair of tongs and a paper grocery bag. He stops, trying to understand what she is doing, bending over every few steps to tweeze something from the grass and drop it in the bag.

Then he hears her dog barking inside the house and he knows.

'Picking up dog logs,' he says, laughing. Of course! Why hadn't he thought of this earlier? Half the people he mows for own dogs, and no one likes picking up dog logs. If he'd offered this service on top of the mowing for a dollar more, he would've hit his goal a month ago.

Adam hurries over to the woman and presents his case. She is almost finished, she explains, but okay, sure, if he finishes it for her and does the backyard real thoroughly, where she probably missed some, she will pay him two bucks. Adam takes over the tongs and runs around like a boy on an Easter egg hunt, rushing to finish before the school bell rings. But he is thorough too, because this is his last chance. So thorough, he manages to fill the rest of her bag and half of another.

'I guess I didn't realize how much I was skimming over,' the woman says when he knocks on her door and asks where is her trash bin. She shows him in the garage and he gets rid of all the dog crap. 'Thank you so much for that. You're a hard-working kid, aren't you?'

'No problem, ma'am,' he says, nodding politely. 'I wish there was more. I need one more dollar.'

He meant it offhandedly, not expecting her to pay him more than the agreed upon two, but she digs back into her billfold and plucks out an extra single.

'Call it a tip,' she says.

'Are you sure?'

'Yeah, honey. I'm sure.'

$579, officially. Adam wants to kiss her, and she really is pretty, somebody's young wife or older daughter, but he only thanks her and runs off to school, landing in his chair one minute after the second bell.

Mrs Fletcher eyes him skeptically but says nothing.

And the day passes in an agony.

And when the final bell rings and the kids are excused for the school year, Adam runs home, before Sheila can get home from Casey, the junior high school she is already failing out of. His dad's brown Ford truck is not parked out front, but that doesn't mean his mom isn't home. Miriam doesn't have her own car, and she sleeps most days. Inside he forces himself to act casual, but there is no need.

The trailer is empty.

They are probably out drinking. Celebrating the end of school, as if they had been the ones to suffer through it. They don't need an excuse to party. They drink most nights and do drugs whenever they can find them. Good days or bad, though the good are few and far between.

Once he is sure he is alone, Adam goes to his bedroom. Pulls the mattress back, rams his arm down into the box spring. He searches around but cannot find the sock. He begins to panic. His fingers scrape along the wooden slats and he gets a splinter. His heart races and sweat pops from his brow.

'Oh no, no, oh no, pleeeeease . . . '

His fingers snag on the sock. He pulls it out, relieved beyond words.

But . . . what . . . his eyes want to jump from their sockets. He is holding it but no, no, there must be some mistake. It is the same sock, his old white tube sock with brown and orange stripes. It has no holes, but he lost its match a long time ago. Just this past Sunday night it was plump as a sausage, packed to bursting with five-dollar bills.

Now it is limp. Empty. Even the single silver dollar Mrs Heritage gave him for carrying her groceries into the house is gone.

Adam rips away the mattress, heaving it against his bedroom wall, but already he knows the truth. Sheila found it. Tattled on him, thinking it would win her some favor. His parents took it. And somewhere right now they are drinking it, inhaling it, smoking it, dancing with wads of it raised in their fists, and they will not come home until every one of his $579 is gone. He can rage and scream and cry and plead and his parents will only look away, pretending not to know what the heck is the matter.

'We put a roof over your head, clothes on your back,' they told him three years ago, when he yelled at them for taking the twenty-dollar gift certificate he earned selling Little League candy bars. The gift certificate was for Grand Rabbits Toy Shoppe and Adam was going to use it to get himself some binoculars, to watch birds. Another activity that would keep him away from home. His mom found it in his jeans and made the woman at the store exchange it for a cash refund. 'You're getting old enough to contribute your share, and why would you want to go and do a faggoty thing like watching birds anyway?' his mother said. 'You're a weird kid, you know that? Sometimes I wonder who the hell made you.'

That night they went out to the BustTop titty bar on North Broadway and came home plastered. He never got his Grand Rabbits Gift Certificate or the binoculars, and he never played Little League again.

That was twenty bucks. This is the Cinelli.

His dreams. All of them.

Gone.

37

Sheila watched, and waited, and struggled to control herself. It was going to happen soon, but it had to be just right, and they couldn't put it in motion until they understood every angle. Things were shaping up differently than she imagined, but there were exciting new elements to consider.

The Family had found the Lynwood place several hours ago, about forty minutes after bottling up as much of Tommy Berkley's blood as they had time to preserve before leaving the farm. Sheila had checked the Boulder County phone book in Tommy's living room, but found no listing, so she used her cell to call information. She was given an address on Linden, in North Boulder, which she knew was only about a mile from where she had grown up. Fate working in their favor.

But when they arrived, parking two blocks up the quiet street, the signals she was receiving immediately crossed and combined and confused her. She made sure Miriam and Ethan stayed in the back of the Tercel while she walked to the Lynwood house. She confirmed the address on the mailbox, even though the house was emanating for her. Someone of importance was inside. She was preparing to Crawl around back, and perhaps inside for a look around, when she heard voices on the front porch. The door closing. Quiet voices, young, coming near her at the end of the drive.

Dressed all in black, Sheila backed into the side of the yard and pressed herself to the ground. A boy and a girl walked to a used gray Saab. The boy hugged the girl and whispered to her. Sheila heard the name Raya. She was excited by the sight of the boy. Was this him? Could it really be so simple?

But he did not emanate strongly enough to be Adam. Still, there was power here. The girl?

These were someone's children. Darren Lynwood's son or daughter?

And then it all became clear, and Sheila knew this was a symbol of a kind. Seeing the girl and the boy before she had the chance to Crawl the house.

In some ways this was better than stumbling across Adam, even finding him in his bed to slit his throat. This was an opportunity to hurt him in ways she had never imagined possible. This was leverage. The power she might reap ...

Sheila waited until they were inside the Saab, the boy opening the door for the girl, because he was crafty too, and then she ran back to the Tercel.

The Saab drove down Linden, and the Family followed.

And then there was a new house, a party, with too many people, and she was forced to wait. She was tempted to leave, turn back for the Lynwood residence, where they were keeping Adam, but she knew this was another symbol, a reminder to think bigger. If she could control herself, and her parents, she would control the final ceremony.

The hour grew late, but eventually her persistence paid off.

38

The party Raya and Chad attended at Taylor Pultz's house over on 9th and Evergreen turned out to be a disappointingly well-behaved affair. Taylor's parents were home, as it turned out, though they allowed several of the more brazen kids to drink a beer or two out in the backyard. It was a combination of liberal parenting policy (better to do it in front of us than out where we can't supervise you) and general aloofness. Father Pultz was busy manning the grill on a small deck without a spotlight; mom was in the living room chatting with a group of girls, listening to their stories from the school year and contributing a few of her own. But most of the fifteen or so high school kids who showed up did so without illicit beverages of their own, and what little was smuggled in dispersed thinly and quickly.

Chad and Raya spent most of the time sitting in the lawn chairs in the backyard with four or five other friends, talking of summer plans, who had broken up already since school let out, and who was looking like they might be hooking up tonight. Chad was his usual upbeat self, talkative, cracking jokes. He'd convinced one of his friends to spot him three beers, and when Raya declined to join him, he pocketed two while nursing the one.

Raya felt she shouldn't be here. She was worried about her parents, especially her dad. She knew by now he was dealing with something more than nightmares or insomnia. The words 'mental illness' kept appearing in her head like a dimly glowing green sign, the sort of broken-down thing you saw in the window of a scary bar or cheap motel. The letters fuzzy, some of them turning from green to gray to black, the light inside them dying. It was difficult to think of her dad as someone with mental illness, and no one had called it that yet, but after tonight's outburst at the dinner table it was impossible not to start framing it this way.

Whatever was going on with him was getting worse. Her mom was scared. Raya had been feeling that for days. She'd tried to ignore the vibe her mom was giving off, but it was out in the open. For the first time in her life, Raya understood that thing kids at school are most ashamed of – *problems at home* – and she wondered how other kids learned to live with this feeling, day in and day out.

We should go now, she thought every fifteen minutes. Even though Mom said they needed some time to themselves, this doesn't feel right. We need to stick together, like a family, no matter what's happening or how bad it is.

Raya kept looking at her phone, checking for a voicemail, a text. She'd called twice as she had been asked to do, but her mom wasn't answering. She left a voicemail assuring them that she and Chad were being safe, and later sent a text letting them know she and Chad were still at the Pultzes' house.

Be home soon unless you want us to give you some space?

But she got no response.

They were either in bed by now, or in the thick of some discussion, the crisis.

'You okay?' Chad asked her again, around midnight. He had finished his second beer and he looked a little flushed. He wasn't slurring or anything, but Raya knew he was feeling it. Maybe it was his way of pretending nothing serious was happening. 'Did you hear from your mom yet?'

'No. It's fine. It's got to be fine, right?'

'Yes,' Chad said, kissing her on the nose. 'I'm sure they're just talking it out, you know? Sounded like your mom is on top of it. If he needs help, he'll get the best help.'

'Don't say that,' Raya said. 'I don't want to hear that right now.'

Chad leaned down beside her. 'Sorry. All I meant was, this isn't going to be a big deal. They have medicine for this stuff, for everything. You're dad's not sick sick. He probably just has some anxiety issues or something. Half the world does these days. It's gonna be okay, babe.'

She didn't respond.

'Do you want to go home?' he asked. 'It's cool if you'd rather be there. I don't mind. We can leave anytime.'

His understanding of how she was feeling made her feel a little better. 'No, not yet. We should give them some space. If I haven't heard from her in half an hour or so, maybe we'll head back?'

'Whatever you want,' Chad said. 'I'll be over here with Sam and Emma.'

'Are they smoking pot?' Raya said.

'No, just cigarettes.'

'Are you smoking cigarettes?'

'No. I don't like 'em. I told you that, remember?'

'You can smoke if you want to. I'm just asking.'

Chad laughed at her but not in a condescending way. 'I know. Why, do you want a cigarette?'

'Yes,' she said, surprising herself. 'Can you bring me one?'

Chad frowned. 'Absolutely not.'

Raya smiled. He kissed her again and went back to his friends.

She checked her phone again. Nothing. She sat by herself for a few minutes, everyone else preoccupied with some other corner of the party. She watched them all, some of her friends and some of them just faces she recognized but had not gotten to know. Most were older, Chad's year, but she didn't feel out of place. All in all she'd had a really good first year in Boulder, this new place that felt like their inevitable home, even to her mom and herself, who hadn't grown up here.

Then she looked away from her friends, to a small grove of trees near what looked like a garden, the trellis thingy already turning green with new vines of some sort. It was dark in there along the fence stretching back to the garage, and she thought about exploring it, walking back into the garden to see where it led. But she didn't want to stray too far from people right now. The night felt hungry, like it was waiting for one more little thing to go wrong, and when that happened, the worst would come true.

But why did she want to know what was back there? The urge to step past the trellis was stronger now, despite her caution. Part of her wanted to know how bad it was, that's why. Not in there, but out here, everywhere, at home.

She wanted to know the truth. But it probably wasn't waiting for her inside the garden. If there really was a little boy, a lost boy named Adam, he wouldn't wait for her in there, would he?

Raya got up from her chair and walked closer to the trellis, looking around to see if anyone was watching her. She stepped past the vines, onto a path of maroon brick stones leading back between rows of weeds that had not been pulled this spring. The light from the party did not reach more than a few feet, and the darkness at the end of the path was so deep, she couldn't see to the end of the garden.

What was back there? Something watching her? She could feel it beckoning to her. Just a few more steps, and she would know. She would meet him, Adam, or whatever was making it possible for him to enter their lives.

Raya took another step, and another, until she was standing out of the light, concealed completely from the rest of the party. See paused, feeling a strange energy inside her, around her body, calling to her, inviting her deeper.

She took two more steps and paused, the smell of flowers and something richly composted reaching up to her.

Yes, come say hello. We're family, after all. Don't you want to meet your real family? Don't you want to be my sister?

Who was that speaking to her? Inside her? Her own mind, or someone else's? Was this Adam? Was he here, the way he had been there in her phone, and crying in the living room? Somehow this didn't seem like him either.

Her real family . . . ?

She thought about Chad and her family and the way she felt every morning, waking up to face the day. Suddenly she needed to know if she was happy, really happy. She didn't know how to define real happiness, but she suspected it had something to do with being content, grateful, having things to look forward to. Feeling loved and being able to love others.

Which meant she was happy, wasn't she? She knew she was going to have a good life, a life filled with a lot of advantages, thanks to her family's money, and her own hard work in school. But she would work for it too. She would set her own goals, reach for big things, like her father had done, as he had encouraged her. She wanted to travel all over, to Europe and Asia and Africa. She could picture herself running a business. She didn't want to be an artist, she wanted to be an entrepreneur, engaged, moving and shaking, doing deals under deadline. She wanted to build something that would last.

She loved her mom and dad so much, though, she couldn't imagine moving away. To spend even one year away from them seemed, in this moment, like a terrible waste. It wasn't that she couldn't make it on her own. She knew she would be able to survive out there, somewhere in a city or a small town, wherever she ended up. But she would miss them too much. Every day. Little things. The trust they put in her. Their conversations, they way they made her feel she could talk to them about anything, no matter how silly or frightening, and they would never judge her. They're my real friends, she realized with something like inner shock. My mom and dad are my best friends, and they always will be. I need them, I will always need them.

And right now they need me.

Raya backed out of the garden, along the path, afraid to turn her back on the darkness at its end. She couldn't explain what had changed, but she knew she had almost made a terrible mistake. She had to go, but something back there did not want her to go. It tugged at her with each step, pulling at something inside her, asking her to come back, stay a while, meet her real family.

But no. Her real family was at home.

'Chad,' she called across the yard, hurrying away from the trellis and its twisting vines. 'We need to go home.'

Chad nodded and gave her the 'one second' cue with his finger, then resumed his conversation with Sam Penrose.

It's not mental illness, the boy's voice said from somewhere inside her. *It's death, hell in human form, and it's on its way to get your daddy.*

'Now, Chad. It has to be now!'

Chad crossed the lawn and met her on the way into the house. She walked faster and he followed her through the kitchen, the living room, past the girls chatting with Mrs Pultz, and she didn't wave or say goodbye.

'What is it? Did you hear from your mom?'

'No, someone else,' she said, pushing through the front door.

'What's going on?'

She stopped at the street, turned, and snatched the keys from him, because he'd been drinking. 'Something bad is happening at home. Right now. Get in the car.'

Chad obeyed. His Saab was an automatic, which was good because she didn't know how to drive a stick shift. She'd had some practice in this car, unbeknownst to her parents. She resisted the urge to speed, but it was nearly impossible. They turned from Evergreen, onto Broadway.

'It's gonna be all right,' Chad said. 'Don't panic. We'll be there in five minutes.'

'We should never have gone to the party. What was I thinking?'

They had gone only six blocks up Broadway when a pair of headlights behind them drew closer, turning bright and enormous in the rearview mirror.

'Someone's following us,' Raya said. 'Like, way too close.'

'Might be a cop,' Chad said. 'Are you speeding?'

'A little.'

'A little's okay,' he said. 'We're fine. Just be cool. You're doing great.'

'I don't have my license yet.'

'We'll tell them I've been drinking, which is true, and you're being responsible – also true. It'll be okay, I promise.'

'Why is he so close?' Raya said. 'The lights are messing with my eyes.'

'He's looking to see if you're swerving or whatever.'

'I wasn't, until he started following us. Now I can't hold the wheel straight.'

'Raya, sweetie, you're sober. Don't worry.'

Then the rearview mirror went dark. The headlights behind them had shut off. The car behind them was driving in darkness, but still tailing them dangerously close.

'Is that really a cop?' Raya said. 'It doesn't look like a police car to me.'

Chad turned in his seat to have a look through the rear window, straining against his seatbelt. 'Oh ... oh, man ...' he said quietly. He turned around and looked at her, forcing himself to speak softly. 'Stop the car.'

'What?'

He continued to whisper. 'Raya, pull over. Get off the road, now.'

Raya looked back over the console, to the back window, where the car was, but when she turned back to face the road, something else caught her eye and she did a double-take.

Then she saw what Chad had seen, and she understood the whispering.

A scar-ravaged face attached to an old woman was lying across the backseats, inside the car with them. She wasn't moving and Raya thought, *there's a decaying dead body in the car.* Then the old woman's arm came up, a wrinkled hand flicked something at them, and something thin went *zzzzziiiip* around Chad's neck. He began to thrash and kick the dashboard.

Shock was all that had kept Raya from screaming, and that shock was stripped away now. She released a scream and drove off the road. Chad's Saab bucked under them, up over a curb and the sidewalk, and she saw houses too close, lawns, bushes. She screamed again and swerved away, back toward the road.

Something tickled at her neck, digging under her hair. Hands, fingers. Nails clawing at her throat. The old woman's hands.

Raya screamed again and thrashed away from the seat, losing her grip on the wheel. The Saab's back end skewed sideways over a patch of lawn and there was a thick tree in front of them. Coming at them, too fast. A loud heavy crunch. The Saab's hood folded up. Chad snapped forward in his seat and something hard smashed Raya in the forehead. Her teeth cut into her lips, her brain seemed to be rocking back and forth inside her skull, and she couldn't tell what happened after that.

39

Adam searches anyway, tearing the place apart. Their bedrooms, the living room, the bathroom, under every cushion and in every drawer. He ransacks the entire trailer in a fury, but he does not find his $568.

He will never get there again. Not with this family, not in this life. Even if he mows lawns all summer, for a whole other year, it won't matter, they will just take it again. He will never mow another lawn or ride another bike as long as he lives.

His Cinelli is gone. Everything is gone.

He can't live here anymore, never again. The bike was going to take him far away, he realizes now. Once he had the Cinelli, he would never have come home.

Adam doesn't cry. The thing inside that allows children to cry is broken.

He sees red, then yellow, and then he sees streaks of white like falling stars. He finds his old Little League bat in the shed out back and uses it to destroy as much of the trailer's insides as he can. Bashing out the front of the TV, the dinner plates, the family photos on the walls. Holes in the cabinets. He smashes his sister's

Barbie collection to limbs and pieces and knocks her bedside lamp to smithereens. The liquor bottles in the kitchen explode with glory. When he is too tired to swing the bat, he staggers and falls onto the couch, exhausted. He stares into empty space for a few minutes, and then his focus comes back with precision.

On the coffee table beside the ashtray is a half-empty pack of his mom's cigarettes, and beside those, a little yellow Bic lighter.

Adam picks up the lighter and thumbs the metal wheel.

A tiny flame curls up and wavers meekly. The lighter is almost out of fuel, but there is enough. Just enough.

He removes the last eleven dollars from his pocket and holds them over the flame, watching the money shrivel and darken, transforming from a piece of the Cinelli, enough for maybe the grips, into fire. When the flames reach his fingertips he drops the bills on the coffee table and watches them consume themselves until there is only a spiral of smoke and a layer of black ash.

In his bedroom, he fills his backpack with a few necessities. A change of underwear and socks, his jean jacket, his favorite issue of *Questar*, and some beef jerky and crackers he has kept in his dresser so that his sister won't find them when they run out of food, which happens for days and sometimes weeks at a time. Lastly he adds the knife, in case they come for him. It is not the pocket knife his Grandpa gave him when he was still alive. It is the evil-looking knife he found in his dad's truck one night, the one he kept for the eventual night they came to kill him.

Then he walks to Miriam and Ethan's bedroom.

'I'm sorry, Arnie,' he says, and holds the Bic flame under the curtain. Holds it there until he doesn't need the lighter anymore.

Adam runs for a long time, thinking of nothing. He runs past Crest View, the school that has done nothing but make him feel ashamed of his family and his life. He runs into Wonderland Hills, where the rich kids live, where Darren Lynwood and Tommy and the rest of them are leading protected lives so removed from Adam's experience they might as well be princes. He runs northwest, past Wonderland Hills pond, toward the rising Foothills of the Rocky Mountains, through fields of prairie grass turning steep into the first woods. He climbs a plateau until he can look back and see the entire town of Boulder, and then moves deeper, to a place where he can hide all night, for days, weeks, the rest of his life.

He hides and shivers through the night, an endless night, and all through the next day.

In the afternoon he searches for a stream where he might fish for dinner, but he doesn't find one. He searches for berries to eat, but there are none.

As the second evening comes, he hears noises, monsters coming for him in the pine trees, his raging father hunting him with a knife, and he runs some more, until he finds this fallen log on the other side of a stream.

He burrows into the brush and keeps perfectly still, sometimes crying, sometimes laughing, and finally sleeping for a few peaceful hours, until something wakes him in the middle of the night. He sits up, listening as a creature drags itself through the sparse forest, stalking him.

Adam is confused, expecting to find himself at home, that this was all a dream, a nightmare. But no, he is still in the hills. Something has come for him. He will surrender. If it is a bear or a cougar, he will not run from it. He has nothing left.

But the creature stalking him is not a creature at all. It's a boy.

One he recognizes.

'You?' Adam asks the shadow watching him from behind the first thin strand of trees. 'What are you doing up here?'

'I followed you,' the shadow responds, and steps into the moonlight. He is wearing faded Levi's jeans, red and white checkered Vans, and his Patterson Racing BMX jersey and his blue Haro gloves. His hair is longer, his frame leaner. He looks so damn cool, and his presence is such a surprise, Adam finds it impossible to be angry at him for ruining his bike. That day in Palo Park seems like something that happened ten years ago. 'I know what happened and I want to help you. I know there's no going back, but there's a better way. We can sort it out.'

Glad of the company, Adam crawls up from the muck and sits on the log. Darren moves a little closer, using a pine needle to pick his teeth. Even this is a cool move. Everything Darren Lynwood does is confident and cool.

'I'm sorry about the Cinelli,' Darren says. 'That would have been rad to see you on that ride.'

'I was hoping you would like it,' Adam confesses, as much to himself as to Darren Lynwood. He realizes for the first time that this is what he wanted. Not just the Cinelli, but the Wonderland Hills Gang's approval. Darren Lynwood's approval most of all. He didn't want to beat them. He wanted to join them. 'You always have the best bikes, the best everything. But I thought you would, you know, respect it.'

Darren steps a little closer. 'I did. I do. You have the eye, man. You have the killer instinct. You just need the right bike to work on your skills. I'm sorry it didn't happen.'

'Wait,' Adam says. 'How'd you know about it, the Cinelli?'

'Arnie told me. He was real proud of you. We all were.'

Adam wants to cry but he wouldn't dream of doing so now. He's already cried in front of Darren Lynwood once. Never again.

'I guess I should say I'm sorry about your family, too,' Darren says, looking around the woods. 'I heard what happened. It's all over the news. But I understand it. I know you didn't mean it, but maybe it's for the best, right?'

He looks down into Adam's eyes, and Darren Lynwood's eyes are black with fire, dark and serious far beyond his years.

Adam says, 'I didn't mean to burn it all. It just ... I lost control.'

'No doubt, no doubt, bro. But how could you have known they were in there? Your sister in the closet, where they kept her. Your folks passed out in the bathroom. Knocked out on heroin or whatever that stuff is they smoke? Smells like a chemical factory. Probably would have done it to themselves if you hadn't done it for them. Like I said, for the best.'

Adam cannot speak for a moment. 'Wait, what? You're saying ...'

Darren Lynwood peers down at him, nodding.

'They're ...?' Adam asks. 'My family, they were home?'

''Fraid so.'

'But I checked. I swear, they weren't.' And at the same time, Adam thinks, *Did I really check everywhere? Or did I skip the bathroom and Sheila's closet for a reason? Because maybe I didn't want to know. Because maybe I wanted them to feel the full force of my—*

'Firemen found the bodies, dude. It's over. They're charcoal.' Darren Lynwood laughs heartily, the same way he did when Adam's bike tumbled into the ravine.

Adam laughs too, because to do anything else, to think about the reality of what he has done, would send him down a dark hallway to Hell for the rest of this life.

'So, the good news is,' Darren says, clapping his gloves together and taking a seat beside Adam on the log. 'You're free. You finally got away from them, in a

414

way not even the Cinelli could have done for you. You can do anything you want now.'

'Whattya mean?' Adam says.

'I mean, you can go anywhere, stay out late, and ride for ever. You'll find another bike, another path, new friends. The world is waiting. No more abuse, no more drugs, no more séances and all that twisted business with your sister. You are better than that, always were, and you proved that today.'

'You knew about my family too?' Adam is too tired to feel ashamed.

'Buddy, the whole school knew,' Darren says. 'But you know what? Screw them. Because school's over. You're the hero, at least to me. If my family was like yours I would have done the same thing, if I had your guts. But I don't think you and I are made of the same stuff. What you got inside you. Man, that's hardcore.'

'Are you kidding me?' Adam blurts. 'I worship you!'

Darren looks him in the eyes again, and this time his eyes are not black or dead, they are blue, crystalline electric blue. Adam is not attracted to him, he has had crushes on girls, but nevertheless Darren Lynwood is beautiful. His cheeks glow. His skin is clean. He is all style. From the way he rides to the way he talks, his taste in bikes and clothes and a thousand other details, it's what everyone at school knows. Darren Lynwood is not only going to live an amazing life and be a star, he is already a star.

'I know you do,' Darren Lynwood says. 'That's what I wanted to talk to you about. I have an idea. It might sound crazy at first, but hear me out. Think about the long term. This is your life we're talking about.'

'Okay.' Adam is puzzled and excited. He feels as if Darren Lynwood knows him, knows his thoughts, because whatever is coming, Adam has felt it too. It's been building for the whole year, before the day in Palo Park. Maybe since the first time he ever saw Darren Lynwood. He wonders if Darren Lynwood is going to invite him to live with the Lynwood family. They can become brothers.

'I'm moving away,' Darren Lynwood says. 'My dad, he works for Mountain Bell, you know. And he got a new job, in Albuquerque – that's down in New Mexico. We're leaving in a week. He was supposed to leave a month ago but he convinced the company to allow him to stay till the end of the school year.'

Adam's heart sinks, remembering the rumors of the Lynwood family's move. Maybe being brothers was crazy, but in the past few minutes he'd started to hope they would become friends at the very least, with or without the Cinelli. Maybe Darren Lynwood would feel bad for him and let him borrow one of his bikes. But he's leaving for real? It's too much sadness in one day. He can't talk.

'It's better this way,' Darren Lynwood assures him, shaking him by the shoulder. 'We will always be friends, but with me gone, you can take over.'

'Take over?'

Darren Lynwood leans in close and whispers in Adam's ear. 'You can be me now.' His breath is warm and smells like candy, orange Gatorade maybe. 'That's what you wanted, isn't it? Not just to be like me, but to be me? To have what I have? To ride my bikes? To have a nice house and a real family who loves you?'

Adam can't bear to look up. He can only nod, and now the tears come regardless of how many times he blinks and how many times he swore he would never cry in front of Darren Lynwood again. Hot tears roll down his dirty cheeks and his chest heaves.

'It's okay. I want you to,' Darren says, hugging Adam close. 'It's my way of making up for trashing your Huffy. For the teasing. For everything. I want you to take it, Adam. Take my life.'

Adam shakes his head. 'I can't.'

'Yes, you can. I want you to.'

'How? How is that possible?'

'Simple. You run away. Not forever, but for a few years. Just long enough for people around here to forget what you look like. To forget what I look like. You have to run away so the police won't find you, and you'll be safer in another state. Then later, in a year or two, you find an orphanage, a shelter, or just call social services. They've been to your house before, you know how those folks work. You tell them you are a stray, a runaway, an orphan who can't remember his family. You forget your family, but when you need one to hold on to, you remember mine. My hard-working father and my sweet mother. My house in Wonderland Hills. You don't tell them any of that, but that's who you are now. Inside you. When they ask your name, you tell them Darren Lynwood, and you can never change that, because your name is who you are. It is your history and your fate. It is your destiny.

'You're a smart kid. All that's been holding you back is your family. They're dead now. Someday you will find a new one. A wealthy family who can't have kids of their own. They will adopt you, and when they try to change your name, you say no, you are Darren Lynwood. Because you have to believe it, Adam. You have to erase everything before today, before this moment, and when you walk out of these woods, you will be Darren Lynwood for the rest of your life.

'When you grow up, you will be handsome, strong, and charming with the girls. You will go to college, you will work hard and get good grades. Your family will set you up, pave the way. You will live the dream life, my life, but you will also earn it. Because I work hard at school, too. One day you will fall in love and be married and have children of your own, and no matter how close they get, they will never know you as Adam Burkett. To them, to the rest of the world, and most importantly to yourself, you will only and always be Darren Lynwood. But you have to believe it. You have to memorize it in your bones. You have to commit everything, Adam, the way you committed to the Cinelli. Because if you don't go all the way, it will all fall down, and one day you will wake up, your life will be hell, you will be a drug addict like your parents, homeless and lost and condemned, forever stuck being Adam Burkett. Now, which would you rather have? My life, or Adam's?'

'Yours,' Adam says. He feels loose, weak, lighter than air.

'Who would you rather be, Adam? A ruined kid from a

rotten home, or me, the kid with all the bikes, all the advantages, all the success waiting for me down the road?'

'You,' Adam says. 'But ... '

'What?'

'What about me? What's gonna happen to ... Adam?'

Darren Lynwood holds Adam's jaw with one of his gloved hands and turns his chin until they are staring into each other's eyes, close enough to kiss.

'Adam is dead. He was lost, he never had a chance. His family tried to destroy him, and they almost succeeded, but he survived a little longer. And then I killed him, you understand? Tonight, at this moment, I gave him my life in exchange for the end of his. He can be no more, not in real life, not in your memory, not anywhere on this earth. Adam is gone to heaven, buddy. He's dead and gone and for ever, amen.'

Darren Lynwood stares into Adam's eyes, making sure he understands.

Adam nods.

'Okay, then.' Darren Lynwood stands and walks a few steps. He takes off his blue Haro riding gloves and drops them on the ground. From his sock he removes a scary-looking street knife, one that looks an awful lot like the one Adam took from his dad's truck, and he flings it in a circle to snap the blade out. He holds the blade up for a moment, then slashes it across his palm. Blood begins to flow. He makes a tight fist, forcing the blood to come quicker.

'You next,' he says, handing Adam the knife.

Adam stares at the butterfly engraved on the handle

for a moment, confused, because something is amiss here. It doesn't make sense, how would Darren Lynwood have the same knife Adam stole from his father's pickup truck? But Darren Lynwood is waiting for him and he can't back out now. Adam cuts deep into his own palm and watches the blood drip to the ground. He makes a fist, just like Darren Lynwood's.

Darren Lynwood comes forward and opens his stark white palm beaded with blood. Adam opens his hand. The boys shake, squeezing hard, making the blood mingle and drip from between their fingers, into each other's veins. It doesn't hurt, Adam realizes. It's warm and soothing and it doesn't hurt at all.

'Stand up,' Darren Lynwood says.

Adam does.

Darren Lynwood hugs him fiercely for a moment, then backs away. He slips his feet from his Vans sneakers. He removes his Patterson Racing jersey and hands it to Adam. He unbuttons his Levi's and kicks them off, then his underwear and socks, until he is standing in the woods bare naked.

Adam thinks one or both of them should be embarrassed, but he's not, and he doesn't think Darren Lynwood is either.

'Those are your new clothes,' the boy says. 'I give you my life. My name. My destiny. The rest is up to you. Can you do it?'

'Yes,' Adam says.

The strange naked boy smiles. 'Then I guess we'll never see each other again. Good luck, Darren Lynwood.'

Adam wants to say more, but he can't think of what.

The boy turns and walks into the woods, his bare legs and butt and back shifting and fading as he winds through the small trees, and only a few steps later he is gone, nowhere to be seen. Adam runs after him a ways, but finds no trace. No footprints, no sound. He walks in circles, his mind empty and no longer searching, just feeling the earth beneath his new feet.

He returns to the fallen log and strips off his own filthy clothes. In the cool June night, he feels something draining from his legs and arms, and something new inching through his veins. He closes his eyes for a moment, swaying on his bare feet, and he turns the name over in his mind, seeing ashes, seeing flames, their burned corpses one final time. There is no goodbye. He has no mother no father no sister. Those people weren't even real. Soon he will meet his real family, when he is ready, and his future with them has already been written. It is only waiting to be lived.

He must say goodbye to the Cinelli. He sees it there on the race stand, perfectly preserved for all time, a kernel of memory he will never visit again, and he knows somehow this is perfect. The Cinelli is another life, one he will never know. He was never meant to have the bike. The Cinelli was not his fate. There will be other bikes, someday, but never the Cinelli. It was too good for him, for all of them, even for Darren Lynwood.

'Darren Lynwood,' Adam says, testing the name, letting it cross his lips, his tongue, floating it out into the hills. 'Darren Lynwood.'

Sounds good. Feels good.

Slowly he pulls on the other boy's clothes, underwear and socks first. The Levi's and the Patterson Racing jersey next. And finally the red checkered Vans. They are all several sizes too large but he knows that, given time, say in a year or two, they will come to fit him perfectly.

It all will.

40

'Here it is,' Darren said, pointing a flashlight at the old rotted log in the woods. He remembered when it used to be thick as three men, but now it was rotted nearly hollow, narrower than a phone pole, the ends crumbling to dust.

Behind Beth, just over the slope, the stream gurgled weakly. This year's run-off from the mountains wasn't what it had been when Darren was a boy, thanks to the drought that had come to afflict Colorado almost every summer.

'This is where it happened?' Beth asked. 'You're sure?'

'This is where I woke up. After that, everything was different. Adam was dead.'

Beth hugged herself and shivered. 'I don't understand. Was he real? The boy who followed you into the woods?'

'He was real,' Darren said. 'But not that night. I worshipped him, the real Darren, and after what happened, something inside me just broke. Split in half, I guess. The boy I wanted to be came to me in a time of need, became my imaginary friend, and I . . . adopted him all the way. To protect me. To save me.'

Beth's face was still a mask of confusion, disbelief. 'How can you be sure?'

Darren walked to her and shined the flashlight onto his left palm. Between the triangle of wrinkle lines was a vertical white scar, thin as thread. He shifted the flashlight to his left hand and shined it down into his right palm. This line was larger, crooked, but also faint.

'The blood oath,' he said, 'Two cuts. Two hands. One boy.'

Beth started to laugh, and he knew she must be on the verge of hysteria. 'You never talked about it!' she cried. 'Since I met you, all you ever said about your childhood was that it was perfect, magical, one long Ray Bradbury story. No wonder. Jesus, Darren! It was all a lie?'

'It wasn't a lie. I believed it. I believed it all the way.'

'How could you do this to me? To yourself?'

'I don't know.' He doused the flashlight. 'I'm sorry, Beth. I'm truly sorry.'

'But what does it even mean? You're someone else? You were an orphan? What in God's name happened to you between the ages of eleven and . . . I don't even know. When was it? When did you find a new family?'

'When I was fifteen, almost sixteen. The winter I gave up living on the streets, I guess it was. Chicago is a very cold place to be a runaway.'

'What about Andrew and Eloise? I suppose you lied to them too.'

'I didn't lie. I couldn't remember. I didn't want to remember. Everything from my Boulder days was a fabrication, Darren's childhood. That was the story I told myself over and over until it was all I knew. By the time I moved into the boys' home in Janesville, I wasn't lying. I was telling as much as I could remember—'

'But your name,' she said. 'It's always been Lynwood. How did that work?'

'It was my identity. It was all I had. My parents, Andrew and Eloise, they understood that. They never pressured me. But they were older, you know. They weren't close to their relatives. They'd never been able to have a child of their own. I came late to them, as a foster child, and I had become so independent by then, it wasn't much more than a sponsorship. When I graduated high school with honors, they took my name as a graduation present to me. So we could be a real fam—'

He stopped, paralyzed in thought.

'What?' Beth said.

'My mom, what she said the other day when we went to visit her. She said his name. Adam.'

Beth stared at him. 'She knew him?'

'She must have known *something*,' Darren said. 'Somehow they knew. They kept the secret all these years, for my benefit, but the disease, her Alzheimer's . . .'

'It just slipped out?'

'Maybe so. I don't know.'

'What happened to the real boy, your bully friend Darren? What about his family?'

'They moved away. I must have picked up on that

rumor as the end of the school year neared. I doubt he ever told me so himself, because we never spoke that spring. But knowing he was leaving, that must have planted a seed in my subconscious. Convinced me, on some level, I could take what wouldn't be missed.'

'But you never looked him up? Don't you want to know what's become of his life? Aren't you curious?'

Darren rubbed his eyes. 'Beth, I haven't had time to process all this. You're already ten steps ahead of me. He could still be in Albuquerque for all I know. Or living some charmed life in another country. Does it matter?'

'It might,' she said, turning and walking a few steps from him. 'I guess I should be relieved you figured this out, but I'm sorry if this doesn't sound like a heart-warming story right now. To me it feels like you've just bent the world and everyone in your life to your will, to continue this, this ... this fabrication. You betrayed us. You lied to me, and to Raya.'

Darren felt impossibly tired. He was starting to get angry, though he knew he had no right to be. 'If I hadn't run away, if I hadn't done it, we wouldn't have met, Beth. If I'd lived Adam's life, I would probably be in jail by now, or dead. There would be no us. No Raya. Do you realize that?'

'But you're not *you*. You're Adam Burkett!'

'No. Just the first ten years, and I couldn't help that. If it were up to me, I would never have been born into that family. But I was, and I did what I had to do. For ten years I was him, and then I made my escape. The

426

rest is me. I am the same man you've always known.'
He moved closer to her, put his arms around her. She
flinched but he held her and eventually she stopped
resisting him. 'I guess it will take some time to get used
to. I'll tell you what I can. Seems like I remember more
every day. I'm still in shock myself, but I promise to tell
you everything that I remember.'

'It almost makes sense,' she said. 'In a weird way.
Your drive to succeed. The company. Your hoarding of
all these bikes, all this stuff from your imaginary childhood. The Radical Sickness Collection was your own
little Pink Floyd Wall? Were you trying to convince
yourself it was real? Is that how it works?'

'It wasn't a plan, Beth. Something in me just broke
that day, and then I became what I became. I don't
understand it any better than you do. But I want us to
sort it out together. I'll see a therapist, a hypnotist,
whatever you want. But I need you, more than ever. I
love you. Will you stay with me? So we can do it
together?'

She looked into his eyes. 'No more secrets?'

'No more secrets.'

For a few minutes they simply stood there on the hill-
side, gazing around, looking up the stars. Eventually she
said, 'So, what about your family? The first ones. What
happened to the Burketts?'

Darren shook his head. 'Gone. In the fire.'

She frowned. 'This had to have been news. We can
find out. We have to look it up. You realize that, don't
you? We have to talk to the police, confirm it all. We

have to bring it all out in the open. If we don't, I'll go crazy thinking about it.'

Darren nodded. 'Of course.'

'How does that make you feel? That they're gone. The way they died?'

Darren thought it over, but not for very long. 'It doesn't make me feel anything at all.'

'But if it's true, if you really started that fire—'

'You'd have to ask Adam about that.'

Beth covered her eyes, released a shrill little moan. 'This is too much. I don't like being out here at night. Can we go home? Now?'

He took her by the hand and they walked out of the woods, down the hill which had seemed so huge thirty years ago. The path led them back to the main trail-head, to the open-space land that used to be truly open but which now was populated by hundreds of new houses built off of Lee Hill Road at the base of the Foothills.

Twenty minutes later they were in the wagon. Beth turned the heater on. She checked her phone. 'Damn it. Raya called three times. She's probably worried sick.'

'She's such a good kid,' Darren said.

'Her last text said she was on her way home, everything is fine.'

'Good. We'll be there soon.'

They did not speak for the rest of the drive. They had talked half the night.

Darren parked in the garage and powered the door down. Seeing the Firebird in the driveway made him

428

think of the backpack, where 'Adam' had left it in the front seat. The magazine, the knife, the sneakers … vintage goods. No wonder it had all seemed so familiar. It was the stuff he owned. Collected. Mementos from Adam's life, preserved.

Beth stopped and looked at the Acura, its ruined windshield.

'This makes no sense,' she said. 'If Adam isn't real, then who'd you hit?'

'I'm hoping it wasn't a "who" but a what.'

'What if you hurt somebody?' she said, and burst into tears.

He came around the front of the car and hugged her.

'No really, what if someone's dead?'

'It could have been a raccoon,' he said, feeling like a fraud. 'A phone pole, a tree, it could have been anything, Beth, but it wasn't a boy. I know that much.'

The angry woman in the Range Rover, flipping him off. Had he run into her? Had she thrown something at him, broken his windshield? He didn't think so, but then, why couldn't he recall anything else that had happened then? Something must have thrown the switch, allowing him to see Adam. To meet him. To take him home.

'You don't know anything,' Beth said. 'Not with any kind of certainty. You can't say that, not right now.'

Darren sighed with frustration, but she was right. He could have killed some kid and he had no way of knowing. Although, if he *had* killed some random kid, wouldn't Officer Sewell have fielded a report from another set of concerned parents? Wouldn't someone have found a body?

'Look, I'll do whatever you want. Tomorrow morning we'll go at this together, from all sides, with the police's help, all right?'

'What about Tommy? You said something about it being too late. We had to come here before it was too late.'

Darren frowned. What had seemed so urgent a few hours ago now seemed a paltry thing compared with what had been unlocked within himself. 'That was before I knew what happened,' he said. 'When I visited him today, I thought Adam slipped away, that maybe he was planning something. Tonight, I felt him again, and I was scared. Literally a scared ten-year-old kid. Those monsters, his parents—'

'Your parents,' she said.

'Fine, *my* parents. They're long gone. Dead. Tommy said so himself. Three bodies were found in the fire's remains, right? Tommy knew it. And I must have known it back then, even when I was Adam. That's what my friend Darren Lynwood told me up in the hills, that night I became him. But he was imaginary, springing up from the trauma I'd just been through, right? And if *that* Darren was a product of Adam, he couldn't have known anything that Adam didn't. So if Darren said the bodies had been found, then Adam must have known. I must have found out at some point. It had to have been in the news. Tommy only confirmed it yesterday. And that means they're really gone.

430

There are no parents, no monsters. The monsters were a figment of Adam's imagination. That's what his parents had become to him. It's over. Now, can we please go to bed and talk the rest of this through tomorrow morning?'

She opened her mouth to argue, but instead pushed past him. He followed her inside. They dropped their jackets and keys on the kitchen bar counter. The clock over the stove said 4:23 a.m.

Beth walked around the counter and looked down at something sitting near the end, a piece of mail or a slip of paper. Darren watched her, a bad feeling building inside. But no, it was going to be okay now. Raya was home, he and Beth were home, they had confronted the beast. His past. Things would get better now. They could deal with the loose ends in the coming days. Everything that mattered was right here, safe.

Beth's brow folded over itself. She covered her mouth. She whirled and stared toward the rear of the house.

'What is it?'

She handed him the slip of paper, one sheet taken from the notepad they used for grocery lists, reminders, appointments.

Beth didn't wait for him to read it. She bolted for Raya's wing of the house.

'Beth!' Darren called, but she was already running down the hallway. He looked at the paper. It was a note. Scribbled with the penmanship of an unwell mind.

bring Adam to school or Raya will have a
ceremony
   no pigs or else daddy will give her an
education before we eat whats left of her
   Love,
   yer big sis

Darren ran to Raya's bedroom, where Beth was screaming at the top of her lungs.

41

Raya woke up choking on water, her face and hair drenched. Soon as she cleared her throat and caught her breath, another blast hit her in the face. She turned away and tried to use her arms to push herself up, but her wrists were tied together, behind her back. Her feet were similarly bound. She was lying on a mattress of some kind, or a rubber pad. She coughed out more water and shook the drops from her eyes, sending a massive bolt of pain from her forehead to the back of her skull, pounding without mercy.

Something bad had happened to her. She remembered being at the party with Chad, asking for a cigarette, worrying about her parents, walking into the garden and then she ... lost track.

Is that where it had happened, whatever it was? In the garden? That was the last thing she could remember. Something had been waiting for her in there, hadn't it? She'd felt it, and now it had her. Something evil.

She was in a big dark room now, the ceiling two or three times higher than in a regular house. What was this? A warehouse? Keep calm, she told herself, keep calm until you know what's happening. Breathe. Don't say or do anything stupid.

'She's awake,' a woman said from somewhere close, but not in front of her. 'The kid is still conked out. I told you not to put that cord on too tight, you stupid old cow. Almost killed him before I cut him loose.'

Raya didn't like the sound of this voice. The woman sounded her mom's age but the voice was rougher, raw somehow, the voice of a lifelong smoker or a woman with too much testosterone in her system. Hard, mean, lacking all humanity.

'Jes 'ill him now, why don'cha?' a much older voice said, this one a man's. 'Please, darlin', let us 'ill him now.'

This angered the woman. 'No, goddamnit, I said. Not until we secure the prize.'

Chad? Were they talking about Chad? Oh God, they were going to kill Chad. Which meant they were probably going to kill her too. Someone had kidnapped them. Sick people here, at least two of them.

Raya tried to sit up a bit, but every time she moved another massive round of throbbing kicked inside her head. The pain was so severe she thought she was going to throw up. Before she leaned back, she peered across the room, a vast, almost empty space except for some kind of equipment at the far end. Rails going sideways, ropes hanging from the ceiling, stacks of something else she couldn't make out, more mattresses maybe. She wanted to scream for help, scream Chad's name to make sure he was okay, but she was afraid of setting them off.

Bootsteps click-clocked behind her, around to her right side, and a skinny form came into view, at the foot of whatever they had set her on. Who was this? Man or woman? Raya thought it was a woman but she couldn't be sure. She was dressed in black, tight-fitting clothes. Wearing a black mask, or so it appeared. She looked down at Raya for a moment and Raya realized it wasn't a mask, but tattoos, black make-up, some kind of patterns and symbols all over her cheeks and forehead, around her mouth. Her face was sharp, her nose a slim edge between closely set eyes.

Raya began to tremble. She couldn't control it. It shook her legs and arms, made the rows of her teeth grate against each other.

'Don't fuss,' the woman said. 'If you try to get up or run, I'll set these two on your handsome boyfriend here, who's lucky to be alive. Understand me, little twat?'

Raya nodded quickly, and that hurt too. Tears swelled up and ran from her eyes. She squeezed her mouth shut, trying not to make a sound. Please, God, let Chad be safe. Please protect him from these people, whoever they are.

The woman had something in her hand. Short, black. A gun or a knife? She switched it from hand to hand as she talked, in the same emotionless tone as before.

'We don't care about either of you. We just want Adam. If he's not here soon we will start the ceremony, and I promise you, he'll feel that from twenty miles away. He'll come. Only question is whether he gets here before I let Ethan and Miriam do what they want, which is a lot. You're very pretty, you know that?'

Raya didn't say anything.

'Adam is lucky. I bet he loves you. I bet he loves you all kinds of ways, doesn't he?'

Raya didn't like the sound of that, but her mind was swimming in another direction. She was trying to piece this together. They wanted Adam, the boy her dad had been obsessed with. Did that mean he was real? Had her dad done something to him to make these crazy people angry? What could he have done to deserve this?

The crazy woman kicked Raya's leg, just above the ankle. She must have been wearing boots, because it felt like she'd been hit in the calf muscle with a hammer. She cried out and the woman kicked her again, harder.

'Please . . . ' Raya said. 'I'm sorry!' Please don't hurt—'

'Answer me, bitch. Does he love you? Does he touch you the way he used to touch me? Did he teach you what you needed to learn to be a woman?'

No, Raya wanted to scream, but she sensed this was not the answer the psycho lady wanted to hear. She didn't want to get caught in a lie but she couldn't bring herself to agree with what this monster was suggesting.

'I don't know him,' Raya blurted. 'I don't know who Adam is.'

'Uuugghhh,' the woman growled, lunging toward Raya. 'Don't fucking lie to me! We know where he lives. We've been inside his house. He got rich and thinks he's special now, but he's a Burkett, just like us. He thinks he got away, but you can't escape who you are. You didn't escape, did you, spoiled twat?'

Raya pressed herself into the mattress. She wished she could disappear through the floor. Working her hands behind her tailbone, she tried to feel her way around the cord. It wasn't rope. Or tape. It was thin, cutting into her skin like a wire. Her fingertips brushed against a hard line between her wrists, plastic notches. If she didn't get free soon, this woman was going to lose control and kill her. But the cord wouldn't budge.

The woman stood back. She spat and something warm and sticky hit Raya in the cheek, across her nose. 'Your daddy's a dead man,' she said. 'You're all dead. Do you know that? We're going to take everything he's got, we're going to drain your blood, clean out the entire family line, and I will be the last thing you ever see.'

Raya cried harder, and she couldn't tell whether she was faking it or not. She had decided to let the woman think she was too scared to try anything, but this was also true, she was terrified. Even so, she continued to swipe at the cord with her fingertips, testing the band around her wrists, using all the strength she could muster without showing it. But still the cord would not give an inch.

The woman walked behind her, out of sight.

'You don't know Adam,' she said. 'But I do. We all do.'

Her clothing creaked as she kneeled, her mouth suddenly close against Raya's ear. She tried to turn away but the woman yanked her by the hair and pressed her lips to Raya's cheeks, mashing into her, her hands running along her throat, lower, squeezing her breasts hard, pinching her skin, pulling it, and Raya shrieked. She thrashed, but the woman was too strong. She dragged her tongue across Raya's lips and up the side of her cheek, to her ear. Licking and licking like a dog.

'He burned us out,' the woman said. 'Tried to burn me like them, but we escaped. Because we're stronger. He's no Saturn. Never was. When he comes for you, he's going to learn what it feels like to be burned by your own kin.'

The woman bit into Raya's ear, her teeth like a blade, drawing blood. She licked the ear again quickly, moaned with pleasure, then shoved Raya's head aside. She stood and her footsteps went the other way.

'Now!' an old woman said. 'We did our job, let us do it now!'

Raya flashed back on the old woman in the back seat of the car. Her ruined face. The corpse-looking thing sitting up in the car.

'All right. A taster to hold you over. Take her clothes off, Ethan,' the young woman said. 'No more than that. If you jump the gun, the gun's gonna shoot you, I promise.'

The older ones, the ones Raya could not see, began to squeal with excitement.

42

Adam came back, but it wasn't like before, waking up in the woods. This time he woke up in a house, on his feet, and there was a woman screaming right in front of him. She was on her knees, hanging over a bed, clawing at the sheets.

Adam looked back down the hall. He remembered the house. He knew who this must be – Darren Lynwood's wife, Beth. Something terrible had happened. She was shrieking. Darren wasn't home, otherwise he would be with her. He looked around the room, taking it in. The pretty bed, the girl's clothes everywhere, posters of bands on the walls. This must be their daughter's room. Raya, her name was Raya, the one he had seen in his dreams of a new family. But Raya wasn't here, so this must be the problem. Something bad had happened to Raya.

The monsters had come for him, and when they couldn't find him, they took Darren's daughter. All because of Adam.

'Why did you do this?' Beth cried into the bed. But it seemed like she was yelling at him. 'How could you let this happen? Where is she? What have they done to her?'

Adam didn't know if Beth – Mrs Lynwood – knew he was here. He didn't know what to say. He only knew he couldn't run away this time.

Something in his hand. He looked at it. A note. He recognized the handwriting. He knew who it was. He remembered them. His mother and father and his sister. They were supposed to be dead, like him, but they weren't. Somehow they had survived the fire. They wanted him. They were holding Darren's daughter hostage. Bring Adam to school – that meant Crest View. Had to be their elementary school. Crest View seemed right, because it was close to home, to the trailer court where they had burned, and because he and his sister had hated school. Hate was power for her, and the school was filled with dark memories, ill will, the teasing and cruel things the other kids had done to her, to both of them. How she used to wet herself in class, only to be laughed at and sent home, their angry mother shouting at the teachers, causing a spectacle in front of the class, making it worse.

Sheila would have chosen home if it hadn't burned to the ground, and probably been replaced by a new house by now. School was the next-best thing. For her.

She was going to use it somehow.

'I know where she is,' Adam said. 'I can get her back.'

Mrs Lynwood pushed herself up and grabbed him by the shirt, yanking him back and forth, screaming at him. 'What have you done? Why didn't you tell me? You lied to me! None of this would have happened if you told me the truth!' She raged and swore at him, babbling her fury.

'I'm sorry,' was all Adam could say. 'I'm sorry, Mrs Lynwood. I'll go find her. They want me, not her. I'll get her for you.'

Mrs Lynwood stopped shaking him and stared, her eyes wet and swollen red. She was beautiful, the mother he'd always wished he had, and his stomach churned for how sad and frightened he'd made her. She studied his face, placing a palm on his cheek.

'Even now?' she said. 'You're still doing it? Do you think this is a game?'

'No, I—'

She slapped him hard across the mouth. Again. A third time, until he tasted blood and his ears rang.

'Stop it! Stop playing games!' she screamed at him. 'This is our daughter's life at stake!'

Adam let her slap him over and over. He forced himself to stand still and take it, but he tried to warn her. 'I have to go now, as soon as possible. I will get her back. They just want me, Mrs Lynwood, I promise.'

She reared back and laughed, but her laughter turned into another scream. She pushed past him, moving down the hall, into the living room and then the kitchen. He ran after her. She reached for the phone, started to dial.

'Who are you calling?' he said.

'The police, who do you think?'

'Don't do that. You can't.'

'Watch me.'

'If you call the police, they will kill her.'

She hesitated, fingers on the cordless phone. She stared at him, her face drawn, pale. She began to moan like a wounded animal.

'They will kill her,' he said again, slowly, forcefully, to make sure she understood. 'They will cut her open and dig out her organs. They are monsters, Mrs Lynwood. I've seen them do it. I was there that night, at the Kavanaughs'. They used to practice on homeless people when we were kids. Sheila is as bad as they are. Probably worse now. You really can't call the police. Don't do it.'

She couldn't speak. She stared at him again, deep into his eyes. 'It's you,' she said. She looked him up and down. 'It's really you.'

Adam looked down, to his dirty jeans and ruined sneakers, his faded Creature From the Black Lagoon T-shirt. He didn't understand what she meant. Who else would he be?

'Adam?' she said. 'Is that you, Adam Burkett?'

'I'm sorry we had to meet this way, Mrs Lynwood.'

This seemed to calm her somewhat. She was still scared, but she spoke quietly, choosing her words carefully. 'Where's Darren? What happened to him? Can you tell me where he goes?'

'I don't know,' Adam said. 'He's not home with you? Did he go look for her? Does he know? I tried to tell him about them but I never knew if he believed me.'

Mrs Lynwood looked around the living room, toward

the bedroom, as if she were expecting Darren to appear at any moment.

'I didn't hurt him,' Adam said. 'I would never do that.'

'Who are they? Who took our ... my daughter? Are they your parents?'

'Yes, and my sister,' Adam said. 'We have to go. Can you drive me to Crest View? I'd take one of the bikes, but it will be faster if you drive me.'

'We have to call the police. You can't, not like this ... you're a child.'

'I know them better than anyone,' Adam said. 'No police. They will never surrender. They will kill her and themselves before they ever let the police take them.'

'Oh my God. Oh my God.'

He took the car keys from the counter and handed them to her. 'You don't have to go inside. In fact, I can't let you. I have to go alone. It will be safer that way. But can you drop me off at the school?'

She nodded slowly. He knew she was in shock, too scared to think clearly, and he would have to help her. She accepted the keys. 'But what are you going to do? How can you deal with them?'

He forced himself to sound a lot more confident than he felt. 'I know their weaknesses. Just get me there. The rest will be okay.'

She started to cry once more, then swallowed it. 'Are you sure? There's no other way? You can't be wrong, Adam. Not about this.'

'I'm sure. But I need my backpack. Is it still here?'

Mrs Lynwood shook her head. I don't know.

'Maybe he left it in the Firebird,' Adam said. 'I need it. We can't go without the stuff in the backpack.'

They went into the garage. Adam's backpack was on the passenger seat. He checked inside, to make sure everything was in its place.

'It's all here,' he told her. 'Let's go.'

They got into the wagon and backed out. Mrs Lynwood had never been to Crest View, but Adam pointed the way for her. It was a good thing he'd stopped there to steal the bike recently, otherwise he might not have been able to find it, not at night anyway. They drove up 19th Street.

She asked, 'Was it you? Are you the one who stole the groceries at Safeway a few days ago?'

Adam felt himself blush with shame. He looked down. 'Yes.'

'And the running away at night. Sleeping outside. You've been doing that?'

'Yes.'

'For how long?'

'I don't know,' he said. 'Every night feels like the first time. But then, sometimes it feels like I've been running for ever.'

She looked away from him, shaking her head.

When they arrived, the clock inside the station wagon said it was 4:42 in the morning. The parking lot was empty. The low little school looked like a flattened prison in the night, its long rows of windows all black.

'What if they're not here?' Mrs Lynwood said, easing

into the parking lot. Her hands were shaking. She kept squeezing the steering wheel, it seemed, to keep herself from flying apart. 'They could have taken her anywhere.'

'They're here,' he said.

'How do you know?'

'I can feel them.'

She pointed at the school. 'Does that mean they can feel you too?'

'Yes.'

'Because you're different. You have something the other kids don't. Is that right?'

Adam nodded.

'She got it from you,' Mrs Lynwood whispered, covering her eyes. 'I didn't want to see it, but she's like you.'

'Who got it?'

'Raya's hunches,' Mrs Lynwood said.

He gave her a questioning look.

'You don't remember – no, of course not. Our daughter has it too. Like you and your family. Something different, a sense of things that haven't happened yet. She got it from yo— from Darren.'

Adam's thoughts spun in confusion. Darren Lynwood had it too? Is that why they were connected? A vision flashed behind his eyes. For a moment he saw the log in the mountains, the woods where he had been hiding. In the trees was another boy, a boy in a Patterson Racing jersey. Was it him? For a moment it was like looking into a mirror, the two boys were one, and then the boy moved and the same boy split in two—

445

'I could ask you questions all night. But we don't have all night, do we?'

Adam blinked away the confused memories. 'No. I'm sorry. I'm going in.'

He pushed the door open. Mrs Lynwood opened her door too.

'No,' he said, reaching for her. 'You can't.'

'I'm not letting you go after her alone.'

'You have to. If they see anyone else, they will kill her instantly.'

'Stop saying that, please stop saying that.'

'I'll get her back,' Adam said. 'I promise you that. But if this is going to work, you need to stay here and wait.'

Something in his eyes must have convinced her. She shut her door.

'Ten minutes,' she said. 'No, five. You get a head start, and then I'm coming to get my daughter, do you understand me?'

'Yes, ma'am.'

Adam exited the car and shut the door quietly. He pulled the straps of his backpack tight against his chest. Ducking as low as he could while still moving on his feet, he jogged to the school's front doors. Being quiet and trying to mask his arrival wouldn't matter, he knew, but he couldn't help it.

They were expecting him, and they would be prepared.

43

Chad was in the corner of the gymnasium, where they had dumped him. He knew that the car wreck and the plastic loop around his throat had knocked him unconscious for at least thirty minutes, maybe more. If the younger woman hadn't cut it off to spare him, or keep him going until they had no more use for him, he would be dead by now. For the past hour or so he had been awake, listening, trying to think of a way out. The others didn't know he was back, alert, and he intended to keep it that way until he could use the element of surprise to some kind of advantage.

When he'd come around, he was in the back of his own car, the woman driving, Raya unconscious in the front seat. He had been too disoriented to react. At first he'd done nothing more than listen. Slowly he'd opened his eyes, just wide enough see up through the side window as they turned from Linden onto 19th Street. He wasn't sure it was 19th until they started to climb the hill heading north. He'd reached for his phone, but his reach went only about two inches before his wrists caught inside another of the plastic ties.

He had played dead (or at least passed out) as they parked and dragged his limp body from the Saab, across the parking lot, into what he gradually realized was Crest View Elementary School. Chad had gone to Douglas when he was younger, but he knew Crest View. Why they were taking him and Raya here, not to mention who they were, what they were planning – none of it made any sense to him. But he knew it had something to do with Darren, and Adam, the boy that had come to mess up their lives somehow. He'd heard them asking about him.

Where is he? What's taking Adam so long? Are you sure Adam wasn't home when you stopped to leave the note?

The connections were there, but Chad couldn't afford to focus on the larger scheme right now. The point was, he and Raya had been kidnapped by some very deranged people. Two elderly sickos and what he was starting to realize might be their daughter, who was about to explode with insanity and violence. Chad had seen the woman's face in the backseat, right before they crashed, and it was like something out of a carnival. She had long black hair and a face of melted wax, and when she sat up to throw the collar on him, her hair had fallen off. A wig, part of some disguise, and there was no mystery to why they needed one.

The old man was like her, scarred bald, both of them quiet, following the daughter's orders. She made them hold him and Raya while she kicked in the front window and unlocked the door. She led them down the main hall, turned right into another hall, past classrooms and walls lined with art projects and paintings, the library, and finally into the gym.

Why wasn't the alarm ringing? Or was it the silent kind? Chad could only hope so, but after another twenty minutes had passed with no sirens coming to the rescue, he had to conclude that the woman had either found a way to disable the alarm or there simply wasn't one.

Thinking he was less important and not much of a threat, they dumped him in the corner, on a hard tumbling mat that smelled like rubber sneaker soles. They had dragged Raya to the thicker mat on the other side of a pommel horse. Chad knew Raya's head was injured but he didn't know how bad. She must have hit it on the steering wheel when they collided with the tree. On the way in he'd caught a glimpse of blood on her face. She had been in and out of consciousness, until the woman came in with the cups of water and started to splash her, kick her, shout at her.

Now he could hear Raya crying, and Chad wanted nothing more in the world than to get up, break free of the ties around his wrists, and attack them with his fists and feet. Elderly or young, male or female, it did not matter. A line had been crossed and he imagined beating the shit out of all three of them. Poking out their eyes. Breaking their necks. It wasn't just about Raya. The whole family was under some kind of attack. The stuff with the kid Adam, Darren's psychological problems, even the Kavanaugh murders. Chad knew it was all connected somehow.

These people were the weak ones, just like Darren

had said. They were dangerous, yes, but they were weak and giving in to their animal nature. The Lynwoods were good people who had worked hard and made a family and the offense here was against the sacred values Darren had spoken about.

Chad wanted to give in to killing them, and if that was a weakness, so be it.

But he had to be smart. Find the right moment.

Were the old ones watching him now? Or only watching Raya? The lights were off and the gym had only a few windows. The people were hardly more than shadows to him, and so he must be to them. But if they saw him moving . . .

To hell with it. He couldn't wait all night for help to arrive.

He had to try.

Chad bent his knees and flexed his shoulders, pushing his hands down under his butt. So close, but he couldn't get his wrists under his ass and legs. If he could get his legs through the hoop of his arms, hands in front of him, he might be able to use them to hold a weapon. Swing a baseball bat, if he could find one. It was an elementary school gym. There had to be some kind of equipment in here.

The woman raged some more and Raya shrieked again. Chad could see her squirming on the other side of the gym as the woman leaned down to her and . . . what? Bit her? Whispered to her? Something vicious.

Chad repressed a growl and once again tried to separate his wrists from the cord. The hard plastic cut into his skin again but he ignored it. The bleeding had started a little while ago. His skin burned. There was just a little wiggle room and he began to shift his wrists against one another, back and forth, until his wrists turned wet again. More blood. Good. Make it slippery. If he bled enough, maybe his hands would slide through.

He flexed his wrists outward, then back and forth, outward, back and forth, and the cutting sensation slipped a little ways up the backs of his hands, the plastic wire grinding against the bones there, digging in, peeling his skin up like a slice of cheese. The pain turned into a searing fire as his skin tore again, blood wetting the back of his pants now, and he ground his teeth to keep from yelling. He was breathing hard from the exertion. If he wasn't careful they would hear him. Check on him. Shut him down.

He relaxed, concentrating on getting his breathing under control, but the pain did not relent. His wrists were screaming at him, his hands covered in blood. He couldn't wait too long or else he would injure himself too severely or lose too much blood to do any good.

Don't be stupid. Wait for help. You can't risk her life trying to be a hero.

But if there was a way to get free, without them knowing...

If you want to be good, he remembered Darren saying to him the morning of the last day of school, *and I'm not talking about being rich or successful, but good at something, and good to the people you love, then the single most important thing to do is resist your own weaknesses. We all have them. Some of us work at rising above them, others don't. And that's all I want you kids to remember, okay? Before you cut a corner, or do something that seems too good to be true, take a second. Stop. Think. Is this the right thing to do, or just the easy thing to do? Because, son, those two things are almost never the same thing.*

It was that simple, Chad realized. He had a choice now. The easy thing or the hard thing. The right thing or the wrong thing. And it wasn't a difficult choice, not at all. It was the easiest choice he had ever made, and probably would be for quite some time.

He would be strong.

The pain would go away, eventually. Someday.

Raya would be for ever.

Chad took three deep breaths, then held all the air he could. He closed his eyes and gritted his teeth, and then he used every muscle from his chest to his shoulders, down through his arms. Slowly but steadily, he pulled his wrists apart and one hand over the other, sliding them in his blood, visualizing the skin, his own skin, coming away in a long peel. One over the back of his left hand, the other along the side of right thumb. His jaw locked tight, the pain turned electric in his arms, sending white flares through his brain. He pulled and pushed, and pulled harder.

I am stronger than plastic. I am stronger than them.

My skin is soft but my bones are stronger than—

Crack.

Chad froze, the pain blowing all the way up his arms,

452

into his spine, pushing against his eyes. Bones in his hand, at least two of them, had just snapped like pencils.

The plastic cord jumped to his knuckles and he sucked in deep lungfuls of air. He felt the floor spinning beneath him. He was going to pass out, would have if not for the pain. The pain was like nothing he could have imagined. His hands felt simultaneously as though they were being skinned alive and smashed in a vice.

He pulled again, hard and fast, and the cord fell off.

His hands were free.

He almost screamed with joy and relief, but he forced the scream back down inside himself and trembled, quivering with excited fury. His throat was still sore from where the cord had been and he almost coughed.

Slowly, Chad brought his hands around into his lap. They were shaking violently. He glanced at them for a moment before balling them into the front of his shirt. Within seconds his shirt filled with blood.

He was glad, so very glad, that it was dark in the gym.

He tilted his head back and looked across the floor.

The woman shouted something more at Raya and then stood. Chad froze, certain she had noticed his movements, heard him squirming. Maybe even smelled his blood.

The old man laughed like a dying coyote and moved with an excitement Chad had not seen him capable of until now. He was going for Raya, bending over her, pulling on her, throwing her shoes aside. He was taking off her clothes, dragging her pants down, and Chad saw Raya's feet up in the air.

Chad started to rise.

'Stop,' the woman said. 'Be quiet!'

Chad froze. Everyone froze. Once again he was sure they had noticed him, but that wasn't it. Something else caught their attention.

'He's here,' she said.

The three of them turned to face the double doors leading to the hall. Their backs were turned to him.

In the corner of the gym, Chad stood up.

44

Sheila shoved the .38 into the waistband at the back of her pants. The mace canister was in her right front pocket. The first knife she kept in her left hand, tucked into the cuff of her black sweater. The second, her daddy's straight-edge used for backup, was in the ankle of her black hiking boot. She had six zip-ties in each back pocket, each one looped but loosely so, open to receive his limbs, his neck. Taped across her stomach was a line of six double-sided razor blades, in case the struggle came down to matters of intimacy.

There hadn't been much time to prepare the symbols, things had moved too quickly. But once she had him secured there would be plenty of time to properly set up the ceremony. She was sweating with excitement. She had never felt so alive, or ready.

'You two stay with her,' she said over her shoulder, one hand on the double doors. 'Stay behind the doors unless you hear me yelling for you. But it won't come to that. He's soft now. He always was. He won't risk her life.'

Disappointed, Ethan attempted one last lunge at the

girl, but Miriam pulled him off and slapped the back of his head. He relented, but stayed close to the girl. Miriam moved between them and the doors, ready to enforce a second line of defense. Sheila knew they were tensed, ready for the reunion, but maybe a little scared. She would have to forgive them that. They were old. When she was finished securing Adam, she would finish them quickly, mercifully.

Sheila peered through the windows of the double doors, up the dark hallway. He would be here any moment, at the intersection where the main hallway split left and right. Would he sense which way to go? She hoped so. She wanted to see his face when she stepped out and presented herself. But if his back was turned, if he went the wrong way, she could use that too. She would hog-tie him and sever his hamstrings, just enough to take the fight out of him. The rest she would savor all night, perhaps for days.

She looked down. On the hallway floor, six paces in front of the doors, was the symbol she drawn for him, the only one she had time for.

His Saturn.

Three feet across and close to six feet high, stroked out in shoe polish.

To let him know she wasn't afraid of him. To remind him of the curse he had been blessed with since birth. Of the way she had drawn on him when he was tied up in the closet, their parents out late, with no one to hear him crying while she had her fun.

He was hers now. He belonged to her. He always had, but when he saw what she had become, what she had done for him, there would be no doubt.

A hundred feet away, down the hall, a shadow moved. He appeared, encased in darkness, but a body his own, there was no doubt. He was standing sideways to her at the intersection. He had not chosen yet. He walked a few steps and looked both ways.

Could he see all the way down here? To her darkened face in the window?

Probably not.

Sheila smiled. Her skin burned with longing. Heat inside her jeans, strength in her arms, it was all so deliciously powerful.

He turned toward her, watching, unmoving for a moment. Then he chose, walking toward her. He wasn't trying to hide, walking alongside the walls or ducking down as he passed the first classroom window. He wasn't running in a panic.

He was walking.

Sheila opened the door and stepped into the hall.

45

Soon as the door closed behind the younger woman in charge, Chad saw the old crone look back and he heard her whisper something.

The old man shuffled over, until he was looming over Raya, and then he kneeled at her side, gazing down at her bare legs.

He wheezed something and started to laugh.

The woman whispered again but it sounded like gibberish, excitement or a warning, he could not tell which. Something urgent. To Chad it sounded like hurry, and that was enough.

Chad stepped off the tumble mat and walked toward them. He kept his hands balled inside his shirt to minimize the bleeding, to muffle the sound of his blood dripping on the floor. He went quietly, slowly, as the woman alternately turned from the window at the double doors to the man leaning over Raya.

It was the longest walk of his life.

On the way, he thought of the first time he saw Raya, on the first day of school last September. He had been walking back from third-period English, on his way to his locker, which was just around the corner from the cafeteria. He didn't have a girlfriend, not since last spring, and he had never been in love. He put his English textbook away, talked to his locker mate for a minute or two, and then Kennedy slapped him on the back and ran off to gym class. Chad had been hungry and decided to head over to the chow line to grab a bagel before fourth-period chemistry class started. He moved through the throng of students loitering and catching up in the cafeteria, and he saw her back first, her hair pulled into a French braid, which he always liked but didn't see many girls wearing these days.

The French braid of dark blonde hair, a soft light blue sweater, and the backs of her legs under the table's bench seat. She was seated alone, leaning forward, reading something. Under the yellow denim skirt, her calve muscles shone with glare from the overhead lights, her skin a soft brown from summer, and she wasn't wearing socks, just a pair of old-fashioned deep red penny loafers. He didn't know he was going to talk to her, only that he wanted to see her face. Somehow he knew before he stepped in front of her that she was new here, not any of the girls he knew from the past two years at Boulder High, and he had the craziest idea that if he hurried and got there before anyone else, he would be the very first person to see her here.

Then he was standing on the other side of the table, looking down at her, gawking without realizing it, and the book she was reading said Paris Trout on the cover. For some reason this made him laugh, not because she was reading but because the title sounded funny, Paris striking an exotic chord while Trout rounded it off in a humorous, down-to-earth way, and it sounded like her French braid and her yellow skirt and newness in his brain, on his tongue.

That's when she'd looked up, hearing his laughter, and her eyebrows came together, and he said the dumbest thing he'd ever said to a girl in his life.

Are you from Paris?

She had no idea what he was talking about, but the question made her smile too. And it had been so easy. He said hi, my name's Chad. Are you new here? And she said yes, and introduced herself, and he asked her more questions, he didn't know what, because he was fascinated by how she didn't seem shy or guarded, but nor was she flirting. She was just being nice. She's a nice girl, he thought. There is no wickedness in her, no deception, and her face was like purity itself. When she smiled he felt like his head was being pumped full of a miraculous gas. They were headed the same way, which turned out to be in the same hall, and then the same room, Chemistry I.

In the classroom she thanked him for introducing himself, very businesslike, and then she walked to her seat, and he was in love, so doomed in love. Raya was the only reason he'd passed that class this year, because he had to stay in it to be closer to her and she helped tutor him, and it took four months of polite friendship before he had the nerve to ask her out, and every day he had come to love her more than the last.

He saw that now, remembered it as clearly as anything in his life, and he relived it for three or four seconds on his way to fix this problem she was in, the situation he would accept not one second more.

Chad was only two or three steps behind the man leaning over Raya when the old woman turned from the doors and saw him. She started to hiss.

Chad ignored her and reached over the old man's shoulders, his bloody hands sliding over the old man's ears, until his fingers hooked into the old man's mouth, inside his cheeks, beside his teeth. The old man clawed at Raya's shirt, at the same time biting Chad's fingers. He groaned and shook his head from side to side, but he would not release Raya. Chad dug his fingers into the cheeks, against the jaw.

Raya was staring up at him, over the man's head, her eyes huge pools of shining life in the dark, and he saw her bare legs on the mattress, and she was saying no, no, no, and he knew she didn't want him to get hurt.

Chad tensed his chest and arms and ripped both ways until his hands slipped free, and the old man had a mouth three sizes too big after that. He rolled on the floor and covered his face, his breath too high and stolen to scream.

The old man rolled to his hands and knees, pushing himself from the floor. He reached into his boot cuff and came out with a long knife, the metal blade dull silver in the dark. He rose to his feet and pointed the knife at Chad's heart.

Chad danced to his right like a boxer and then shot forward, down low like he had learned in wrestling practice back in junior high. He caught the old man's legs and swung them out from under, simultaneously lifting, his shoulders hitting the man in the hips. The blade snagged on his side, along his ribs, and the pain was sharp but brief as Chad lifted the old man up and threw him over his shoulders, dropping him to the floor, onto his head.

The old woman threw herself at Chad and he jumped aside, caught her by the back of her lowered neck and flung her away, using her momentum to send her sprawling to the floor.

The old man pushed himself to his hands and knees once more, breathing hard, coughing, swaying, and this time Chad did not let him make it to his feet. Blood poured from the old man's mouth and Chad ran at him from five steps away. He punted into the exposed teeth and chin and the head snapped back. The old man flipped onto his back and gurgled out a series of choking sounds.

The old woman came crawling forward stabbing through the air, the curve of her arm with knife in hand a scorpion's tail, slashing toward Raya. She was grunting and whining and the blade stuck in the mattress, less than a foot from Raya's side.

Chad rushed in beside her and he jumped his right leg into her lower back as hard as he could. Her hips smashed down and he jumped her again, higher, into the back of her neck. Her arms shot out, the knife flew free, and her hands slapped to the floor. She tried to get up but her legs were spasming.

Chad looked to Raya, then at the old woman, and he had to be sure.

He ran up beside her and kicked her in the jaw. There was a loud crack and the woman's head lolled to one side.

The old man was on his back, staring up, arms and legs reaching for a hold, for a knife, for anything, and it did not matter. All that mattered was that he was still moving.

Chad ran to him and stomped another heel into his chest. A great gust of sour breath shot from the ruined old face and the man's hands clenched his shirt, digging as if trying to find the heart beneath.

Raya's crying pierced the quiet.

Chad ran to her, leaning down to her side. She was bound at the wrists, but they had cut the cord at her ankles, the man had, to open her up. His mind raced for something to cut her free but he couldn't stop himself, not when he saw her bare legs again, her underwear, which she had never let him see. The sight of them now, in this context, was such a violation, so unfair to her, he looked away and wanted to scream and go on stomping the old fucking monsters until their eyes popped.

Instead he bent and lifted her in one motion, carrying her high against his chest.

'You're bleeding,' she said, crying with relief.

'No, I'm not. Are you all right?'

'I think so.'

He ran with Raya in his arms, carrying her like a

toddler, to the opposite corner of the gym, where the moonlight beamed down at the small window in the door. He raised his right leg again and kicked the door, but it didn't open. It was locked.

Keeping Raya snug against his chest, he turned sideways and leaned down to flip the deadbolt lock. His hand was wet, a section of skin flapping over his knuckles like a torn glove. His fingers slipped. It was hard to grip the lock. But he kept going until at last the tab flipped sideways.

'It's okay,' she said. 'You can put me down. I can walk. Let me go.'

He would not.

'You're hurt, please, put me down.'

'Never gonna happen.'

Chad squeezed her tight and kicked the door open. He ran out cradling her, onto the playground, beyond the asphalt basketball court, into the gravel soccer field, into the weeds. He ran two hundred yards away from the obscenity, carrying her. He found the split two-way partition in the fence and twisted them through. He carried her away, and when she started to cry with relief and kiss him on the ears and said *I love you I love you I love you please stop you're hurt please baby please still he did not set her down.*

Away was all that mattered. He ran.

A half a block further down 19th Street, the red and blue flashing lights found them, and Beth was there, yelling for them not to shoot, the policemen had guns drawn, and only then did Chad set his Raya down.

46

Sheila heard the commotion behind the doors but she could not look away from him, from her baby brother. Ethan had probably lost control and started in on the girl. Well, that was to be expected. Miriam would try to hold him back, either out of some ancient jealousy or because she wanted them to stick to the plan, but in the end she wouldn't bother trying to keep him from his dinner. He was an old pig daddy and he took a lot to get riled up, but once he'd forged his pig iron he wasn't coming back down until he'd released his sap.

Miriam would back her up if things got out of control, if Sheila screamed for her, but she didn't want to scream. Not now.

Sheila had known it would come to this. Her and Adam, alone together.

He had paused when he heard the commotion behind the doors, and she knew he was scared. He was still at least seventy feet down the hall, more shadow than body, but Sheila could smell his fear from here. She waited for him, in front of his symbol, beckoning with her hungry eyes, one hand flat against the mace in her pocket, the other fondling the Buck knife's handle inside her cuff.

He began to walk toward her again.

'Yes,' Sheila whispered, and shuddered with anticipation. But she said no more than this. She had no words for what she felt now. She was emanating for him, sending him everything she had stored up and refined these past few days, and for the past thirty years. Her hatred and vengeance and her rotten love, she wanted him to have it all. It would overwhelm him, burn his skin before he was close enough to touch.

He walked toward her, head up, and one hand was set at something on his chest, near his shoulder. Was he wearing a backpack? What had he brought to the ceremony?

A few steps later, something unexpected happened. A fine line of white-blue light began to glow at his hands, around his feet, and then up his legs, snaking like threads of fire up, up, higher to his shoulders and neck and over his head, until he was surrounded by the thinnest, finest aura she had ever seen. She had never seen its color or beauty before, not on him, not on anyone.

Inside the vessel of light his features became visible to her, at last. She saw his face, his young skin, and he was exactly as she remembered him, the last time she had seen him at home on the morning of the last day of school. He had been so excited that day, for what he was planning, but she had already discovered his secret and given it to her parents. All his stupid money for his gay little bicycle. And it had filled her with a calm she had never known, knowing he was about to be crushed.

This is what she saw now, except that he was not smiling now, and did not look happy. His cheeks were the same, glowing, and his eyes were the same soft brown. Even his clothes were the same. His silly T-shirt with the monster on it, with its dirty joke about pee, so faded because he'd worn it a thousand times. And his ragged Levi's, everything was the same, down to his brand-new white Puma sneakers, the ones he had saved for because they wouldn't get him any new ones, and why should they? She didn't get new shoes, so why should he?

Adam walked toward her, and something confused her, his size. She was enraptured by his clothes, the outfit he had worn that day, she hadn't noticed how short he was. From the end of the hall he had looked smaller, small as a boy, but she thought that had been the distance and the shadows. He was supposed to be a man. He had to be a man, adult-sized like her.

Now, when he was fewer than thirty steps away, she saw that she had been wrong.

Adam was a boy. A small boy, a runt for his age, not yet eleven years old.

He was still young and beautiful, and she had grown old, ugly.

Sheila's hands began to shake.

47

Adam was twenty steps away and still walking. Twenty steps away from a woman he no longer recognized, a hideously stunted creature with the blackened face and flat gray eyes of a demon. She seemed enormous, towering above him, and every time she spoke her coarse voice sent ripples of ancient fear through his skin, down into his bones, cooling his blood. There were many things he did not know, did not want to know, but he did know one thing.

He was going to die here tonight.

He took another step.

She pointed to the floor. At his symbol. 'See what I made for you? This is where it will happen. Are you ready to die for me, sweet little brother?'

He didn't bother looking down. He kept his eyes on her, staring at her, his face set like alabaster glowing in the reflection of her eyes. The white-blue filaments of fire circling and circling him, surging stronger with each new step.

Sheila bared her teeth.

'Your bullshit doesn't work on me,' he said. 'I never

believed in it. I didn't believe in any of you. You aren't capable of magic. You're nothing but trash, Sheila. Your parents too.'

Sheila gasped. Her eyes were full of fury.

Adam stopped and set his backpack down.

He could see that she was trembling with desire to attack him, end him, slaughter him – yet something held her in check. She wiggled her left arm and a knife slipped into her palm. She waved the blade before him. He was only four or five steps away, and the blade was longer than the one he carried in the pack.

'I missed this school,' he said, looking at her pants. 'I'm surprised you chose to come here. Isn't this where you learned to hate them all? Isn't this where you always lost control?'

A wet stain bloomed between her legs, through her dark jeans. She lost control again now, and the laughter of fifty children filled the hall.

'Stop it! Stop it!' shrieked the woman who used to be his sister, covering her ears and stomping her feet. 'Shut up!'

'I left you behind,' he said, speaking softly. 'Because you never took care of me. I have a new family now. If you don't let Raya and her friend go, if you don't kneel now and give up, I will be the last thing you see.'

'Kill her!' Sheila screamed over her shoulder. 'Kill her now! Kill his bitch daughter!'

But there was only silence in return.

She faced him again, removing a canister of something from her front pocket. She held it out, aiming a nozzle at him while her other hand quivered with the knife.

Adam opened the top of his pack. She thought he was going for a weapon and lunged at him, stepping into his Saturn symbol. But he did not flinch. He dug into the pack, searching for the last item, the only one he had not figured out. He had the ability to learn things by touching them. He knew it was a talent that could be used for good or evil and if he chose to use it only for good, it would take him far in life. But one object remained in his pack, and he had not yet fathomed its meaning.

His fingers hooked into its three pieces now and for a moment he was yanked out of the school's dark hallway, cast into light.

Into Dave's Bike Store, on a cool late spring Wednesday after school, the rain coming down hard. He had sacrificed fifty cents from his savings to take the bus because there could be no mowing today, and the rain was depressing, and because he needed something, another look at the Cinelli. He had been in a funk, the dream half completed but still so far away, weeks that seemed like years, and life at home had been one sad horror after another. Three nights ago his father had come home drunk in the middle of the afternoon, berating Adam for sneaking a slice of leftover pizza, punching him in the chin, not hard enough to leave a visible mark but hard enough for him to see stars. One of his teeth cracked.

'Why don't you go on and kill yourself?' his father said, shaking his fist out. 'Get it over with. You're useless to us now. You don't even exist.'

He enters the shop this day dripping wet and now he is standing at the counter, staring into the glass at a row of free-wheels. He can't bring himself to walk to the Cinelli, to look up at it. He feels beaten, lost, unworthy. And then Arnie is there, on the other side of the display case, looking down at him, sighing heavily. Adam can't speak and Arnie doesn't need to ask. It is written on his face. Arnie disappears behind the saloon doors to the parts storeroom and reappears seconds later with a small paper envelope, wrinkled and faded blue. He takes Adam's hand and shakes the tiny bag.

Three gold rings tinkle into Adam's palm.

The bag says Campagnolo, Made in Italy.

'I was saving these for the big day,' Arnie tells him. 'The perfect final touch. They're brake cable clips, like the World Champions use. Normally they're silver, but I have an uncle in New York, he's from the Old Country, and he is personal friends with Tullio Campagnolo himself, the legend, the God. I asked my uncle for a favor and he reached out, to see what he could do. The guys at the factory had those done up for me personally. Dipped in 24-karat gold. Those three rings are the only Campy clips of their kind in the world, Adam. And they were made for your Cinelli. What do you think about that?'

Adam hiccups, swallowing his tears. He can't bring himself to look up at Arnie, not yet.

'The final touch,' Arnie says. 'But I want you to take them now. Something in the rain tells me today is the day they'll do some good.'

With that, Arnie closes his fist around Adam's fingers, sealing the rings inside his palm. His hand is thick and hairy and

471

stained with bicycle grease, but it is warm, so warm, and Adam doesn't want him to let go.

He looks into Arnie's eyes, blinking.

Arnie nods. Whispers, 'Don't give up on me, son. Don't ever do it.'

They stare into each other's eyes a few seconds more, then Arnie releases his hand and walks away, into the repair bay.

Adam shuffles across the showroom floor, to the exit, and when he steps outside, it is no longer raining, it is no longer cold, he is—

Here, in the school, staring at the rings, hypnotized. The gold has faded, chipped off, flaking away like fake jewelry. Adam understands now that Arnie made it up. These aren't real gold. They were not specially made for him by Tullio Campagnolo himself.

Arnie did this. Dipped them in brass, in his own shop.

For Adam.

He smiled broadly and looked up at the woman in her black make-up.

'What the fuck are those supposed to be?' she screeched.

Adam raised his palm before her and the light followed his hand, encircling the rings, until they glowed a brilliant blue-gold.

'These are my magic. The kind you will never understand.'

Sheila laughed. Adam did not.

He moved closer to her, raising the rings, until she stopped laughing.

'Go on. Take them,' he said. 'I want you to have them.'

Sheila snarled and dropped the mace, reaching to snatch them from his palm, but at the last second her hand froze. She scowled at him, sensing a trick.

'There's nothing left,' he told her. 'My pack is empty. These are my gift to you. I forgive you, Sheila, if you give up now. You have one last chance to be saved. Take them. Take my forgiveness.'

He could see something giving way inside her.

'Forgiveness is real,' he said. 'If you believe in it.'

The hand holding the knife continued to shake. She bit her lower lip. She was losing her hold. She backed up one step, then came forward again and reached for the rings. When her hand was inches from his palm, the blue-white light flickered and leaped to meet her, delicately attaching itself to her fingertips.

Her hand quivered, her knees buckled, and at the last second she lunged, dipping her left hand beneath his arm, under the rings, and drove the blade into his stomach. The blade tore through his T-shirt, into his belly, and when the handle slammed into his hot skin, Adam's fingers closed around the rings, squeezing them tightly in his little fist.

He did not cry out. He did not scream or fall.

He looked up into her eyes.

'Everything,' he said. 'For the ones who saved me. For Andrew and Eloise. For Bethany. For Raya. For Chad. For Darren Lynwood. For the bicycles, and for Arnie.'

And then he smiled again, gazing into her eyes, marveling at all she would never understand.

'You're finished,' he said.

Sheila released the knife handle and backed away, repulsion and a crawling terror making itself known upon her features, and the blue fire around her little brother flared, turning orange and red like the flames of a burning house. The flames leaped from his fist clutching the gold rings and crossed the air between them like a serpent, until the fire attached itself to her and set her skin ablaze. The light left him and surrounded her, darkening to the color of a blood sunset, and Sheila screamed, turning away, shrieking as her hair burned to her scalp.

'Help me! Put it out! Oh God it burns! Help meeeeee!'

She clawed at the double doors, pushing and pushing as the fire ate her alive, and finally she remembered to pull. The door swung at her and she screamed.

Miriam was there, filling the doorway, and she ran into her daughter with a dull grunt. Sheila's feet left the floor as the old woman hefted her up, and then she could not hold her and Sheila fell down, rolling onto her back.

The fire was gone, the blue and white light as well as the flames, doused, as if they had never been. No trace remained on either of them.

Sheila's hair lay in disarray across her left eye, her mouth. A hunting knife stood from her diaphragm, angled up under her sternum, its blade sunken into her heart.

The old woman saw what she had done. She looked

at Adam, then down to her dying daughter. She fell to her knees and began to breathe heavily.

Adam watched her for a moment, not moving as her hand reached for the knife handle. She squeezed it and pulled. The blade came away dripping deep red. The old woman raised the blade and kissed the blood, closing her eyes, swaying on her knees.

She looked to Adam. Her eyes were moist but no tears flowed.

Adam shook his head. 'No. No more.'

The old woman turned the blade around and plunged it into her own throat. Animal sounds came from her mouth and she fell forward, collapsing onto her daughter.

Adam walked past her, through the doors and into the darkened gymnasium. He looked everywhere, calling out for Raya, but the girl did not answer.

The room was empty. There was no one in here.

No, that wasn't true. There was a lump of shadow, a man on the floor, lying on his back. Adam walked to him. The scarred face stared up at him, mouth agape, torn beyond recognition, the cheeks split. His eyes were two dim black pools. One hand, scarred from the fire, was clutching his shirt at his chest, as if the real and final pain had visited him there. Adam leaned down and put his hand around the old man's neck. He held it there for a while, feeling nothing.

He stood.

A door in the corner of the gym opened with a bang and a paler shaft of night light cut through, making a triangle of reversed shadow across the floor.

Mrs Lynwood ran in, stopped, and looked toward him.

'Where's Raya?' Adam said.

'She's safe. They're outside. We're all safe. Are you hurt?'

'No,' Adam said, and fell to the floor.

Mrs Lynwood ran to his side and set down on her knees. He could smell the outdoors on her skin, in her hair.

'You're hurt. Where is it? Tell me what to do.'

'Not hurt. Free.'

She hovered above him, her hair falling around her face, and she was not an angel. She was a living, loving human being. She felt pain and cried and loved and tried to do good for the people in her circle. She cupped the back of his head in one hand and with the other held his right hand, squeezing. He stared into her beautiful eyes, seeing all he had never seen before, all he had ever wanted from a mother, and he knew he was in trouble. He was falling in love.

He coughed.

'Don't go,' she said, wiping his hair from his eyes. 'The ambulance is here. They're coming. Hold on. Please don't go. We can't make it without you, sweet boy.'

He smiled.

She kissed him on the lips, and for the second time in his short life Adam Burkett died.

FALL

And then the summer ended, and the leaves began to change from green to gold and red, to yellow and brown. The lawns dried and leaned over for want of mowing.

Darren Lynwood had nothing to look forward to in those days. He checked the mail in the morning and evening, and in between made the usual phone calls. But there was nothing to be done. He was going to lose the house. Maybe that was for the best, because it was too much for one man and he had grown tired of living here alone. Tired of living, so tired.

His wife and daughter had gone back to North Carolina, to live closer to the rest of the family, and he missed them too much to stay in this house another year. He needed a plan for winter, but he couldn't figure on one.

He continued to work, though the garage was also failing. No one was interested in paying a lonely middle-aged mechanic with no personal relationship skills a hundred and ten per hour to fix their vintage motorcycles. The guys who collected vintage cycles, most of them knew how to do their own repairs.

So, while the bank closed in on the house, the shop

was dying too, and that was fine, because he didn't feel much like working anymore. He didn't know what he felt like, except for drinking. He had his beer, cases and cases of it, which was silly when you thought about it, because there were a dozen liquor stores within walking distance, here in this tired old neighborhood off East Colfax in Denver. Lately he had begun switching from beer to cheap tequila, the only liquor his sensitive stomach could handle. The ulcers had started two years ago, but they hadn't really flared up until the girls left.

He watched the TV, flipping channels from late afternoon until midnight, searching and searching for something, a sign, a story that made sense, but there weren't any on offer.

That was the hell of it. Nothing made sense. It just happened to you, and your life went upside down, and then you had a chair and a TV.

Outside, on the street, a large engine growled down the block. Pneumatic brakes squealed and then hissed. Was today trash day? He hoped not, because he hadn't taken the trash out this morning. Wasn't going to do so now. He could put that off another week. It was mostly bottles and cans anyway. A few pizza boxes.

He heard a metal door jarring open, the racket of one of those old garage doors, maybe. Or one of those big brown UPS vans making a delivery. Voices. Men talking.

Darren turned the volume on the TV up a little louder and tilted back his beer.

Knock-knock-knock. Someone at the door.

He ignored it. Wasn't expecting anyone. No one

knocked anymore, no one he wanted to talk to. Probably the bank. Had to start sometime.

But they turned persistent. *Knock-knock. Knock-knock-knock*. Over and over, and then he was angry, shoving himself up from his chair, beer in one hand as he stomped to the door. He opened it.

Darren stared at the man on his porch. Oh, I see.

Him. The man in the park.

'What is it?' Darren said. He was taller than the visitor, by several inches. 'What else do you need?'

'Nothing,' the man said. 'Nothing at all.'

Behind the visitor, down the sloping dead lawn, out on the street, someone had parked a twenty-four foot Van Lines moving rig. The back door was up and two guys in blue coveralls were unloading boxes onto his yard, crowding his sidewalk.

'And that?' he said, pointing his beer at the movers.

'A little payback,' the man on his porch said.

'Sure. And for what?'

'Saving my life.'

Darren held the visitor's eyes as long as he could, but it unnerved him to do so. He looked back to the movers.

'What's in the boxes?'

'Collectibles. Things most people don't understand. Thought you might.'

Darren sighed.

'Do you remember my name?' the visitor said.

'I thought it was Darren Lynwood. That's what the paper said. Darren Lynwood, entrepreneur turned BMX bike guru or some damn thing. I saw that and had a real good laugh. I said, now that's interesting, because my name is Darren Lynwood too, and I used to be into BMX bikes. I better go on down to Boulder and see what this is all about.'

'I'm glad you did,' Adam said. 'You unlocked something very valuable for me. For my family.'

Darren nodded. 'And now you want to give it away. Out of what? Guilt?'

'To say thank you.'

'Don't want 'em.'

'Why not?'

'Didn't earn 'em.'

'I think maybe you did.'

'Nope. Your life, not mine.'

'Are you sure? Because it was lived in your name, your spirit. The spirit I knew, anyway.'

Neither man spoke for a moment.

'A lot changed for me this summer,' Adam said. 'I woke up to a lot of things. And one of them is, what happened to that kid? What became of the Darren Lynwood I knew?'

'He grew up with too many advantages,' Darren said. 'And not enough discipline. Everything good that came to him, he pretty much fucked up on his own.'

Adam scratched his cheek. 'Well, maybe some of this stuff can help.'

'I don't think it works that way.'

'Sell them, then,' Adam said. 'Give them away. Do whatever you want with them, but they belong to you now.'

'Uh-huh. What's the catch?'

'The catch is, there's about three hundred thousand dollars worth of goods there in that van, and I don't know your situation, but I know mine. I need to move on. I'm asking you to do me one last favor and give this stuff a home. Put it to use or put it where you think it belongs, because I know it doesn't belong with me.'

Darren opened his mouth but the visitor cut him off.

'But you can't have them all. I'm keeping one.'

Darren's eyebrows lifted but he said nothing.

Adam hitched up his pants, wincing as he did so, as if there was something paining him in the gut.

'It was you, wasn't it?' Adam said. 'You had it all this time. You found out where I lived and delivered it yourself.'

Darren Lynwood said nothing.

'Why?' Adam said. 'Please. I have to know how you wound up with it. It's the only thing I don't understand and I won't sleep until I know.'

Darren took a swig of his beer and set it down on the table beside the door. 'The first time I read about your family in the paper, thirty years ago, I knew what happened. I knew why you did it. I felt responsible.'

'You were just a kid,' Adam said. 'We all were.'

'But that was me, kid or not. I ruined your bike. I played a role, you see? And then you were out of school, and then a family was dead. A few days later, when the cops hadn't found you, I got real nervous. Seemed like God was onto me, or fate, something bad. I had the money, or my folks did. I knew the story behind that

481

little Italian job. Arnie had told me. I went down the shop and had a talk with Arnie. He told me about the promise he'd made to you, and I said I'd keep her safe. If and when you ever surfaced. He didn't believe me until I put up two of my bikes as collateral, 'cause he was stubborn like that. Took a little longer than I thought for you to turn up, but there you were in the park that day, and I said yep, that's got to be him. No other dipstick would be dumb enough to take my name.'

Adam laughed. 'You were right about that. Thank you for taking such good care of her. I hope you don't mind if I keep her. I waited a long time.'

'Knock yourself out,' Darren said.

'You have others to choose from. That truck is full.'

By now there were over a dozen boxes stacked on the lawn and more coming out.

'You still ride?' Adam said.

'Do I look like I ride?'

Adam turned and whistled. The movers looked up. Adam held up two fingers, like a peace sign. The movers nodded and leaped up into the truck. They reappeared a moment later, wheeling two bikes down the steel ramp.

One was a Kuwahara KZ-1, black with chrome components.

The other a Patterson, yellow and blue, Zeronine plate #1. Darren's memory was not what it had once been, but as the movers rolled the bikes up the walk and leaned them against the stoop, he felt a pang of longing, like seeing a thirty-year-old photo of your first girlfriend.

'That my Patty?'

'I think so,' Adam said. 'I pieced it together this summer, as best I was able to remember. All survivor parts. Era-correct. Lynwood-style.'

From his back pocket he removed a plastic bag containing a new old stock pair of Haro racing gloves. He ripped the plastic, removed the gloves, and handed them to Darren.

Despite himself, Darren felt a smile spreading across his chapped lips, inside his unwashed beard. He took the gloves. 'You're sick in the head, you know that?'

'Take it for a spin?' Adam said.

'I'll kill myself on that thing.'

'Nah. We'll go slow. We have to. I'm still recuperating.'

Darren shook his head, but before he knew it his feet were leading him out of the house, down the front steps, and his hands were on the gummy yellow grips.

Adam hauled one leg over the Kuwi and sat down very gently. He looked sideways at Darren, waiting.

'We're too old for this,' Darren said, straddling the Patterson.

Adam kicked the pedal back, spinning his freewheel. 'Never. Never too old to ride, my friend.'

This, Darren Lynwood discovered, turned out to be true.

ACKNOWLEDGEMENTS

Many thanks to my new editor at Sphere, Ed Wood, who helped me develop more than a few of the scenes in this novel more thoughtfully and with increased fidelity. It was a pleasure working with you and I hope we get to do many more books together. Mad props to Thalia, as always. At this point you may be my most senior reader at LB and I am always grateful for your help.

Special thanks are also due to my old school BMX comrades, the original NoBo-Wonderland Hills Gang from BITD: Jeff Metzger, Mike Wozniak, Jack Shrine, Troy Hamilton, David Christie, Jason Berkley, DJ Menzel, Tommy T., Eddie, Jesse Morrow, Chopper, and Al down at Dick's Bike Shop. And to my new friends via BMXmuseum, where we keep the faith and fuel the obsession: PlanetX, who sold me the coolest JMC known to man and told me of his own search to reclaim; Leviathan, my go-to guy for Race Inc. and some Vietnamese lunch; to Nikbsnjk for the Quad; Vazquizzel for the Diamondback; HUGE love to JT, who hooked me up with a Cinelli almost as cool as the

485

one I had when I was 11. And to its-all-good, Joe Buff-ardi, CRUZR_ADDICT, route66, NORCAL BOYZ, Arizona Louie, The Man Himself Jim Melton, and dozens of other guys who shared their childhood riding stories, memories and bike parts (which are really one in the same). Your infectious passion for collecting and love for the bikes stoked me and helped me remember so many things that went into this book. Ransom515 owes you a debt of gratitude for welcoming me back into the community and helping to keep the past alive.

Stay rad.

Have you read The Birthing House?

When Conrad and Jo move into the historic Victorian house,
it seems like a new start for them. With its fairytale porch,
wooden floorboards and perfect garden, it feels
as though they have finally come home.

But when Conrad is given an old photo album, he begins
to discover what dark secrets the house is harbouring.
Looking through the cracked, hundred-year-old pages,
he finds a photo of a group of Victorian women
standing outside his house.

And his heart nearly stops when he sees
that one of the women – raven-haired and staring
at him with hatred in her eyes – is his wife . . .

*

'A stunning debut – swaddling the reader in dread from the very
first sentence, and spiralling into a heart-stopping climax'
Michael Marshall